* * * * * * * * * * *

"Tim?"

Odd, Tim thought, peering out from the wings of the backstage area. Usually, the lights were so bright onstage that the audience beyond the stage's edge was obscured to the actors, let alone the tech crew. Yet a pair of vibrantly blue eyes shone from the darkness of the mezzanine. From the moment the curtain had gone up, the sensation of being watched had returned, but it wasn't the same as before. Instead of the sick feeling in his gut, Tim felt excited. Breathless. Every time he was onstage moving scenery, he could feel those eyes burning into him and it was exhilarating. He couldn't wait for the show to end. He stood at the edge of the wings for most of the performance, squinting into the darkness beyond the stage, willing to risk Nikki's wrath for a moment of connection. When it finally came, it was electric.

"Tim?"

A strange sense of belonging spread from his middle towards his extremities. The experience was odd and uncomfortable and wonderful and he wanted to explore it further.

"Tim."

A dormant part of him stirred, awakened. He stared directly into the blue depths, willing more to come.

"Tim!" The sharp insistent hiss broke through his reverie and he painstakingly turned from the welcome blue to be met by a pair of stormy brown eyes.

* * * * * * * * * * *

BOOK ONE IN THE STAR CHILD TRILOGY

RISING SIGN

JARED R. LOPATIN

RISING SIGN

http://starchildtrilogy.com

Cover Art by Kathryn Allen Ferguson
Interior Layout by Thomas J. J. Ferguson, V

ISBN 978-1442177000

First edition: May 2009

Printed in the United States of America

Thank you to all who believed and supported this dream.

*A special thanks to the three Pisceans
who helped make the dream real:
Jon, TJ, and Mom.*

Prologue

The woman screamed and grabbed her head. She fell backwards onto the floor, stiff, her eyes open wide, but unseeing.

Sereny clutched her mother's hand, cringing as the ice cold flesh touched her own. The night wind howled around the house and, not for the first time, the girl wished her father wasn't away, but a special order had taken him out of the country. His amulets were famous all over the world. She remembered their conversation before he left.

"What if it happens while you're away?"

Her father had held her close. "You've seen what to do. Hold her hand and always have pen and paper nearby. You're twelve years old, Sereny. Soon, you'll be going through the same thing and we'll do the same for you."

She looked up into her father's face. "What if something else happens?"

His expression was serious. "You have this." He touched the hematite hawk amulet at her throat. He kissed her lightly on her forehead and added, "Take care of each other. I'll be home before you know it."

Sereny's fingers found the amulet, drawing comfort from the fact that a part of her father was still present. Stroking the back of her mother's pale hand, she waited for the psychic's vision to pass. As instructed, Sereny's blue notebook and favorite pen rested within reach.

Sounds began to emerge from her mother's open mouth. They were deep, gutteral moans that slowly became words. Loath as she was to let go, Sereny released her mother's hand and grabbed the notebook and pen. The wind screamed as though attempting to drown out the woman's voice, but was no match for

Sereny's concentration. Her hand scratched the words onto the page with careful precision.

"When thousand spins of Terra twins..."

The howling increased and with a sudden crack, the window shattered, bathing the pair in glass. A figure in a grey cloak swept through the room, shrieking. It saw the young girl and flew at her with a malicious cry.

While part of Sereny was frozen with fear, her instincts took over. She grabbed the amulet around her neck and yelled "Release!" An enormous hawk manifested before the girl, wings spread wide in a shield, just as the attacker reached for her throat. Repelled, it found itself next to her mother's body. The girl flew into a terrified rage and cast her arms around her mother, seeking to protect her.

The woman awoke, color and warmth returning to her flesh, and found herself face to face with the creature, her daughter desperately clinging to her. Quickly, she invoked her own amulet and a bear erupted into being, snarling. Finding itself blocked by guardian spirits, the creature retreated. Instead of leaving, however, it flew towards the back of the house, to the room that Sereny had never been allowed to enter.

The spells that sealed the door held, though the figure beat furiously at them. It no longer seemed to care about the other occupants of the house, which proved to be its mistake. The girl's mother spoke in a firm, but clear voice, invoking not only the power within her, but the untapped spell on the door, set in place for just such a situation. The door flashed, blinding all three of them, but when the flare subsided, only the girl and her mother stood before the forbidden room. Sereny coughed as the smell of sulfur washed over her. She felt pain in her fingers and became aware that she was still gripping her notebook, the rings biting cruelly into her hands. Relaxing her fingers, she looked down at the almost blank page and despaired. With the attack, she hadn't been able to record all that had been said. Her mother caught the expression and gently took the notebook from her. Upon reading the six words, she frowned slightly, then stepped forward to the door.

As her mother placed a hand on the knob, Sereny's heart skipped a beat, but there was no flash. The doorknob turned and with a squeak, the door opened. Her mother turned on a lamp.

Sereny entered the room with anticipation pounding in her heart and questions caught in her throat. She eagerly searched the room, hunting for forbidden secrets, but found only filing cabinets. Frowning, she watched her mother move with a careful step, her sharp eyes peering about.

Stopping at a nondescript cabinet, the woman opened a drawer and reverently removed an ancient piece of paper bound by a silver ribbon. She solemnly placed this into her daughter's outstretched hands and nodded.

The girl pulled gently at the ribbon, giddy with excitement. The ribbon fell to the ground and unrolled the crackling paper, revealing lines of scrawl. Her eyes widened in surprise. She read the lines upon the page, her mouth silently shaping the words.

When thousand spins of Terra twins...

She read them again, then looked up at her mother.

"What does it mean?"

Her mother spoke for the first time since her vision.

"It means that it is starting."

Chapter 1

Damn, damn, damn! Tim cursed in time with his feet slapping the pavement as he made a mad dash down the street to the theater, his shoulder bag swinging in his hand. The rain splattered his face and hair, darkening the brown locks to an almost jet-black. He dodged around an elderly couple, silently cursing everyone on the sidewalk, the rain, and his boss. Especially his boss. Sprinting down the entire last block, he threw open the ancient door, taking satisfaction in hearing it clang against the side of the theater, then quickly surveyed the backstage area, relieved to find no sign of the stage manager in sight. Nikki was a stickler for punctuality. He started towards the room reserved for technical staff, but halted after three strides. "Forgot to sign in," he murmured aloud. Frantically digging in his bag for a pen, he hurried back to the stage door.

"Well, well, well. How kind of you to show up." The silvery voice dripped with derision. Tim groaned inwardly. *Please,* he thought. *This isn't fair. I shouldn't have to deal with her right away.* He forced a smile onto his face and turned to face the speaker.

"Cassandra," he greeted her. "How are you this lovely evening?"

"On time," the actress responded, placing an emphasis on the words. "I realize this is the first time that you've worked in a professional theater, but that's no excuse. The stage crew is supposed to arrive before the actors. It's opening night. This is not a good way to start the run!" Cassandra emerged from the shadows like a predator stalking its prey. She posed, leaning slightly forward and causing her robe to fall partly open, exposing a generous amount of cleavage. Her movements were careful and calculatedly seductive, demonstrating a high opinion of her own beauty. *Too bad most of it's fake,* Tim thought, but he didn't dare say this out loud. Her face glazed over in a perfect simulation of sympathy. "Oh, dear me, little boy, what happened to you? You look like a drowned rat."

"It's raining," Tim muttered through gritted teeth. His eyes darted left and right, expecting Nikki to appear at any moment. Cassandra didn't seem to notice.

"Oh, is it still raining? I could barely feel it through the furs. Of course, I arrived early, ready to warm up, and nothing is ready for me! The stage is dusty and you know how dust affects my voice. If my performance suffers tonight, it's your fault."

I'll take that chance, Tim thought to himself, but kept his mouth shut as he sifted through his bag, removing contents and shifting others in what was swiftly becoming a fruitless search. Cassandra seemed oblivious to his actions.

"When are you going to get to the stage, Timothy? I can't let your incompetence get in my way."

Tim continued to rummage through his bag while the actress sighed theatrically and lightly tapped the toe of her stiletto. Finally, he resurfaced with a pen. "As soon as I sign in," he answered.

She observed him with a false, cold smile. "You might want to dry off. You're going to have to mop back here as it is. Make sure you get to the stage immediately. I need to warm up. And by the way, looks like someone already signed you in." With that, she turned and strutted off to her dressing room, her stilettos clicking on the boards, leaving Tim seething.

Shutting his bag with a vengeful tug, Tim stormed his way in the opposite direction towards the tech room. Latwanda was waiting for him when he opened the door. She was dressed in all black – the stagehand's uniform – her long hair braided and held back in a tight bun. Her look was reproving, but all she said was, "Hello."

"Hi. Don't even say anything. Mark was being such a jerk today. He knows it's opening night and he still wouldn't let me go until my replacement came in and she was twenty minutes late. I didn't have a choice. There's no reason for it either; he could handle things at the store by himself for that little amount of time, but of course, he won't do that. He wants to squeeze every last second of work out of us." He slammed his bag down on the table with a bang and tore through it, yanking out black clothing. He paused. "Thanks for signing me in. You're a lifesaver."

"Tim, you have got to get here before Cassandra," Latwanda begged.

"I know, I know, I have to set things up before the actors get here and–"

"No, I just can't deal with that prima donna by myself." Tim laughed, feeling his frustration mitigate with commiseration. "I mean it. She's a pain in the ass. She asked if I could collect rainwater today so she could observe it and see if there was anything in the rain that might affect her voice."

"You've got to be joking." Tim pulled out the rest of the required outfit.

"I wish I were. That woman is a bitch. She has no heart." She went over to the kitchen section. "Want a cup of coffee?"

"That would be awesome. I'm wet to the bone." Dry clothing in hand, he headed for the bathroom. "Be right back."

Latwanda hummed to herself as she started the coffee and Tim emerged a few minutes later dressed in his new outfit. "Beautiful," she said. "This is the perfect look for you. Slicked back hair, all black clothes. You look like a rebel of some sort."

Tim laughed. "Yeah, that's me. Rebel Tim. Well, I was going to wear my robe and stilettos, but..." Latwanda snorted. "Does she really think that's a normal outfit?"

"Who knows what she thinks? Or if she thinks." She handed him a mug. "Drink quickly; we have work to do." They could hear the familiar noises of other people arriving and getting ready for the show. As if on cue, the door opened and Nikki entered.

"I need coffee," she said, making a bee-line for the kitchen. She quickly filled a mug and sipped at it. Turning to them, she added, "And the stage needs sweeping and mopping, the props need checking – there are things to be done."

Tim and Latwanda looked at each other. "Yes, Nikki," they said together, dumping their mugs and heading for the door.

* * * * * * * * * * * *

Tim spent as little time at the opening night festivities as possible. It just wasn't his idea of a good time to stand around watching Cassandra being fawned over by her entourage. As one man from the audience knelt and kissed Cassandra's hand, Latwanda said, "There isn't enough alcohol at this party. I'm outta here."

Tim was right behind her. "Wait for me." They gathered their things and left the theatre, walking out into the cool night. The sky had cleared, but the ground was still wet and shiny in the moonlight. They walked in companionable silence, each enjoying the outdoors. At the corner, they parted ways and Tim made his way back to his apartment.

As he put the key into the lock, he was met by a barrage of meows coming from the other side of the door. He chuckled quietly and opened the door with a practiced foot to keep the cat from escaping. He dropped his bag and scooped the tawny ball of fur into his arms. "Hello, Harmony. Miss me?" The cat nuzzled his face, purring. Shutting the door with his shoulder, he chuckled again and set her down on the floor where she immediately began weaving in and out of his legs, purring all the while. He flicked on a light and looked around his apartment.

On the walls hung poster after poster of various Broadway shows; some with autographs. Playbills littered the tables and floor. Pictures with friends and cast members shared the bookshelves with books of theatre history, acting techniques, and librettos. A stack of original cast albums claimed a spot by the couch.

Inhaling the familiar scent of his living space, his body relaxed. The highs and lows of the day paled as the simple desire for a glass of water took over. He noticed the answering machine light flashing, and hit it en route to the kitchen.

"Hi honey."

"Hey, Mom." He always talked back to the messages.

"Just wanted to drop you a line and say happy opening night." *Thanks.* "I hope everything went well." *For the most part.* "Anyway, your father and I have been thinking about you, wondering how you're doing." *I'm single.* "Seeing if there's anything exciting going on." *Nope, Mom, still single.* "Anyone special?" *Ha, that's what I thought. No – single.* "Well, hon, as I said, hope you had a wonderful opening night. I love you and good luck." *Mom, not 'good luck'. Say 'break a leg'.* He'd never cured her of the habit.

He took a large gulp of water and strolled back into the living room, grabbing his bag and flipping on the television. Harmony jumped up and curled onto his lap. Absently stroking the cat, he let his eyes follow the pictures on the screen.

The film featured a handsome man striving desperately to save his love from evil's clutches. It was a stereotypical hero/villain story and just perfect for Tim's tired brain. He found himself engrossed in the film, silently cheering on the hero. Tim's heart squeezed as the villain caught the heroine in his trap. The music built, adding suspense to the scene and though he was aware of the convention, Tim's pulse quickened with anticipation.

A sharp pain in his legs made him sit up with a start. Harmony was standing on his lap, claws extended into his skin, fur fluffed out. Her head swiveled back and forth, scanning the room. The hair on the back of Tim's neck stood up and he echoed the cat's scrutiny. Harmony moved to the arm of the sofa and, as quietly as possible, Tim stood. He tiptoed to the edge of the room and peered down the hallway. There was nothing.

A gunshot rang out and both of them turned sharply to face the television where the hero and villain faced off. Neither of them moved. Harmony turned back to Tim and with an almost apologetic air, settled on the sofa as if nothing had occurred.

Only partially comforted by the cat's manner, Tim performed a quick search of the apartment. Nothing out of the ordinary. Tim rejoined his companion for the rest of the movie, letting the fictional characters play out the tension that had arisen within the room. By the time evil had been vanquished, both Tim and Harmony were feeling calmer. Tim sat for a moment, then glanced at the clock. 1:00 am. "Well, Harmony, it's time for bed." The cat looked at him with unblinking yellow eyes.

He stood, dislodging the cat, put his glass in the sink, and crossed into his bedroom. A large red circle on the wall calendar caught his eye. *Dinner with Nell;*

Ilene's. His best friend had complained about never seeing him recently, but she always did that during the week before a show opened. She knew he disappeared from the face of the earth during that week. So, he arranged dinner at their favorite place, Ilene's, for between work and the show.

As he was undressing, a movement at his bedroom window caught his eye. He moved closer to the window. Harmony was already perched on the windowsill, watching intently. Tim observed the cat, his apprehension returning, then turned his gaze back to the city. Nothing. Just the same skyline he saw every night. Without warning, something swept by the window, grey against the blackness. Tim jumped back with a startled oath and Harmony streaked by him, screeching. Blood thundering in his ears, he crept slowly towards the window and peered out. The skyline greeted him, undisturbed. He squinted into the darkness, daring something to come again, willing it to appear. Nothing. Just a peaceful city working, celebrating, slumbering.

Heart pounding, Tim looked around for Harmony. She had disappeared. He called for her, but she didn't come. Uneasy, he went to the kitchen pantry and grabbed her bottle of treats. Shaking it while moving from room to room, he called her name over and over. Silence. *Tim, you're scaring yourself,* he thought. *She's probably just hiding from that thing.* He knew he had seen something – no, someone. That shape had had a face. He didn't know who or what it was, but it had some kind of face.

There was no sign of the cat anywhere. His unease increasing, he put the treats back in the cabinet and returned to his bedroom. Swallowing his panic, he continued to reassure himself that Harmony had been scared and was now hiding somewhere he was unable to look. His heart fluttered against his ribcage like a frightened moth and he thought about calling Nell. *No, she's probably sleeping and anyway, what can she do?* he thought. Shivering, he crawled under the covers and stared at the window, half-hoping the figure would come again, half-afraid that it would. Against all expectations, eventually his eyes closed.

Chapter 2

He probably should have noticed the strange surroundings first, but he was so happy to see Harmony that it was awhile before his brain registered anything else. She capered about his ankles, glad to see him as well. When he went to reach for her, she bounded away and he struggled to follow. She eluded him, staying just out of his reach, a tawny flash among a dirt road. The dirt got all over his sneakers, but somehow, Harmony remained clean and pure. She led him down a path lined with oddly shaped plants. They glowed with a phosphorescence that lit the path ahead of him, dimming somewhat as he passed. Harmony scampered all over the path, pausing every so often to sniff the air. If he stopped for any reason, she swatted him with a paw, keeping claws in so as not to hurt him. The path appeared endless. The sense of being watched overwhelmed him and he turned to face his stalker, but found only the path.

Tim looked up into a multicolored sky. It was a patchwork of constellations and each constellation was illuminated by a softly glowing sphere. He stopped to scrutinize the pairing, but felt a paw swipe at his ankle and kept moving.

Glancing back down, he found that his surroundings had changed. There was no more path. He had come to the center of a very large, circular canyon. Turning around, he saw that the way in was now blocked by a thick mountainside and just inside of the wall was the faint outline of a figure. It flickered for a moment and disappeared. A meow sounded. Tim turned around again. In front of him lay an enormous set of scales carved out of the mountain, but so delicately done that it looked almost fragile. One plate was slightly lower than the other with a grey-cloaked figure upon it. Harmony hissed at the figure, and leapt onto the other plate, weighing it down enough so that the scales balanced and Tim could see that

Harmony wasn't the only thing balancing them out. On the plate with the cat was an infant. Helpless, but silent, with intelligent eyes, the child reached towards him. Tim stretched out a hand to touch the infant.

His alarm blared. Frustrated, he hit the snooze and tried to go back to the dream, but even as he turned over, he knew it was useless.

He slid one leg, then the other, over the side of the bed and pushed himself into a shaky standing position. Stepping on clothing, Tim stumbled his way towards the bathroom and flicked on the light. Squinting in the fluorescent lighting, he started the shower and twisted the knob until the water was just the right temperature. The spray massaged his muscles, relaxing them to a state unachieved during sleep. Suddenly, his mind snapped alert with the memories of the previous night, as if the water had washed the dream from his mind. He felt a rush of adrenaline sear his chest. He wondered if he had dreamt the entire occurrence. That speculation triggered a fresh flow of adrenaline as he remembered Harmony's disappearance, only to reappear in his dream.

He tried to recall all of the details of the dream, but his mind seemed to rebel, remembering only Harmony, constellations, and an infant. He struggled, attempting to discern the meaning behind it, but the more he thought about it, the more slippery and evasive it became. Eventually, his concern turned to focus upon his missing cat and he quickly finished the shower, wrapping a towel around his waist. He grabbed his toothbrush and began brushing when an odd glow in the steamed mirror caught his eye. Squinting at the skewed image of his face, he wiped his hand across the mirror, clearing it of steam.

His eyes were glowing lavender.

He drew a sharp breath and moved closer to the mirror. The familiar flecks of brown, grey, and green stared back at him, but now with an added uncertainty that hadn't been there before. Concentrating hard, he willed his eyes to change color again, but they refused. *What is going on?* he asked himself, his heart resuming its terrified beat.

Immediately, Tim headed for the kitchen and grabbed Harmony's treats. Searching underneath furniture and opening all of the doors and drawers, he scoured the apartment. His fears steadily gained strength. He finally had to admit defeat and get ready for work, but in the back of his mind, he made a promise to make "Lost Cat" posters when he got home. It felt better to have an activity planned. Glancing at the clock, he threw on his work uniform, snatched his bag, and dashed out the door.

At first, he thought it would be a great job working at the local bookstore, but after three and a half months, it had become wearing. True, he loved people and he loved books, but combining them in a capitalist market situation ruined both, at least while he was at work.

That morning, his frustrations were not completely work related. Very few customers came into the store, and after the usual morning setup, Tim was free to read for his own pleasure, but he had trouble concentrating on the book in his hand. He wanted nothing more than to escape thoughts of the previous night and his growing sadness at Harmony's vanishing act. He'd finally slip into a story, just as one slips gently into a warm bath, and without fail, there would be an interruption. It was torture trying to calm his mind long enough to return to the fictional world. The afternoon continued much in the same way and he groaned when the phone rang, tearing him from his safe novel.

"Good afternoon. The Book Nook, Tim speaking. How may I help you?" He practically spat the words into the receiver.

The voice on the other end was pleasantly cheerful. "Yes. Um, do you have *A Cat Collar for All Occasions?*"

He relaxed. "Hi, Nell."

"How'd you know it was me?" She sounded put out.

"Who else would make up a ridiculous name like that?"

"You. You're the cat-lover." Tim's heart squeezed. His mind delved into possibilities for Harmony's disappearance. "Hello? You still there?"

Trying to sound normal, he stammered out, "Yeah, yeah, I'm still here. What's up?"

"Thought I'd lost you there for a second. Where'd you go?"

"Just thinking about something."

"Yeah, I could smell the smoke all the way over here."

"Ha, ha, very funny. You've been using that joke since we were six."

"And, after eighteen years, it still works."

"Shut up." It was on the tip of his tongue to tell her about Harmony and the strange events of the past day. True, Nell was his best friend, but her views were unpredictable. She could be whimsical and eccentric one moment, then turn stubbornly logical at the drop of a hat. Depending on her mood, there was no telling which way she would go with this situation. He wanted her to say that he was just being silly, that Harmony had probably gotten out and she'd be back, that he only imagined the figure at the window and his eyes changing color. But he was terrified that she might believe him and that would make it real, so instead he asked, "We still on for tonight?"

"Yeah, about that – I can't make it."

"What? You were the one who whined about how you haven't seen me and now you're breaking our date? What's going on?"

"Don't be mad at me," Nell pleaded, "but Gary called and he has tickets to a *People Litter* concert downtown. I can't miss it!"

"Some best friend. You're ditching me for a concert."

"I could've lied and said I had a family emergency or something stupid like that. I should at least get points for honesty."

"You get very little points at all, Nelly."

"Don't call me that, Timothy Jason Dalis, I mean it." Her voice took on a hint of steel.

"You're blowing me off," Tim argued. "I have every right to call you whatever I want."

"Fine, Elf." It was Nell's childhood insult for him, referring to his ears, which hinted at a point. "Can we reschedule? It's not like you have a life or anything."

"You sure know how to charm a guy, Nell."

"Tell that to Gary."

"I'll be sure to tell him when I see him." Tim pointed a customer down an aisle for the "Self-Help" section.

"How about tomorrow?"

"Work, then the show."

"What about Monday, then?" She sounded exasperated, but Nell was always dramatic.

"Working the evening shift," Tim told her.

"Perfect. Let's do brunch. Ilene's?"

"Do you have to ask? Of course, Ilene's."

"Deal. I'll meet you there at 11:00." Nell told him.

Tim rang up a copy of *Cat on a Hot Tin Roof,* trying not to think about Harmony. "Sounds good to me."

"I'll see you then."

"Have fun at the concert."

"Miss me."

"Always. Talk to you later."

"Have a good show. Bye." Tim stood for a moment, listening to the dial tone on the other end. He still felt uneasy about keeping secrets from his best friend. Resolving to tell her in person, he replaced the receiver with a sigh and turned back to his book when a new voice interrupted him.

"Excuse me?" He glanced up. A spiky-haired woman stood before him, smiling kindly. She was probably in her late thirties, early forties, if he had to guess, but with a distinctly younger style of dress. She wore jeans that were ripped at the knees and frayed at the bottom of the cuffs. The cuffs almost completely covered her feet, but when Tim looked down, he could see the toes of her sneakers poking out from underneath the pants, one red, and one blue. Her black t-shirt was faded and covered with symbols in silver sequins, a pairing that was mirrored by the grey streaks in her raven-colored hair. Her earrings were mismatched; the right ear contained a diamond stud, while the left was weighed down by a long dangling teardrop. Around her neck, she wore a hawk made from a dark grey stone. A few wrinkles betrayed her age, but most were laughter lines around her eyes and mouth, which was painted a frosted baby pink. Hazel eyes twinkled with merriment. He blinked.

"Excuse me?" she repeated.

"Yes?"

"I'm sorry to bother you, but could you tell me where your New Age section is?" She shifted her feet, and her bag, covered with drawings that she had obviously done herself, swung into view. It was packed to the brim with various books and instruments that Tim didn't recognize.

"Oh, um, sure. Like, astrology and tarot cards and all that?"

"And all that," she agreed with an obscure smile.

"In the back, near the Religion section." He pointed vaguely towards the back corner.

"Are you sure?"

He stepped out from behind the desk and found that she stood eye to eye with his 5'5 stature. "Well, it's not really a section I go into all that often." He led her past New Fiction, Romance, Mystery, and Science Fiction to the back of the store. He shrugged apologetically. "There's not a lot in this section. We don't get a high demand for books like these. I guess most people don't really believe in this kind of stuff these days."

The woman turned to him. "What about you?"

"Me?"

"Yes. Do you believe in astrology and tarot cards and all that?" she asked.

He had to grin in spite of himself. "Not really. I mean, no offense, but I've never really seen how my life could be controlled by something as distant as the stars."

The woman seemed amused. "Not controlled, really. Influenced. In a very strong, but ambiguous manner."

"If you say so, but I think a lot of it is self-fulfilling. We make our own destinies."

"Sometimes." She began to hunt along the shelves.

Feeling oddly defensive at her seeming dismissal, he continued, "Look, I just don't agree with it. The stars can't explain my life."

The woman studied him for a moment. "Is everything in your life so easily explainable?"

Up until recently, Tim would have responded with a resounding "Yes!" but the previous night had shaken him. His mouth flopped helplessly as his brain strove to find an answer. Finally, he muttered, "I don't get how everything can be told by a horoscope."

"Yes, I know. Many people read their horoscopes in papers and magazines, though they don't believe in them either. However, there are many more people that do believe. The art of prediction is a branch of astrology that, when used properly, will reveal certain information, but the horoscopes that you find in a newspaper aren't this kind of art. You understand?" Only marginally interested, Tim made a small noise of assent.

The woman went on. "There's another branch of astrology that is closely linked to psychology. The astrologer uses information like birth date, time, and location to construct a chart for the exact moment of that person's birth. This is called a natal chart or a birth chart and it's a picture of the sky that reveals certain things about the person." Tim surreptitiously glanced back towards the front of the store. He felt trapped by this woman and wanted to find an opening in the lecture that would enable an excused exit. Unfortunately, she didn't pause.

"This kind of chart is difficult to create accurately because there are a lot of mathematical calculations in order to get the exact locations of the planets for a given moment down to the second. Nowadays, we have computer programs which do it for us. A person's psychological makeup is contained in that chart. Each of the ten planetary influences has a place in one or two of the twelve signs of the zodiac."

Despite his eagerness to escape, Tim's curiosity prompted him to interrupt. "Ten?" he asked. "How can there be ten planetary influences when there are only nine planets?"

"Good question. Well, first, the Earth isn't included as a planetary influence because the birth chart is located on Earth looking out at the heavens. Earth can't influence its own inhabitants because the Earth is always in the same position in everyone's life at all times so there's nothing to differentiate its influences on us."

Tim wrapped his mind around that concept. Constant things aren't noticed. "Okay, I think I'm with you on that. But that only leaves eight planets then."

"Right. The remaining eight planets, plus two – the sun and the moon. Granted, these aren't actually planets, but they're included in the planet group. Some astrologers strongly suspect that there are still two planets to be discovered, but until then, we have these ten, and all have a major impact on a person's life.

"The Sun is the most basic and commonly known influence. When most people identify themselves astrologically, they are identifying their Sun Sign, or where the Sun falls in their chart. If someone says, 'I'm an Aries', they are really saying, 'My Sun is in Aries'. Most people don't worry about the other planetary influences. When you read your horoscope in the paper, you are looking for your Sun Sign."

"Okay, got it." Although he remained skeptical, his curiosity was aroused. He wondered where the other planets fell in his own chart.

The bell at the door to the store rang and Tim was almost disappointed as he excused himself. He found a young man looking for books on unsolved mysteries. Tim led him towards Non-Fiction and by the time he returned to the New Age section, the woman had gone. Both disturbed and relieved, he went back to the desk and dove into his book, determined to escape the frenzied thoughts of his mind. The end of his shift came quickly after that, with minimal incident, and he headed off to Ilene's to grab something to eat. He felt fresher once he stepped outside into the evening. The breeze flew through him, purifying his thoughts. He walked the two blocks down to Ilene's, his heart lightening. On such a clear night, it was easy to pretend that everything was fine, but underneath, there was a layer of apprehension and every so often, he'd glance at the sky. It looked less and less as though anything would appear and by the time he reached the tiny diner, he felt halfway normal again.

The sight of his favorite waitress, Lena, was enough to put a smile on his face. She smiled back as he entered. "Tim! Good to see you, honey. How is everything?"

"Hey, Lena. Not too bad, not too bad. Any of your tables available?" They had a familiar routine they enacted every time he went to the diner.

The grandmotherly woman loved every minute of it. She looked around the near-empty restaurant and shrugged. "I guess I can find a table for my favorite customer."

"Oh, is Bette Midler here?" They both laughed. Every time, it was a different celebrity or someone they both knew. Tim loved to see Lena laugh. She was a sweet woman who'd been working at the diner for almost thirty-five years now. He never took anyone else's table and he always knew when she was working. She'd been serving him and Nell since the first time they went to the diner, the night that Tim moved to Philly.

Tim loved Ilene's. There were always a few patrons, but it was never crowded. The food was good, but he really came for the comfort it gave him. Stepping into Ilene's was like returning home and he could almost completely ignore the nagging doubt at the pit of his stomach that told him something strange was going on underneath the façade of normalcy he was desperately maintaining.

"And where is the lovely Nell?" Lena asked, grabbing two menus. "Late as usual?"

Tim followed her to the table. "Not tonight, Lena. Nelly ditched me." He pouted.

Lena laughed. "Oh, she'd kill you if she heard you call her that."

"That's half the fun," Tim admitted. "I think I'll just have the original, please." The 'original', for Tim, was what he ordered that first night, which was chicken parmagiana. For Nell, it was a burger and fries with a glass of red wine. Tim always made fun of her for the combination.

"One original, coming up." Lena wandered back to the kitchen.

Tim checked his watch. 6:00 pm. He had a little time, so he reached into his bag, opened his book, and began to read. He hadn't read more than a page when he felt someone staring at him. He looked up from his book to the front of the diner, heart in his throat, expecting to see a grey-cloaked figure there. There was nothing. Just the storefront window providing a view of the street. Quickly, he glanced around the room, wondering if anyone saw his panicked reaction. There was a couple by the door, obviously interested only in each other. On the other side of the room was a boy around his age, a knapsack at his feet, writing in a notebook. *Probably some kind of student or something*, Tim figured. Behind him was a family of five. The father was trying to keep control of two young kids, while the mother fed the baby in the high chair. The little boy from the family met his eyes. Tim told himself that he was being paranoid and returned to his book. About half of a page later, the hairs on the back of his neck stood on end and his head snapped up from the book, ready to catch someone's eyes. Nothing at the window. The little boy was happily eating his dinner. Everyone was involved in their own lives. He was beginning to feel hunted. Unnerved, he went back to his book, but the words swam before his eyes and he put it down. Fortunately, Lena chose that moment to arrive with his food.

"Here you go, honey." She stood for a moment, plate in hand. "You alright?"

Tim opened his mouth to confide in her, but he realized that she would think he was crazy. If he couldn't tell Nell, he certainly couldn't tell Lena. He swallowed and nodded.

She set the plate down in front of him with a flourish and said, "Eat up. You're beginning to look like a bag of bones, young man."

"I work it off at the gym," Tim told her, but he obligingly took a bite of the food. He drew comfort from the familiar taste. "Delicious as always. Mom worries that I might starve up here on my own, but I keep telling her that as long as I have you around, Lena, she has nothing to worry about."

"Hmm. You're still getting skinny. You'll have to come in here more often." She poked him in the ribs, tickling him. He swatted her hand away. "How dare you strike an old woman!?"

"Oh please, Lena, you're not old. You're vintage." They both laughed.

"Well, I have tables to take care of. And you have food to get through before your show." She bustled off with a washcloth, wiping down one of the tables.

Tim attacked his chicken. He relished this dish, but there was more to it than that. It was mindless action that granted him reprieve from the odd occurrences. He was clinging to anything that resembled a normal life. Chicken parmagiana was a perfect specimen of normalcy. It was one of his favorites from home and Ilene's made it almost exactly the same way his mother made it. His mother refused to believe that, but she was glad he was eating. Halfway through the chicken, he felt well enough to focus on the book. He had to stop eating every so often to flip a page, but that never bothered him. He had that down to a science, having always brought a book to meals whenever he had to eat alone. It got to the point where he almost felt naked without a book at a table. He finished eating with a moan of appreciation. Lena chortled behind him. He jumped and turned around. *Calm down*, he told himself. *She already thinks something's wrong.*

Meanwhile, Lena was talking. "My, my, when you enjoy something, you really enjoy it."

"Nah," he said, "it was awful. I just ate it so no one else would have to touch it."

"Oh, get out of here, you." She made shooing motions with her apron. "I ought to never serve you again."

"Don't say that, Lena. You're the reason I come here. I wouldn't be served by anyone else." He always won her over in the end.

"Mmmhmm. Well, we'll see about that, next time." Then she opened her arms for a hug, which he happily obliged. "Oh, my dear, I do adore seeing you." She held him at arm's length, scrutinizing him. "You're sure you're okay?"

Tim decided not to say anything about his unease. He plastered a smile on his face. "Happy as I could ever be, Lena. I've got you and chicken parm. Who could ask for anything more?"

"I'll take rhythm, music, and a man." The fake smile became real as Tim recognized the Gershwin lyrics, immediately beginning to hum the tune. "In the meantime, you better pay for that chicken parm and get on over to the theatre. It's almost twenty to 7:00."

Quickly digging in his wallet, Tim snatched a bunch of bills and thrust them at her. "I know how much it is. No change. The rest is for you." Swinging his bag up onto his shoulder, he dashed for the door, yelling back over his shoulder, "Thanks for everything, Lena! Take care!"

"Bye honey! Break a leg!" came the response, and Tim's grin widened as he ran down the street towards the theatre. *At least it isn't raining this time*, he thought.

Chapter 3

"Tim?"

Odd, Tim thought, peering out from the wings of the backstage area. Usually, the lights were so bright onstage that the audience beyond the stage's edge was obscured to the actors, let alone the tech crew. Yet a pair of vibrantly blue eyes shone from the darkness of the mezzanine. From the moment the curtain had gone up, the sensation of being watched had returned, but it wasn't the same as before. Instead of the sick feeling in his gut, Tim felt excited. Breathless. Every time he was onstage moving scenery, he could feel those eyes burning into him and it was exhilarating. He couldn't wait for the show to end. He stood at the edge of the wings for most of the performance, squinting into the darkness beyond the stage, willing to risk Nikki's wrath for a moment of connection. When it finally came, it was electric.

"Tim?"

A strange sense of belonging spread from his middle towards his extremities. The experience was odd and uncomfortable and wonderful and he wanted to explore it further.

"Tim."

A dormant part of him stirred, awakened. He stared directly into the blue depths, willing more to come.

"Tim!" The sharp insistent hiss broke through his reverie and he painstakingly turned from the welcome blue to be met by a pair of stormy brown eyes. Abruptly realizing the scene had ended, his mind went numb. The dark stage filled with tension as he racked his brain to remember what scene change came next. Cassandra lost patience. She shoved him hard in the back, causing him to fall onstage. He struggled in the blackness to figure out what to move.

Latwanda was already starting the scene change. "Act two, last scene change," she muttered as she passed him.

His mind whirled, cleared. "Thanks!" he exclaimed, relief washing over him as he took a desk into the stage right wing. He set a chair in place and escaped to the cool darkness of the wing again. The scene change complete, he took a deep breath. *That was close.* Latwanda came quickly around from backstage.

"What happened to you out there? Are you okay?" She looked concerned.

Tim put his hand on her upper arm. "I'm fine. I was just thinking about something and I got lost in thought."

"Well, you better snap out of it. Cassandra's going to flip on you. The critics are here tonight and she wants everything to be perfect. She was steaming when she entered." Indeed, the air onstage was fairly crackling with tension, radiating from the tall blonde. The other actors were maintaining a safe distance.

"I better come up with an excuse before she comes offstage."

"Which is any minute. I'll see you after bows. If she doesn't kill you." Latwanda retreated quickly, as Cassandra bore down on him, fury blazing in her eyes.

"What in the hell were you doing? Where were you? Were you daydreaming? How could you let that happen? The show is timed perfectly, you imbecile, and now you've thrown it all off! There's no way the critics missed that. Did you know we had critics here tonight? Does your tiny little brain comprehend what that means?" She continued to rant and rave at him, and at first, Tim backed away, hardly daring to look her in the face. He finally looked up and met her smoldering brown eyes, brows knit together so closely that they almost became one. His mind was abruptly shunted to the side as a new awareness took control. The sensation was not unpleasant and when he analyzed it later, he found that he couldn't really say that the awareness was not part of him. So he stayed docile as this new part of him stood up straight and calmly faced the actress. Cassandra sensed the change. "What is *with* you?" she asked.

Tim began to smile. "I'm sorry," he said in his most contrite and sincere manner. "I made a mistake and you're right, it did make a difference in the timing, but I guarantee you that every critic out there is so mesmerized by your performance that they won't even notice the scene changes at all." He felt as though he were split in two and a part of him he had never known, never consciously accessed, was dominating the situation while the rest of him sat back and watched.

Cassandra's eyes took on a lavender hue and her wide smile mirrored Tim's own. "You think so?"

"Of course. Honestly, who's going to pay attention to what's happening in the scene changes when Cassandra LeVoe is coming onstage? No one would be able to notice anything else." *That was laying it on thick,* the rest of him said.

Cassandra practically preened herself. "You're right." The awareness disappeared as quickly as it had manifested and Tim was left before the diva with no clue as to how to proceed. Cassandra seemed to recover herself and assumed a haughty air, her eyes brown once more. "Just don't *ever* let that happen again, Timothy Dalis!" She stalked away, but her heart wasn't in it.

Latwanda came out of the shadows. "What in the world did you say to her that didn't get your eyes scratched out?!"

Tim looked at her, bewildered. "'Wanda," he said. "I honestly don't know."

After the show, Tim searched the lobby for the blue-eyed stranger, but found no one. Irrationally feeling rejected and dreading the walk home alone, he decided to call Nell and tell her what was going on. The phone rang and rang, finally going to voicemail. *Oh, damn!* he thought. *She's at the concert.*

"Nell, call me back. I'm having the weirdest couple days. There was this thing...and Harmony...and blue eyes...I need to talk. I don't care what time it is. Just call me back when you get out of the concert. I hope you're having fun. Love me, miss me."

He walked into his apartment with a bit of trepidation. No meowing came when he put the key in the door. No cat came to greet him when he entered. Harmony was gone. The apartment felt hollow without her. Sad and lonely, he went right to the computer and pulled up pictures of Harmony, using them to create a "Lost Cat" poster. Then, not wanting to think anymore, he set the printer to print fifty copies, pulled the blinds down on the window, shut them tight, and went directly to bed.

Harmony reprised her dream cameo and she wasn't the only one. The figure from the mountainside stood beside her at the entrance to a large castle. Tall and willowy, the young man opened his mouth, but no sound came out. Harmony rubbed against the boy's ankles, a sign that this person, whoever it was, was friendly. The boy went into the castle and Tim followed. He found himself in a cavernous hall, sparsely lit by a torch here and there. There were paintings on the walls, but he couldn't make out what they were. The boy went over to one of the murals, pointing insistently at something, but Tim didn't understand. Harmony was meowing at him and he was trying to read the boy's lips, but in the flickering light, it was near impossible. There was a rumbling throughout the hall and the ground began to shake. Cracks appeared in the floor, widening at an alarming rate. The boy vanished. A bright flash of light caused Tim to stumble backwards and with a cry, he fell into a newly formed chasm.

* * * * * * * * * * *

Upon waking the next day, Tim immediately reached for his phone. There was no message from Nell. Annoyed, he threw it against his bag. He kept his anger for Nell at the forefront of his mind the entire morning; it felt good to be righteously angry. It also kept the other emotions at bay. He grabbed the stack of posters and a roll of tape, posting them every ten steps on trees, posts, and whatever else he thought he could get away with. He even posted one in the window of The Book Nook when Mark wasn't looking. For the first time, he did whatever his boss asked him to do without complaint. Physical activity kept his mind from working. He organized bookshelves, helped customers, checked books against the database, anything he could do to keep himself occupied until he could talk to Nell. He was stacking books in the Mystery section when he was paged to the front by his boss.

The phone was placed in his hand. "It's a customer who said you helped her with her last purchase. She asked for you specifically." Mark walked off, but not before grumbling out a grudging, "Well done."

Tim watched him go for a minute before saying loudly into the phone, "The Book Nook. This is Tim. How can I help you?"

"I'm looking for *Circus Clowns of the Middle Ages!*"

"You are a circus clown, Nell."

She laughed. "I'm not the only one. You sounded like a clown in your message last night."

"So you got it. Why didn't you call me back?"

"I put the phone on silent for the concert."

"You're supposed to turn it back on after the concert!" he yelled, earning him a look from Mark. He lowered his voice.

"I forgot, okay? Geez. Besides, I don't know what you're upset about. You said something about someone with blue eyes." Her voice held a hint of teasing.

"Yeah, about that – are you free for dinner?"

"Well, I have to cancel my massage appointment, my facial, and my combination pedicure and bikini wax, but I guess I can fit you in."

"You're so funny. Why in the world would they combine a pedicure – you know what? Forget it. Thanks, Nell. I really need to chat." He realized he was twisting the phone cord around his wrist so tightly it was beginning to hurt. He quickly unwound it.

"No problem. I'll meet you at work and we can go over to Ilene's. Lena working tonight?"

"Yeah, perfect. I'll go straight from there to the show."

"Again with this show. Haven't you kicked the habit yet?"

"You think you're so clever."

"That's because I am. See you at Ilene's. Bye." Without giving him a chance for a rebuttal, she hung up. Hanging up the phone, he felt a little better. He'd explain things to Nell and she'd help. He hoped. Mark came back over.

"Were you able to help her with her book?" His tone suggested that he knew the nature of Tim's phone call.

Once again, Tim played backseat as the new personality took over. Smiling, he lied, "I was. There were two more books in the series and she wants all three of them. She says she'll come in to get them. In hardback," he added. Tim thought he saw a slight glow appear around Mark and the distrustful air shifted into approval.

Mark smiled greedily. "Nice upsell, Tim. Good job." And as the lavender glow faded, he strode over to a new customer, smiling his used car salesman smile. Tim winced and retreated to the back shelves to stack more books, which was where he hibernated for the rest of the afternoon. His mind worked on trying to understand what this new awareness was. Was it dangerous? What did it want? It had taken over during two very awkward situations and he couldn't deny it was effective. He resolved to be more alert for the next time it happened and in the meantime, this new personality seemed to be, if not beneficial, then harmless. *First that thing at the window, then Harmony, then some stranger. Is it any wonder I'm developing a split personality?*

As it was getting close to the end of his shift, Nell showed up. Slightly taller than Tim with honey-colored hair and light blue eyes, she was sporting a new *People Litter* shirt with a picture of a stick figure in a litter box. Mark had left, so Tim and Nell were able to make small talk while Tim finished his shift. He went into the bathroom to change out of his uniform and when he returned, Nell was browsing through a book. Knowing that she would immediately start asking him questions, he led off with one of his own.

"Whatcha readin'?" he inquired.

"Just checking something I read in the newspaper this morning," she answered, flipping a page.

"What?"

"They were saying that we would be able to see Neptune in the upcoming months."

"That's impossible. You can't see Neptune from Earth," Tim scoffed. "Not without a telescope anyway."

"Well, that's what the paper said."

"So, what exactly do you think you're going to find in...," he grabbed the book and laughed, "*Astrology for Dummies?*"

"Huh?" She grabbed it back. "Oh, damn. I thought it said Astronomy. I'm an idiot."

"Dummy, technically," he pointed out.

"Shut up." She slapped his arm. "Let's go to dinner."

Tim opened the door and gestured for her to leave. "After you, m'Lady."

"You're such a gentleman." She sauntered out. "When you want to be."

Tim made a face and followed her down the street. The silence stretched between them; Nell giving Tim the time to say whatever he needed to say, Tim not so sure he knew how to start. Lena smiled broadly at them as they entered the diner.

"Well! What a surprise! Twice in one week? And Nell this time! Is it my birthday?"

"Yes it is," Tim told her. "Happy 29th."

Lena swatted him on the arm. "Twenty-nine, indeed! What I wouldn't give to be twenty-nine again!" She wrapped her arms around Nell. "You're getting skinny too, missy! I was just telling this one that he was getting too skinny, but it seems that like everything else, you're doing that together."

Nell disengaged and pouted, waif-like. Affecting a small voice, she said, "Well, we have no food where I live and if you don't have a table open, I'm just going to waste away from hunger."

Lena went into her routine. "We can't have that!" She looked around the diner, saying, "I guess I can try to fit you in somewhere."

"Oh, thank you, Lena! You're my savior!" Nell was overacting and she knew it. Tim rolled his eyes.

Lena tried to keep a straight face, but a laugh escaped her. "Oh, you are something else, Nell! Let's get you two something to eat." Taking two menus, she started towards a table.

As they settled into their seats, Nell ordered her "original" and after a moment's deliberation, Tim also ordered a hamburger. Nell raised an eyebrow; Tim rarely ate red meat. "I need it tonight," he explained.

"I see." There was another moment of silence, and then Nell prompted him, "So?"

Tim didn't know what to say. Now that he had Nell in front of him, it seemed completely ridiculous to bring up the subject in the middle of Ilene's. It was too familiar, too comfortable. Inwardly, he was screaming at himself to start the story, to confide in his friend. Yet he heard himself say, "So...still no job?"

Nell's expression was quizzical as she assessed this change of possible subject. "No, still no job. I still can't believe we got shut down." She took a sip of her wine. "A few temp positions, but they're few and far between."

"How are you paying for anything?"

"I'm not spending a lot. Gary's helping me out too."

Tim wasn't exactly happy about this new development in Nell's life. It wasn't that he disapproved of Gary, but he just didn't feel that he was good enough for Nell. Nell was constantly falling for deadbeats that did nothing for her and though Tim admitted that Gary was a step up for her, he thought she could do better. He wouldn't tell her that, however. They had had a fight about one of her boyfriends early in their friendship and didn't speak for almost a year. Since then, he had learned to keep his opinions about certain subjects to himself and react noncommittally. "That's nice of him. The tickets for the concert must have cost him a fortune."

Nell shook her head. "He got them through a friend at work for free. It was complete luck that we were both available."

"Except you weren't available," Tim pointed out.

"Okay, yes, you're right. I'm sorry. But it was *People Litter*! The only concert in their 1999 tour that I could go to!" She pointed to her shirt with a pleading look. "You know I have no willpower!"

"Can't argue with you there. How is Gary?"

"He's good. He was very nice. Brought me a rose when he picked me up."

Tim took a sip of his wine. "That's sweet."

"It was really sweet. He even bought me this shirt at the concert. Now, *that* cost a fortune. He said, 'If you want it, it's yours'." There was a contentment coming from her that Tim wished he could take part in. "What about you? Seeing anyone special?"

He groaned. "You sound like my mother. That was one of the questions she left me on my machine on opening night."

"Oh, shit, I forgot to ask. I'm a bad friend. How was opening night?"

"Funny you should ask, actually. I mean, the show went fine. Cassandra was a bitch, but that's nothing new."

"Definitely not," Nell agreed, drinking more wine.

"I didn't stay long at the party after the show. I went home, listened to Mom on the machine. The usual crap. She still says 'good luck'." He made a face and Nell laughed. "But then I was getting ready for bed–"

"Ooooh, it's a sexy story," Nell teased. Lena's interruption stalled a retort from Tim.

"Here you are, kids." She set a plate down in front of each. "Another glass of wine for the meal?"

"None for me, thanks, Lena," Tim declined.

Nell drained her glass quickly and held it out. "Yes, please." Lena took it from her to refill.

"Don't drink too quickly, Nell," Tim warned her. "You can't handle a third glass."

Nell's voice was filled with disdain. "Oh, please. I can drink you under the table and you know it. A third would be nothing to me." She picked up her burger and took large bite.

"I don't mean alcohol-wise. I mean money-wise," Tim corrected her.

With her mouth still full, she responded, "This from Mr. Spending Spree himself."

"I have a job. I have income." Tim took a smaller bite of his own burger, relaxing in the familiar company.

Lena returned with the glass of wine and set it down in front of Nell. "If you need anything else, guys, all you need to do is holler."

"Thanks, Lena. Tim's paying for this glass of wine, by the way. He's the one with income." She grinned mischievously across the table at him. Tim snorted. Lena shook her head and left. Nell raised her glass. "Here's to me having no income, but having a best friend who's willing to support me."

"As if I have a choice," Tim grunted, but he obligingly raised his glass and clinked it against hers. Taking another sip, he added, "Besides, you have a boyfriend now who can pay for you."

"Yes, but I wouldn't want to deprive you of the privilege."

"Poor Gary. I hope he knows what he's getting himself into." Tim started in on his fries.

"I want to know what you're getting yourself into. We were at the point in the story where you were going to get naked and get in bed." She took another large bite and mixed it with the wine in her mouth.

Tim grimaced. "You've definitely had too much to drink already. That's not the point of the story."

She groaned. "What is the point of the story? Get to it." A loud insistent beeping filled the air. "Actually, hold that thought." She dug through her purse, while the beeping got louder and louder. Tim continued munching while she pulled out a cell phone the color of sunshine with daffodils on it and checked the screen. "It's Gary." She flipped it open and raised it to her ear. "Hello?"

"Could that thing be any more disgustingly cute?" Tim wondered aloud. "It looks like a care bear vomited all over your phone."

Nell threw him a look of death. He smiled back as innocently as possible and took a sip of his wine. She gasped. "Really? Are you kidding me?" *Oh, geez,* he thought. *Knowing Nell, this conversation could take awhile.* He sat, watching her talk, lost in thought. His stomach twisted and he turned over his shoulder to glance behind him. The eerie feeling of being watched had suddenly returned, but the diner window provided him with a view of an empty street. He turned back to Nell to ask her if she'd seen anyone looking in, but she was completely involved in her conversation and wasn't paying attention to him. He quickly took another sip of wine, but it tasted bitter in his mouth. He finished off the burger to get rid of the taste. All the warmth he'd been feeling vanished and he shivered.

"Tomorrow? Yes, we're still going." Now anxious to talk to his best friend about events, Tim was drawn back to Nell's conversation. "Of course she knows we're coming; that's her job, isn't it?" Catching Tim's questioning look, she said, "Hold on." She placed a hand over the phone. "We're going to a psychic tomorrow."

Tim raised an eyebrow. "You're going to a what?"

"A psychic. Hey, why don't you come with us?"

"You want me to go on a date with you and Gary to a psychic? You've got to be joking." Tim took a large gulp of wine.

"It's not a date. Not officially, anyway. C'mon, it'll be fun. What time are you working?"

"5:00."

"Perfect, you're coming." Ignoring his incredulous look, she turned back to the phone. "Still there? Yeah. Yeah, Tim's coming with us. See? That's what I said. Okay, call me later. Bye."

"You didn't give me any choice," Tim complained.

"Shut up. Do you really have anything better to do?"

"No, but–"

"I didn't think so." She looked smug and took another large bite of her hamburger. "Our appointment's at 1:15 tomorrow. Be ready to go around noon."

"She lives that far away?"

"No." She eyed him. "But I know you. If I tell you to be ready to go at noon, you'll actually be ready to go around quarter to 1:00 if I'm lucky. So, be ready to go at noon."

He wanted to steer the conversation back. "Fine. I really don't believe in any of that shit though and you know that." His unease returned. "But there has been weird stuff happening lately."

"Yeah? Like what?" Nell leaned forward.

"Well, some woman was in the store yesterday asking me if I believed in this kind of stuff. And now Harmony's gone."

Nell paused in the act of taking a bite. "She's gone?"

"Gone. I put up posters. Didn't you see them?" Tim worried that someone had torn them down.

"Tim, you know I turn my head when I see those posters!" It was true. Nell had a huge soft spot for animals and couldn't bear to think of a pet wandering the streets alone, away from the family that loved them. She always avoided looking at the pictures because she claimed they made it worse. "When did she leave?" Nell's eyes were moist.

"The other night when I came home from the show. Nell, something weird happened that night."

Lena reappeared at the table's edge. "All done?" she asked. Nell wolfed down the last few bites of her hamburger and chased it with the rest of her wine. Putting the glass back down on the table with a clang, she nodded, her mouth full. Lena shook her head and began removing plates. "Well, I'm glad to see that you're eating as well, missy."

"It's good food," Nell responded, her mouth still full. Agitated, Tim watched Lena clear the table, wishing she would hurry up. He didn't feel that he could talk to Nell in front of Lena.

The waitress turned a discerning eye his way. "And you have a show to get to." She jerked her head towards the clock.

Nell laughed smugly. "Told you. You're always late, Tim!" Tim stifled a curse as he stood and fumbled for his wallet. "Don't worry about money. I'll cover you and you can pay me back." She gestured for him to leave.

"Nell, you can't afford that. You have no income!"

"So you've mentioned. I have enough to cover this right now. You have to promise to pay me back though."

"I don't have the time to argue this out with you. I promise I'll pay you back. Thanks, Nell!" Snatching at his bag, he leaned across the table, gave Nell a quick kiss, tossed a wave at Lena, and headed out the door.

Nell hollered after him, "Call me later! I want to know what's going on!"

* * * * * * * * * * *

He was on his way into the tech room when a voice he knew all too well rang in his ears.

"Timothy? Timothy! May I have a word?" He halted in his tracks and slammed a smile into place before turning around.

"Of course, Cassandra. How are you today?"

"I'm just lovely, as always. The question is, Timothy, how are *you*?" Concern filled her eyes, but Tim couldn't tell if it was sincere. He decided he didn't care.

"Fine. I'm fine, Cassandra."

"I just wanted to make sure we didn't have a repeat performance of last night, Timothy. I'm sure last night's mistake was a fluke and will never happen again. Things might get ugly if it did and neither of us wants that, now, do we?" Her voice was pure steel.

"Not at all. I promise. I'm feeling completely on top of my game tonight," Tim assured her, using all of his willpower to maintain his smile and keep his tone pleasant.

"Good boy. I'd hate for what happened to color our experience for the entire run." Leaving him standing there, she clicked her way to her dressing room.

Insides churning, he spun on his heel and went to the tech room. In a way, he was half-hoping that what had happened the night before would happen again. He wanted to get another glimpse of the blue-eyed stranger. Yet he knew that if anything went wrong, Cassandra would eat him alive. He was almost willing to risk her wrath in order to see his blue-eyed friend. Almost, but not quite.

As soon as he was able, Tim scanned the audience. Nothing out of the ordinary. Apparently, the previous night had been a fluke as Cassandra had said. Luckily for him, the show went beautifully. Cassandra even thanked him for not screwing up, which he took to be a compliment.

On the way home, he decided that he needed a beer. Slipping into a nearby bar, he plopped down onto a stool and grabbed a drink menu.

The bartender, silent and watchful, plodded over. "Whatcha want?"

Tim pointed to one of the local beers and the bartender nodded. Within minutes, Tim had a beer in hand. He downed the drink, barely tasting it, and ordered a second. Nursing it, he reviewed the events of the previous days in his head. The alcohol was swiftly working its way through his bloodstream, making his thoughts muddled and blurry. He couldn't remember having ever gotten so intoxicated in such a short time. As he finished his second drink, his head was pleasantly humming. He hummed along, providing a harmony to the music playing in the bar. Harmony. She passed into his head, batting a paw at him as if trying to stimulate his brain into action.

Before he could wrap his mind around what she was trying to communicate, the bartender returned and placed another beer in front of him. Tim stared. "Next beer's paid for."

"By who?" Tim wanted to know, but by that time, the bartender had traveled down the bar and was taking care of someone else. Tim's eye followed him, trying to assess who might be his benefactor, but the faces ran together. He shrugged, not in any condition to question his good fortune, and took a swig. He brought the bottle in front of his face and tried to read the label, but it swam before his eyes. He only made it halfway through his beer before sleep began to overtake him. *This is weird,* he thought groggily, *I've never felt this drunk and definitely not from three beers.* He felt a hand on his bicep and turned to face the person, but the movement made him dizzy and he passed out before he could see who had a hold of him.

Chapter 4

He awoke to the warmth of sunlight streaming through the window onto his body. He opened his eyes very gently to meet an anxious face peering down at him. A face with piercing blue eyes. Confused, he blinked. When he reopened them, the face was gone. There was no one in the room. His head was pounding and his ears were ringing. He sat up gingerly and put a hand to his head. His throat felt raw, as though he had screamed throughout the night. As he tried to stand, a wave of dizziness enveloped him and, groaning, he laid back down, cradling his head with a pillow. The ringing persisted and it occurred to him that the ringing was outside his head. When he looked at his bedside table, he discovered that his cell phone was the source of the noise. He snatched at it and flipped it open. "Hello?" he managed to scratch out.

"Tim! What the hell is going on?" Nell sounded concerned.

"Huh? Nell, not so loud." Her voice was making waves of pain crash through his head.

"DID YOU JUST WAKE UP?!" she screamed into the phone. Tim yanked the phone away from his ear and clenched his teeth as a waterfall of pain cascaded over him. When it had diminished to tiny rivulets, he spoke again.

"Mmmmhmmm. What time is it?" He searched for the clock.

"It's 12:20, you stupid elf! You have fifteen minutes to get ready! I'm on my way over. Now, get up!" The click blasted into his ear and he moaned, gently closing the phone.

"Damn!" he muttered. Tim tried to remember what had happened the night before, but his mind couldn't focus. He remembered being in the bar, but after that, the night was a haze. *That's why you don't mix alcohol,* he told himself. He found his way down the hall to the bathroom, every muscle groaning in protest. Cupping his hands under the faucet, he gulped water directly from the sink. The cool water went a long way to soothe his parched throat and his headache began to subside as the moisture made its way through his body. A short shower did a lot to massage his sore muscles but he could not relax. There was a nagging feeling that something was off. He was heading back down the hall to get dressed when a knock at the door made him jump. He crossed the living room and opened the door to find Nell glaring at him.

"You're still in a towel?! Tim, we have to be at the psychic's by 1:10! I told Gary we'd be there by 1:00 and you're not even dressed! I swear, I'm gonna shoot you if you don't get dressed right now!"

"Hello to you too, Nell," Tim responded. "Don't worry," he added, walking towards his bedroom, "if she's a real psychic, she'll know we're going to be late."

He dressed in record time as Nell screamed death threats through the door. They were on the road soon after, Nell driving at warp-speed. Tim was used to her driving habits, but his body was still delicate and every jerk of the wheel caused at least one muscle group to complain. How she still had her license remained a mystery to him. Cars, buildings, and people whizzed by as she flew through the streets, muttering obscenities under her breath the entire way, half of which sounded newly invented to him. The nagging feeling persisted, but as they pulled up to a small, one-story stone house, Tim gave up. The house looked cozy with a wagon wheel table on the porch and lacy curtains on the windows. It was definitely not the sort of place that Tim ever imagined a psychic would live, let alone work from. They hopped out of the car and started up the walk, underscored by Nell's complaining.

"We're five minutes late. He's gonna be so mad that we're five minutes late."

"Who? Gary? Five minutes is nothing." Tim stopped on the porch before the worn wooden door. "Besides, technically, we're five minutes early, now aren't we?"

Nell turned to him, tight-lipped. "Tim, do I seem like I'm in a rational mood right now?"

"Um, no."

"Take the hint," she warned, raising her hand to ring the bell. A pleasant chime sounded throughout the house. The door opened, and Tim beheld the sweetest-looking elderly woman he had ever seen.

"Hello? Do I know you?" she warbled, peering at the arrivals through her glasses. Her hand was entangled in the chain attached to them.

"Um...Are you Madame Sereny?" Nell inquired doubtfully.

"What?" The older woman blinked her confusion.

"Nell?" A young man rounded the side of the house.

Nell flung herself at him and hugged him fiercely. "Gary! Where have you been?" Tim waved a greeting.

"Now, don't get mad," Gary pleaded. "I got stuck in traffic."

"Well," Nell pretended to mull it over. "Don't let it happen again." And she winked at Tim, who rolled his eyes. She turned back to talk to the woman only to find the door closed in her face. "What the–?" She knocked on the door. No answer. "What is going on?" She banged on the door as loudly as possible.

A muffled voice responded from the inside. "I'm on my way! Trines and quincunxes, I'm coming – you don't have to pound on the door!"

Nell looked at the boys. "Tri-what?"

"Must be some psychic term," Gary suggested.

The door opened a second time to reveal a younger woman in jeans and a dark blue t-shirt with hot pink letters declaring *Seers Are Believers!* upon it. As luck would have it, Tim happened to be looking down when she opened the door, so his first view of the woman was of her mismatched sneakers – one blue and one red. He raised his eyes to meet the gaze of the spiky-haired New Age customer. She smiled. "Hmm. If it isn't the non-believer. Nice to see you again." Tim's mouth flopped helplessly.

"You two know each other?" Nell looked from one to the other.

"In a manner of speaking," the woman explained. "We met briefly at his bookstore."

"Oh, yeah?" Nell asked. Tim looked down, avoiding Nell's inquiring gaze.

"Maybe you can help us." Gary stepped forward to relieve the awkward tension. "We seem to have the wrong address. You see, we're looking for a psychic."

"That's me. I'm Sereny." She held out her hand.

Gary shook it. "I'm sorry, but you don't look like any kind of psychic I've ever seen, Madame Sereny."

"Just Sereny, please, Gary." Gary exchanged a slightly surprised glance with Nell and Tim as Sereny ushered them inside. The hallway was lined with antiques and beautiful black and white photographs. Towards the end was a series of pictures whose subject could only be Sereny at a very young age. The hallway emptied out into a den-like room where they found the elderly woman sitting in a rocking chair, crocheting. Sereny walked over and knelt beside her. "Mom," she said loudly. The woman turned to face her daughter. "Mom, these are Gary, Nell, and Tim." She gestured to each in turn. "They're clients. I have work to do. I'll be in the back if you need me." She beckoned to the three. "Follow me." They obeyed, moving through another doorway into a small room, sparsely decorated, containing a few chairs. "This is my waiting room. Readings are private. If someone wants to share the information they learn at the reading, that's their choice."

"This is kind of an odd...I mean, interesting place to hold psychic readings, isn't it?" Gary asked Sereny.

"I don't believe in creating atmosphere for money, Gary. I am who I am and I just happen to be psychic as well." Gary looked doubtful, but said nothing. "The people who truly need me find their way to me. As for the place, this is where I grew up. My parents have lived here all the years of their marriage. I moved out when I was twenty-two, but after my father died a couple of years ago, my mother's health began to fail, so I moved back home." Sereny's hand unconsciously stroked the hawk at her throat. "I converted the back area into my own private room to do readings. My mother does not hear very well, so don't worry about her overhearing. About the only sound she seems to still pick up is the doorbell." She delivered this with no sense of loss or pride, but stated it matter-of-factly.

"I'm sure she heard you introduce us. I guess you really are psychic since we never told you our names," Gary noted.

Sereny laughed merrily. "Yes, I am, but that's not exactly damning evidence. I take the appointments myself and you have to give your names when you make the appointment. As for Tim, I met him the other day, as we mentioned already."

"But I never told you my name," Tim protested.

The corners of Sereny's mouth twitched. "Then I guess I really am psychic." Her manner turned business-like. "Now, enough chitchat. Who would like to go first?"

"Ladies first," Gary offered, gently pushing Nell forward.

"Too kind. Yes, too kind, I'm sure," Nell announced dramatically, affecting a British accent. Sereny put her arm around the young woman's shoulders and led her through a doorway. Tim caught a flash of red and white before she closed the door firmly behind them.

Gary and Tim turned to each other. "I guess we should sit down," Tim suggested. Gary nodded and they both took seats, leaving a seat between them. Tim cleared his throat. "So, how was the concert?"

"It was awesome. Everyone was jumping up and down and one girl jumped onstage to dance with Paul Whittaker."

"Lead singer?"

"Lead guitar," Gary corrected. "She got pulled off by security."

"That must've been fun for her."

"I guess." There was an awkward silence.

"So," Tim started, grasping for a topic, "How did you hear about Sereny?"

"Actually, I heard about her through a friend. I'm not really into this stuff either, but I mentioned it to Nell and..."

Tim chuckled. "I know what you mean. Once Nell gets an idea into her head, there's no getting around her. It takes some getting used to."

"Yeah, I can see that."

"Good luck," Tim offered.

"Thanks." And that more or less exhausted the conversation. Tim looked around the room. The beige walls were illuminated by sunlight streaming in from a window and a skylight. There wasn't much in the room besides the couple of chairs and a stack of rather ordinary magazines. He picked one up and paged through. Nothing particularly interesting caught his eye. He started reading an article on Chihuahuas just to keep his mind on something. After a short while, the door opened and Sereny led a stunned Nell out. Without a word, she gestured for Gary to enter the room. Gary glanced at Nell and stood. As he went inside, Tim saw black and yellow from the room. Shaking his head to clear the image from his mind, he moved to Nell. She sat, stock-still, staring at the door.

"Nell?" When she didn't respond, he took her hand. She faced him, her eyes still somewhat vacant. "Nell, are you alright?" Nell began to shake. Tim swallowed hard, his unease returning. "What happened?"

"The– the–" She choked off the words and leaned against him. He held her tightly, memories of the past few days flashing through his mind.

"The what?" The shaking was becoming more pronounced. What had she seen in that room? He slowly placed a hand under her chin to tilt her face up to him and was shocked to see that she was smiling and shaking with laughter. "Nell!" Disgusted, he shoved her away from him. His heart was still pounding. "Don't you take *anything* seriously?"

Still laughing, she answered, "Not if I can help it! Tim, I'm sorry, but the look on your face was priceless. For someone who doesn't believe in this, you sure looked scared out of your mind!"

"It wasn't funny, Nell. I told you something weird is going on. I really thought something horrible had happened." He went and sat down.

She sobered and took the chair next to him, laying a hand on his wrist. "Concern noted. And I still want to know what's going on, but the reading was fun. She told me all kinds of interesting stuff."

Despite his anger, he was curious. "Like what?"

"First, she asked me if I wanted cards, crystal, or stars. I asked for crystal and she made me look into this ball. I was kinda disappointed. Crystal balls and cards and all that – it just seemed so...I don't know, traditional, I guess. She seemed so much like a New Age kind of psychic, you know what I mean?"

Tim wasn't sure what the difference was, but he went along with it. "Yeah, I guess so. Anyway, what did you see?" When she didn't respond, he clarified, "In the ball."

Nell looked uncomfortable. "I really don't want to say. It was kind of personal."

"Something too personal for me to know?" Tim wondered. "I'm your best friend."

"I know that, but this was something that you don't know about." Nell's eyes took on a faraway look

"Something with your love life? 'Cause I have every right to know about that."

She snapped back. "Oh, please, you know more about my love life than my boyfriends do."

"Best friend privileges," Tim claimed. "You know all about mine."

"And what's there to know?" Nell teased. "There hasn't been all that much to talk about from your end of the table."

Sheepishly, Tim agreed. "Yeah, I know. Whereas you, on the other hand, seem to have a new boy every week."

"Not this week. It's still Gary." She moved closer to the door and tilted her head towards it. "Gary is so much better than all of the others, Tim."

Tim snorted derisively. "Nell, a fish would be better than some of the guys you've dated."

"Shut up, Elf. You're just jealous." Tim snorted again. "This one's gonna last. I have a good feeling about Gary." As if on cue, the door opened and Gary stepped out, glowering. Nell jumped back and immediately began reading a magazine, pretending, not very successfully, that she had been doing that the entire time. Sereny appeared in the doorway, her face an emotionless mask. She crooked a finger at Tim. As he stood, he heard Nell whisper urgently, "What did she say?" before being hushed.

Tim walked past Sereny into a room containing a small round table with two chairs on either side it and a dresser off to the side. The table was covered with a violet cloth that draped down to the floor. There were numerous candles scattered about the room, throwing flickering light upon the blue and lavender walls. Tim was confused. There was neither the glimmer of the red and white he had seen when Nell entered the room, nor the black and yellow for Gary.

"The room fits the personality of the person that I'm reading," Sereny explained without being asked. "Please have a seat." She offered the chair closer to the door. Apprehensive, Tim slowly lowered himself into the chair. Sereny smiled reassuringly and took the other chair.

"What did you tell Nell and Gary?" Tim couldn't help but ask. "Nell wouldn't tell me when I asked her and we share everything. Gary didn't look much better."

Sereny tsked. "I told you before: readings are very personal experiences. I'm glad you're concerned about your friends, but don't worry. They'll be okay."

"Are you really a psychic? I mean, you do seem to know things, but you certainly aren't what I'd picture a psychic to be."

"Does everything fit so easily into what you picture it to be?" He had no answer for that. "What I look like has nothing to do with what I can do. What I am is called by many names: seer, medium, clairvoyant, psychic, and so on. I am gifted with abilities to gain information in unusual ways, mostly through the vibrations of the universe, but having these abilities means that I also have a responsibility. You'll understand that soon enough."

Tim groaned. "Are you naturally cryptic or does that come with the job description?"

"If I told you everything at once, you wouldn't be able to handle it. Trust me. I'm giving you information in pieces that you can handle. Learning more about me makes it easier for you to learn about you."

"'Learn about me'...'learn about you'...What are you talking about?" Frustrated, Tim was no longer wondering why Gary had such a negative look on his face when he emerged. *This woman is impossible to understand,* he thought.

Sereny just smiled. "Soon. Now, you came for a reading, yes?"

"Not by choice," Tim muttered. Realizing the possible consequences of his being rude, he looked up to Sereny still smiling at him, though he noticed a glint in her eyes. "Yes, thank you." Remembering what Nell had told him, he added, "I choose the cards."

"The cards are a choice," Sereny agreed. She reached into a drawer, removing a deck of cards. "Pick four cards from this deck and give them to me." She placed a second, smaller deck beside the first. "Just pick one card from this deck. You can shuffle either deck, but make sure you're not looking at the cards when you pick."

Tim studied the two seemingly normal decks of cards. On the back of the larger deck was a pattern of intertwining vines. The other showed the solar system. He picked up the vine deck and shuffled it thoroughly. Almost hoping that something amazing would be the result, he removed four cards at random and handed them to Sereny. Taking the other deck in one hand, he fanned out the cards with the backs facing him. He selected a card from the middle and handed that across the table as well. She laid the five cards down in front of her and put the other cards back in the drawer. Shutting it, she turned back to the cards and studied them for a moment, concentrating. Tim watched her intently as she slowly raised a hand, slipped a fingernail beneath the first of the vine cards and flipped it over, revealing the Seven of Hearts.

"Wait," Tim said, confused. "This is just a regular deck of cards. I thought there would be pictures on them or something, you know, like Tarot cards. I didn't think it would be normal playing cards."

"Does everything fit so easily into what you picture it to be?" Sereny repeated softly, not looking at him. She turned over a second card. Seven of Clubs.

"So, what does that mean? Are Sevens good or bad in this deck?" Tim wanted to know. He didn't know why, but he was beginning to get nervous.

"We'll see," was the short response, and the Seven of Diamonds lay face up next to the other two.

Tim stared at the table. "Three Sevens? Weird. What are the chances of that happening?"

Sereny seemed to be beyond hearing. She was silent as she revealed the Seven of Spades. Tim filled with curiosity and apprehension.

"Now, it is complete, except for one card," she breathed. Her hand was steady and sure as she reached for the final card. Tim's gaze was fixated upon it and he was almost disappointed when it was revealed, but Sereny's face broke into a smile that was both relieved and anxious. It was a symbol: ♎. There was no significance to the symbol for Tim, but Sereny clearly understood what it meant. He looked at her, then back down at the symbol. It hadn't changed.

"I – I don't understand," Tim ventured.

To his surprise and annoyance, Sereny laughed. "No, I guess not. I'll explain all I can, and I need for you to keep an open mind. Will you agree to do that?" Her voice was triumphant.

Tim's mind was awash with confusion. "I can't promise I will. But I'll try. As long as you promise to be clear. No more obscure messages."

With childlike solemnity, Sereny crossed her heart. "I will do my best." Tim nodded, but didn't smile. "Make yourself comfortable." He tried to relax and wasn't very successful. With everything that had happened to him, the last thing he wanted to do was prepare for a lecture. He wanted to ask the psychic questions. Maybe she would have some answers. He felt a war inside of him between frustration and respect and in the end, respect won out. So he sat there quietly as Sereny stood and began to pace about the room.

"I'm don't know how much you remember from our conversation the other day." Tim was silent. "I explained about Sun signs. Was I clear?"

"Crystal."

"Good. Now–"

"No. Crystal," Tim corrected, pointing to the table. The crystal ball had appeared on the table and was glowing. Sereny moved towards it cautiously.

"Shhh," she warned. "Don't make a sound." Tim watched as she and the crystal held some kind of silent communion. After an unbearably long moment, Sereny nodded and the crystal dimmed. She faced Tim. "Now, where were we?"

"Wait just a moment. What the hell was that? What did it say?" The questions came pouring out of him.

"Nothing that you need to know." She moved to the back of the room, seating herself at the computer. "You were born on the eleventh of October, yes?"

"Yes, but–" Sereny was already typing away.

"1975?"

"Yes. Sereny–" More typing.

"2:42 pm?"

"Yeah."

"36 seconds?"

Tim stopped trying to ask about the crystal. Stunned, he whispered, "How do you know all that?" For a moment, there was no sound but the clicking of Sereny's fingers on the keyboard. She made a few final strokes and next to the computer, a printer lit up and filled with room with its whine. Sereny stood, retrieved the paper from the printer, and then moved slowly towards him with a tender smile on her face.

"You are a very special person, Tim. An extremely unique individual in this world."

"Why? What are you talking about?" Tim's heart skipped a beat and he was beginning to sweat.

Sereny sat down across from him and laid the paper face-down on the table, folding her hands on top of it. "I know this sounds odd, but there is a prophecy that gives your birth great significance." From memory, she intoned:

"When thousand spins of Terra twins,
Twelve years ere Waterbearer,
All on the Earth will see rebirth
And yet, be forced to share her.

"The stars are born in human form,
Their power quite divided.
The Twelve, forewarned of coming storm,
Are powerfully united.

"The guide and guard of fledgling charge
Inherits power unmeasured.
So molds the will, for good or ill,
Of precious ether treasured."

Tim sat for a moment after the last word fell from Sereny's lips. Those twelve lines, supposed to explain everything, left him bewildered. He had no idea what any of it meant, but he could feel a growing sense of apprehension as he reviewed the ominous words in his head. He stared up at her, waiting for an explanation.

Sereny did not disappoint him. "I'm not just a psychic. I work within an organization called The Gathering. We are a select handful of minorly gifted individuals who keep an eye out for strange occurrences. This prophecy fell into our hands near the end of the 18th century. It was studied at great length and the members, noting that it referred to the end of the 20th century, put it into a vault and it was forgotten.

"About thirty years ago, Tim, our astrology wing recorded something incredible. Contradictory to all beliefs and previous astronomical and astrological studies, the planets had shifted position in their orbits. For a mere second in time, they aligned. One second later, they were back in their original positions, continuing along their original orbits. Everyone on Earth experienced disorientation, and I'm told most people passed it off as a personal moment of dizziness. However, this event sent waves of energy throughout the psychic world. Similar waves swept through The Gathering; waves of information centered on the astrologers. They were besieged by demands for an explanation, but no one could explain it. So we went on alert, keeping watch for a repeat occurrence. It happened again. And again. Every year at a different time for eleven subsequent years." She unfolded her hands and flipped over the paper. "One of those times was October 11th, 1975, at 2:42 and 36 seconds in the afternoon." She slid the paper across the table to him.

Tim stared at the paper. It was a chart like the ones she'd mentioned. There was the symbol from the card on it, along with other symbols that he didn't recognize. There didn't seem to be anything special about it. As with the prophecy, he didn't understand the chart, but he knew there was a great significance to it. He studied it for a few minutes, pondering the story Sereny was telling him. When his eyes returned to her face, she continued. "If you were ever to have your birth chart done by a computer program, it would print that out. A computer, being a logical machine, would keep the planets on their regular course. That chart is false. Your true chart, the chart that belongs to you only, looks like this." She reached into the dresser again and retrieved a much older piece of paper, folded many times over. She reached across the table, holding it out for him to take. Carefully, he took it from her, unfolding it and laying it down on top of the other chart. The chart he looked at now had the same symbols as the one he had just studied, but in this chart, ten of the symbols were grouped together near the symbol from the solar system card he had chosen originally.

He frowned at his birth chart, trying to figure out the significance of the difference. Finally, he looked up. "I don't know what any of this means," he said.

"You're about to find out," Sereny told him. She held up the card he had chosen with the symbol facing him. "This," she started, "is the symbol, or as we call it, the glyph, of the sign, Libra. The chart that you hold shows that the position of the planets – all ten of them – aligned under Libra at the moment of your birth. Not only that. Libra, and therefore all of the planets, are in the Seventh House, which is Libra's natural house, Libra being the seventh sign of the zodiac." She held up the other four cards, displaying the sevens. "That is the significance of these. This is a complete aberration, of course. It had been thought impossible for all of the planets to align under one sign. The influences would make an individual extremely one-sided, or, in this case, blessed with certain abilities."

Tim felt as though he were drowning. "Abilities?"

"In order for the universe to exist, it has to move forward. Everything has to die so that more life can come forth. Even stars. When a star explodes, pieces spread out to become other stars. Yet, by hoarding power, one star was able to stay in existence long after it should have dissipated. This star was Merel." The name sent chills down Tim's spine.

"It escaped to a fledgling blue and green planet and continued to grow in power. This situation has had major repercussions throughout the universe. In fact, there is speculation that the eradication of the dinosaurs is a direct result of further power gain." She paused. "I'm getting off topic. If Merel is left unchecked, the universe and everything in it will be annihilated.

"According to the prophecy, at the turn of the millennium, the person destined to stop Merel will be born. This child will have gifts from the stars. At the moment of this individual's birth, each planet will be in its natural sign and each sign will be in its natural house. A child with this kind of power is volatile and cannot be left to fend for herself. She will have the potential to do incredible good or cause harm unseen to date. The ultimate result depends on the guidance that she has. Our goal is to find the Star Child and teach her to use her power to preserve the universe. Naturally, we first thought Merel's goal was to kill the child, but the prophecy suggests that Merel also wants to harness this power. 'So molds the will for good or ill of precious ether treasured,'" she quoted. "Whoever teaches the Star Child is the one who will ultimately preserve or destroy life."

"Why does she need to be guided at all?" Tim asked, curious.

"Without guidance, she will destroy herself. Power like that needs a purpose," Sereny told him.

Tim felt a glimmer of an idea in the back of his brain, but he stubbornly flicked it away as a horse flicks a fly. Already suspecting the answer, he asked, "Who is supposed to care for the kid on your side?"

Sereny gazed at him thoughtfully. He had an uncomfortable feeling that she knew he was being purposefully obtuse. "To protect and teach this infant, twelve guardians were born. As the child will be blessed astrologically, so are the guardians. This is why the planets aligned, each under a different sign. When one of these individuals names their sign, they are truly the personification of that sign for not only the Sun, but every planet falls into the sign at their time of birth. The sign has, in a sense, been brought to life. Similar to those with psychic gifts, these individuals were each born with a talent, stronger than common psychic talents, which is innate and natural to the person and suited to the sign they were born under."

Sereny held her peace as she watched comprehension light Tim's eyes. Incredulity washed over him. "Are you telling me that–?"

"Yes." She reached across the table to take his hand. "Yes, Tim. You are Libra."

Chapter 5

Tim sat, stunned. The full impact of what he had just been told still hadn't hit him. His mind warred with the possibility that what Sereny told him was a lie. He wasn't sure whether he wanted to believe her or not. He desperately wanted to contradict her, to call her a fraud, to make it not true. Yet, he knew, deep down in his soul, that this was the part of him that had been awakened the other night. He hadn't even known it existed until a few days before, and now it had a name. Libra. He thought again of the strange connection he'd felt in the theatre, and considered asking Sereny about it, but he couldn't bring himself to do it. *Does this have something to do with the grey-cloaked figure?* he wondered. His head was swimming with questions and he became painfully aware that Sereny had been silent for a long time. She was waiting, watching to see what he would say, what he would do. He cleared his throat and pulled his hand away.

"I, um, I mean, this wasn't what I was expecting when I came here today."

Sereny laughed. "No, I guess it wasn't. I'm sorry if it comes as a shock."

"Shocking?" Tim asked sarcastically. "How could this possibly be shocking?"

"Again, I'm sorry. I tried to prepare you as much as I could."

Tim tried to put sincerity into his voice. "No, you were okay. I mean, how can you prepare someone for something like this? I don't know if I even believe it."

Sereny's voice took on a serious quality he hadn't heard yet. "This is real. Your gift is real, the infant is real, and there are real dangers involved."

"Are the guardians – am I in danger now?"

Sereny hesitated. "You are." Tim's skin crawled. "And anyone who knows about you will be in danger."

"In danger from what? From who? How can I protect myself if I don't know what I'm protecting myself from?"

"Keep an eye out for anything out of the ordinary."

A dam inside of him broke. "Things haven't been ordinary for awhile! There was this thing and Harmony disappeared and I feel like I'm being watched all the time–"

"Yes. The crystal mentioned that."

"That's what the crystal told you?!" he raged, standing. "You could have mentioned that earlier!"

Sereny was unmoved. "You will find help soon."

"Why can't you help me?" he pleaded.

"There's nothing I can do," she replied calmly. "Tim, I wish that I could do more, but I'm a psychic. All I can do is tell you what I know and what I know most of all is that help is on its way."

He put his head in his hands. "So I'm just supposed to what? Sit tight and wait for someone to come up on a white horse and fight a battle in my honor?"

"Well, yelling at me isn't going to get you anything," she said coolly.

He glared at her, his rage spent, but still unsatisfied. Another thought came to him. Sullenly, he said, "You said we all have talents. Gifts of a sort."

"Yes, you do."

"What's my gift? Am I allowed to know that?"

Sereny smiled. "Of course. Libra is known for its charm. You, as Libra, have an immeasurable amount of charm at your disposal. This may not seem like any kind of true talent," she said, watching his face regain its skeptical look, "but it is a subtle and powerful gift. Anyone who you come across can be charmed. You simply have to exert your will on them and they will become compliant, so that someone who might have argued with you will suddenly acquiesce to your whims. It's not mind control; it's an appeal to their emotional nature, so that you become someone that they want to please. As you learn to use this gift, you will be able to force even enemies to not only do your bidding, but take pleasure in doing so. This is not a gift to be used lightly or abused. So far, you have used it in very small doses and quite unconsciously. In fact, I believe the first time you used it consciously was on your friend, Cassandra."

Tim barked out a laugh. "She's not exactly a friend." Then he understood what she was referring to. "You mean the other night? I just smiled at her and she..."

"She suddenly was very understanding, wasn't she?"

"Yeah. I felt like I had split in two and this other part of me was doing something to her. Her eyes changed color and then she was so nice." Tim began to wonder at the power within him. "But then I was back in control. It happened again with my boss. He actually glowed. I mean, I think he did."

"It's possible. You said you split in two, but your talent is yours, Tim. You are Libra. Make sure you connect with this talent because you will need it."

Tim's anger and frustration were trickling away as things fell into place. "Yeah. I felt connected, but detached at the same time."

"The more you accept the situation, the better off you will be."

Tim thought of something else. "Sereny, the infant about to be born: who is it?"

"We don't know. We only know it'll be at the end of this year." She gestured for him to sit and he obeyed. "All twelve Signs will be needed for the rescue and protection of the Child. We have until the end of the year to gather them all together."

Curious, Tim asked, "How will I know who they are? Do they look any different?"

"Do you?" Sereny countered. "No, they look just like everyday people, but there will be something more to them. You will be able to feel it."

"Like some kind of connection? An awakening? A bond?" Tim asked alertly.

"Yes. Exactly. How did you know?"

Tim tried to make his response as nonchalant as possible, taking pleasure in knowing something she did not. "I may have met one of the other Signs already."

"That's highly improbable, though not altogether impossible. Where did you meet?"

"Well, we didn't actually meet, but it was at the theater where I work. I was backstage and I could feel it from the audience. I couldn't see anyone else in the audience, but there was this pair of eyes that I could feel staring right at me. I felt this part of me wake up."

"It's entirely possible that you may have indeed met one of the Signs, but the chances of it are very slim." The doubt in Sereny's voice was reflected in her expression. "If you have, though, there is a way to check." She produced another piece of paper and handed it to him. "This is a list containing the birthdate and birthtime for each of the Signs. If you come across anyone that gives you that feeling, check their birthdate and time against this list. If they match, you'll know you have found a Sign. Remember that all twelve Signs must be present at the birth of the Star Child or all is lost. In the meantime, learn all you can about the influence astrology can have on our lives. It will help you to better understand your fellow Signs and the Star Child.

"Also, keep the group together. Libra is the born diplomat and the charm you possess is a huge part of it. It is most important that the group keep some kind of harmony." Tim gave a start. Sereny glanced at him sharply. "Is there something else I should know?"

"Harmony. My cat. She's gone. She disappeared a couple of days ago," Tim told her.

"A cat?" Sereny arched an eyebrow.

"Yeah," Tim said, feeling silly. "Just that you're saying that we need harmony and Harmony just disappeared from my own life."

"Why did you name her 'Harmony'?"

Tim shrugged. "I don't know, actually. A friend told me that the best way to name a pet was to pick the first word that you see that you like and make that the pet's name. Seemed stupid to me, but the first word I saw was 'harmony'. It was in one of the shows I was working on at the time." His mind was sinking back into memory. "I know I laughed and said it out loud. But when I said it, she sat up, came over to my lap, and put a paw on my knee. I know she was looking at me and trying to say something. I said it again and she meowed, so it became her name." His mind returned to the present. "I don't know why she ran away."

"It's possible that she didn't just run away, Tim," Sereny reassured him. "Something monumental is about to happen and very often, animals can sense things like that before humans can. They're very sensitive to the vibrations in the air. Harmony may have sensed something coming and headed out either to face or escape it."

"Well, she could have told me she was going," Tim grumbled.

"She might have done just that. Her leaving may very well be a warning to you." Sereny was serious.

"I just wish I knew what," he said, frustrated.

"It's very likely that you'll find out," she told him. "Now, we really are out of time and you must rejoin your friends. Remember, though, that anyone who knows about you is in danger."

"I get it. It's the Superman syndrome. At least *he* had some idea of what he was doing." Tim stood, folded the papers and put them in his pocket. Sereny opened the door, gesturing for him to go through. Nell and Gary had obviously been deep in conversation, but went quiet as he entered. Gary gazed at him with curiosity, while Nell's face reflected more concern. She moved towards him, but a look from Sereny halted her.

"I will see you out. Follow me, please." Without waiting for a response, Sereny started off back the way they had come. As they passed through the den, Tim paused to look at Sereny's mother. She was lightly snoring in her rocking chair, her crocheting strewn across her lap. He opened his mouth to say goodbye to her, but then he realized he didn't know what to call her, so he satisfied himself with a small wave in her direction. The corners of her mouth curled faintly at the edges, but she didn't wake up.

"Charming," he heard her say and startled, he hurried after the others, catching up to them as they reached the end of the hallway. *Looks like psychic gifts run in the family*, he thought. As they stepped out onto the porch, Sereny looked at each of them in turn. "I wish all of you luck. Perhaps we shall meet again." Her gaze lingered on Tim as she closed the door before any of them could say anything. The three stood in silence.

Finally, Nell said, "I guess we should go." The boys looked at her. "I mean, you have to work tonight and we have a date. I need to get ready."

Gary nodded. "And I have things to do before then. See you tonight, Nelly." Tim looked at Nell, expecting to see the usual annoyance at the nickname, but her expression was one of great affection as she stepped into Gary's embrace. Tim started off down the path as they began to kiss. His thoughts were a jumble. It suddenly occurred to him that he never asked Sereny what the figure outside his window was and he felt his chest constrict with the frustration that had become habit over the past few days. He consoled himself with the knowledge that although it sounded impossible, there was an explanation. Libra. He was Libra.

Nell met him a few minutes later at the car. He went on the offensive before she could start to question him.

"Nelly?" he inquired sarcastically.

"It's a pet name. Only someone I'm dating is allowed to use it," Nell informed him. "You lost your chance, Elf." She unlocked the door and they got in.

Tim assumed a long-suffering look. "I guess I'll just have to survive without it then. I probably wouldn't have survived this long if I had dated you." She slapped him on the arm and started the car. "Ow! Both hands on the wheel when you drive."

"That's rich coming from you. You can't even back out of a driveway." She smirked and gunned the engine.

"At least I don't drive like a maniac." As if to emphasize the point, the car flew over a bump, causing both of their seatbelts to constrict against them. "Why are you in such a hurry?"

"I told you. I have to get ready for my date tonight. Gary's taking me out to a fancy restaurant." She made a sharp right from the left lane, cutting off another car, honking her horn through the entire turn.

"He can finally afford McDonalds?" Tim joked. That earned him another slap on the arm. "Ow! Cut it out! It was a joke!"

She ran a red light, ignoring the glares and honking from the other drivers. "You know, there aren't many guys who are willing to take me to a nice dinner, Tim. I'm a little nervous."

"There's no need to be nervous. It's a dinner. Just like all the others you've had. If you want," he suggested, "I'll come to the same restaurant and sit at the next table and tell you what you're doing wrong. It could be an acting exercise."

"Timothy Dalis, don't you dare come on this date! I will make your life miserable. Don't think I can't!"

"Don't think you don't!" He dodged the slap this time and laughed, beginning to relax for the first time since he sat down in Sereny's waiting room. This was normal life for him, joking with Nell, worrying about trivial things. He did his best not to reflect on the weightier information he had just been given.

As if she were psychic herself, Nell asked, "So, what did Sereny tell you?"

His good mood evaporated as quickly as it had come. "She said my best friend is too nosy," he replied.

"You're one to talk!" she shot back. "Honestly, what did she say? You were in there for forever!"

"It's personal. Too personal, and no, I'm not saying that just to spite you," he added as she opened her mouth to protest. "I'm being honest." He wanted to tell her, but Sereny's warning about people getting hurt was still fresh in his mind and he loved Nell too much to risk that. He wasn't sure if she'd believe him anyway. True, Nell was always studying odd phenomena and appeared to be a true believer in otherworldly influences, but when it came right down to it, Nell could be more practical than anyone he knew. She liked knowing about the occult, but he wasn't sure she really believed whole-heartedly in it. He wasn't even sure he was completely convinced yet. His whole world had been turned upside-down by what Sereny had told him and he wasn't prepared to take all of it as truth just yet, but neither was he ready to discount it as lunacy.

"Fine." Nell stopped the car. "Get out."

Anger flared in his heart. "Nell, you wouldn't tell me what she said to you, so why should I tell you what she said to me?"

Nell laughed. "Of course you don't have to tell me. Sereny told us that we didn't have to reveal what the readings said. We're at your apartment, you ninny. Get out. I have things to do."

"Oh." Tim looked out the window. Nell had pulled up right in front of his door. He leaned over and kissed her on the cheek. "Have fun on your date. Call me afterwards."

"That might be tomorrow." She smirked mischievously.

"Nell." Tim rolled his eyes.

"Shut up and get out of the car." She started to push him as soon as he opened the door. "I'll talk to you later."

"Talk to you later." Tim shut the door and she roared off down the street. He started up the stairs to his apartment. A thought came to him and he checked his watch. Almost 4:30. He had a little time. He decided to go over to The Book Nook and do a little research before his shift. Sereny had suggested that he learn all that he could about astrology and that's exactly what he was going to do. He headed back down the stairs and along the sidewalk in the direction of the store.

Sheila, who was working the desk, looked up in surprise as he entered. "Tim! What are you doing here? No one ever shows up early to work!"

"I have some research to do first," Tim answered.

"Oh. Well, you're lucky. Mark called about an hour ago telling me to lock up early. He wouldn't tell me what it was about, but I'm thinking that he's finally getting nailed on building code violations." She sounded pleased at the thought.

"How nice of him to forget that I was scheduled for tonight," Tim grumbled.

"Well, yeah. That's typical Mark. Does this mean that I don't have to lock up?" Hope bloomed on Shelia's face. They all hated closing the store. If even one thing was out of place, Mark would yell at them the next time he saw them. There were a few instances where money had been taken out of their paychecks. Tim thought about it and though he winced inwardly at having to lock up, he relished the idea of being alone to do his research without customers bothering him.

"Sure, I can take care of that for you. No problem. You get out of here."

"Are you sure you don't need any help?" He recognized this for the insincere offer that it was and he fulfilled her expectations and hopes by declining.

"Nah. I can handle it. Better get out of here before I change my mind," he threatened.

"Sure. Thanks, Tim. Been a slow day." She indicated the handful of patrons milling about. "I'll see ya later, okay?"

"See ya." She grabbed her purse and shot out the door, practically pulling it off its hinges in her haste. "Easy enough," Tim murmured to himself. As the hour drew to a close, he shooed the last few patrons out of the store and locked the door, flipping the OPEN sign to read CLOSED. He went through the minimal cleaning exercises and double-checked the finances in the cash register. *Sheila's right,* he thought, *it hasn't been a very busy day. Mark's not going to be happy about this.* He finished everything about a half an hour later and made his way over to the New Age section.

Even when he had been helping Sereny, he hadn't realized how many books there were on the occult. He searched the subsections, making his way through Dream Interpretation, Wicca and Witchcraft, and Tarot, before reaching Astrology. *These really should be organized,* he decided. In the Astrology section alone, he found a wide variety of books. Some were generalized astrology. Some focused solely on certain signs or planets. There were a few on casting horoscopes and others about constructing birth charts. Curious, he opened one on birth charts and found a baffling series of mathematical formulae. He shut it quickly and headed back towards the shallower waters of general astrology. He was tempted to get a book purely on Libra, but Sereny had told him that all of the Signs would be needed and the least he could do would be to learn a little bit about each Sign. He took a few general-seeming books and went back to the front of the store. Settling into a chair, he opened the first book. Although he wanted to read about all of the Signs, he was curious about Libra, so he flipped through the book until he found that section and began to read aloud, thoughts flowing freely as he went along.

"Libra," he read. "The seventh sign of the zodiac is the most charming of all the signs. Ruled by the planet Venus, it concerns itself with harmony and beauty." *Weird. Now, I know why Sereny asked about Harmony.* "It has an eye for aesthetics and often has luxurious appetites." *I do have good taste.* "Being an air sign, it is primarily a mental sign, and deals with situations intellectually rather than emotionally. Libra, as a masculine cardinal sign, has a strong desire to make a change in the world." *Who doesn't?* "Libra is a born diplomat." *Yeah, she said that too.* "Through their charm and open mind, the Libran is usually able to see both sides of an argument and tactfully explain either side to the opponent, whether that opponent wants to listen or not. Libras like balance and will use every power at their disposal to keep it. They won't fight unless they feel strongly about something, especially in a case of fairness. If they feel they've been unfairly wronged, they will come out swinging, claws extended." *That's certainly true.*

A tapping sound interrupted his studies. He raised his head to see a middle-aged couple peering in at him through the window. The woman was mouthing something. He couldn't make it out, so he rose and unlocked the door, poking his head out. "Can I help you?" he inquired politely.

"Are you open?" she asked.

"No, I'm sorry, we're not. We closed early today. Inventory," he added on a whim.

"Oh, I'm sorry. You looked like you were open." She indicated the light.

"Nope, just doing some last minute work." He was beginning to get impatient.

"When do you open?" the man queried.

Tim pointed to the store hours listed on the door just below the CLOSED sign. "We open tomorrow at 9:00 am." It was taking all effort to be gracious.

"Okay, we'll come back tomorrow then."

"Have a good night."

"You too." They moved off through the night and Tim locked the door behind him. He returned to the book.

"Libras can be indecisive and often get a reputation for being so," he continued. "Being able to see different sides of a situation can inhibit them from making a decision, even in trivial matters, such as what to eat for dinner or what movie to see. It can be frustrating and stressful for them if they're forced to make one quickly." *Definitely. I hate making decisions on the spur of the moment.*

"In addition, Libras are reputed for being shallow and vain." At this, he laughed. "They love to pamper themselves with expensive items, but as they have excellent taste, their money is usually well-spent." He snorted. "They enjoy long baths and showers." *True.* "Any kind of pampering they can have, they adore."

"Libra is also the sign of relationships and the House of Partnerships is its natural home." *Wouldn't Mom love to hear that?* he thought, amused. "Libras are happiest when in a relationship. They love to be a part of a two-some."

"The parts of the body ruled by Libra are the lower back, the kidneys, and the buttocks." *The signs have parts of the body connected to them?* he wondered.

More tapping on the window made him look up. Three teenage girls were looking in at him. One of them mouthed something and pointed to the door.

"We're closed," Tim said loudly. He pointed to the sign on the door and repeated, "Closed," exaggerating it so they could read his lips. The girls moved over to read the store hours. One of them looked up at him again and he shook his head. She shrugged and turned to the other two and they left, chatting animatedly.

"Geez." Tim turned back to the book to read about the health factors involved in being a Libra. Foods that he should be eating, foods that he should stay away from, health risks that Libras are specifically prone to. Grabbing another book, he started reading about Libra and its compatibility with other Signs. There were a few decent pairings, he discovered. He opened a third book to read about the influences of the other planets when they were in Libra. He had just begun the information on Neptune-in-Libra when knocking disturbed him yet again. He threw the book down in frustration, exclaiming, "Look, I'm sorry but..." The words died on his lips as he met a pair of familiar blue eyes staring at him through the glass.

Chapter 6

For a moment, neither one moved. Then, as if someone had electrocuted him, Tim shot out of the chair and dashed to the door, keys in hand. He unlocked the door and ushered the stranger inside, locking the door behind him. Adrenaline shot through Tim's chest. The stranger held out his hand. "Xander," he introduced himself. "Alexander Conlyn."

"Uh, Tim," Tim responded, robotically shaking the proffered hand. "Timothy Dalis."

"Nice to meet you," Xander said politely.

"Same here." Tim's mind was awhirl with incoherent thoughts. Xander stood at about six feet, smiling an easy smile down at him. He was wearing a brown leather jacket that accentuated his muscular frame. His long legs were encased in a pair of flared jeans and he wore a grey ribbed v-neck with a light blue stripe across the chest that complimented his eyes. Tim noted that he could have been quite intimidating if he had wanted to be, but Xander had such a laid-back manner that he found him instantly likable. Xander's calm demeanor was betrayed by the fact that he kept pulling gently at his shoulder-length light brown hair. Again, there was a strange sense of connection that he'd felt in the theatre and he wondered if this was a Sign. Suddenly very aware that he was staring more intensely than was polite, he dropped Xander's hand, blushing furiously. "Sorry." Xander's smile merely widened slightly. "Um, you know the store's closed, right?"

"Then why'd you let me in?" Merriment twinkled in the blue.

"Well, I...I mean...," Tim stammered, at a loss for words. The truth was, he didn't know why he had let Xander in.

"I was teasing," Xander reassured him. "I knew you were closed. I read the sign." He pointed back towards the door.

Tim was even more thrown by this confession. "But if you knew we were closed, then why did you even come to the store? Why did you knock?"

"Because you were here," was the rejoinder.

"Were you at my show a couple nights ago?" Tim circled him to end up back in his chair behind the desk. He relaxed a little once he sat down.

"Yeah, sorry about that. Hope I didn't get you in trouble or anything." Xander leaned over the desk towards him.

Tim licked his lips, trying to appear nonchalant. "Hey, no problem. It wasn't too bad." Xander picked up one of the books on the desk and examined it. "Uh, I was just doing a little, uh, research." A thought hit him. "Did, uh...did Sereny send you? I mean, is she the reason you came here?"

"I told you, Tim, that you're the reason I came here."

Tim flushed. "It's just that...I mean, she just explained that...well, never mind. It doesn't matter." He stood and gathered most of the books.

Xander went to take the three that he had left. "So you're really into this astrology stuff, huh? You believe in it?"

"Leave those," Tim told him. "I'm going to take them with me." Xander raised an eyebrow but said nothing. Tim started for the New Age section, trying to get away from Xander's inquisitive gaze. "Nah, not really. I mean, it's all new to me. A friend was telling me about it. There's a whole lot more to it than I ever thought. I guess I'm sort of having a change of heart."

Xander followed behind him. When they got to the stacks, Xander reached out and took a book from Tim's arms and placed it back on the shelf. "I see. Why is that?"

Tim put a book next to Xander's. He shook his head. "It's not important. I wouldn't want to bore you." He put another book on the shelf.

Xander took the final book from Tim's hands and reached out across Tim to put the book in its place, stepping in closer to do so. Tim suddenly became very aware of how close they were. "You couldn't bore me, Tim. Try me." He smiled his easy-going smile.

The blood was thudding in Tim's ears, giving him a heady feeling. Somewhat dimly, he found himself saying, "You wouldn't believe me."

"Try me, Libra."

It was as if someone had thrown icy water down his collar. "What did you just call me?" Tim whispered.

"You are Libra, aren't you?"

He was shaking. "How did you know?"

"Oh, that's easy. I'm Sagittarius." Xander delivered this news with a casual toss of his hair.

It was too much for one day. Tim's mind struggled with the concept of meeting another of the Signs, but couldn't hold it. Dizziness overtook him and he began to fall. Xander grabbed him and half-dragged him towards the front of the store where he settled Tim back into the chair. Tim could feel the strength in the slender arms. It was comforting and somewhat familiar. He placed a hand on the desk to steady himself. Xander grabbed another chair and sat across from him.

"I didn't mean to startle you," he said. "I thought you might have recognized what I am because of what we felt. When two Signs are near each other...this isn't the time to explain any of this, is it? Do you need anything? A glass of water or something?"

Tim waved away his concern. "I'm okay. It's just a lot to digest at once. I only found out today. Sereny, the woman I mentioned earlier, is a psychic, and she was the one who told me about me being Libra."

"Yeah, I know Sereny. She's nice. She's part of The Gathering." Xander smiled uncertainly.

"You know about The Gathering, too?" Tim was stunned. "How long have you known about being Sagittarius?"

"A long time. Listen, I know it's a lot to take in. Destiny isn't an easy thing to be confronted with. The nice thing about your destiny, Tim, is that it's shared. You're not ordinary," he admitted, putting a hand on Tim's shoulder, "but you belong to a unique group of people."

"Oh, please stop," Tim moaned, breaking the contact and putting his head in his hands. "If I hear one more time about how I'm unique or special, I think I might just throw up."

"I know it's hard, but you can't just run away." Xander's voice was compassionate, but firm. "We have too much to do so you can't waste time feeling sorry for yourself."

That brought Tim up short. "I'm not. I mean, I'm trying not to. It's just that I feel like all of a sudden, the world expects me to be someone that I never even knew I was. Like everyone else has a head start and I didn't even know we were racing. It's not fair. I don't know even who I am anymore."

"I'm trying to understand, Tim, but I grew up knowing who I was. Who I am."

"Then tell me, Xander," Tim begged. "Tell me what you went through. Tell me how I come to fit in all of this."

Xander leaned back in his chair and took a deep breath. "My parents are members of The Gathering. Dad's a precog. It means he has visions of possible futures."

"'Possible futures'? How can there be 'possible futures'?" Tim asked.

"Well, if there's a set future, but then someone finds out what it is and acts to change it, then the future that was, isn't there anymore. It was a possible future. Get it?"

"I hate that people keep asking me that. If I don't understand, I'll ask. I promise." He knew he was being rude, but he didn't care. It helped relieve the pressure to vent. Xander sighed.

"Well, there are an infinite number of possible futures out there at any given time. Dad can get glimpses into those possibilities and change the future if he wants."

"But if you change the future by knowing the future," Tim argued, "then the future is now different and you still don't know the future, so what good does knowing do?" He felt like he was talking in circles.

"I said you *can* change the future. Knowing doesn't always change the future though. Sometimes, you just know what's coming. When my mom was pregnant, my dad had a vision of a young boy and he knew that he was going to have a son.

"Mom's an astrologer. Did Sereny tell you about the planets aligning?" Tim nodded. "Well, the first time that happened, the astrology wing went crazy. Mom says that everyone was running around trying to figure out what was going on. When it happened again and again, the astrologers were able to see a pattern starting, but it wasn't until someone remembered the prophecy that they were able to figure out why."

"Sereny told me the prophecy," Tim interrupted, "but I didn't get it. She said that a kid's going to be born and that the planets aligning is how we were born."

Xander pulled at his hair. "By the time the planets aligned for my birth, the pattern was strong enough to tell that this was because of the prophecy. So, to almost everyone inside The Gathering, I am Sagittarius. I grew up knowing that I had a great destiny, but my parents did their best to give me a normal upbringing. They refused to call me Sagittarius, naming me Alexander. They made sure I had a normal education in addition to the education that I was getting in the occult. I grew up with strange things happening around me. I don't even notice it half of the time.

"So, I had a mostly normal, happy childhood. Except I felt like something was missing. I had a few friends among the kids at The Gathering, but I was never really part of the group. It's one thing if you're psychic or the kid of a psychic. Being Sagittarius, there was always this distance from the others. When I met you, I felt part of the emptiness vanish. I guess when all the Signs are together, I'll feel complete in a way.

"About a year ago, I started getting ready for the time when the Twelve would come together as one. I was given all of the information that The Gathering had on the Twelve (which isn't much, by the way) and tuned into the call in each Sign's soul that constantly searches for the other eleven souls. When two of us get close enough to each other, that call becomes a compulsion. I felt your soul call mine and I followed it to the theatre. That's where you first felt the call in your own soul. I felt it echo mine. I never meant to distract you. I just couldn't ignore it. You have a very magnetic pull."

"Thanks, I think." Tim laughed.

"I wanted to talk to you without other people around. Merel's followers can disguise themselves as anyone and I couldn't take the chance that we would be overheard. They will stop at nothing to get their hands on the Star Child."

"But who are 'they'?" Tim prodded.

Xander's voice dropped to a whisper and Tim had to strain to hear the word. "Astranihl." The room suddenly seemed colder. "Stars whose lights have gone out. Their power is less than ours, but they are far more ruthless with it. They have a bit of magic of their own and they can assume human form, but it takes a lot of effort for them to do it."

"Can they fly?" he asked hesitantly.

"They can and they do."

"I think I saw an astranihl," Tim ventured.

Xander nodded. "You did. I was there when you saw it."

"You were stalking me?" Tim wasn't sure whether he was bothered by that thought or not.

"Not stalking, Tim. Once I'd identified you, it wasn't hard to know where you were. I just had to tune in to your call. I've had training to hone my skills in that department. Lucky thing for you that I did, too, or else you wouldn't be here. That incident in the bar was nasty." He shuddered.

"In the bar? What happened in the bar? I'm talking about outside my window at my apartment."

Xander swore. "They were at your apartment? Oh, great," he muttered to himself. He turned back to Tim. "Listen, Tim, they're following you. The night you went to the bar, someone bought you a drink."

"Yeah, the bartender wouldn't tell me who." His memory was fuzzy, but he recalled that fact.

"That's because it was an astranihl who had been drugging you from the second you got in there. That third drink knocked you out completely and the astranihl came out to take you back to the rest of them." Tim started shaking again. "I was able to get you away from it and bring you back to your apartment. I stayed with you that night to make sure nothing else happened to you."

Despite the chilling news, Tim felt a warmth begin to grow around his middle. "Then it wasn't a dream."

"It wasn't a dream," Xander agreed very solemnly. "It was real and it means we need to get out of here."

"Where am I going to go? I have a show, a job..." He almost added a cat to the list, but sadly, he remembered that Harmony was gone.

"You have to leave that behind. I know it's hard," Xander empathized, placing a hand on his shoulder again. "We'll go to The Gathering. It's the safest place for anyone with talents like ours."

"Xander, I don't even know what your talent is." Tim was intensely curious about his new companion. "I was doing research, but I didn't get past Libra. I didn't even make it all the way through Libra; there were interruptions." He pointedly directed a mocking glare at Xander, who laughed and held up his hands.

"Okay, okay, I'm sorry. Sagittarius is the sign of higher travel. That's my gift. You're the charmer; I'm the traveler."

"How does that work?"

"I can journey to almost anywhere I want. The only thing I need is a picture in my head of where I'm going. Once I've been somewhere, I can go back to that place instantly. As soon as my talent revealed itself, my parents took me all around the world, showing me different cities and countrysides. I haven't been everywhere, of course, but there are many places I can get to easily." Xander tried to keep his pride down, but Tim could see that he was excited to share this information. "I don't think there's a state in America that I haven't been to."

"Impressive," Tim commented.

Xander's stomach growled. "Come on, let's get something to eat. We can discuss this over dinner. I can take you anywhere you want to go." His eyes sparkled.

"Anywhere?" Tim asked archly.

"Almost anywhere," Xander qualified. "Where would you like to go? I'm paying."

Tim shrugged. "That's an offer I can't refuse. And I thought I was the charming one." Xander chuckled. "What about after dinner? What then?"

"Then we find the other Signs." Xander moved towards the door. Tim restrained him with a hand on the arm.

"Wait. Xander, what do I do about the show?"

Xander thought for a moment. "How about a family emergency? You don't have to go into detail and most people understand that sort of thing."

Tim hesitated, then unhooked the phone from his belt. Hitting speed dial, he took a breath and tried to put as much emotion into his voice as possible. "Hey, Nikki? Hey. Listen, I have a problem. A family problem. I don't really want to talk about it." He listened to Nikki's sympathetic clucking on the other end. Then she asked the question he dreaded. "Yes, well, I don't know how long I'll be gone. They need me." More sympathy with a hint of frustration in it. "I'm really sorry, Nikki, but I can't ignore this. If I can come back before the end of the run, you know I will, but you might want to see if there's anyone else that can take the job." More frustration this time. "Yes, I understand, but I don't have a choice." Xander was watching him anxiously. "Thanks for everything, Nik. I hope things get better too. Thanks for understanding. Best of luck for the rest of the run." He closed his phone. "Well, there goes any kind of career I had in theatre," he bemoaned the loss. Moving back behind the desk, he took the three books that he had left and rang them up.

Xander shook his head. "Very dramatic. You belong in theatre. Don't worry. They'll find someone else. Besides, you have another job now and another world to explore." His stomach growled again and Tim's answered with a growl of its own. Xander looked significantly at Tim's middle. "Looks like I'm not the only one who hasn't eaten in awhile."

"Yeah, I meant to eat, but I forgot." Tim was surprised at himself. He rarely forgot to eat. Food was a great source of comfort for him, and although he tried to eat healthily, he always enjoyed his meals.

"Where do you want to go?" Xander asked him.

"Wherever you want. Let's just go." Tim grabbed the keys. He took his credit card out of his wallet and swiped it through the machine. Taking a plastic bag from underneath the desk, he quickly stuffed the books into it. "Do you have a bag or anything?"

"Yeah, but it's with my parents. I can get it anytime," Xander replied.

Tim unlocked the door, let Xander out, and locked it behind them. "Where is The Gathering? You never said."

"I never worry about where," Xander answered with a grin. Tim rolled his eyes. During this exchange, they were off down the street. Tim felt strange; as if all of his emotions were running at high levels. He felt excited and nervous, exhausted and content all at the same time. The city, so familiar to him, was suddenly a stranger. Other people seemed alien and he unconsciously moved closer to Xander. He knew that nothing had really changed, just his perception of things. He didn't know where they were going, and he didn't care. He was looking forward to traveling with Xander. It seemed like a much more powerful talent than his own, but Sereny had told him that his power was more subtle. He couldn't wait to experience traveling the way that Xander did. In his mind, they were winking out of one place and popping into another. He was quite disappointed, therefore, when Xander stopped in front of an ordinary restaurant called La Bella.

"This looks like a nice place. Have you ever been here?"

Tim folded his arms across his chest. "Are you kidding? I can't afford places like this."

"I can," Xander told him. "Let's check it out."

"But, aren't we going to..." Tim made a waving motion with his hands.

"What? Travel?" Tim nodded. "We're going to travel a lot, trust me. Right now, we need food more." He opened the door and they stepped inside. The hostess greeted them and took them through the dimly lit room to a booth in the corner. A busboy appeared out of nowhere and filled their water glasses.

"Good service," Tim commented, taking a sip of water.

Xander did the same. "I hope the food's just as good." He scanned the menu. "Looks like they've got some decent dishes. Oh, this one sounds good." He leaned across the table to point to a dish on Tim's menu.

Tim read aloud, "'Penne and chicken with wild mushrooms and capers in a marinara sauce'. It does sound good. I was looking at the seafood lasagna."

"That sounds good too," Xander admitted. "Tell you what: you get that and I'll get the chicken dish and we can split both. What do you think?"

Tim found he liked the idea a lot. "Good plan," Tim complimented Xander.

"Every so often, a good one comes to me," Xander replied modestly. He took the napkin from the table, folded it, and draped it across his lap. "So, how did you find out about being a Sign?"

* * * * * * * * * * *

"...and then she told me who and what I am." Tim reached over and speared a piece of chicken from Xander's plate. "It wasn't exactly the easiest thing to swallow."

"I can imagine," Xander agreed. "I bet that chicken is much easier."

"Yes, it is. Do you like it?"

"Yup. Chicken is one of my favorites," Xander answered through a mouthful.

"I wouldn't have ever guessed," Tim teased.

"Wow, no wonder they call you the charmer," Xander shot back.

"Am I being too charming?" Tim inquired, overly polite. "Maybe I should tone it down a little."

"Don't. I don't mind at all." They smiled at each other. Tim became self-conscious and worked frantically to find something to say. He was saved by the return of the waitress.

"How is everything?"

"Everything's wonderful. Thank you." Tim told her. Xander agreed silently, his mouth full.

As she moved on to another table, Tim pulled out the list that Sereny had given him. "So, which one are you?" When Xander gave him a look, he explained, "Sereny gave me a list of the birth dates and times of the Signs. I already checked mine off." Unfolding the paper, he asked again, "When's Sagittarius?"

"December 3, 1974, at 6:30 am and 23 seconds," was Xander's reply. He was thoughtful. "Sereny's great. She's a close friend of my parents and very devoted to The Gathering. I'm glad you met her. Maybe I'll pay her a visit soon."

"She'd like that, I'm sure." A beat, then, "Wait a second. You said you didn't know her."

"I never said that. I just didn't want you thinking that Sereny had sent me."

Tim relaxed slightly and continued eating. "Yeah, I guess so." Lacking more to say on the subject of Sereny, he settled on, "She seemed nice."

"She is. She's also extremely protective of me, but then, I'm sure she'll be just as protective of all the Signs." Xander took a sip of his water.

"Protecting the protectors, huh?"

"Yeah, I guess so. All of The Gathering is pretty much the same way," Xander admitted.

"Has Merel ever tried to attack The Gathering?" Tim had visions of a large castle fighting off raiders.

Xander put down his fork with a sigh. "Not directly, no. They can't. The Gathering has protection from an attack like that, but the astranihl can hurt us in other ways. The Star Child is key and it's gonna take all of our powers to keep her safe. Merel's gonna try to keep that from happening. If even one of us is missing, they gain a great advantage. So they're out to capture or kill any number of us, putting us all in danger. That's why we need to find the other Signs as soon as we can. Once we're all part of The Gathering, we'll have protection from Merel."

"Great. I feel like a prisoner," Tim grumbled, his outlook souring.

"It's the opposite actually, Tim," Xander said earnestly. "We have a lot of freedom. More than most people." The sour look stayed on Tim's face. "We'll have even more once all of the Twelve are together."

The drowning sensation had returned. "How did you deal with people coming after you all the time?"

"It wasn't 'all the time', and my parents took care of my safety. They also had endless help from the rest of The Gathering. I was the most protected of all of the Signs because I was lucky enough to be born right into the one group that would understand my purpose." Xander's smile was beginning to irritate Tim.

"So the rest of us were just left to fend for ourselves while you were pampered and made a fuss over? That's not fair." A piece of the book came floating back to him about Libras and fairness, but he brushed it aside. He didn't want to think about the Signs anymore, and he was certainly sick of discussing the trappings of destiny. He felt backed into a corner and all of his frustration built up inside of him, so he lashed out. "You had the benefit of knowing exactly who you were and why you were on Earth and what's to come. The rest of us are in the dark, struggling just to eke out a normal existence, and now you come floating in here, telling me that I have to abandon everything I know to go join a crusade that I barely understand. That I have power I wasn't even aware of, so I may have cheated my way through life without even knowing it. *And* that I can't tell anyone else about it. Not my parents, not my best friend, no one. What would happen if someone found out, Xander? What? What would happen?"

Xander's face clouded over. "I know this is hard for you, but you can't let anyone know, Tim. Anyone who's not a Sign or a member of The Gathering is either an enemy or a victim. Anyone who knows is vulnerable."

Tim stood up. "I barely know you. I've never met anyone from The Gathering besides Sereny and we're not exactly the best of friends, and you're saying that I can't trust anyone else in my life? There isn't anything fair about any of this." Tossing down his napkin, he added, "I don't think I'm very hungry anymore."

Xander tried to restrain him. "Wait, Tim..." he pleaded, but Tim was having none of it.

"I don't care," Tim cried desperately, but even as he said it, he knew it was a lie. To avoid the hurt on Xander's face, he hauled the door open and left. He wandered to the park across the street and sat down on a bench.

The truth was that he did care. He cared much more than he wanted to care. He knew he had behaved like a child back in the restaurant and that Xander was only trying to help, but he was overwhelmed. *It's too much*, he thought. He looked around. There was a couple sitting on the bench near him, holding hands, totally oblivious to the world around them. He wished he could ignore the world around him as they were doing and just concentrate on something he loved. *What the hell am I doing? At least a year with a bunch of people, most of which I haven't even met yet. What happens if we fail? What happens if we die? My parents would never know what happened to me.*

The thought of his parents reminded him of something his father once told him. He had asked whether his father was happy with the way his life had turned out and his father had replied, "Tim, I wouldn't change who I am. You can change what you do, but always be proud of who you are. Then do things that make you even prouder. Destiny will reward those who follow her. I should know. I have you." *Always be proud of who you are and do things that make you prouder,* Tim thought. A breeze blew through the park, bringing with it the fresh scent of the gladiolas that grew along the walkways. They were his favorite flower; his mother used to plant them in her garden and their presence always comforted him. He breathed in their scent, letting it fill him, cleansing him. He wanted to sit there in the park forever, not worrying about everything that had just been dumped on him. Yet logic slowly overtook emotion and he knew he had to go back and accept responsibility. He cringed at the thought of how he had treated Xander. He stayed in the park a little longer, just breathing in the cool air.

When he got back to the restaurant, he was surprised to find Xander waiting for him outside.

"Hey."

"Hey."

Tim put his hands in his pockets. "Look, I'm sorry for what I said in there."

"Nah, it's okay." Xander waved it away and handed the plastic bag to him. "I've had a lifetime to deal with it. You haven't even had a day."

Tim slid his arm through the loop and put his hands in his pockets. "Well, I'm still sorry. I know you're just the messenger and I shouldn't have yelled at you. It's just a lot, y'know?" Xander nodded sympathetically. "Anyway, we should probably go back in and pay for dinner or there'll be trouble that has nothing to do with Merel."

Xander held up a shiny credit card. "Already paid for. Courtesy of The Gathering."

Tim was surprised. "The Gathering has funds?"

Xander chuckled. "The Gathering has everything it needs. Gifted people need to eat too. They're not the best chefs though, so enjoy the good food while you can."

"No wonder you're so eager to dine out," Tim teased. "And the check's not exactly coming out of your pocket, now, is it?"

"If you'd rather pay for yourself..." Xander left the statement hanging.

Tim held his hands up in surrender. "No, no, I appreciate it."

"I thought you might feel that way." He looked up at the sky. "Clear night," he noted. "Full moon, too."

"Yeah. Does that affect us? As Signs, I mean."

Xander looked thoughtful. "I think so. I bet Cancer's feeling the effects. Cancer is ruled by the Moon."

"Now what?" Tim turned to Xander, but he was still staring at the moon, pensive. "Where do we go from here?"

"We relax for a night. Tomorrow, if you're up for it, I thought we might go find another member of our little group of friends." His gaze left the moon and he started to walk. Tim followed behind, excited.

"Yeah, I'm definitely ready." Xander threw him a look. "No, really. The more I learn about this, the weirder it is, but I'm starting to get used to it. Give me a couple of days. I mean, I'm a Cardinal Sign, right? I should be good with change."

Xander arched an eyebrow. "Listen to you: 'A Cardinal Sign'. Okay, we go find another Sign tomorrow." He yawned. "I'm gonna crash soon."

"Where are you staying?"

"Family. If they'll take me in." Xander's statement held the open-ended tone of a question and Tim glanced at him. "Do you mind? I mean, I can go back to The Gathering, but I think it's important that we spend more time together without other people."

"Of course you can stay with me," Tim told him. In the back of his mind, he could hear his mother's warning about bringing strangers back to the apartment.

But Xander wasn't a stranger. He really hadn't ever been one. Taking the lead, Tim turned right and headed for his apartment, the plastic bag bouncing against his hip.

Chapter 7

"I sort of remember the apartment from when I brought you back the night of the bar incident, but I really didn't take the time to see the place," Xander told him, looking around. "You don't like theatre, do you?"

Tim followed his eyes to all of the posters, pictures, and books, and had to laugh. "Just a little. Would you like the grand tour?"

"That shouldn't take too long," Xander joked.

"Be nice, Xander. I thought Sagittarians were supposed to be nice."

"I thought you didn't get past Libra," Xander countered.

"I didn't. I made it up," Tim admitted.

"Well, it was right on. Good job."

"Glad you liked it," Tim said. "Now, this is the living room. It doubles as the den and triples as a sitting room."

"It's so multi-faceted. Who knew a room could be so many things?" Xander picked up a magazine from the floor, leafed through it for a few pages, and tossed it onto the couch.

Tim clapped his hands together and pantomimed a megaphone. He walked backwards to another door and opened it to reveal a toilet, sink, and shower. "Okay, people, let's keep the voices down on this tour! On your left, you'll see the bathroom."

"I like the rubber duckie shower curtain." Xander walked in, feeling the plastic between his thumb and forefinger.

"Not my choice. I just never got a new one after my roommate moved out." Reassuming the tour guide stance, he called out, "Keep moving!" Xander saluted as he left the bathroom and Tim shut the door behind him. "As you exit the bathroom, you will see a door to your right. That is the linen closet where we keep all kinds of sheets and towels. Beyond that, we have the kitchen where all kinds of concoctions have yet to be made."

"Do you cook?" Xander opened the refrigerator and grimaced at the lack of items inside.

"Not very well. I like to cook. I just don't do it often. I'm hardly what you'd call an experienced chef," Tim admitted. Xander closed the fridge and opened a cabinet.

"Nice assortment of cereals, though," he commented.

Tim laughed. "I like cereal, but I don't like the last bit at the bottom of the box because then all the crumbs get into the milk and make it lumpy and gross." Xander took a box and shook it, demonstrating how little there was inside it. He placed it back on the shelf and closed the door.

"Are all of them like that?" he asked.

"Most of them." Embarrassed, Tim cleared his throat and led Xander out of the kitchen. "Next on our tour, you will see the door to the bedroom. I'm sorry, but this exhibit is closed during this time."

"Why?" Xander's interest was piqued.

"Because it's a mess," Tim explained.

"Oh, come on, I was here before and I don't remember it being that bad. Besides, you can learn a lot about a person from their bedroom." Xander tried to dodge around Tim to open the door, but Tim was quick and matched him move for move. Soon they were wrestling and Xander, being bigger, got the best of Tim, throwing him onto the couch, crushing the magazine, and dashed for the door, Tim in pursuit. Xander threw open the door and stopped dead, his mouth open.

The bed was unmade, sheets strewn about haphazardly, some hanging off of the bed frame. The hamper was overflowing and clothing littered the floor, only allowing the wood floor tiny pockets to peek through. The desk was obscured by numerous receipts and other miscellaneous pieces of paper that spilled off onto the chair. A filmy glass stood watch over a food encrusted plate. The bookshelf, which clearly used to be white, was now turning a mottled brown and its top shelf was slowly being taken over by hardened wax from half-melted candles. Cardboard boxes peered at them from underneath the bed, some of them with their contents practically crawling to get out.

"Wow."

Tim quickly reached across Xander to close the door. "Yeah. Learn anything?"

Xander turned to him with barely suppressed amusement. "That you're a slob. That room is a mess."

Tim punched him on the shoulder. "I told you that. You're sleeping on the couch anyway."

"That's okay, I don't know if I could have been able to make it to the bed without breaking my neck." He walked over, removed the crumpled magazine, and laid down on the couch, testing it out. "I guess this'll have to do."

Tim rolled his eyes. "Are you always like this?"

"No. Sometimes I'm obnoxious." Xander grinned up at him, but the grin turned into a yawn.

Tim announced in a loud voice, "This tour has ended due to exhaustion on the part of the patron." Then, in a normal tone, "What time did you want to wake up tomorrow?"

"How about 10:00?" Xander yawned again, covering it with the back of his hand.

"Shit. I'm supposed to work tomorrow."

"Don't worry about money. Everything's taken care of," Xander reassured him.

"That wasn't the point. Someone has to do the job..." Even as he said it, a thought crossed his mind and he reached for his cell phone. "I have a really good friend – my best friend, actually. Her name is Nell and she's currently out of work. She could be a good replacement."

"Great. Give her a call."

Tim settled on the arm of the couch and opened his phone. He punched in the number and listened as the voicemail picked up immediately. He closed the phone. "Phone's turned off. She's out on a date. I'll call her tomorrow morning; I don't have to work 'til 1:00 anyway." He checked his watch. "Okay, so it's almost 10:30 now. Was there anything you had planned for the rest of the evening? Maybe see more of the city?"

"Actually, there were one or two things I had in mind, but they can go in any order," Xander answered.

"Oh?"

Xander gazed up at him through half-closed eyes. "For one thing, I'd love to take a shower, if you don't mind. And you know my background now and I still don't know yours, so I'd like to remedy that."

"That's understandable. Why don't you shower first? That'll give me time to get your bed set up. Then you can be comfortable and we can talk." Xander agreed and Tim rose from the couch, heading for the linen closet. Xander stood as well and followed him, stepping into the bathroom. "Hold on a second," Tim stopped him, taking a large towel out of the closet and tossing it to him.

"Thanks. Be out in a bit." Xander disappeared into the bathroom.

Tim grabbed a bunch of sheets and pillowcases from the closet and shut the door. He threw these onto the couch and went into his room. Removing two pillows from his bed, he returned to the living room where he stripped them and resheathed them in the fresh pillowcases. He unfolded the couch into its bed form, thinking about how ordinary this action was in light of the strange events of the day. *It feels like Nell picked me up a year ago.* He considered the differences between Nell and Xander. Nell had been in his life for years. Xander had been in his life for hours and yet he felt closer to Xander than he'd ever felt with someone before. He stretched the fitted sheet over the corners of the impromptu bed. *If this is what it's going to be like with twelve other people, my life is about to get really strange.* In spite of this, he felt comfort when around Xander and he was looking forward to feeling more of that. He threw the second sheet on top of the first, tucked in the sides, then lobbed pillows towards the head of the bed and headed back to the closet to get a blanket. As he removed the blanket, he realized that he hadn't heard any water running. He knocked lightly on the bathroom door.

"Xander?" No answer. Knocking harder, he called again. "Xander? Are you okay?" Still no answer. Tim tried the doorknob, but it was locked. Ice cold fear spread through his veins. "Xander!" he screamed, dropping the blanket and pounding furiously on the door. "Xander! Open the door! What's going on?! Xander!" Closing his eyes, he collapsed against the door, his head in his hands. *We shouldn't have come back here. That thing was already here and now it's got Xander.* A deep sense of loss enveloped his heart, mixed with the fear, and formed tears which threatened to spill down his cheeks. Abruptly, the door opened and he fell onto the bathroom tile. Xander jumped back with a shout. He hurried forward to help Tim to his feet, his face a mask of worry and confusion.

"Tim! What happened? Are you alright?" Tim smiled wearily at the inadvertent echo of his own words. He placed a hand on the doorframe. "Tim, do you have a habit of fainting?"

"Not normally, but nothing's normal anymore. I thought you were going to take a shower, but I didn't hear any water running so I knocked on the door to make sure everything was okay. Why didn't you answer me?" he accused, quickly wiping his moist eyes.

"I was. I am. Taking a shower, I mean. Sorry. I went back for supplies for tonight and tomorrow. I had just gotten back when I heard you screaming and pounding on the door." He spread his hands in apology.

"You went home?" Tim was surprised.

"Yeah, I was just getting this." He held up a backpack that had lain by the bathtub, unnoticed by Tim until now. "It has my bathroom items. I figured I wouldn't bother you for those. I also told my folks where I was."

"Always the dutiful son."

Xander ignored the comment. "Are you okay?"

"Yeah. I didn't know what had happened to you and I– well, I was worried." Tim walked out of the bathroom and picked up the blanket that had fallen.

Xander followed him to the doorway. "Aw. You were worried about me?"

"You said we're in danger and I know they've already been to the apartment. So, yes, I was worried." He folded the blanket over his arm.

"Oh." Xander looked disappointed.

"Yeah. I'm just going to finish setting up your bed. You enjoy your shower." When Xander didn't move, he said, "Go. I'm fine."

"I'll be quick." Xander's frame vanished from the doorway, and the door closed. Tim returned to the living room. Almost immediately, the sound of running water could be heard throughout the apartment. Tim took a deep breath, taking comfort in the sound. Throwing the comforter onto the bed, he tucked it in, folding it down around the pillows and leaving a triangle of an untucked corner as an invitation. He went into his room and closed the door, quickly stripped off his clothing, and hauled on a pair of sweat-pants and a large tee shirt. Running a hand through his hair, Tim examined his reflection in the mirror hanging on the back of his bedroom door. He thought he looked different somehow. All of the new information that had recently been revealed had changed him. There was a new understanding in his eyes, a comprehension of something larger. With it was determination, and not just a little apprehension. Though he was daunted by the task ahead of him, a large part of him was excited. He wondered what the other Signs were like. Curious, he left his room, grabbed the plastic bag and pulled out the first book. Plopping into a chair, he flipped to Sagittarius and began to read.

Sagittarians are usually happy-go-lucky creatures who like to have fun, he read. *Ruled by Jupiter, the planet of luck, they are used to being lucky and depend on it. They are seldom content with where they are and have a strong case of wanderlust, traveling to as many places as possible. Their obsession with exploration and expansion gives them a more worldly view than most other signs.* He was so avidly into the book that he didn't notice Xander stepping out of the bathroom dressed in purple pajama bottoms and a black tank top, hair still wet. He padded silently over behind the chair. A drop of water splashed onto the page, startling Tim. He slammed the book closed and turned around.

"Reading up on me?" Xander asked, amusement heavily evident in his tone. "I told you that I'd tell you whatever you wanted to know."

"Just researching," Tim muttered.

"Uh huh." Xander walked around the chair and sat down on the bed, pulling his long legs up and crossing them in front of him. "Okay, my turn for research then. Tell me about you."

"What do you want to know?" Tim's fingers nervously stroked the book's spine. "I can't just talk about myself."

"Just start at the beginning. We'll see where it goes from there."

"That could take awhile," Tim warned.

Xander settled back against the pillows. "We've got plenty of time. Let's start with the easiest – were you born here?"

"No. I was actually born in some little town in Delaware that no one's ever heard of. My parents are a bit older than most people's parents our age. They weren't supposed to be able to have children, so I was kind of a surprise. My dad's a retired mailman and my mom's a fifth grade music teacher. I know it doesn't sound glamorous, but actually, I had a really great childhood; my parents went out of their way to make me feel special. Birthdays were always huge occasions with colorful decorations and lots of company. Christmases are extra special, even though we aren't religious. We just like the holiday. There's an annual tradition in my family that started when I was little. Just before midnight, my parents would wake me up and we would head outside to lie down on the ground and make a wish on the moon. If it snowed, we'd make snow angels too. I know it sounds corny, but when I was a kid, I always believed that my wish would come true. I never believed in Santa Claus or Rudolph or anything like that, but those snow angels always held special meaning for me. I never grew out of it. Nowadays, I have to wake them up to do it, but we still do it. Sometimes, we stand for a bit, holding hands, just being together before going back to bed. The next morning, there are so many presents underneath our tree. Usually more than they can afford, and ever since I was old enough to realize that, I've reprimanded them." Tim laughed. "They always say the same thing: 'We'd spend even more if we could. Our wallets know limits that our hearts don't.'" He sobered, adding softly, "This might be the first year that I'm away from them for the holidays."

Xander sat up. "If it's possible, you will be there, Tim."

Tim tried to brush it aside. "More important things to do this year." But it sounded hollow even to his ears.

Xander took a picture from a nearby end table. "You look so young in this picture," he changed the subject.

Tim held out his hand for the picture. He studied it, a faint smile on his lips. "I was young. Eleven or twelve. All I wanted at that age was to be on the soccer team at school. I was so happy when I saw my name on the list." He handed the picture back to Xander, who looked at it again and then replaced it. "Of course, I quit a month into it when I found out I wasn't good at it."

"Of course. How did you end up in Philadelphia?"

"After I graduated college, I wanted to live in a city, but I wasn't ready for New York."

"I've been to New York several times," Xander told him. "Trust me when I say that no one is ever ready for New York."

Tim smiled. "Yeah, I guess you're right. Someday though. Anyway, Philadelphia has a pretty big theatre community and a friend needed a roommate to defray costs, so I went. I ended up here in this apartment with my friend and former roommate, Jack. This was actually my room." He gestured to the living room. "Then he got a girlfriend and went off to live with her and by then, I had the job at the bookstore and I worked part time for a theatre box office. Now, I work backstage, so with the two jobs, I've been able to hold the apartment financially. Plus, I have a really great relationship with my landlady. She seems to like me and, come to think of it, I just might have poured on a little charm. I can't really complain. I like the neighborhood; the people are nice, and of course, I like having a place to myself."

"I'm sure it has advantages," Xander agreed. "Like a place to bring strangers who treat you to dinner."

"Oh, please," Tim retorted. "This is the first time *that's* ever happened." Xander looked skeptical. "It's true. Besides, this is hardly that kind of situation and you know that. If there weren't some kind of cosmic destiny between us, you would have never gotten an invitation."

Xander pouted. "Never?"

Tim colored slightly. "Well, okay, maybe *eventually*, but definitely not after one random dinner."

"I guess I'm lucky that cosmic destiny plays a role, then, huh?" Xander grinned.

"So you could see the mess that is my apartment? I wouldn't exactly consider that lucky, but you're entitled to your opinion." Tim threw a leg up over the arm of the chair in one of his favorite relaxing positions.

"Gee, thanks." Xander inclined his head ever so slightly in a mock-polite bow. "So, Philly's been good to you?"

"Yeah. I like living in a city." He scratched at an itch on his ear. "More people."

"Different kinds too. I've noticed a wide variety of people when I've visited. I like the diversity of Philadelphia and New York is even more diverse."

"New York is an entity unto itself," Tim observed and Xander nodded in agreement. "Is there anywhere you haven't been but you've really wanted to go?"

"I've been to every continent. Except Antarctica, of course," he clarified. "I've pretty much been to most of the major countries at least once. I don't know where I'd want to go next if I had my choice."

"You're lucky. There are so many places I've always wanted to visit. I mean, I'm not obsessed with traveling, but there are definitely parts of the world that I want to explore." He stifled a yawn.

Xander hugged a pillow to his stomach. "You'll probably see many of them and probably some things you don't want to see before this adventure ends."

"How do I sign up for this tour?" Tim joked.

"Your name's already on the list. You don't have much of a choice."

"Well, I'm sure the company will make this journey worthwhile." Tim smiled warmly. Xander returned the smile. "Let's hope the good company continues."

"Well, we'll find out what one of them is like tomorrow." Excitement sparkled in Xander's eyes. "Speaking of tomorrow, it's about midnight and I don't know about you, but I need to get some sleep. Traveling is exhausting."

"Yeah, it's been a long day." Tim left the chair. He put the book back in the bag and started towards his room. When he got to the door, he turned around. Xander looked up at him inquisitively. "Uh, do you need anything else? Another blanket? Something to drink?"

"No thanks," Xander declined. "I'm good with this." He patted the blanket.

"Okay, then. Pleasant dreams."

"You too."

Tim shut off the light and went into his room, closing the door gently behind him. He was so used to living alone that the knowledge that someone was in the apartment with him made him feel strange, but in a way, it was reassuring. He set the alarm and crawled into bed, his mind awhirl with the events of the day. He wondered what tomorrow would hold, and what the new Sign would think of him. He tried to remember the relationships between the other Signs and Libra according to the book, but the information escaped him. He hoped that they would get along. Curling into his favorite position, he automatically reached out to pet Harmony and froze as his hand met air. Placing a pillow where she normally slept, he squeezed it tight. *It's not the same.* With only that thought to keep him company, he drifted off to sleep.

His dreams were haunted by the cries of a child. He knew he had to find the child at all costs, and he went tearing up and down the streets of a foreign city, searching for the source of the wailing. The familiar figure of a young man flickered at the edge of his vision, but he assumed it was a distraction and tried to ignore it. The crying grew louder until it became a painful keening that was ultimately eclipsed by the screaming of his alarm.

He stretched and slammed the alarm off. Running a hand through his unruly hair, he made his way into the living room. Xander sat upon the bed, now converted back into a couch, a pile of the sheets and blanket folded next to him. A small knapsack lay on the floor by his feet and he leaned against the pillows he'd slept on. He smiled as Tim blinked in the daylight.

"Morning, sleepyhead," he greeted him brightly. "Sleep well?"

"Not so much," Tim growled. "Had a weird dream. Need coffee and shower."

"You go take a shower and I'll make us some coffee," Xander offered.

Tim shuffled towards the bathroom, then stopped and turned around. "Do you know where anything is?"

"No, but I'm sure I can figure it out by the time you finish your shower."

Tim nodded and headed into the bathroom. "Sure."

* * * * * * * * * * *

About an hour later, showered and groomed, Tim was at the kitchen table with a cup of coffee in front him. He sipped gratefully. Xander leaned against the counter with his own coffee, watching Tim wake up with each sip.

"Ready for another adventure?" Xander broke the silence.

"Just a bit of unfinished business before we go," Tim replied, holding up his phone. He punched in Nell's number. "She's going to kill me for calling her before noon," he added, relieved to hear the ring that told him her phone was on. It rang four times before a groggy voice answered.

"Hello?"

"Hey, Nell."

"Tim?" She groaned. "Oh, dear Lord, Tim, if this is you calling to check up on me or hear details..."

"Hang up on him and let's go back to sleep," interrupted a male voice in the background.

"Shhhh."

"Is that Gary?" Tim asked. When no answer came, he pressed a button on the phone, forcing a loud sound into her ear.

"Ow! Yes! Yes, it's Gary, and what business of yours is it anyway? Why the hell are you calling me at the crack of dawn? Are you insane?"

"First of all, Nell, it isn't the crack of dawn. It's almost 11:30," Tim pointed out, conveniently forgetting his own loathing of the morning.

"Same thing."

"Don't be a smart ass. Listen, do you still need a job?"

She snorted loudly. "Stupid question. Of course I still need a job."

"Take mine," he suggested.

A beat, then, "What?"

"I have to leave for awhile to take care of some business. I need someone to cover me at the store and you've already applied, so it works out perfectly. I get a cover and you get money." He tried to make his voice light and pleasant, dreading the inevitable question.

Nell wasted no time. "Where are you going?"

He hesitated. "I can't tell you."

"Timothy Dalis, I'm your best friend! I have a right to know!" Gary hushed her.

"Nell, it's something very important. It's personal. If you value our friendship at all, you won't ask me."

"That's so unfair," she protested.

"Yes, it is. It's really not fair. Please trust me though. Maybe someday I'll be able to tell you and you'll understand, but right now, I just can't. Please, Nell." Xander was looking sympathetically at him over his coffee mug.

"Could you be any more dramatic?" she wondered aloud. "Oh, fine. But there better be a huge explanation with lots of details when you get back." Pause. "When *are* you coming back?"

"I don't know. It might be a year..."

"A *year*?!"

"...or it could be longer. I don't know right now. I'll try to keep in touch," he promised.

"Tim–"

"No. Don't even say it. I won't say goodbye to you over the phone." He took a breath. "I'm not saying goodbye to you at all. The time will fly."

She laughed. "Tim, you are an overdramatic sap. I wasn't up to saying goodbye yet. I was going to ask what time I have to work."

"Oh. Glad to know you care, Nell." He was smiling though. "You have to be at work at 1:00 today. You work until closing. Make sure you dress in uniform – you know the uniform – and if there's anything you need to know, I think Mark is working today. Maybe he'll help you out if he's in a good mood."

"Tim, I've visited you at that job practically every day since you started there. I can probably do that job better than you do." He could hear the challenge in her voice and he knew the source of it. She was frustrated and upset with him for leaving so suddenly.

"Well, here's your chance to prove it, Nell. Be there ten minutes early if you can."

"Will do. Thanks, Tim." Another pause. "I guess now is the time to not say goodbye."

"Yeah." He bit his bottom lip. "I'll see ya, Nell."

"See ya." The line went dead and he slowly closed his phone. Xander put his hand on Tim's shoulder.

"I know."

Tim stepped away from him, fighting the feeling of loss that threatened to overwhelm him. "It's all for the best."

"Right." Xander hefted his knapsack. "It won't be so bad–"

Tim stopped him. "Don't. Let's just go."

Xander nodded, understanding. "Are you ready to go?"

"Not yet. I have to throw a few things into a bag. What should I bring? Are we coming back here?" Tim started for his room.

"Eventually."

He whirled around. "Eventually?"

"It's a good idea to have a place to go to in different cities around the world. This can be the Philadelphia base." Moving into the living room and sitting, he tried to lighten the moment. "Hey, you won't have to worry about rent. And The Gathering can provide almost anything you need, so pack light."

Tim was already throwing pieces of clothing into a bag. "Okay, I just have to put the books in here and I'll be ready to go." When he had finished, he stood and observed his apartment with a wistful mien.

Xander caught the expression and suggested, "What do you say we get something to eat before we go?"

Tim looked at him gratefully and thought for a moment. "I know just where I want to go," he said.

* * * * * * * * * * *

The cashier behind the counter waved to Tim as they entered. "Hey," he shouted, "Lena's not in yet, but she'll be in in a couple of minutes if you want to wait."

"Long as it's not too long!" Tim yelled back.

"You know Lena. She'll be in early, if anything. She's due in about ten minutes so she should be here...now," he finished, pointing behind them to where Lena was bearing down on him with arms outstretched.

She enfolded him in a rough hug, exclaiming, "Tim! This must be my lucky week! What's the occasion?" Appraising Xander up and down, she clicked her tongue in what Tim hoped was approval. He was justified in this line of thinking when she added, "And who is this strapping young man? Friend of yours?" She winked. Tim felt the heat rise in his face.

Xander spoke up. "Alexander Conlyn, ma'am. Pleased to meet you." He held out his hand for her to shake it, but found himself hugged as well, while Tim stood to the side and grinned.

Eventually, she released him and stepped back, pursing her lips. "Please, honey, call me Lena. We're not so formal here at Ilene's. Any friend of Timmy here is a friend of mine. I've known him for years."

"Lena's the best," Tim chimed in, and Lena shoved him playfully.

"Get on with you. Get over to that table you like to call home and I'll bring you whatever you like." Giving Tim another push, she took Xander by the hand and half-dragged him to the table, asking him, "Where did you and Tim meet? How long has this been going on? And why didn't you say anything?" This last question was directed at Tim.

Both boys started to answer at once. "Oh, we're not together...," Tim corrected, just as Xander explained, "We just met yesterday, actually..."They looked at each other. Lena took a breath.

"I can see that this is a story for another time." Brusquely, she changed the subject. "You boys must be hungry. Tim? The 'original'?"

"Can I do it as a sandwich, Lena?" Tim asked.

Lena nodded. "Sure, honey, anything for you. Alexander? What can I get you today?"

Xander looked at Tim. "I don't know what's good here. What would you recommend?"

"Well, I haven't tried much on the menu," Tim admitted. "I always get the same thing. Lena, what's good today?"

"We have a special for lunch that's a chicken sandwich with a peanut sauce," she suggested.

"Oh, I can't," Xander declined. "I mean, it sounds great, but I'm allergic to nuts."

"Oh. Well, there's always the club sandwich. That's a big favorite around here." She pointed to the item on Xander's menu and he read the description.

"That sounds great." Xander handed his menu over to her and she turned to leave.

"Lena, I think I'll try that too," Tim stopped her.

Xander asked, "What's the 'original'?"

"Chicken parm," Lena answered for Tim. "It was the first thing he ever had in here and since then, he rarely has anything else."

Xander grinned across the table. "Wanna split again?"

Tim smiled. "Sounds great." Lena glanced at Xander, then back at Tim, but said nothing as she moved towards the kitchen, grabbing an apron on the way.

"This is a cute place," Xander observed. "Small, family oriented."

"Yeah, I like it. Reminds me of home." Tim looked around the diner, trying not to think about the number of times he had come here with Nell and how that part of his life was behind him.

"Lena seems nice. I can't believe you have your own waitress." Xander squeezed a lemon into his water.

"She's been waiting on me since the first night I came in here. I've never wanted anyone else." Tim picked up a lemon and mimicked Xander, taking a sip of the flavored water. He smacked his lips. "Even the water's good."

Xander laughed as Lena returned with their food. "Enjoy, boys."

Xander lifted two quarters of his club and placed them on Tim's plate. "Here."

Responding in kind, Tim cut his sandwich in half and put one on Xander's plate next to the remaining quarters. "I hope you like it. It's so good." Xander obligingly took a bite.

"Mmmm. It is good. Hope the club is just as good."

"I'm sure it is."

Lena came over to the table a short while later. "How's everything, boys?"

"It's okay. The service is somewhat lacking," Tim teased her.

Lena tugged her glasses down on her nose and stared at him over them. "You could do a lot worse than me, kiddo."

"Don't I know it," he placated her.

"This is amazing," Xander added, indicating his club. "And the service is impeccable."

Lena smacked Tim lightly on the back of the head. "See? At least one of you knows how to charm a lady." This comment sent the two Signs off into gales of laughter. "Well, I don't see what's so funny about a little charm, but I'm glad you enjoyed it." She left them still laughing.

Tim had almost finished his fries when he felt his face growing hot. He looked across at Xander. The Sign was turning red and his eyes were widening in panic. Sweat poured down Tim's face and soaked his shirt. He could feel his body rebelling against him. No one seemed to notice. He could see Xander struggling to keep himself conscious. They were both fighting a losing battle, but Tim wasn't ready to give up just yet. He was exhausted, but more than that, he was angry. He was sick and tired of not being in control of his life. All of his frustration went to fuel his muscles and he fought his way to his feet, pushing down on the table for leverage. He watched Xander roll out of his chair. Step by painful step, he attempted to cross the short distance between them, but his legs weren't obeying him. As the world grew blacker around him, he could only focus on finding help. His grip on the table tightened. His other hand moved towards his cell phone. He managed to get it out of his pocket before collapsing in a heap.

Immediately, Lena came running over from the kitchen and she bent quickly to check on the prone Signs. A mirthless smile stretched across her face.

Chapter 8

The world was blurry when Tim opened his eyes and pain seared his body. He groaned and closed them again. *This isn't happening.* He prayed for it all to be a dream. Cautiously, he reopened his eyes and looked around. He was alone, lying in a four-poster bed with heavy, dark indigo curtains. The windowless walls were constructed from dull, rust colored brick, giving the room a drafty feel. The only light came from a lit fireplace directly across from the foot of the bed, which threw odd shadows on the wall. Despite the heat, Tim shivered. A frantic voice screamed in some part of his head, but his brain was so foggy that only a muted feeling of unease was able to get through. His distress increased as he discovered that his clothing had been taken from him, as had his wallet, his phone, and his keys. He was dressed in a long, white robe that was too big for him and two silver bracelets encircled his wrists.

Pain lanced through his chest as he sat up and he opened the robe. Red welts decorated his skin, tender to the touch. He didn't know how they had gotten there and he grimaced as horrific scenarios barged into his mind. Gingerly, he tightened the robe about his body. Wincing as his feet touched the cold, uncarpeted floor, he moved closer to the fire, bending to examine the bracelets further. They glowed in the flickering light. He turned them over and over. There was no clasp, no catch, nothing to release them. Panicked, he tried to remove them by pulling them over his hands, but they were too small and he only succeeded in scratching his wrists. A glint from across the room took his attention and looking up, he saw a wooden door with a brass handle in the corner of the room. He straightened, ignoring the pain, and took a few cautious steps towards the door. He stretched out a hand to take the handle, expecting some kind of punishment. When nothing happened, he gripped the handle and turned. The door opened easily and silently. Surprised, Tim peered into the darkness beyond the door.

As his eyes adjusted to the blackness, he found a tiny room with a porcelain tub in the center of it, filled with water. He tiptoed forward and looked down into it. A shadow of his reflection stared back at him. He dipped a finger into the water. Warm, but not burning hot. Suspicious, he looked around the room. There was a sink with a small glass next to it and a large, fluffy towel on a peg. The room was bare except for that. He moved to the tub again and untied his robe. Sighing as he slipped into the warm water, he could feel his muscles relax and the pain melt away. He closed his eyes, luxuriating in the sensation. The room suddenly filled with the smell of gladiolas, lulling him into further bliss. He sank lower into the water, breathing deeply. Sleep beckoned to him, opening its arms and inviting him in. He dearly wanted to sleep for a long time. His awareness began to drift in and out. He felt the water caressing him, soothing his body, whispering to him. It was the most pleasant feeling he had experienced in a long time.

His eyes flew open in shock when he felt himself hauled from the warm water. Frigid air bit at him as he fought a losing battle to stay in the tub. The water itself seemed to cling to him, willing him to stay, but the hands that gripped him were too strong and he found himself roughly dumped on the floor. He stared up at his attacker and his eyes widened further when he met Xander's eyes, fairly crackling with anger. A similar robe hung on his frame and Tim fairly flew across the room to snatch the towel from its peg and wrap it around himself. Shivering violently, he glowered at the Sign.

"What the hell do you think you're doing?" he demanded.

Xander stepped towards him, his voice deceptively calm. "I was just going to ask the same of you. Be happy you have charm; it makes up for your lack of intelligence."

Tim was bewildered. "I was just taking a bath."

Xander strode over to the tub and pointed down into it. "This is enchanted water, Tim! It makes you relax so much that you can't fight it or anything else. You would have relaxed until they could have asked you anything and you would have told them." He pointed to the sink. "That water is tainted as well. Don't touch anything they offer you. Any of it could be a trap."

Aware of how close he had come to disaster, Tim shook with more than just cold. "I...I didn't know."

"I know." Xander saw the fear in his eyes and softened. "You have to understand, they are not your friends. Whoever they were in your life before, they can't be trusted now. I know how painful that is for you, but you have to believe me."

Tim took a deep breath. He thought about the dangers that surrounded him. He thought about how Xander had already saved him. Twice. "I believe you." He moved closer to the other boy. "I'm sorry, I didn't mean to–"

"I know, Tim." Xander reached out and ruffled his hair. Tim could see that a pair of bracelets also decorated Xander's wrists.

"How touching," came a familiar voice from the doorway. Lena leaned casually against the doorframe, her arms folded underneath her breasts. "It's so nice to see harmony among the Signs."

"Lena." Tim was dumbfounded.

"She's an astranihl, Tim," Xander warned him.

"A what?"

"One of the chosen," Lena said, moving smoothly into the room and picking up the discarded robe. Her eyes shone with religious fervor. "An honored person, chosen to serve Merel." She held the robe out to Tim. "Come now, we wouldn't want you getting a cold, now would we?" When he hesitated, she shook it at him, an edge entering her voice. "Take it." He accepted the robe. Lena waited, silent, her hand still outstretched. Xander politely turned away and Tim realized she was waiting for the towel. He put the robe on, then slipped out of the towel and handed it over to her, tying the robe tightly around him. She took the towel and folded it across her arm, looking every inch the grandmother, but Tim could see malevolence glittering in her eyes. "Follow me," she said, and Tim experienced a warped echo of following Sereny. *Had it been only the day before when Sereny had told him about the Signs?* He had no idea how much time had passed since his breakfast with Xander.

They followed her back through Tim's room to another door that he hadn't noticed. She threw open the door and stomped on through it without checking to see if they were still behind her. The short hallway was lined with other doors. Xander nudged Tim and gestured to the door next to the one they had just come out of, indicating the room to be his. Tim wondered what was in the other rooms. The doors were all the same wood with identical brass handles. The hallway opened into a banquet hall, hosting a long table with many high-backed chairs, the top of each bedecked by a hideously deformed gargoyle. They were positioned in such a fashion that it appeared as though they were about to devour whoever was unfortunate enough to be sitting in front of them. Banners hung upon the walls between stained glass windows. Each held symbols that Tim didn't recognize, but Xander obviously did and scowled up at them. Lena went directly to the far side of the table and took a seat. She beckoned them over and bade them sit next to her. They crossed the room and took the proffered chairs. As Tim lowered himself into the seat, he felt a pull in his heart and, looking for the source, was startled to see another person across the table, previously hidden by the chair.

A tiny person, smaller than Tim, sat quietly at the table, her hands folded on the table in front of her as if she were in an elementary school classroom. She had short, straw-colored hair and cat-shaped brown eyes. Her face was much too angular to be considered beautiful, with sharp features that did nothing to help that cause. A large robe hid most of her body from view, and upon her slender wrists were the same silver bracelets that he and Xander wore, but there was a chain that bound them to the table. She observed the newcomers with great interest, looking neither left nor right. He saw the reason why; her head was held firmly in place by the stone paws of the gargoyle perched upon her chair. The pull grew stronger, and he thought he recognized it. It was similar to, but not the same as, the bond between Xander and himself. This was a Sign. He wanted to say something, but one sideways glance at Lena forced him to swallow the impulse.

Lena sat tall and rigid next to him, completely unlike the woman who had greeted him warmly every time he entered the diner. Inwardly, he mourned the loss of a friend. He looked to his other side. Xander was imitating the young girl, folding his hands on top of the table. He was trying to affect an easy-going manner, but the tightness in his jaw belied his tension. The silence stretched on.

Just as it seemed to become oppressive, a howl echoed throughout the hall. Figures swept into the room, floating and flying about the table, but keeping a safe distance from the four human beings. They screeched and screamed as they flew by. Tim knew them: astranihl. Xander stiffened beside him and even the girl's expression hardened in fear and anger. Only Lena remained unaffected. Astranihl filled the air, tattered ribbons of cloth trailing from their bodies. Tim tried not to stare, for fear of being reprimanded in some way. Each one landed in front of a stained glass window and bowed down before it as if in worship. Then they rose and turned towards the table, their grisly visages taking on an expression of ghastly pleasure. Those closest to the four already seated figures made a wide berth around them and settled themselves at the other end, leaving as many seats as possible between them. A hush fell over the room and the doors at the other end of the table opened.

A small blond boy was lead through by a middle-aged woman who could easily have been his mother. Tim guessed him to be about eight or nine. He tried to stop when he saw the astranihl, but the woman's grip tightened and he was inexorably brought to the table. The girl across the table gasped involuntarily and as Tim looked at her, he saw that the gargoyle had twisted her head painfully to the side to watch. The little boy tried to run, but two astranihl grabbed him, laid him on the table, and held him there. The woman bowed and left the room, ignoring the boy's whimpering. At the click of the door, the astranihl fell upon the boy with a fury. The boy began to scream in absolute terror and pain and Tim knew he would never forget that sound. The girl cried out and tried to shut her eyes, but at a whispered word from Lena her eyes snapped open, tears flowing freely. The sounds of bones cracking and flesh tearing filled the air and though he couldn't see Xander's face, Tim saw his hands clench into fists. It only lasted a few minutes. The smell of rotted meat assailed their nostrils and the astranihl departed as swiftly as they had come, leaving nothing left of the boy but a piece of a bone here and there and the echoes of his screams still ringing in the hall. Tim shuddered involuntarily and he looked across the table to see that the girl was shaking violently, her face contorted in a silent scream.

"Foolish boy," Lena whispered contemptuously, her eyes glittering. She turned to the others. In a macabre imitation of her former persona, she asked, "Can I get anyone something to eat?" They shook their heads. "No? Ah, well, I'll leave you to explore your new home. Jamee here can show you the way around." The girl, now freed from the gargoyle's grip, turned her head at the sound of her name, her face streaked with tears, fury written in her eyes. She met Lena's cool gaze and found a threat. Cowed, she nodded slightly. Lena nodded back curtly and the chains fell open. The elderly woman stood and followed the length of the table. As she reached the section where the horrible feast had transpired, she stopped. She reached out, snatched a piece of bone, and shoved it into her mouth. Chewing and humming to herself, she continued out the door through which the boy had been brought, shutting it behind her. The sound echoed harshly throughout the hall. The boys turned to their new companion.

"What was that?" Xander asked just as Tim asked, "Are you okay?"

She merely stared at the spot where Lena had stood moments before.

"What was that?" Xander repeated.

There was no response.

"We can leave you alone if you need privacy," Tim offered, rising to his feet.

Jamee held out a hand. "No, please, I'd prefer to be with people right now." Her voice trembled like a leaf in the fierce autumn wind. "Real people. It's been so long since I've seen a real person." Her eyes went to the site of the massacre and she stood up so fast that she almost knocked the chair over. Shaking, she backed away from it, suggesting, "Let's get out of here. I can't stay in this room."

"Where will we go?" Tim got to his feet as well, moving around the table towards Jamee. Curiosity for their surroundings beat back the horror that was welling up inside of him. Xander followed.

Her answer was short. "My room." She set off at a brisk gait, surprising them. *For a tiny person, she moves very quickly*, Tim thought.

Meanwhile, Xander was saying, "Is that a good idea? Shouldn't we be trying to find a way out?"

Jamee's eyes darted from side to side, quick and alert. "No. Not here. Not now." She took them back the way they had come, into the hallway of doors. They came to the door directly across from Xander's room. She opened it and stepped inside. Her room was furnished exactly the same way that Tim's was. A fire crackled in the fireplace. Jamee crawled into the bed and pulled the covers up around her, hugging herself as if she couldn't get warm. She patted the covers, inviting them to join her, and they obliged, Tim taking a place at the foot, with Xander between them.

The fire stretched towards them, heating and lighting them with its glow. Tim held his hands out to it. "How long have you been here?" he asked Jamee.

"I think two years. I can't really tell, except for the little bits of news that I get from the astranihl."

Xander jumped on this comment. "You know what they are?"

"Yeah. I know who you guys are too," she responded solemnly.

"Did everyone know before I did?" Tim complained. Jamee's face froze in an odd expression, then she laughed a merry tinkle that was almost too ladylike for her, gasped, and the tears began to flow again.

"I haven't laughed since I've been here," she explained, hiccupping. "It feels weird. Good, but weird."

"You said you know about us," Xander reminded her.

She turned to him. "Yeah. Lena's talked about you."

Tim grimaced. "Lena. I can't believe she's an enemy. She seemed so nice. Don't even say it," he threw over at Xander.

Xander, to his credit, did his best not to look smug, and almost succeeded. "I wasn't going to say a thing," he protested innocently.

"Yeah, right." Then he sighed. "Drugged. Again. They have no imagination."

"Right," Jamee agreed. "The astranihl don't have imagination. They try the same plan until it works or fails so badly they have to try something else. They can't think outside the box."

"Maybe we can use that to escape," Xander mused.

Jamee shook her head and held up her wrists. "These aren't just pretty decorations. They're a special form of handcuffs. They match our energies, and their magic works against our powers, making us as helpless as anyone else. With these on our wrists, we can't leave. There's a field around the building and anyone wearing them can't get through. Anyone else can pass through, so if we could figure out a way to get them off, we could escape." She dropped her hands back into her lap. "And I know a way," she whispered.

"If you know a way, why didn't you escape?" Xander asked.

"I couldn't. My younger brother—" She choked back a sob. Tim crawled across the bed to put his arms around her, understanding.

"The little boy?" he asked gently. She nodded and leaned into him, weeping. He held her tightly against him. Xander moved next to them and rubbed her back, repeating, "It's okay. It's going to be okay." They stayed there for an immeasurable passage of time. The fire crackled.

"You've been here for two years? Why didn't they kill you?" Tim was shocked by Xander's blunt question, but Jamee lifted her head, seeming relieved to move on with the conversation.

"I don't know. Maybe I'm bait. If they could harness our powers somehow, the Star Child is theirs." She looked doubtful though.

"Are there any more of us here?" Xander was insistent.

The door opened and they jumped apart from each other. Lena entered, smiling with a warmth that didn't reach her eyes. In her hands, she carried a tray laden with food. She said nothing, though her smile widened when she saw the anger burning in Jamee's eyes. The door closed behind her and Jamee took a deep breath, crossing the bed to get to the tray.

"Wait," Xander stopped her. "That could be drugged."

"They've been bringing me food for years and nothing's happened to me. I understand if you don't want to eat it, but if you don't eat now, you don't get another chance." She grabbed a hunk of bread and spread butter on top of it. Tim and Xander exchanged a look and then shrugged and grabbed bread for themselves.

As they sat on the bed, chewing, Jamee explained what had happened. "My brother was their hold on me. They knew the time was coming when the Signs were supposed to come together and they believed that I had somehow been in contact with the rest of you. I told them that I didn't know where you were or anything about you. They didn't believe me and told me that if I didn't cooperate, they were going to...kill Joey." She swallowed hard. "I couldn't escape without trying to figure out a way to free him as well." Her eyes were wet.

Tim asked tentatively, "What are you going to do now? I mean, now that it's just you."

Astonishingly, Jamee smiled. "Well, it's not just me."

"But I thought you said there were no more of us here," Xander accused.

"True," she agreed. She changed the subject. "Which ones are you?"

Tim was still focused on trying to figure out who else was with them. "Huh?" he grunted, reaching for a second piece of bread.

"Which Signs are you?"

"Sagittarius."

"Libra."

"I'm Gemini," she said.

"The Twins," Xander breathed, picking up on something that eluded Tim. Tim swiveled to focus on Xander.

"What does that mean?" he asked.

"It means that there are two of us," said a fluty tenor voice. Tim whirled back to see that Jamee had disappeared. In her place lounged a young man with the same straw-hair and sharp features. Mischief shone in his brown eyes and the corners of his mouth twitched with amusement. He snapped a hand out and crammed a slice of bread into his mouth.

"What the–?" Tim was flabbergasted.

"I can't stay long. Not here," the boy said, his mouth full. "Jamee will explain everything. But it's nice to meet the both of you." Then he blurred and Jamee was tugging the robe closed around her chest and chewing. She swallowed. "I hate when he does that," she muttered.

"Um, Jamee?" Tim wasn't sure if what he had just seen was real or a trick of the firelight.

"Yeah, sorry about that. He wanted to meet you guys in person. That's my twin, James."

"James and Jamee?" Xander laughed.

"Yeah. Our parents named us when they thought we were still two. The doctors told them it was vanishing twin syndrome when James disappeared in the womb. They never realized that we had merged into one body and we never told them. It was our little secret." She smiled sadly. "Only Joey knew."

Xander broke in. "Why isn't James able to come out for long periods?"

"Huh? Oh, right, he said that."

"You can hear each other?" Intrigued and curious, Tim wondered what it must be like to have someone watching and listening to your life.

Jamee was happy to explain her unique situation. "We experience everything together. I mean, if there's something we don't want to be a part of, we can turn off awareness and sleep, but most of the time, we sleep at the same time and stay awake at the same time."

Xander jerked a thumb towards the door. "Do they know?"

She became wary, lowering her voice a little. "No, and that's part of the reason that he can't come out a lot. In normal situations, we can switch back and forth with no problem."

Xander pounced. "What's the other reason?"

Jamee held up her wrists and grinned mischievously. The silver bracelets glinted in the firelight, but upon closer inspection, Tim could see tiny cracks along them. "It puts too much strain on the bracelets. They absorb our powers if we try to use them. If you do it too long, they can heat up and burn you." Xander nodded and Tim glanced askance at him. Apparently, he had experimented. "But like I said before, they're connected to our specific energies. Since the astranihl didn't know that we were two, they attuned the bracelets only to me. James started out a separate person from me and still is in a lot of ways. When he wears them, his energy overwhelms them and they don't work. They keep trying, though, which is what makes them crack. As soon as we discovered that, we decided it was better for him to stay out of sight until we could find the right time to escape. We wanted to take Joey with us, but..." She trailed off, but no trembling accompanied this comment. She was entirely in control now.

"Don't the astranihl notice that there are cracks in the bracelets?"

She shook her head. "They're regenerative. As long as they are still sort of together, they can repair themselves, feeding on the person's energy. In that sense, they're almost alive."

"So, if you were to change into James," Xander said slowly, "you could escape."

"Yes."

"Why doesn't it absorb your talent of changing forms?" Tim wanted to know.

She laughed. "That's not our talent. That's just our nature. Our talents are much more powerful." She paused and the boys waited in anticipation. Her voice dropped again to a conspiratorial whisper. "We can change things."

"Gemini is the Sign of change and adaptability," Xander agreed, "but what do you mean you can change things?"

"We can change one object into another. Transform them. The bigger object, the more energy it takes out of us and the longer it's going to take to make the change. We haven't come across an object that we can't change, but we haven't tried really big changes."

Tim's mind was racing ahead, formulating a plan. "Can you change people too?"

She frowned. "No, we can only do inanimate objects."

Tim persisted. "But you can change any object, right?"

"Yes."

Xander was looking at him curiously. Tim was trying to think. "You said you can use your talent on anything? Even something enchanted?"

Jamee's eyes widened. "I'm not sure about that, Tim. We're playing with forces we know very little about. We've never tried anything like that." She went silent for a moment and closed her eyes. The boys waited. Her eyes opened. "James says he's willing to try it. He's sick of being stuck in this hell. I hope he's referring to the building and not the body." She smiled.

"When?" Xander nibbled on a fingernail.

"Tonight," Tim said firmly. "We don't have much time. The other Signs could be in similar danger."

"He's right," Jamee agreed. "You've been here for almost a week now. At least, that's what I can tell from the talk of the astranihl. It has to be tonight."

"We were drugged for a week?" Xander did not look pleased with this news.

"You were drugged for a week," Jamee confirmed, "but they didn't leave you alone. They had to put you through the same experiments that I went through to get your bracelets working right. One of you was more difficult than the other. Lena kept saying how the machine almost rejected you."

Xander looked over at Tim, who slowly revealed his chest. Both Signs gasped. "I guess it was me," he said.

Jamee was the first to recover. "Tim, I'm so sorry. That machine is horrible. They don't care about us except as vessels of power, and ordinary people are less than animals to them." Xander was silent, staring at Tim's chest until Tim closed the robe again. "Does it hurt?"

"It hurt a lot when I woke up, but since I had the bath, it's been sort of a dull ache instead." His hardened his will. "I can handle it." Okay, so we leave tonight. What do we do?"

"For now, just act like everything is normal. As normal as it can be in this place," she corrected herself. "I'll come get you after they put us in our rooms for the night and we'll get out of here. Once I get those off of you, you'll have to follow me to the exits."

"No need." Xander sat up proudly. "My talent comes in handy at that point." He explained it to Jamee, who hugged herself with excitement.

"That'll make things much easier." She faced Tim. "What about you?" Another explanation followed. "Charm, huh? I guess that'll be useful."

"Trust me, once you've seen him in action, you'll see how useful it is." Xander winked at Tim, who tried to shrug it off, but couldn't restrain a flush of pleasure. "Meanwhile, what do we do until then?"

Jamee thought for a moment. "Dinner was just served, so they'll come around in about two hours to separate us. They'll check on us an hour after that and then we're on our own. I'll come to you after then. We have two hours to kill together. The best we can do is learn about each other."

So Tim found himself telling his story again. He knew he was going to have to tell it a number of times throughout this adventure. Then he sat and listened while Xander talked about his background, interjecting every so often to voice his opinion. They learned that Jamee and James were from California. They had been taken in their sophomore year of college while home on break watching their little brother.

"Joey tried to fight the astranihl, but he was knocked out and brought with us. Apparently, that wasn't part of the plan. I don't know what Merel did to the bastard who kidnapped us, but I could the hear screaming from my room. Later, I was told that Joey was ransom for my good behavior." She took a breath. "I never got to see our little brother except on very rare occasions and he was always surrounded by astranihl. We couldn't get close enough to get away. I was promised that I could have visits with him if I let them experiment on me. That's how they created the bracelets. I was poked and prodded, there was blood taken. James never tuned out. He suffered through all of it with me." There was fierce pride in her voice.

"Once the bracelets were made, they let Joey visit for a limited amount of time and always with an astranihl in the room, so James couldn't show himself. Joey spoke to him through me anyway. He was a very bright little boy. Too bright. One night, about a week ago, he hurt one of the astranihl and tried to escape. I still don't know how he did it. He wouldn't tell me. When the astranihl came after him, he spit at them. He was brought before Merel and I was given a choice: one of us would die."

"So you've seen Merel?" Xander asked, his face intense.

She shook her head, sadly. "No, orders were always passed down through the astranihl. I never had any contact."

"How could you choose?" Tim asked tentatively.

Tears shone in Jamee's eyes. "Joey begged me to let him die. He said that he was just holding us back and it would be easier for us if he weren't there." Tim's heart ached with sympathy for the tearful Sign. She hugged her knees to her chest and wouldn't look at either of them. "He was so brave. So brave."

After that, Xander and Tim steered the conversation to lighter subjects until Lena returned to the room. She didn't say anything, but the look in her eyes was unmistakable and the boys reluctantly left the bed with a glance at Jamee. She smiled thinly as she watched them disappear from the room. Tim saw her roll over to stare at the flames and then the door was shut. "To your rooms," Lena ordered them curtly. They separated and obeyed, avoiding each other's eyes so as not to give anything away. Having shared the company of the other two Signs, a sense of abandonment overtook Tim as he entered his room. He went directly to the bed and laid down, settling the robe about him. The fire crackled and hissed. He closed his eyes and thought about all that had happened, grimacing as Joey's screams echoed in his memory. He shook his head to clear the thought and focused his thoughts on what would happen when Jamee came for him. The overwhelming events of the previous days took their toll and he dozed off.

The boy was back. They were in a meadow and the boy was beckoning to him. He seemed really desperate for Tim to understand something. Tim crossed the meadow, but as he got closer, there was a sudden barrier. He couldn't see it, but he could see the boy on the other side calling silently to him. He struggled against the barrier, but it held fast.

He was awakened a short while later by a hand on his arm. "Jamee?" he murmured. A slap across the face sent his head rolling and a harsh voice said, "Quickly, Stark."

"He's beginning to wake up, doctor." Tentatively, Tim opened his eyes. A white-haired, aged man leered down at him, the light gleaming from a gold ring through his left nostril.

The harsh voice spoke again. "Then he will have to experience it awake."

The man's leer grew more spiteful. "Morning, sunshine," he sneered. Tim opened his mouth to yell, but the man brandished a wicked looking, three-pronged knife about his throat. "One sound, little boy, and you're dead." Tim shut his mouth and the man nodded his approval. He took each of Tim's arms and, using a thick rope from his pocket, he tied Tim to the bedposts by his forearms and ankles, taking care not to touch the bracelets. He then took the robe and tore it, baring Tim's sore-ridden chest. Tim hardly dared to move.

"Stark, is he prepared?" the voice demanded.

"He is, doctor." Stark moved off of the bed with some difficulty and Tim could see a younger man, though still middle-aged, standing there, holding some kind of contraption. The machine in his hands blinked and whistled. It had two long cords with clamps on the ends and numerous shorter wires that terminated in what looked like suction cups. The sight of the machine struck a chord of terror in Tim and he started to struggle again.

Stark quickly returned the knife to Tim's throat and the cold steel prickling his skin forced his obedience. "Do you think it will work, doctor?" Stark asked with glee. His other hand freed the ring from his nose and handed it out for the doctor to take.

"I do not know, Stark, but if it does, it will gain us a large advantage. He is the most resistant so far and if we break him, we will be able to harness the power of all of them. Remember, do not touch him once it has begun. The magic from the bracelets will temper the machine's hunger and the boy's power will be trapped in this." Pressing a button on the machine, he held up the tiny gold ring. A cord snaked out of the machine and wrapped around the ring, taking it from his hand. Remember that neither boy nor bracelets will have any power while the machine is running. The machine does not discriminate between energies and it will just as easily take from you as it would from him." Tim saw a shudder shake Stark's body. "Do not touch it once it begins," he repeated. He set the machine on the floor, saying, "Go to it, my beauty." The machine skittered sideways on tiny metal legs like a living creature, moving towards the bed as Tim watched with growing panic.

Stark laughed a high pitched whine of a laugh and moved away from the bed. Their anxious voices made Tim's blood run cold and he tried to distract himself from the events that were taking place in front of him, but his mind would not cooperate. A clamp appeared, taking a part of the bedspread. The machine hauled itself up onto the bed and slowly crawled towards him. Tim struggled minimally, but Stark flashed the knife and he laid still, letting the electronic animal make its way up his body. It was cold to the touch and he felt numb wherever its metal met his flesh. It straddled his chest and the suction cups extended. At such a close view, Tim could see miniature needles in the center of each cup. His mind gibbered in terrified anticipation. The machine affixed the cups to his chest, one to each welt and jammed them in. Tim gritted his teeth, determined not to make a sound. The clamps stretched towards the bracelets on his wrists. As they latched on, a jolt of agony shot through him and he threw his head back, grinding his jaw. His body was wracked with pain and tears were streaming from his eyes, blurring his vision. It was beyond anything he'd ever experienced. Dimly, he could hear shouting, but he couldn't focus on it. His mind went numb as a fresh flow of anguish seared him, his back arching involuntarily. Then, blessedly, the pain was gone. Cool air rushed over his skin, making him gasp as it stung his chest. His mind hummed with the pain-soaked memory and he closed his eyes, unable to focus on anything except shallowly taking in air. His chest felt like it had been ripped open and it hurt to take even the smallest of breaths. Slowly, he became aware of words through the humming in his brain.

"Tim? Can you hear me? Xander, I don't think he can hear us." "We have to get him back to The Gathering." *Xander*, Tim thought gratefully.

"Tim?" Tim opened his eyes. Xander and James peered down at him, worry clearly written on both faces. "Don't worry, Tim," Xander said, "we're going to get you back."

"Xander," Tim managed to croak.

Xander turned to James. "You have to hold onto him tight. I can take people with me, but we have to stay in contact the entire time. Remember, *don't* let go." James nodded and each took one of Tim's hands in their own. The door burst open and Lena stormed in, shrieking incoherently at them. It might have been a trick of the light or of his mind, but Tim swore he saw her lift into the air, streaking across the chamber towards them, wailing like a banshee all the while. Xander and James quickly joined hands, and the room around them blurred and vanished, Lena still shrieking and grasping at the air where they had been. Tim closed his eyes as his stomach heaved, protesting loudly. He felt like he was floating, weightless. Then there was a jolt and voices were shouting. He opened his eyes to many people converging upon the three Signs at great speed. A middle-aged man with light blue eyes and a loping gait was the first to reach them. He grabbed Xander's arm, drawing him out of Tim's line of vision. James was quickly swallowed by the mob. Tim strained to sit up to see where his companions had gone but he was pushed back down and all sounds were drowned out by a woman's voice.

"Medical!" she screamed. A clanging noise filled the air, hurting Tim's ears and giving him a headache. More figures appeared in his limited line of vision. He was beginning to feel claustrophobic and twisted to get away from the hands holding him down. Then something sharp jabbed into his arm and his eyes fluttered shut.

Chapter 9

When he awoke, he was in a strange bed. There was a middle-aged woman he didn't recognize sitting in a chair beside him, holding his hand. She looked at him as he turned his head towards her. She was a handsome woman with waves of light brown hair streaked with gray cascading down around her shoulders. Her eyes were a light hazel color and creased with years of laughter. The same lines framed her full lips which opened into a tentative smile as she stroked the back of his hand.

"Welcome back," she said.

Tim tried to wet his lips to respond, but his tongue was dry. The woman let go of his hand and took a glass of water from the bedside table. Using one arm to help him sit up, she poured the cool liquid into his mouth, some of it running down his chin. "Thanks," he whispered. His limbs felt like lead, but with effort, he lifted a hand and took the glass from her, tipping a bit more into his mouth before lowering it to his lap. As the water made its way to his stomach, he took in his surroundings.

He was in the last of many beds lining a wall. Most of them were unoccupied, but there were a few down at the far end that had a person in them. Across the room were shelves stocked with metal instruments, gleaming in the early morning light coming in through large arched windows. A few people bustled about the large room, taking instruments down, putting them back, carrying charts back and forth, talking in corners. Their shoes made no sound on the stone floor.

To his right, there was a tapestry depicting a large tree. Underneath the tree were people in varying states of repose, consuming the fruits of the tree, smiles woven onto their faces. The sun shone brightly down upon them, seeming almost to smile itself. Animals capered about the figures and flowers grew around them. All in all, it was a pleasant scene. If one looked closely enough, the trunk of the tree took on the shape of a beautiful woman gazing benevolently down upon the people in her shade. The woman noticed him observing it.

"The Dryad, Rythsinda," she said gently. "Patron of the healers. It is said that one fruit from Her Tree could heal any wound, cure any infliction. It is from Her that all healers have their gifts. Only the pure of heart and body are able to follow Her. The Dryad never took a man to bed and out of deference to Her, the healers are chaste. They also choose not to eat meat. For the healers, to break either of these conventions would be a violation of the gift given to them by the Dryad and Rythsinda does not tolerate deviations." She paused and the corners of her mouth curled slightly. "I guess you don't really want to listen to healer lore for the duration of your recovery?"

"No, thank you. I mean, it's fascinating to hear, but I have other things on my mind," Tim declined.

"Such as?"

"Where am I? Who are you? Where are Xander and James? Are they okay? What's wrong with me?" The words tumbled from his mouth before he could think about them.

The woman held up her hands, laughing. "One at a time, Tim! For goodness' sake, take it easy or you will wear yourself out before you have a chance to recover!" She gestured for him to drink more water, which he obeyed. "You are in the hospital wing of The Gathering. You suffered multiple injuries from a *psyphagyte.*"

"A what?"

"A machine that feeds on energy. The *psyphagyte* was originally designed to mix energies and thereby imbue the users with properties of both kinds of energy." She paused. "Let me go back. In the world most people live in, the base of the human being is blood and the blood types. In our world, a person's energy is what defines him. Where there are only a few types of blood, though, each person has a specific kind of energy that is unique to him. No two energies are exactly alike, but those who share an emotional relationship have complementary properties in their energy flow. Therefore, in most cases, it's much easier to transfer energy from a family member or a friend than from a stranger. The closer the relationship between the two people, the more easily the transfer is made. In very rare cases, an enemy will be the easiest transfer because of the strength of the emotion between them, even though the emotion is negative. Healers take the energy given by a person and augment it with their own, then transfer it to the patient, thereby giving the patient the energy he or she needs to recover without diminishing the energy of the giver to a critical level. In extreme situations, a person can transfer energy on his own, but there are very few recorded cases of this and most end in disaster.

"Sometime back around the mid-80s, a scientist named Dr. Harry Ventnors made forays into the psychic world and learned of the powers of the healers. He wanted to capture it for himself, so he created a machine called a *psyphagyte*, which would do the work that a healer would normally do, but faster and more cleanly. It was also intended to be able to mix the energies of two people, so that those of us who were gifted would be able to share our gifts with those who weren't. If this weren't bad enough, another suggestion for the usage was to put the properties of gifted individuals into common objects that then would be sold to the public for a profit. This caused an uproar throughout the psychic world, especially among the healers, who felt that it was a degradation of the Dryad. There were a few, however, who supported Dr. Ventnors' invention and were willing to submit themselves for experimentation. Dr. Ventnors had done some minor testing with various animals and was ready to try it with human beings. He decided he would make this first test open to certain invited members of the medical community and government officials.

"The experiment went horribly awry. Some say the Patrons themselves were angry with the scientist and cursed the project. Another theory suggests a group of telekinetics got together and focused their energies upon the machine, hoping to destroy it. Whatever the reason, instead of multiplying the mixed energies and sending them back into the people, the machine drained them of all energy, leaving them mindless shells. The machine then turned on Dr. Ventnors, doing the same to him as hundreds of horrified spectators watched. The government was able to cover it up and no more was heard of Dr. Ventnors, nor of his machine, but it appears by the marks on your chest that the machine was not destroyed as it was commonly believed." She carefully opened the robe at his chest and he could still see the tiny holes where the needles had pierced his skin, ringed with redness. Quickly glancing at his wrists, he noted that they were red and raw as well, but there was no evidence of the bracelets that he had worn.

"What happened to the *psyphagyte*? How did we get away?" He flexed his wrists. It was uncomfortable, but not painful.

"When a *psyphagyte* is in operation, nothing can interrupt it, lest the energies be lost forever. The people who were using it on you found a way to keep the machine from sapping your energy entirely. It was explained to me that the bracelets prevented you from using your talents. These bracelets were created with the same properties as the *psyphagyte*, but they were only able to take energy from you when they needed to repair themselves and only over a period of time. The reason that you were unable to use your powers was because they were designed to take energy from that aspect of your being first without hurting your life force. You were unable, therefore, to tap into that specific kind of energy it takes for you to use your talents. I assume that the bracelets would give enough energy to the machine to satiate it, thereby ensuring the entrapment of your own powers within some object.

"James and Xander broke down the door to your room and attacked the men who were doing this to you. That's one powerful talent the Gemini has. I'm told that they had to pry the machine off of you before he was able to act. Then he laid a hand on it and transformed it into a harmless little box." She gestured to the box sitting on the bedside table. "James says that had he tried to transform it while you were interconnected, you might have been transformed as well." Tim shuddered. "As for the bracelets, it seems that they were able to temper the machine long enough for James and Xander to get it away from you for transformation. I can only assume that, having been drained by the machine, they could not regain the energy fast enough to regenerate so they disintegrated.

"Xander knew that you needed a healer, so he and James brought you back here to The Gathering. His father had had a vision and was heading to the spot where you appeared, informing everyone he saw on the way. Medical was called, and you were brought up to the hospital wing where healers were ready. Xander himself volunteered to give the energy necessary to heal you." She beamed with pride.

"Where is he now? Can I see him?" Tim was anxious.

"My son is sleeping," she answered and smiled as Tim started. "As is James. It was a long night."

"I didn't realize. You should be with Xander, Mrs. Conlyn," Tim told her.

She shook her head. "My husband is with the boys, keeping an eye on them. I volunteered to keep an eye on you, Tim." The affection was clear in her voice. There was so much that Tim wanted to ask, to say, but he didn't know how to express it, so he stayed silent. She seemed to understand, though, and nodded at him.

A commotion at the other end of the room caught their attention. An older woman with wiry graying hair was shouting at one of the healers in a scratchy voice.

"I know he's awake, Lisa! Just because I've aged doesn't mean that I've lost my eyesight!" She gestured towards Tim with a lit cigarette clutched in a gnarled hand.

Lisa was obviously trying to be respectful. "He needs time to recover, Professor. You can see him later today. And there's no smoking in the hospital wing. You *know* that!"

The woman huffed indignantly. "You think now that you're a fully invested healer, you can give orders to those who taught you your craft. You had better let me by, young lady, before I speak to Carlotta about reassigning you to dung duty!" When Lisa hesitated, the woman moved around her with remarkable speed for someone her age and size. She traversed the long room to stand at the foot of Tim's bed. Up close, she was even more formidable. Her almost violet-brown eyes were magnified by oversized glasses. Jowls drooped, bookending her lips, which were painted an unruly shade of red. The same red was painted onto her nails, giving them the semblance of the bloodied talons of a bird of prey. A necklace made of limestone quartz hung about her neck, dipping between her sagging breasts. The black sack of a dress she wore billowed around her chest with a shawl tied about the middle to give her a waist. "Rachel," she greeted Tim's companion.

"Blanche."

The woman stared down at him. "Well?" she rasped. "Don't just sit there marveling at my beauty, boy. Who are you?"

Tim cleared his throat. "Uh, I'm Libra, madam. Er, Professor."

"Professor Galten," she informed him. "And I couldn't give a parakeet's wings which Sign you are. I refuse to call you by such a ridiculous title. You're no different than the rest of the gifted people around here, except that you have more responsibility. If you are to be a part of The Gathering, and I assure you that you have no choice in the matter, I shall need a suitable name to call you by." She peered intently at him through her glasses.

"It's Tim. Timothy Dalis."

"Much better, Mr. Dalis, much better," she wheezed, taking a long drag of her cigarette.

"If you don't mind, Blanche, I think I'll go check on Xander." Mrs. Conlyn rose with a wink for Tim, and gestured for the professor to take her seat.

Professor Galten lowered her bulk into the chair with a thud. "Not at all, Rachel. By all means, go see how your son is doing. Check on the other one while you're at it," she added.

"I will. Tim, listen to Professor Galten. She's one of our best instructors."

The professor's lips quirked in such a way that, had her mouth not been permanently frozen in a grimace, might have been a smile. She bobbed her head curtly in acknowledgment of the compliment. "Off with you." Mrs. Conlyn nodded and departed, moving gracefully towards the door. Tim watched her go until a loud cough brought him back to the professor. She looked him up and down. "You're smaller than I expected, but with your gift, size doesn't make any difference. It's a very subtle but effective talent. Essentially, you're forcing people to like and trust you so that they'll accept your version of the truth. You may even have the power to change emotional memories."

"My version? The truth is the truth no matter what, isn't it?" Tim took a sip of water.

"Foolish boy." She laughed coarsely without smiling. "Use your head. There is no singular Truth. If there were, there would only be two decisions in this world: right and wrong. And that's assuming that the Truth would include free will. Quite to the contrary, there are many choices in this world between black and white, and what is right for one may not necessarily be right for another."

"Then, if there is nothing that is definitely right, how do we know that what we are doing is right?" he challenged.

Professor Galten took a long drag on her cigarette, watching him intently. He waited patiently. "Now, that's a good argument, boy. Much better. The truth is," she continued as she opened the tan box that used to be the *psyphagyte* and flicked her ashes into it, "we don't. The only thing that we know for sure is that if the other side gets a hold of the power, then they will use it to unmake the universe as we know it. We're fighting for our very existence and that's something worth fighting for. Wouldn't you agree?" He nodded. "Glad you see it that way. The truth is malleable. Anyone can twist things in order to make the truth work for them."

"Kind of the way that the future can be changed?" Tim asked.

She bobbed her head. "Very good comparison. Just as John Conlyn can affect the future by seeing the future. As the future has different possibilities, so does the truth. Your particular talent enables you to make people see the truth that you want them to see."

"I'm getting that. How do I do that?" he wondered aloud.

"You befriend people through their hearts and minds. A feeling emanates from you, surrounds them, and takes them in. They have no choice but to find you in a position of some authority, and anything you say is immediately accepted as truth because they trust you."

Tim had a chilling thought. "Then I actually have no real friends? They're all under mind-control?"

"Of course you have real friends. Without exerting your desire to charm, you're an ordinary person." She took another drag.

"Thanks," Tim said sourly.

"Don't be petulant," she reprimanded him. "You are not ordinary. You wished to know if you had legitimate friends, and the answer is yes. Don't believe what you do is mind-control, though. You are appealing to their emotions. It's not the same. Instead of altering someone's actual memories of an event, for example, you would be able to alter their feelings about the event."

He scratched his nose. "How could that possibly help anyone?"

"How a person feels about their past affects how they will act in the future, Timothy. If you are scared by a spider in the past, you are going to be more wary of spiders in the future. If that fear is taken away, you won't be nervous to go near a spider in the future. Certain behaviors are learned." She pointed at him with the cigarette, spilling ashes onto the bed. "That is what your power holds. Just as erasing that memory would have a similar effect. This will not always be an easy thing for you to do. Powerful enemies will be harder to charm. You'll need to practice."

"Great. I feel like I'm back in school," Tim muttered.

"All of life is a school," the professor noted. "We learn from our experiences. However, sometimes, it is necessary to impart information in a more direct manner, which is why I'm here right now. No time to waste."

"What kind of information?" Tim was curious.

"History."

Tim cringed. "History?"

"Yes, Timothy. Had you been listening more carefully to what I have been saying, you would understand that history affects the present. Knowledge of the past is a vital tool that you will need in order to perform well. The history of The Gathering is what you are to learn today."

"Now?" he asked incredulously.

"Now," she confirmed. "You have nowhere to go and nothing to do. There is no better time. The healers tell me that you will be recovered enough by the end of the day to attend dinner. We'll take our lunch up here while you learn the history of this magnificent place." She put her cigarette out in the box and pulled another cigarette from underneath the voluminous folds of her dress. Grasping a silver dragon-headed lighter in one talon, she drew the flame across the cigarette, closing her eyes and drawing in a deep breath. Placing the lighter back amongst the blackness of her dress, she raised a claw and snapped her fingers. The sound resonated through the cavernous room and a young healer at the other end jumped and hurried over to them.

"What can I get you, Professor?" he asked, bowing respectfully.

"Lunch," she grated. "What do you want, boy?"

"Oh," Tim stammered, "Uh, I dunno."

"How about some soup and a sandwich? We have chicken noodle." the healer asked kindly.

"Yes, please." Tim suddenly realized how long it had been since he'd last eaten and his stomach rumbled in agreement.

"For the sandwich, would you prefer turkey, bologna, salami, or ham?"

"What are the chances I could get all four? I'm really hungry," he apologized.

The healer smiled. "That's natural after what you've been through. We'll get you back on your feet in no time."

"Ham on rye for me, Joe," the professor ordered. The healer bowed again and went off. She turned back to Tim, exhaling and enveloping him in another cloud of smoke.

"Before we start the lesson, are there any questions that you have?"

Tim hesitated. "How did you come to be here?" he asked tentatively. "What gift do you possess?"

Professor Galten's eyes took on a faraway look. "If I so wish, my body can be immune to potions and herbs. Therefore, I've devoted my life to the study of wortcunning, or herbalism. I can evoke hidden properties of various plants by mixing them together in infusions or potions. I create many potions for The Gathering."

"How long has The Gathering been here?" Tim queried.

"The Gathering was formed in 1575 by a group of individuals who found that they were unlike other people. At the time, the Church was out to destroy all heretical ideas. Since all ideas that originated from outside the Church were considered to be heretical, the group went underground for protection and preservation. They called themselves The Gathering because there was a call in each of them that gathered them together.

"One member, Eva Braith, had visions. Her dreams told her things about the different members of The Gathering. Early in the formation of the organization, she had a dream about the origin of the members' gifts. Braith's Vision is possibly the closest thing that The Gathering has to a bible. It is our lore. It is the only thing that we, as members, adhere to, as far as an ancient text is concerned, although it has never been formalized into any kind of religion. The story has been passed from generation to generation." Her voice took on the quality of a priest in its reverence and familiarity with the well-worn tale.

"In Eva's dream, she stood in an open field. The members of The Gathering surrounded her, a few people at each point on the compass. To the South, a volcano cracked the ground, spewing lava down into the field. A few members cried out, but those standing at the southernmost point did not move. The lava flowed over them and yet they were not burned. It touched no other members. From the bowels of the volcano appeared a great Flame. The Flame slowly moved down the side of the volcano, beckoning to those who the lava had touched. The others watched silently as their lava-struck members met the Flame at the base, where it formed into the figure of an elderly man with a long, flowing beard and proud bearing. He flickered once and they bowed to Him. 'Ye of the Fire shall be blessed with the gift of mobility,' He said, His voice crackling. 'The world is yours to arrange as you like it. Be wise with this gift, my children, and never try to move something beyond your power, or the energy will consume you. This is the will of Andoleen, Fire-Spirit, and so shall it be.' From the volcano's side came rocks of various sizes. They flew through the air towards the followers of Andoleen, each of whom stretched out a hand and halted a rock in mid-air. Andoleen nodded once and led the newly formed telekinetics up into the folds of the volcano to watch and wait."

The healer returned at this point with their breakfast. He carefully placed Tim's tray table on the bed so that it straddled his body. The aroma hit him full in the face and his stomach rumbled loudly. He lifted his spoon and attacked the soup with vigor. The soup warmed him as it traveled down his throat to his stomach and he sighed contentedly as he started in on his sandwich. The professor kept one claw tightly wrapped around her cigarette, grasping the sandwich in the other hand. She continued speaking between mouthfuls, frequently gesturing with the sandwich and causing bits of ham to fall from between the bread.

"From the East, a breeze picked up, bringing flower petals upon it. The petals swirled about those standing at the eastern point. Though it did not reach the others, they could see hair and clothing whipped into action by the wind. The petals began to come together, weaving into a pattern. As the pattern became clearer, the figure of a middle-aged woman was formed. She turned to the mountain and spread Her arms towards it. Andoleen inclined His head. She turned back to those of the East. Plucking a seed from Her person, She bade them open their hands. Into each hand was placed one of the seeds. 'Taste,' She breathed. 'Taste and behold the gift of communication. Ye of the Air shall have a sense of understanding each other that will be unheard by others. With this gift comes the danger that others with the gift will be able to hear you when unguarded. Be sure to keep that which you do not wish known deep down in your heart where it cannot be touched. This is the will of Manaran, Seed-Keeper, and so shall it be.' She took the telepaths to a hill covered with all of the flowers known to man. They settled there among the blooms and turned back to face the center.

"In the North, a great Tree sprang from the ground. The branches stretched out to the sky and over those standing to the north of Eva. The foliage was all colors and from the branches dropped a young woman the color of the bark."

"Rythsinda," Tim interrupted, swallowing a bite of turkey.

"Rythsinda," Professor Galten agreed. "The Dryad. She dipped low into a curtsey to Manaran and Andoleen, who bowed back. Rythsinda turned to the Tree and a stag emerged from behind the large trunk. He was magnificently colored with all of the hues of the Earth in him. His antlers were iridescent and shone in the bright sunlight. The Dryad strode over to him and held his head in Her hands, stroking the muzzle and whispering in his ear. Then She turned and held a hand out, calling those of the North to come to Her. As they drew near, She slashed her hand across the beast's chest and he fell to the ground with a scream of pain. There was a gasp of horror from a few members, but the Dryad's followers kept on, standing in a circle around the wounded stag. Weeping, Rythsinda raised Her head to look each in the eye. 'Ye of the Earth are both blessed and cursed with feeling. Touch him,' She commanded them. Each knelt and placed a hand upon the dying animal. 'Feel the lifeblood flowing out of him. Feel his pain, take it into yourself and know what it is like to be dying. Join hands.' There were tears streaming down each person's face, matching the Dryad in her grief, but they obeyed. 'Feel each others' energy and feed it back into him.' The members closed their eyes. Slowly, the skin knitted itself back together and the wound closed. The stag got to its feet and trotted off. Rythsinda smiled. 'Beware the dying creature, for it cannot always be saved. Ye must learn to judge how much energy to use lest you lose your own life in the attempt to save another. Trust what ye feel. This is the will of Rythsinda, Dryad, and so shall it be.'" She gestured for the fledgling healers and empaths to take refuge in the branches of

Her Tree while She Herself settled down against the trunk to watch what would happen next.

"Eva turned to the West, where a lake was already forming. The water spread over the field, growing in size until it spanned the western horizon and she stood at the edge of an ocean. Those standing to the West were suddenly waist-deep in water. A small boy swam up. In His hand, He held a trident, and they could see that His nether region was comprised of scales. He smiled a boyishly shy smile at the other Three and They smiled back. He turned to Eva and she stepped forward to join the others in the water. He laid His trident upon the surface of the ocean and it rose up, cascading over them and encasing them in a sheath of solid water. Before any of them could cry out, the water was absorbed into their bodies. He smiled. 'Look, ye children of Water. I give the gift of knowledge. Water is endlessly flowing, constantly moving. It has knowledge of past, present, and future, and so shall ye. Yet, know that knowledge does not necessarily include goodness. It is up to ye to choose what will be the correct course of action. Choosing certain actions based on the knowledge ye have, ye might change the future. Knowledge is a very powerful tool. Use it wisely. This is the will of Niole, Mer-Child, and so shall it be.' He wrapped the psychics and precogs in a dome of water and turned back to where Eva had stood moments before.

"From the stars above, a beam of light spiked down. A figure began to form within the light, but the light grew so bright that the members of The Gathering had to shield their eyes. The Four recognized the figure, however, and bowed Their heads in respect. Then the Four left Their disciples and moved towards the light. When They reached the light, it flashed, blinding the members. When they recovered, the light and the Four were gone. In Their place was a small scrap of paper with the word *Protect* on it.

"Thus ends 'Braith's Vision'."

Tim was intrigued. "Who was the figure in the light? The God of the astrologers?"

"It is unknown who that figure was, but there are theories. And these are not Gods. We call them Patrons. Without them, we would not be who we are, but we do not worship them and we do not follow any rules that were written down in a book. Only the healers make sacrifices, and that is their own choice. There is no law requiring that they be celibate. They choose it out of respect for Rythsinda." She tapped out the long strand of ashes that had formed upon her cigarette during the story.

"So, who is the Patron of the astrologers?" Tim wanted to know.

"The astrologers have no Patron. Astrology is not a gift innate to certain human beings. It is a matter of knowledge and mathematics. While it has more of an occultish bent than astronomy, it is one of the more decidedly scientific branches of The Gathering. Granted, there are those who have a penchant for it, but they are not gifts from the Patrons. Herbalism is in a similar vein." She puffed on her cigarette and indicated the room that they were in. "True, my immunity makes my chosen study of herbcraft safer. It allows me a deeper study of what the properties of certain objects taken from the natural world will do when treated in specific ways. I can heal certain illnesses through the use of my potions, but I cannot take energy from one human being and transfer it to another. Only a healer has that ability. Do you comprehend the difference?"

"Yes, but I have another question. I noticed that each of the Patrons were associated with an Element. Does that mean something?"

"Each Sign is also associated with an Element. There are three Signs that fall under each Element, and each of the Elements brings a certain character to the sign. Fire signs are passionate and impulsive. Earth signs are stolid and practical. Air signs are eccentric and intellectual, and Water signs are intuitive and emotional."

"So, do we connect to the Patrons in some way?" Tim was fascinated with the idea of the Patrons and wanted some kind of personal link with them. He looked down at his plate, pressed a finger onto one of the crumbs, lifted it to his mouth, and sucked it down.

"That is as yet unknown. We do know that the abilities that you possess are not connected to the gifts from the Patrons. Else, all Fire Signs would be telekinetics and you would be a telepath. No, you are not of the Patrons, but of the zodiac. You are a Sign. Whether your status as an Air Sign has a connection to the Patron Manaran has yet to be determined, but one thing is for sure, Tim: the Patrons are gone. There are speculations as to whether the Patrons had some say in creating you. The most popular theory is that the blinding white figure is the universe Herself and the Patrons were created by Her to help keep the balance. We are an extension of that. The last message that they left for us was to protect, and protect we will. Our job is to protect the Star Child. We will do this with every last bit of energy that we have." Her voice was magnified by pride until it rang throughout the chamber. The healer looked up and saw that they were finished. He swept through, removing the tray without a word.

"And the first step to doing that is to collect all of the Signs together, right?" Tim observed.

She nodded. "Right you are, boy. Right you are."

"Tim!" Tim followed the call to see Xander running across the floor, James in tow. James's jeans were torn at the knee.

"Alexander Conlyn, there is no running in the hospital wing," the professor reprimanded him.

"There's also no smoking, Professor Galten," he pointed out with a grin. She stared hard at him for a moment.

"Well, you've a point there, I suppose," she wheezed grudgingly. "I see that there's nothing more I'll be able to teach you while this maniac is here," she said to Tim, who shared a grin with Xander and James.

"Professor, this is James," Tim introduced them. "He's the Gemini. James, this is Professor Galten."

She held out a hand. As James took it, she added, "I'd like to meet both of you." Startled, James glanced at the other two Signs, then shrugged and blinked into Jamee. She continued shaking hands with the professor.

"It's nice to meet you, Professor," Jamee said smoothly. She flashed back to James, who disengaged from the contact. "I'm sure we'll see you around," he said.

"Yes, I'm sure you will." She faced Tim. "We'll speak more tomorrow. Perhaps I will see you at dinner." Taking another long drag of her cigarette, she barreled towards the door, healers scrambling to get out of her way.

"You look better," James told him.

"I feel better," Tim admitted.

"The healers say that you'll be out of here by tomorrow," Xander chimed in. He sat on the edge next to Tim as James took a spot on the foot of the bed.

"Thanks to you, I'm told. I owe you big time."

Xander shook his head and his arm brushed against Tim's. "Nah, I didn't do anything."

"Your mother might disagree with that," Tim argued. Xander's touch was making him light-headed. He tried to focus. "She's very nice, by the way."

"Yeah, I'll keep her around. You'll meet Dad at dinner."

"He's really nice too," James informed Tim. Tim nodded and yawned.

"I think he needs more sleep," said a healer who had come up from behind them.

"Come on, Lisa, we just got here," Xander protested, but she took a hold of his collar and tugged.

"You want him to heal completely, don't you? He's got to be on his feet soon so he needs his rest now. He'll be down for dinner." Her tone brooked no argument. Xander and James reluctantly left their positions, promising to come back to get him when it was time for dinner.

When they had gone, Tim asked the healer, "Is it true that you don't eat any meat?"

She smiled at him. "Get some sleep now," was all she said.

Chapter 10

His sleep was dreamless and when he awoke, Xander was by the bed, keeping watch. Tim smiled tiredly at him. "Where's James?"

"Dad wanted to talk to him and Jamee, and Mom had work to do, so I volunteered to watch over you," Xander explained.

"That's sweet of you," Tim told him.

"Well, it was either me or Professor Galten and I figured the smoke would get to you," Xander joked. "Hungry?"

"A little, yeah."

"Good, it's almost dinner time. The sleep did a lot of good. The healers explained it to me. When they took my energy and placed it into you, at first, your body was too weak to do anything with it, so it just went to keeping you basically functioning. Then, when your body had enough strength, it sent my energy to start the healing process." Xander took Tim's robe in his hands, mirroring his mother's actions from earlier that day. The wounds were still there, but much fainter and the redness had vanished. His wrists were still tinged with pink, but there was no scarring.

"It's amazing," Tim breathed.

"You'll be completely healed by tomorrow, which is good because we have more Signs to find." Xander removed his hands, and as he did, Tim saw a flash of red and black. He grabbed Xander's forearm and pulled it closer. A ring of blisters decorated each wrist, some black and scabbing, others red and weeping pus. Xander winced and tried to pull away, but Tim held him fast. He could feel heat emanating from the sores.

"How?" he whispered.

Xander swallowed, hesitating. "We didn't understand the bracelets properly," he confessed. "When Jamee became James, the bracelets lost their hold and fell apart without a problem. In order for me to get free, James had to transform the bracelets. Jamee had discovered that when she tried to use her talent with the bracelets on, they heated up from the energy they were absorbing." Tim's eyes widened with horrified understanding as Xander continued. "Then James tried to use his talent on my bracelets, and they resisted at first, instead trying to absorb his abilities. It felt like a fire crawling across and under my skin. Eventually, the pressure was too much for them and James was able to change them, but they left mementos of their presence." Catching sight of Tim's expression, he quickly added, "The healers say that I'm going to be fine. They just haven't really been working on me yet because they needed my help in healing you first. Not that I'm complaining. You're needed here."

"So are you. You're needed here much more than I ever was," Tim argued, holding tightly onto Xander's hand.

"Don't say that. I need you here. When you were laying there with that awful machine–"

"Just don't think about it. I try not to." They looked at each other. Footsteps came pounding upon the floor and James appeared at the foot of the bed as the boys sprang apart.

"What's taking you guys so long?" he panted. "Everyone's ready for dinner. They're waiting for you." He paused, his mouse-like face taking on a concerned cast. Tim and Xander were staring at each other. "Is everything okay?"

Xander broke the connection and turned to James. "Sure. We just got caught up talking is all. Ready to see more of The Gathering, Tim?"

Tim slid his legs over to the side of the bed. Xander moved closer so Tim could use him for support if he needed to. He pushed off the bed and found that he was much stronger than he had originally thought. He waved Xander off. "Lead the way."

James coughed delicately. "Um, Tim, you might want to change for dinner, don't you think?"

Chagrin spread through him as he remembered that he was wearing the robe that had been given to him by Merel. "That might be a good idea," he said. James produced a bag of clothing that he had been holding at his side and took out fresh jeans and a polo.

"Did you want me to take out the underwear too, or can you do that yourself?" James teased.

"Give it," Tim snapped, stealing the clothing from the boy.

"Come on, there's a bathroom near the end of this room." Xander started across the floor.

"Great," Tim grumbled. "Communal bathrooms. I feel like I'm back in college."

"Oh, no, each of our rooms has its own bathroom," James contradicted him, excited. "It's awesome. Wait until you see the rooms. They're huge." James continued to talk about how wonderful their rooms were as they crossed the infirmary. A few patients sat up to observe the Signs as they passed by. Tim tried to ignore their stares. The healer, Lisa, met them at the end of the room.

"Authorization requested for patient TD-S7 to go to dinner," Xander said formally.

"Authorization granted," Lisa replied. "Return by 11:00 pm."

"Hey, thanks, Lis. We'll have him back as soon as we can." Xander led the way out of the room.

"By 11:00 pm, Sagittarius, or else!" The shout echoed in the room and a few patients stirred at the noise. Xander rolled his eyes and shut the door behind him. They moved down the hallway. There was a blue and green carpet running the length of the room. Another carpet ran along the ceiling, mirroring the first in reds and golds. A lamp hung down every fifteen feet casting light along the hallway. The walls were painted with various murals of the Dryad, Rythsinda, most of them showing Her in the process of healing a person or animal. Xander stopped at a door, saying to Tim, "If you want to change in here, we'll make sure no one disturbs you."

Tim turned the handle and looked inside. "This is the bathroom?"

"No, this is a broom closet." He held up his hands when Tim glared at him. "Yes, it's a bathroom. Go ahead. We'll wait for you out here."

Tim entered the room, which turned out to be a spacious and private bathroom. He quickly removed the robe and changed, enjoying the sensation of fresh, clean clothing against his skin. He was fascinated with the story of the Patrons and curious to learn more about the building which was to be his new home. A warm feeling grew within his chest as he considered his companions and what they had gone through for him. Splashing cold water on his face, he looked in the mirror. He saw a joy in his face that he hadn't had before. The sense of belonging and purpose had added a new dimension that he hadn't even realized had been missing. Grinning, giddily aware of his brush with sudden death, and happy to go back to the people who had protected him, Tim emerged from the bathroom, robe in hand. "What should I do with this?" he asked.

"I say we burn it," James suggested fiercely.

Xander shook his head. "Trash it." He took the robe from Tim and, suiting action to word, threw it into a nearby receptacle. Wiping his hands on his pants, he added, "I'm starved. What about you?"

Tim nodded. "Definitely. Lunch was pretty good, so I hope dinner's even better. I was so hungry at lunch that I could have eaten a whole buffet."

"Let's go eat," James said, taking off down the hall.

Xander and Tim followed him, Tim thinking aloud, "He certainly learned his way around this place pretty quickly."

Xander heard him. "You'll figure it out. There are all kinds of secrets to be discovered in this place. I spent a lot of my childhood exploring and discovering places that no one else knew about. Drove my parents crazy."

"I'm sure. I'll have to see if I can find any."

"Maybe I'll show you a few of my favorites sometime," Xander offered. Tim nodded.

"Are you guys coming?" James yelled from the end of the hallway.

* * * * * * * * * * *

Tim was escorted into the banquet hall by his fellow Signs, one on each side. They stood in the shadow of the enormous arch that marked the entrance, giving Tim a chance to rest and take in the scene before him. A frenzy of activity met his eyes. Tables of all shapes and sizes littered the floor, each one packed with people eating, conversing, laughing. In one corner, food was floating through the air to and from members. A roaring fire inhabited the fireplace at the far end of the room bringing warmth to the otherwise drafty room. It was tended by two young boys who were covered from head to toe with soot and appeared happy to be so. An enormous rug carpeted the stone floor, almost running from wall to wall. At each corner of the rug, Tim could make out figures that he guessed were the four Patrons of The Gathering. The center held a white circle displaying the word "Protect" woven with black yarn into the fabric, most of the word obscured by tables, but still legible. Tim tilted his head up. The ceiling was painted in the image of the night sky, containing all of the constellations, most of which he did not recognize. A golden candelabra bisected it, dripping with countless crystals that threw prismatic flickers of firelight throughout the room.

Xander steered them to an octagonal table almost directly underneath the chandelier. Four figures were already seated with plates of food in front of them. There was a slight lull in the conversations of the people they passed as various members turned to observe the newcomers. As they neared the table, Tim could see that the chairs were as varied as the people who occupied them. A sharp cough from the table announced the presence of Professor Galten. Tim's heart lifted as a familiar voice reached his ears.

"The question is, John, how do we prepare for the birth when we don't even know where the birth is going to be? You said yourself that you haven't seen anything." Sereny lounged in a La-Z-Boy, her brow knitted in consternation.

"That doesn't mean that we don't have other sources of information, Sereny," said a male voice. Tim saw that it belonged to a middle-aged man with light blue eyes.

He looked vaguely familiar. Mrs. Conlyn sat to his left, one elbow on the table, her chin in her hand, listening. "Why, just yesterday–"

"Good evening, gentlemen," the professor greeted the Signs in a loud voice.

The man noticed the new arrivals, disconcerted for only a second before standing and greeting James with a handshake and Xander with a hug.

"Tim, this my dad. Dad, this is Tim," Xander introduced them. Tim shook his hand.

"Tim, it's a pleasure to meet you. I've heard a great deal about you from my wife and son, as well as Professor Galten." Mrs. Conlyn smiled warmly at him and the professor inclined her head. Mr. Conlyn gestured for them to have a seat, sinking back down into his easy chair. Xander immediately plopped into a kitchen fold out chair, earning him a hard look from his mother. James sank into an enormous bean bag chair, his tiny frame almost getting lost among the folds. Tim lowered himself into a rolling desk chair, putting on a lock so it wouldn't go anywhere.

"You were the one who came running when we arrived," Tim voiced his thoughts aloud. Mr. Conlyn gave him a quizzical look. "Mrs. Conlyn told me."

Mr. Conlyn smiled and took his wife's hand. Plates heaped with food floated in from over their heads and settled themselves at the boys' places. Chicken parm steamed in front of Tim and his stomach growled. "Xander told us that this was one of your favorite dishes," Mrs. Conlyn said to him as Xander beamed.

"Well, don't wait, gentlemen," the professor commanded. "Eat."

Tim tucked a napkin onto his lap and took up his fork. For awhile, the adults talked quietly amongst themselves and the boys ate. Tim didn't really pay attention to the conversation; he was so focused on his food. When he did tune in, Sereny was explaining a reading.

"...and when I cast the dice, 9, 7, and 3 came up, followed by 1 and 5, and then 11. Any further castings brought up the same results repeated over and over. The ball was reading nothing but masculine energy. Everything that I've read points to this outcome. I don't understand why you're fighting it."

"Because it makes no sense," Mr. Conlyn explained. "The vision I had suggested that a feminine energy was being threatened. If we are going to win, surely we must figure out who it is and get them safely within the walls of The Gathering before they are taken."

"John, we don't know which one it is and there are six of them out there," Mrs. Conlyn protested.

"Without all of them, we are doomed to fail," Mr. Conlyn argued. "We have to save the one that is under threat or we run the risk of losing everything."

Sereny disagreed. "The readings couldn't be more clear. For some reason, we're supposed to ignore the threat. What if this is a trap, after all?"

"Are you suggesting that my vision is a trick?" Xander's father asked in an ominously quiet voice.

"Oh, shut up, John; no one's questioning your integrity," Professor Galten snapped. "Sereny has a point. You've had but one vision and she has been delving into the other world by a few paths. All of her paths say the same thing. Now, it could be true that a feminine Sign is threatened, but obviously, we're supposed to obtain the six masculine Signs first. We don't have time to try to figure out which Sign is under immediate threat, because in case you hadn't noticed, they're all under threat as long as they are outside of The Gathering."

"Can I ask a question?" Professor Galten turned, startled, to face Jamee, who now occupied her brother's seat. Her brown eyes flicked from adult to adult, alert and intelligent.

"Uncanny," Sereny murmured, having never seen the twins change.

"Of course, dear," Mrs. Conlyn allowed.

Jamee hunched forward, folding her arms over her knees. "I've been listening to your conversation while James was eating and from what I can make out, it seems that the numbers correspond to each of us here at the table, is that right?" Sereny nodded. "So, it's the order in which we're supposed to join The Gathering?"

Sereny nodded again. "That's right."

"Xander explained the whole duality thing to me. Masculine and feminine stuff. So, you're saying that the masculine Signs come first and then the feminine? That's the order?"

"That's what it appears to be," Mrs. Conlyn answered softly with a glance at her husband, who looked rebellious. Professor Galten was intensely focused upon the Gemini.

"If everyone comes in that order, then we'll have all of the Fire and Air Signs here, won't we?" More nods. "Then there has to be a reason." Xander and Tim had stopped eating by this time and everyone at the table waited as she thought. "I think Fire and Air just have to come first. They're the doers and the planners of the zodiac. At least, that's what I've learned. And 'masculine' just means 'outer-directed'. Who else would start this adventure, but those who were raring to go out and meet it head on?" She shrugged. "I mean, I guess that's why. If there is someone in danger, we're not going to find out who it is in time. Maybe that's why we need to do this in a certain order. Maybe certain talents will be needed to get other Signs." She shut her mouth with a pop and there was silence at the table.

Professor Galten looked at her appraisingly. "This one has a brain, John. You have your answer. Certain Signs must be obtained in order to obtain the rest of them."

Mr. Conlyn stared at Jamee with wonder across his face. "How could we have overlooked it? It seems too simple."

"Probably how we overlooked it," the professor pointed out. "Often, the most simple solutions are those that are hardest to see. The girl has a point. The Fire Signs, while volatile, are passionate and quick to get started. That's why we need the Fire Signs at the beginning of this journey.

"The Air Signs are primarily intellectuals, as evidenced by Ms. Holm here." Tim blinked. He hadn't known Jamee's last name before. "They will be needed for the planning aspect."

"I haven't been very much help," Tim muttered softly. Unfortunately, not softly enough. Professor Galten whirled on him.

"You are here for a reason," she told him.

"Why then?" he asked rebelliously.

"That is not something you need to know. If it were, you would know it already."

"I loathe that kind of answer," Tim grumped.

Surprisingly, Professor Galten laughed her coarse laugh. "As would I, were I in your position. Be patient." The laugh disintegrated into a cough and she regained her usual demeanor. "If I had to guess, I would assume that the Water Signs would be the next group to obtain for emotional power and support. Intuitively driven, those Signs will be devious. The Earth Signs will be the hardest to convince since they're known for practicality and stubbornness, especially Taurus. The power of Earth, however, is arguably the strongest of all the Signs." She rubbed her hands together. "I could use a cigarette."

"No smoking in the dining hall, Blanche. How about coffee?" Mrs. Conlyn suggested. "I could use some coffee myself."

"As could I," Mr. Conlyn agreed. "I still say that we should be more guarded. We are already aware of one plot to harm a Sign." He glanced sideways at Sereny. Mrs. Conlyn laid her hand on top of his in comfort and warning.

Xander broke through the tense moment that followed. "Mom, I have to get Tim back to the hospital wing by 11:00 or Lisa's going to kill me. I wanted to give him and Jamee a tour of the place."

"Go ahead," Mrs. Conlyn assented. The Signs got up from the table. "You know where to go. Don't disturb the psychic wing. There have been strong vibrations in the air, and they have asked that all non-psychics stay out, lest they muddy the readings."

Xander leaned over and gave his mother a quick kiss on the cheek. "Sure, Mom. No problem." Tim noticed that the dining hall had emptied out and there were only a few stragglers besides the four adults. *How long were we sitting there?* he wondered. They exited the dining room and entered the main hallway. The doors to the outside world were down the hall to his right, barred with three bars, each carved to look like a creature of land, sea, or air. There were doors and stairwells all around the room, leading to various wings of the building. Constant traffic moved in and out of the room, up and down the stairs. Conversations had an electric charge to them; there was a nervous energy in the air. Tim could feel it and he knew the other two were affected by it.

"Can we get out of here? There's too much...I don't know, but there's too much," Tim lamely explained.

"I know what you mean," Jamee agreed.

"Don't worry," Xander told them. "I know exactly where to go."

Chapter 11

Tim had never seen so many books in his life. He strained his eyes, marveling at the seemingly endless stretch of knowledge. Tilting his head up, he saw the highly domed room was near full to capacity and his head spun at the prospect of such a dizzying climb. Directly in front of them, a circular desk surrounded a man who appeared the epitome of the librarian archetype. A rotund figure, he sported an argyle sweater vest that stretched tight as it reached his portly middle. Spectacles perched precariously on his nose, which was buried in paperwork. Xander strolled up to the desk with Tim and Jamee and cleared his throat. The man jumped.

"My, my, my!" he exclaimed. "If it isn't three of the Signs!" Tim had expected a British accent from the man, but there was a distinctly southern twang to his voice.

"Yup. And we'll have another one soon," Xander bragged.

"Absolutely splendid! If I may introduce myself, my name is Mr. Pears. I'm delighted to be meeting the illustrious Gemini and Libra." He shook Tim's hand so vigorously that his glasses threatened to fall off. He took a finger and pushed them back up.

"This is Tim, the Libra, and, in her present form, Jamee, the Gemini," Xander introduced unnecessarily.

"Mr. Pears?" Jamee stifled a giggle.

"Yes, like the fruit." *He must be used to any jokes by now*, Tim thought, noting the man's pear-like shape. "Is there anything I can get for you?"

"No, not right now," Xander declined. "I'm just showing them around The Gathering." He turned to his friends. "Pears is a mnemonic."

"Um, isn't that a way to remember things?" Tim asked.

"Yes, that is one definition of the term," Mr. Pears reinforced. "However, Sagittarius is referring to one who has uncanny memory. I forget nothing."

"Nothing?" Jamee looked skeptical.

"Indeed. A noteworthy skill for a librarian. I can accurately tell you the location of every book that lives upon these shelves, as well as those that have recently been taken out. The mnemonics are a branch of the telepaths, but while a telepath is able to access the thoughts of other people, mnemonics have unlimited access to our own memory centers. Everything a person experiences leaves an imprint on the mind. Mnemonics are able to access those imprints at any time, thereby giving us an instant recall of any given situation through our own experiences. There are only three known mnemonics in the world."

"Is every book in here related to the occult?" Tim wondered aloud.

Mr. Pears laughed. "Good heavens, no. We have all genres. Most are dedicated to the arts that we practice and the studies done on them. Others delve into the nature of the universe. Some are written by members of The Gathering." He coughed modestly. "Yet, we also have many books that are purely for pleasure. In fact, I believe that we have the largest collection of books seen since the libraries of Anderson Baker."

"Who?" Jamee asked.

"Ah, Anderson Baker." Mr. Pears' eyes gleamed. "Mr. Baker was a member of a very wealthy family. He was also a mnemonic as well as a devoted bibliophile. In his time, he amassed the largest quantity of books and artifacts the world had ever known and placed them in four libraries scattered across the globe."

Xander suddenly became alert. "Where? And how come I've never heard of him?"

"If you stopped in here more often, you'd have learned about him," Mr. Pears chided. "And we don't know where the Baker libraries are. They vanished when he died ten years ago. Many claim they were destroyed by the Church, but there are those who know that the libraries still exist, preserved in time, containing every item that Anderson collected over his lifetime. The only clue to their whereabouts can be discovered in a book that rested nearby when he was found dead." Mr. Pears sighed.

Tim was curious. "Where is this book now?"

Mr. Pears gestured to the shelves. "The book lies somewhere upon those shelves."

Jamee looked around behind her as if she expected the book to sneak up on them. "But if you know where each and every book is, don't you know where it is?"

"I do indeed know where it is, but I do not know which one it is. If it passed through my hands, I did not recognize it."

"Why? Is it in a different language or something?" Jamee asked.

"The book is indeed rumored to be in a different language."

"Then why wouldn't you just look for the book with a strange title?" That was Xander.

Mr. Pears turned a bland look on him. "Baker was one of the most learned men of his time. Remember that he spent his entire life researching anything and everything. Have you any idea how many languages currently exist? Let's not forget how many languages have risen and fallen throughout time. Which language would you suggest we start with?" Xander colored slightly. "The libraries hold an incredible amount of information within them. Baker knew that was a dangerous prospect in the wrong hands. He had the libraries enchanted, an action that renders them inaccessible to anyone who does not hold with Baker's ideals. There is every reason to think that the book is spelled in a similar way." He removed his glasses and cleaned them with a practiced air, his gaze faraway. "We have performed everything imaginable on the library. Tracking the energies of the books, interpretation spells, rituals to reveal hidden secrets..." He sighed despondently. "We're no closer to discovering the secret than we were ten years ago." He straightened and refocused on the Signs. "Would you like a tour?" Tim started to accept, but Xander shook his head.

"Sorry, Pears. We're on a time limit," he apologized, but Mr. Pears waved a hand.

"No apologies, my dear boy. Please come back and visit when you have the time. If you can put up with the rambling of an old man, that is." He winked at them.

Jamee laid her hand on his arm. "I think it's cool. I might come back a little later, if that's okay with you."

"You're always welcome. Where are you off to next?"

"The astrolab," Xander replied.

"Fascinating place. Never go there much myself, but it's always a pleasure to see the astrologers hard at work. Now, off you go." He shooed them out of the library and the large door squealed shut behind them. There were considerably less people in the hallway than there had been. Xander moved to a large staircase and began climbing. The stairs spiraled high above them.

After passing two floors without a word, Xander stopped before an unobtrusive-looking door and faced them, one hand on the doorknob. "The fourth floor belongs to the astrology wing. This is where our rooms are." He opened the door and led them down a hallway filled with doors that reminded Tim eerily of his time spent in Merel's demesnes. There were symbols on each door, and he recognized the last door's symbol as the glyph for Libra. Xander gestured to it. "That's your room, Tim. You can see it later; I want to show you the lab before we run out of time." He bypassed Tim's room and traveled down a hallway filled with portraits until they came to an open door and walked through.

"What's this?" Jamee asked.

"Computer lab," was the answer. "Full access to the internet in each lab. Every wing has one, but they're specialized to meet the needs of the department where they're positioned. For example, each computer in the astrology wing is equipped with an ephemeris."

Tim didn't recognize the term. "What's an ephemeris?"

"It's a book that keeps track of the positions of the planets at all times. Very important tool for the astrologers."

"What about us?" Tim asked. "Are we allowed to use the computers?"

"Of course. Unless you'd prefer the one in your room."

"We have our own computers!" Jamee squealed, delighted.

"Good. I'm sure I have a million emails sitting in my inbox," Tim said. Xander rolled his eyes. They left the lab and made a sharp right, heading down a circular hallway that was also filled with doors. "What are all of these?" Tim asked.

"This is where all of the astrologers stay. The Gathering provides accommodations for each of its members and the astrologers are all in orbit around the astrolab. They can just cross the hall whenever they want, day or night, but access to the lab is strictly monitored." He pointed to a sculpture of an owl sitting on a ledge above a doorway. "All of the doors have specific requirements that don't necessarily match the others. The owl requires a retinal scan and absolutely no talking for at least a minute beforehand. Only certain astrologers are allowed through the owl at certain times. The times change daily, and there's a complicated process for informing the astrologers of the changes that I haven't figured out yet. I never use the owl." They continued around the hall, coming to a door with a fox. "The fox requires an offering of a different food each day. The same process tells the astrologers the food change."

"Why all the doors?" Jamee asked.

"All the information on the Signs is in there and Mom said that there have been times when unauthorized people were caught trying to get the information. She wouldn't tell me who and she wouldn't tell me why, but ever since then, they've been really uptight. So now certain people are cleared for very specific times and they're only allowed through assigned doors."

On they went. The cat required one to scratch an ever-changing pattern on the door. The lark needed a song. An elaborate bow gained access for the snake. A pounding pattern pleased the bear. Tim was having trouble remembering what each animal meant as they went along.

Finally, they arrived at a door without an animal. In its place lay a stone infant. "The Signs have their own entrance. No one but a Sign can enter through this door."

"Is that the Star Child?" James asked, pointing to the sculpture.

"An artist's rendering, yes. Of course, we don't know what she actually looks like, but that's the closest guess anyone has right now." So saying, he stepped forward and the infant's eyes opened, making both Tim and James jump. After an intense minute, the eyes closed and the door opened. Xander stepped through with a smile over his shoulder. Tim and James looked at each other, then Tim sighed and stepped forward. The eyes opened and focused upon him.

An alien awareness swam through his body, flowing along the bloodstream, peeking into crevasses, poking at the muscles, finally settling in his brain and sifting through his memories. He felt it ignore most of his life, focusing on every instance where he used his talent. He hadn't even realized that he'd used it as much as he had. He grimaced at the thought that he had somehow cheated his way through his life. Then the awareness vanished and he stepped through, feeling both violated and validated.

The scene that met his eyes was completely unlike the tranquility of the hallway. The room was huge. Numerous circular, glass table-like structures were in rows throughout the room and people wandered up and down the aisles created by them. Some carried books, others held clipboards, and still others possessed odd-looking disks that Tim could not identify. There was a stack of machines lining one of the walls. Here and there, a few people were conferring. A ladder stood next to the door, leading up to a second level, which held monitors and computers of varying sizes. Some people were typing on them, entering data; others were sitting at tables, relaxing. Lights blinked on and off at indeterminable intervals. The domed ceiling was made up of screens, each showing a different part of the galaxy. The atmosphere hummed with the excitement of the astrologers, moving place to place like bees in a hive. Most of them ignored him.

"Geez, that was weird," he heard muttered behind him. He glanced back to see James standing there taking in the scene before him.

"Hey guys," Xander called, beckoning them over to one of the glass tables where he and his mother stood. They made their way over to them, narrowly avoiding collisions with astrologers, earning them nasty looks.

"What do you think of The Gathering so far?" Mrs. Conlyn asked them when they arrived.

"It's cool," James answered. "Very different from any place that I've ever been. Of course, we've only just begun to see the place."

"I hope you'll make yourselves at home. Tim, how are you feeling?"

Tim shrugged. "No worse, I guess." He pointed to the table-like structure in front of them. Now that he was closer, he could see that there was a ring drawn on the surface about six inches in from the edge. "What is this?"

"This is a natal charter," Mrs. Conlyn responded. "They work in conjunction with the machines you see over there. Those are electrephemerises, or EEPs. Books are wonderful, but we found this to be a lot faster. All you need is an individisk." She held up the odd-shaped disk Tim had noted from before. "Make sure that it's a blank one. It's important never to overwrite a chart with another chart. It renders the disk non-functional. Then you place the disk into the EEP and start entering the required information such as birthdate, birthtime, location, etc. The EEP takes the information and charts it mathematically, but that's not the best way to see a natal chart, so we have these natal charters to display the information in a traditional chart. I actually just got this disk from the EEP and was about to check the information on here. Would you like to see?" Tim nodded and she slid the disk into a slot at the base of the table.

The table lit up and suddenly the ring was split into twelve pie slices. Symbols decorated the insides and outsides of the slices. Tim saw the symbol for Libra. He recognized this as being the same kind of chart that Sereny had displayed, but he could not interpret it. "This is a birth or natal chart," said Mrs. Conlyn. As she went on to explain to James what was being shown, Tim stared at the symbols, willing them to make some kind of sense. "You'll learn more about them while you're here. For now, I'll point out your glyphs to you."

"Our what?" James inquired.

"Your glyphs. The symbols that represent your Sign. Xander already knows his." She pointed to an arrow with a line crossing near its base and it lit up obligingly. "That's Sagittarius."

"I see Libra's," Tim put in, happy for once to know what he was talking about. Pointing to his symbol, he added, "Sereny showed me."

"Correct," Mrs. Conlyn approved. "The symbol for Gemini is over here."

"It looks like the Roman numeral for two," James observed.

"Not surprising when one considers that Gemini is the Twins. You'll learn the other glyphs eventually. Continue on your tour. You don't have a lot of time left," she warned Xander.

"I know, I know."

"See you later." She gave Xander a kiss.

"Bye, Mom." Xander started off.

"And thank you," Tim added, but she was already bent over the natal charter, engrossed in her work.

They went to a circular machine at the center of the room that Tim hadn't noticed before. Xander gestured to the domed ceiling. "The dome always shows the positions of the stars and planets no matter what time of the day it is. You can see any constellation or any planet at any time."

"How?" James asked.

They reached the machine, which was divided into sections each with a number and a letter. "We're at the controls for G-3," Xander told them, pointing to the corresponding section of the dome. "You can enter whatever you want to see on the keyboard and it will appear in that section of the dome."

"How does that happen?" James pressed.

"The Gathering sent tracking devices into space in the early '80s. They're not the bulky satellites that the government has placed in orbit. They're extremely hard to detect and when they show up on radars, they look like pieces of asteroids. There is a tracking device for every known star and planet. When a new star is discovered, a new tracker is programmed. When a star dies, the tracker returns to The Gathering to be reprogrammed. All of the information these devices gather is immediately transmitted back here for the astrologers to view. So, what would you like to see?"

"Venus," Tim answered before James could say anything. James glanced at him in surprise. "It's my Planet. I mean, it's Libra's ruling Planet."

"Taurus' as well," Xander threw in, typing it on the keyboard.

"I have to share?" Tim pouted jokingly.

"So does James. Gemini and Virgo share Mercury. Supposedly, there are two more planets to be discovered, but until then, you're stuck." He grinned. "I'm sure you'll both get over it." He punched a few more keys. "There she is." He pointed to a section of the dome. Venus loomed, cloudy and obscured, and to Tim's eyes, beautiful. He felt an overwhelming desire to go to it, as a child would run to its mother. He took an involuntary step forward, dazzled by the planet.

"Whoa, boy." Xander stopped him by placing a hand on his chest. "I know that feeling, but you'll have to exert a little control, or she'll end up controlling you." He tapped a few buttons on the keyboard and the image vanished. "The pull a Planet has on its respective Sign is a powerful one."

Tim shook his head to dispel the last of the compulsion. "Sorry. I didn't realize that would happen."

"No, it's my fault," Xander apologized. "I should have warned you. Any kind of visual contact with the planet has that kind of effect."

"That's one heavy drug," Tim agreed.

James looked interested. "Could I see Mercury?" he asked eagerly. Xander took one look at his watch and shook his head.

"Sorry, James, but we've got to get Tim back to the hospital wing or Lisa'll kill me."

Tim wasn't ready to go back yet. He felt energized and told Xander so, but Xander said, "That's an effect from seeing your ruling planet. It'll wear off in about a half hour and you'll crash. Hard." Tim started to protest, but Xander cut him off. "Trust me, Tim. We have about fifteen minutes to get you back to the hospital wing. Luckily, there's a more direct route than going all the way back downstairs." He left the machine. Tim and James followed him to a ladder and climbed up to the second floor. They walked past astrologers of different ages, races, shapes and sizes, ignoring the hiss of whispers that followed them.

"I feel like a circus freak," James murmured.

"Make that two," Tim agreed.

"You get used to it. We're something like royalty around here. Don't let it go to your heads," he warned. They came to an alcove.

"What's this used for?" James wanted to know.

"Before this was the astrology wing, it was the telekinetic wing. Alcoves like this were used to protect people from flying objects during training sessions. Few know its secret though." As he spoke, he slid his hand along one section of the wall. The wall became hazy and translucent, displaying a very narrow hallway. There was only enough room to walk single file and Xander gestured for the other two to go first. James walked through the haze with no apparent problem, so Tim nerved himself and stepped through. There was a strange sensation of passing through water, but he wasn't wet. Xander came through after them and there was a popping sound, then he said, "Okay, just keep going straight and we'll get to the hospital wing." James took off down the hall and Tim struggled to keep up.

"Xander, if the machines do all of the calculating, then how can an astrologer be good or bad?" James queried.

"Astrology isn't all math; it has to be interpreted," Xander answered from behind Tim. "Some astrologers interpret the charts using stock interpretations. For those astrologers, a Sun in Sagittarius will always mean the same thing. Then there are astrologers who see the combination of things as important. A Sun in Sagittarius with a Moon in Libra would be different than a Sun in Sagittarius with a Moon in Gemini. Then there's the kind of astrologer than can see even beyond that. He can see what a Sun in Sagittarius will affect years down the line. He can tell what it will mean when that person is around certain other people and how they will react. This intuition gives him the advantage over other astrologers. Anyone can do the math. It's the interpretation that counts." They only walked for two or three minutes more before James stopped.

"Xander, I'm at a wall."

"Oh, right. Okay, you have to stroke the side of the wall from top to bottom, lightly tapping your fingers in order from thumb to pinky." James did as he was told and the wall in front of them turned hazy. They found themselves in the hallway outside the doors to the hospital wing. Xander turned around and repeated the action and the wall turned opaque. Tim had to stifle laughter when he saw that they had come out through the back end of a bear painted on the wall. Reflecting back on the conversation they'd had in the passageway, a thought occurred to him.

"Xander, whose chart were we looking at back in the lab?"

"A world leader's."

"Which one?" James asked.

"I don't know, actually. Mom won't tell me that stuff." Xander opened the hospital wing door with a yank, which brought Lisa running.

"You're lucky, Sagittarius. It's 10:58."

"Hey, I promised I'd have him back by 11:00, didn't I?" Xander grinned at her. She didn't return the grin.

Tim dodged the comforting arm she attempted to throw around his shoulders. "I'm fine. Really." She stepped back and let him make his way to his bed. As he reached it, a wave of dizziness overtook him and he grabbed onto the bed frame. Xander and James were at his side immediately. He waved them off. "I'm fine," he repeated. "I just got a little dizzy is all."

"The effect of seeing Venus is starting to hit you," Xander explained sagely. Lisa was furious.

"You let him see his ruling planet so soon after recovery?" she fumed. "You idiot! What were you thinking?"

Xander managed to look abashed. "I didn't really–" He faltered. "He seemed okay and I thought seeing Venus would help him get a little stronger."

"Sometimes, you don't think at all!" she flared. "He's not as strong as you think he is. He needs at least one more night here under careful surveillance, maybe two now that you've gone and exposed him to his Planet."

"He doesn't have two nights to spare, Lisa," Xander argued.

"Excuse me, but *he* is standing right here," Tim interrupted sharply. "And right now, *he* wants to sleep, so if you're going to argue, go someplace else." He crawled forward over the frame and collapsed into the bed.

"He's right," Lisa agreed with a glare at Xander. "He needs to rest and that requires quiet." Her emphasis on the last word caused Xander to close his already opening mouth and satisfy himself with returning her glare.

"Fine," he whispered finally. Tim closed his eyes. Vaguely, he could sense them leaving and he dozed off into a light slumber. A short while later, he was aroused from his sleepy state. He remained semi-conscious and opened his eyes to see Lisa gently removing his shoes. He closed his eyes again, preferring to drift about in self-imposed darkness. The healer's hands slid the sheet from underneath his body and pulled it back up over him. He felt her brush the hair from his forehead and then her presence was gone. Smiling, he rolled over and fell deeper into a sleep filled with dreams of the Patrons. He stood with the other Signs and watched as the Patrons bestowed their gifts upon the members of The Gathering. He saw them depart, but before they did, it seemed that they all looked directly at the Signs with expressions of confidence. Then they were gone and the command to protect was the only thing left.

* * * * * * * * * * *

"Tim, wake up." Through the haze, he heard the voice calling him and he fought consciousness with a vehemence. He was enjoying his sleep and had no desire to return to the waking world anytime soon. Unfortunately, the waking world had other ideas. He felt someone shaking him, lightly at first, but getting rougher as he refused to acknowledge their presence. "Tim!" He rolled over and pulled the pillows on top of him, trying desperately to shut out the voice. Another voice, said, "Here, let me," and there ensued a few moments of beautifully undisturbed silence. Then, without warning, he was covered in ice cubes and freezing. He leapt out of the bed with a yelp, rubbing bleary eyes in order to stare down his attacker.

James stood there with a mischievous grin on his face, a grin that was echoed by Xander. Cold, wet, and miserable, Tim frowned at them. "Did you have to do that?"

James' grin did not falter. "You are really hard to wake up."

"So you turned my pillows into ice cubes?"

James shrugged. "Worked, didn't it?"

Tim gave up. "What time is it?" he demanded.

"It's just after 5:00 am. Now shut up before you wake anyone else," James warned.

"Oh, yeah, we wouldn't want anyone else to miss this lovely morning," Tim shot back, but he did lower his voice. "Why are we up so early?"

"We have a lot of Signs to find in a very short amount of time," Xander answered.

"Lisa's letting you do this?" Tim was incredulous at the thought of his healer allowing Xander to take him anywhere.

Xander hesitated. "Well, that's the other reason for the early wake up call. Healer bathroom break. Now come on. She'll be back any second."

Tim was still doubtful. "How do you know I'm ready? Lisa said that I might need another night in the hospital wing."

"She was just saying that to scare me. Healers are always over-cautious. You feel better, don't you?" Xander took Tim's shoes from the floor and handed them to him. "Put these on." He looked at him with curiosity. "Do you really want to miss out on this?"

Tim didn't think twice. "Hell no." He shoved his feet into the shoes and tied them tightly. Then they all grabbed hands.

"Hang on tight then."

Chapter 12

The hospital wing shimmered and swam before his eyes. Colors and objects blended, forming a many-hued environment. Tim felt his body begin to melt and, panicking, he tried to get a tighter hold on Xander's hand. A strong grip squeezed back, reassuring him that Xander was there and this was all normal. His hand melted into Xander's and he could feel himself blending in with his environment, losing form. The colors enveloped him, caressing him, running through him. He no longer had eyes, but he could see movement. He heard and felt a pulsing, loud and powerful. He quickly noticed hundreds of thousands of echoes, all surrounding him. There was an amazing conversation going on here and he longed to understand the language. The air, if one could call it air, crackled with power. He tried to listen to everything going on around him, and as he focused his concentration, certain beats called to him. His life force answered. Focusing further, he could feel Xander's beat. From the other side of Xander came a strange double-beat and he knew that to be James/Jamee. He suddenly knew that these were the souls of the Signs. He tried to feel them and communicate with them, but he didn't know how, so he contented himself with just knowing they were there. One got stronger and stronger until it was almost as loud as Xander beside him. Just as he felt that he could lock onto it, the colors separated and reformed into a recognizable surrounding. Xander's hand suddenly felt solid again and the rhythmic beat faded away. His eyes focused and he found himself in a small park in the early morning light. A slight breeze brought the smell of baked goods from a bakery across the street. Xander and James studied him.

"You okay?" James asked.

"Yeah," he reassured them. "That was...I don't know if I can even describe it."

"I know what you mean," James said.

"I don't really remember my first time," Xander admitted. "You guys are lucky."

"So, what now?" Tim asked.

"You guys get a lesson," Xander told them.

"Whoa, wait just a minute," James said, winking at Tim. "You never said that there were going to be lessons. If I'm going to be in school throughout this whole thing, I'm outta here."

"First of all," Xander ticked off on his fingers, "how do you plan to do that? You don't know where you are. Second of all, where would you go? Third, once you get where you're going, what would you do? Right now, you have no job, therefore no income. The Gathering is currently your home."

"Calm down, I was only kidding. Geez," James said, taken aback by Xander's outburst.

"Sorry. Traveling always makes me a little excitable afterwards."

"Duly noted." James mimed writing on a clipboard. "So, what's the lesson for today, Professor Conlyn?"

"You guys are going to hone your skills and find the Sign." Xander swept an arm out, gesturing to their surroundings. "She's here somewhere."

James was surprised. "She?"

"Yeah, she."

"I could feel her while we were traveling," Tim jumped in, excited. "I could feel all of the Signs. I couldn't tell it was a girl, though."

"I felt the Signs, but I couldn't really separate them," James said.

Xander nodded. "When we're traveling, we lose form and can only be found by our souls. You can feel all of the souls in the universe if you want, but I wouldn't recommend it. It's overwhelming. By honing in on certain qualities, you can find anyone. People you have strong connections with will be louder and stronger. That's why the call of the other Signs is so powerful – because of our bond. Physical proximity also helps them to be louder. It's harder to hear when you're not traveling, but it can be done if the need or bond is strong enough. It's how I found you, Tim, and it's how you're going to find the Sign."

"How do we do that?" James asked.

"First, you have to tap into your own soul. It's the key to finding anyone else."

Both boys closed their eyes. Tim tried to concentrate, but all he could hear were the normal quotidian noises of birds singing, people talking, dogs barking. He felt the cool breeze on his face. Willing himself to try harder, he took a deep breath and tried to clear his mind. Slowly, all outside disturbances faded away. Calm descended upon his mind. Then, faintly, a hum sounded. He could feel it as well as hear it. It was warm and welcome. The sound grew stronger and the call more insistent. It surrounded him and suddenly, he couldn't tell where the sound ended and he began. It struck up a beat, filling him with rhythm. There was an odd sense of coming home.

"I think I got it," Tim ventured.

"Yes, you do," Xander confirmed. "You can open your eyes now."

"Will the feeling go away?" Tim asked.

"Not unless you want it to. Also, each time you try to find it, it will get easier. Open your eyes."

Tim did as he was told. "Everything seems so much brighter," he breathed.

Xander walked over to a tree and sat down, leaning back against it. "Your soul is coloring your vision. Each soul sees the world differently. Basically good people see the world a little brighter. Those with darker outlooks see the world in grays. The soul always knows the truth. Some souls even tint the world with a specific color. So it's actually possible to see the world through rose-colored glasses."

Tim stood above him. "What does it mean when that happens?"

Xander shrugged. "I never asked. Most of the people who have been able to do this have been considered crazy by society and now live in mental institutions." Tim shuddered. They both turned towards James, whose face was screwed up in concentration. "You're trying too hard, James," Xander called. James opened his eyes and looked at them helplessly, frustration clearly written across his face.

"I can't get it."

"I can." Jamee's voice came out of James' mouth, startling all three of them.

"Fine, you give it a try, sis." Jamee flashed into existence, cracked her knuckles and closed her eyes. Not even a second passed before the air around her was lit with a yellow radiance. She opened her eyes.

"Got it," she bragged with a tilt of her head.

Tim looked at Xander. "Do I, um, glow?"

Xander nodded and Jamee grew excited. "Do I glow too? Is that how you know that we're in touch with our souls?" she asked. When the boys nodded, she leapt into the air and started turning cartwheels about the park. A few people stopped to watch her, but most ignored the exuberant Sign. Xander and Tim laughed. It was the first time they had seen her unrestrained and happy. She flopped down onto the grass, pulling a few blades to examine them. She danced up to Tim and grabbed him, causing a spark to leap from their joined hands, and pulled him around and around until they both fell down again, giggling. Tim knew they had a huge task ahead of them, but he gave in to her infectious enthusiasm. Then, by mutual agreement, they ran over to Xander and began tickling him. He cried out against their assault, trying to attack them as well and only succeeded in making himself more vulnerable. They rolled over and over in the brisk morning air, enjoying the freedom. Eventually, they wore themselves out and lay on the grass, panting and staring at the sky.

Finally, Tim sat up. "Okay, we found our souls. Now what?"

Xander responded from his lying position. "Now comes the hard part. You have to open yourself up to receive the calls of all the other souls. Before you do that, though...oh, damn, there she goes." Tim turned in alarm to see Jamee already concentrating. She gasped and the aura about her began to fragment, flashing other colors. She contorted in pain, tears leaking from her tightly squeezed eyes. Xander sat up quickly and took her hand, a violet glow flaring into existence around him. "Relax, Jamee. Concentrate on me. Ignore everything else." Jamee's body was shaking and the colors flickered faster. Xander kept speaking to her in a very calm, soft voice. "Focus on me only, Jamee. Find my beat." Tim could feel Xander searching for her soul with his own, forming a link between them. Jamee's soul clung to Xander's, using him as a lifeline to pull herself out of the chaos. Tim could feel the multitude of souls calling at the edge of his perception and he quickly disconnected from his soul. The calls immediately stopped. He watched as, slowly, Jamee's aura began to take on the hues of Xander's and then yellow crept back in until it was whole again and she lay hiccupping on the grass.

"You okay?" Xander asked her, his aura disappearing.

Jamee took a few deep breaths and the light about her vanished as well. "I think so."

"Good." He reached out and flicked the end of her nose with his fingers.

"Ow." She grabbed her nose. "What was that for?"

"Don't ever try something before it's fully explained to you. It's dangerous. We almost lost you." The shaking started again. Xander squeezed her hand.

"Sorry. I was just excited." Her face was a mask of misery.

"I know and that's awesome. Just be careful, okay?" She nodded. "You can't just jump into something like this headfirst with no idea of where you're going. It'll overwhelm you."

"Why didn't we feel overwhelmed when we were traveling?" Tim wanted to know.

"When we're traveling, we become our minds and souls. There is no physicality to be affected. Your body simply can't take the pressure of all of the souls in the universe trying to commune with the soul inside of it. When you're pure soul and mind, it's easier, but there's still a great deal of pressure." He helped Jamee to her feet. "My talent protects us when we're traveling. You don't actually feel the battering of all of the souls, but you can still communicate with them. It's natural for the soul to be open and receptive to other souls, but the body can't take it."

"Okay, no more experiments," Jamee agreed. "I screwed up. I guess that ends the lesson."

"Hardly," Xander said, and smiled at her. "We still have a Sign to find."

"I'm not so sure I want to try again right now," said Jamee. "Can't Tim do this one?"

"You're going to have to learn it at some point, Jamee," Xander told her.

She stood up. "I know I will, but I'm just not ready yet. Please?" Xander turned to Tim.

"You wanna try it?"

Tim wasn't as excited as he had been before he saw Jamee collapse, but he was still interested in learning the skill. "Yeah, I can do this."

"Are you sure? You really don't want to jump in unprepared."

"So I saw. Honestly, I'm ready." Tim stood still and closed his eyes lightly to demonstrate.

"Okay, listen to me. Concentrate on yourself first. You have to reconnect with your soul." Tim was apprehensive, fearing that the attack would continue as soon as he made contact, but as his aura flared into life before the others, he felt no such pressure.

"It was easier this time," he said, opening his eyes.

Xander nodded. "Okay, now, take it slowly. Open your soul up a little bit. Just enough to see if you can find my soul's call. Just concentrate and search for a pulsing that's close to you." Tim closed his eyes again. He felt a tiny little part of his soul open up. Immediately, there was pressure to open it up more, but he held fast, sending sensors out from that tiny part to find Xander's recognizable pulse. It took a lot of willpower to hold his soul mostly closed while sending a probe out for another soul. He struggled at first, but after a while, he managed to balance the two tasks enough to make a link to Xander's soul. Xander smiled as he felt the touch. Jamee, watching, grew excited as she saw part of Tim's aura turn violet. Without a prompt, Tim unlocked another tiny part of his soul, protecting it against attack and searched for Jamee's strange twinned soul. He locked onto it faster than he had with Xander's and Jamee gasped with delight as she felt the bond, and saw another part turn bright yellow. He found that maintaining the connection was a lot easier than trying to find the connection in the first place; once those parts of his soul were committed to a connection, the pressure to make a connection stopped. He opened his eyes and smiled at them.

"I can feel you both."

"We can feel you too," Jamee responded happily.

"It's weird, but I like it. They feel similar to mine, but different in color."

"Color?" Xander asked.

"Well, not color that you can see, but more like you can feel. That doesn't make any sense, does it?" Tim laughed sheepishly.

"No, it makes sense, Tim, 'cause your aura is glowing with our colors. It turned part violet when you touched Xander, so I guess James and I are the yellow." Jamee looked awed.

"What color am I normally?" Tim asked.

"Lavender," Xander responded. "It's time to add another color to the mix. Use the familiarity of our souls as a guide. I know it sounds strange to use something familiar to find someone you've never met, but trust me."

"No, I get it." Tim once again unlocked a tiny part of his soul, putting defenses up immediately and sent his mind out, searching for the new Sign's soul. *She's around here somewhere*, he thought. He moved through the early morning joggers, the dog-walkers, the night shift workers heading home. None were a Sign. He expanded his search, his awareness sweeping up and down the streets and throughout the area. When there was no result, he redoubled his efforts, expanding his territory yet again. From the edges of his awareness, he began to feel a connection. When he headed for that direction, the call suddenly came in so clearly that he involuntarily brought his hands up to his ears as if he had heard the call physically.

Jamee let out a sigh. "Oooh, he's found her. There's red in his aura."

"I've found her," Tim confirmed.

"Hang onto her," Xander told him. "Which way?" Tim pointed and they started off down the street. The sun was climbing into the sky and more people were out and about, which put a lot of strain on Tim who was desperately trying to keep his hold on the Sign. Souls faded in and out, none actually calling to him, but he could sense them. He had to exercise iron control over his desire to make connections with them as well. They walked for awhile before Tim abruptly changed direction.

"She's moving," he explained. Tim followed the signal up and down many streets, finally coming to a halt in front of a strip of clothing stores. "She was just here." They moved on, passing windows displaying preppy clothing, skater caps, and hippie skirts. By this time, there were patrons coming in and out of the stores, chatting and trying on clothing. None of the Signs said anything when Tim stopped in front of a store that displayed the name SPIKE in neon letters. They peered in through the window. An array of leather collars and bracelets met their eyes. A few patrons meandered around the shop, picking up items and examining them. "That one," Tim hissed.

The other two saw where he was looking. A girl, younger than them, stood at the counter, choosing from a selection of nose rings. Her hair was a screaming pink. She wore a studded collar, combat boots, black jeans, and a t-shirt that read *Really... Who cares?*. They watched as she picked up a nose ring and held it up to her nose, checking out her reflection in a mirror. She straightened suddenly and turned towards the window. They ducked simultaneously and moved away from the store. "Okay, we found her," Jamee said. "What do we do now?"

"We wait for the right moment," Xander responded.

From their vantage point, they saw the girl go up to the cashier, pay for the nose ring, and immediately remove her former nose ring, inserting the new one. She put the old one in her pocket and walked out of the store, squinting in the bright sun. She headed right for the Signs and tilted her head so that the nose ring glinted. "Like it?"

The three Signs looked at each other, surprised. Tim was the first to recover. "Like what?"

"The new ring."

"Oh, yeah. Sure."

"Looks great," Jamee added helpfully.

"Coffee?" the girl suggested.

"Huh?" That was Xander.

"Do you want to get a cup of coffee? I know this great place. It's right on the corner." She pointed.

The Signs exchanged another look. "Sure," they said together. The girl led them over to a coffeehouse called *Bean There, Done That*. None of them spoke to each other as they ordered their respective coffees and sat at a corner table away from everyone else.

"Dana Wyntrap," the girl introduced herself.

"Tim Dalis."

"Xander Conlyn."

"Jamee Holm."

"Yeah, I know. It's nice to meet Libra, Sagittarius, and Gemini." The three Signs raised their eyebrows. It was Jamee who finally asked the question.

"How do you know that?"

"Did a psychic get to you too?" was Tim's input.

"No, no psychic. It's my talent. Telepathy," Dana explained. "I'm Aries, the Ram."

"What does Aries have to do with mental powers?" Tim wondered.

Xander opened his mouth to respond, but Dana cut him off. "Each Sign rules a part of the body. Aries rules the head and is also the first Sign in the zodiac or the head of the zodiac. Plus, my glyph looks like the head of a ram." Xander stared at her incredulously as she spouted exactly what he had been about to say verbatim, then told her so. She grinned. "Yes, I know. I figured it was a clear enough display of my talent. I had no idea of any of this before, of course. Your thoughts were reading from miles away."

"So you know everything about us," Tim said.

"No, I can only read surface thoughts," Dana corrected. "I've never been able to go deeper than that. Thoughts that remain blocked are beyond my reach."

"You might be able to develop that part of your talent," Xander told her.

"What's The Gathering?" she asked enthusiastically. "That came in loud and clear. Most people, when they're talking about a topic, will think very clearly about it and I can pick those thoughts up easily."

"Awesome. So we don't have to tell you about everything that's going on." Jamee seemed relieved.

"No, not in great detail. I can pick most of it up if you give me a quick summary."

"There is a great power about to be born," Xander began.

Chapter 13

"And I am your Aries," Dana finished for him. "With a talent for mind-reading."

"So it would seem," Xander agreed.

"When do we get started?" Dana's eagerness showed in her face. *She picks things up quickly*, Tim noted. She turned to him. "I've always been a quick study. It's important to have flexibility and be able to adjust to different situations."

"Can you send?" Jamee asked. "Do you only read thoughts or can you send too?"

Dana frowned. "I've never been able to send. I only know how to read."

"Oh. It was just a thought." The other three stared at her. "No pun intended," she added quickly.

"The Gathering might be able to help with that too," Xander informed her.

Dana was visibly excited by the prospect. "Can we go right now? To The Gathering?"

"Just like that?" Tim was surprised. Dana shrugged. "But, don't you have a job? An apartment? Family? How old are you anyway?"

"Nineteen. The job is something I can leave easily. Besides, The Gathering pays for everything. You thought that at me. As for where I live and family, those go together. I live at home and commute to college. I'm not exactly the most welcome person at my house though. My parents don't like the way I live my life." She said this matter-of-factly.

"I'm sorry," Tim sympathized. "They tell you that?"

"No, but their thoughts scream at me all the time. It's hard for me to be around them. I love them and they try to love me back, but their love is colored by their disappointment. Being an only child, they had put all their hopes and dreams on me and when I didn't turn out the way they wanted, it kinda crushed them."

"Can you block them out?" Jamee inquired, gulping her coffee.

Dana chuckled bitterly. "Not really. I'm pretty good at tuning out most thoughts, but with my parents..." She trailed off. "I've had years to deal with it. College is an awesome escape for me. I can be myself there without worrying about what they're thinking all the time. I only come back to the house to sleep and, once in awhile, eat." She grew pensive. "Guess I'll have to drop out now."

"What's your major?" Xander inquired.

Dana downed the last of her coffee. "Psychology. Perfect for someone like me, right? My professors all love me, but then, I guess I have an advantage, being able to read minds. I do everything I can to avoid cheating, though. I study my butt off. I want to find out why people think they way they do. My parents say I've become a little Freud since I went to college. I guess I can see where they're coming from, but I can't help it. At least classes have helped me understand their disappointment. They're upper class and want me to be a little lady and follow in the traditions of the family, marrying rich and all, but I just don't care. I want to do something more with my life than be a wife and mother." She said this last part with a finality that clearly signaled the end of the discussion.

"Well, you're part of our family now," Tim welcomed her and she gave him a weak smile.

"So, do I get to see The Gathering?"

"Not yet, Dana," Xander told her. "We have to pick up the next Sign on the way, as long as no one feels the need to rest or anything." He looked pointedly at Tim.

"I'm fine. Do I have to keep saying that?"

Xander stood. "Just checking. We need to go get the next Sign as soon as you're ready, Dana."

Tim interrupted. "Take all the time you need to put your affairs in order."

Dana laughed shortly as she stood. "You make it sound like I'm dying."

"In a way, you are," Xander told her. "The girl known as Dana Wyntrap will disappear for most of the known world. To most of The Gathering, you will be known only as Aries. The enemy will know you as Aries as well. There won't be many people who will know your real name."

"Now you make me sound like a superhero with a secret identity."

"Don't think that way," Xander warned. "We are special people, but we are still only people faced with a terrible task. That task is guarding. We don't save lives, we don't right wrongs. Our job is to protect the Star Child. She will be the true superhero. The 'secret identity' idea is a good one, though. No one can know that you're a Sign. The consequences are dire."

"But what if–"

"Please," Xander said bleakly. "Don't ask 'what if', and don't argue. Just trust me when I say that it's not a rule you want to break."

Tim watched him carefully. Xander's face quickly regained its usual sunny disposition, but his eyes still displayed deep pain. He reached out to comfort him, but Xander pulled back slightly, asking Dana, "What do you need to do before we go?"

"I just have to tell my folks that I'll be gone for awhile. I'm sure they'll be thrilled not to have an analytical mind-reader in the house," she assessed.

Jamee stood and went to the trash can to throw out her coffee cup. "Do they know you're a telepath?"

"I don't think so. I think they're too afraid to find out too much about me that they've never dared to pay close attention. They'll be fine with me leaving for a bit." Dana tossed her cup in a high arc towards the trash can and hit her target.

Tim stood and followed her example. His cup crashed into the side and hit the floor, drawing the attention of a few of the patrons sitting around them. He hurried over and picked it up, placing it in the can and returned to the amusement of the other Signs. "Okay, so I'm not a great athlete."

"We noticed," Jamee teased him, then turned to the new Sign. "I guess we should go so you can talk to your parents and get any clothing or stuff that you want. I think you'll be happier once we're on our way."

"Yeah, I guess," Dana agreed. "Let's go. It shouldn't take too long." She exited the coffeehouse and led them off away from the shops. Tim had many thoughts running through his head and he tried to keep them away from the surface. He saw that Dana was talking animatedly with Xander and Jamee. She was nice to be sure, but she had a dangerous talent. Without trust, she could be a troublesome addition to the Signs. *Then again*, he thought, *so could I.* Without trust, the group would never survive. Now that he had three Signs around him, he could feel the differences in their bonds. Jamee and Dana felt different from Xander. Maybe it was a gender issue. He hadn't felt that way with James, but then, James and Jamee were so intertwined that perhaps it was a different feel altogether. He wanted to find another Sign and explore the bonds between them. He wondered if Xander felt a difference. It wasn't something he should be concerned about, but he was curious. He decided to worry about it when they got the next Sign and tuned into the conversation between the other three.

"So I had a double education," Xander was saying. "Regular school by day and occult training at night. I learned about the Signs and the worlds outside of the world we know."

Tim stopped in his tracks. "There are other worlds?"

The others turned around. "In a way," Xander answered. "There is the world we see and accept, but there is far much more in the universe than we can see."

"'There are more things in heaven and earth, Horatio, than are dreamt of in your philosophy'," Tim quoted. The others looked blank. "It's *Hamlet*. You know, Shakespeare?"

"He's into theatre," Xander explained to the girls as they started walking again.

"Professionally," Tim added. "Or, at least, I was."

Dana picked up the pace. "That's cool. I've always wanted to get up on stage and perform, but I don't have the guts. Plus, I bet the audience would overwhelm me with all of their thoughts." The rest of the conversation was taken up with tales of past experiences and mistakes made on the job. Jamee had just finished telling them about her short career in fast food when Dana announced, "We're here."

They'd arrived at a moderately large house with a freshly mowed yard in front and a fence surrounding it. The bushes were all trimmed into various animal shapes. The house was an eggshell color with maroon shutters on the windows and blooms in flower boxes. A porch ran three-quarters of the way around the house with a garden bordering it. Flowers also lined the walkway leading up to the front door and a tree with a swing stood to the side, keeping watch over the house.

"It's like a painted picture," Jamee commented brightly.

"Tell me about it. Mom's a flower nut," Dana grumbled, grimacing at the house. "You haven't seen the inside yet."

Jamee smiled. "It gets better?"

"Worse." Dana led them up the path to the front door and pulled out her key. As she opened the door, she yelled, "I'm home!" The Signs found themselves in a foyer. To their right stood a mirror, and Tim immediately made use of it. In the reflection, he saw a vase of flowers on a small table behind him. Even the wallpaper and carpet had a floral theme. It was almost overwhelming.

A middle-aged woman in a conservative cream-colored blouse with tan slacks and brown shoes descended the stairs. Her shoulder-length hair was showing signs of gray around the roots. She wore no jewelry except for a wedding ring. "Hi honey," she greeted her daughter, giving her a hug. Tim, who was watching Dana's face, saw her wince and withdraw from the embrace as quickly as possible. "Oh, you brought company. Do I get an introduction or do I have to do it myself?"

"Mom, these are Xander, Tim, and Jamee." She indicated each in turn. "Guys, this is my mom."

"It's a pleasure to meet you, Mrs. Wyntrap," Tim greeted her, extending his hand.

"Aren't you charming," the woman commented. Tim shot a glance at the others, who hid grins behind their hands. Xander winked. "Welcome to our house. All of you." She held a hand out to Xander, who took it.

"Nice to meet you," he said. Jamee repeated the action, and then Mrs. Wyntrap clapped her hands together. "You are just in time for lunch," she told them. "Feel free to take a seat at the table and I'll be happy to make you all some sandwiches."

Dana was already heading upstairs. "Mom, we really..."

"...would love that," Tim finished. "That's very kind." Mrs. Wyntrap smiled and showed them into the kitchen. Dana hung back and grabbed Tim.

"What do you think you're doing?" she hissed.

He removed her hand. "Helping. Don't forget my talent."

Each taking a seat at the table, the four Signs watched Dana's mother bustle about the kitchen, removing lunch meat and condiments from the refrigerator. She laid these on the counter, humming to herself all the while.

"Would you like some help, Mrs. Wyntrap?" Tim offered, relying on his talent. He watched carefully as her eyes glowed briefly with lavender effulgence.

"Oh, no, thank you, Tim, but it's very nice of you to ask." When she had everything laid out on the counter, she faced them. "Now, what can I get you? I'm afraid I don't have much, but hopefully, you can find something you like."

Observing his choices, Tim spoke up. "If it's not too much trouble, I'd like ham and cheese, please."

"No trouble at all, Tim. American cheese okay?"

"Sure."

"Mustard?"

"Yes, please."

"Pickles, lettuce, tomato...?"

"Pickles and onions, please." Dana was watching him with a disgusted look.

"Coming right up." She pulled the ingredients for Tim's sandwich into a pile.

"Xander?" Xander placed his order, then Jamee, until three piles sat on the counter.

"Honey, do you want your favorite?" she asked Dana.

The Aries colored, but all she said was, "Sure, Mom. That'd be great."

"So, how do you kids know Dana?"

"We met at school," Dana answered quickly, before anyone could say anything.

Her mother paused. "You've never brought school friends home before."

"They're, um, kind of special friends," Dana said awkwardly.

"Close friends?"

"Yeah. You could say that."

"Are you all psychology majors too?"

"Actually, no," Tim answered. "Theatre major."

"I love the theatre," Mrs. Wyntrap gushed. "In fact, I used to sing when I was younger."

"I bet you have a beautiful voice." He was pouring forth all he could.

"Oh, it's nothing," she demurred, flattered. "Lunch is served." She placed a plate in front of each of them. "Eat up." They obeyed.

"It's absolutely delicious. I wish I could get food like this where we're going." Tim smiled again at Mrs. Wyntrap, who reeled slightly from the force of his talent.

Recovering, she asked, "You're going somewhere?"

"Um, yeah, Mom." Dana coughed. "Xander, Tim, and Jamee are part of a program through school that rebuilds communities that have deteriorated. They've been talking to me about going with them and helping people who've had their lives destroyed get back on their feet."

"Honey, you don't have a medical degree. You're only a sophomore."

"It's actually in place of a few sophomore level classes," Tim lied smoothly, still smiling. "Dana can earn credits towards her major while getting practical experience in her field. Dana's exactly the student that the college wants for this program. She has an intuitive sense of human need that most psychologists or psychiatrists out there today lack. Also, it's clear that she's had a proper upbringing and that's a fine base."

"How much does it cost?" There was no mistaking the suspicion in her voice.

"It costs nothing for Dana. The trip is paid for by the college. Most survivors, once they get back on their feet, are so grateful to have had the help from this program that they often donate money to the cause. In fact, many of them become volunteers themselves. The program only accepts a few students from each department. Dana is one of the lucky ones. I'm sure you wouldn't want to stand in the way of something that could make the world a better place and benefit your daughter at the same time."

"Well, of course not."

"Good, then it's all settled." Tim's smile grew as he watched Mrs. Wyntrap's suspicious expression smooth out into one of acceptance. The other Signs had finished their sandwiches and were staring at him. "Thank you so much for being understanding, Mrs. Wyntrap. You're doing your own part to make a better world for some unfortunate people."

"I guess I am at that," the woman mused. She turned to her daughter. "Dana, you're going to be doing wonderful things. I'm so proud of you."

With an odd glance at Tim, Dana stood and embraced her mother freely and feelingly. "Thanks, Mom."

"Actually, we should get going," Xander said, standing as well. Tim quickly shoved the rest of his sandwich into his mouth and followed suit.

"Aren't you going to say goodbye to your father?" Mrs. Wyntrap asked her daughter.

Dana glanced at Xander and shook her head. "We don't have time," she said. "It's a long journey and our flight leaves in under three hours. We're running late as it is."

"Do you need a ride to the airport? Your father has the car, but we can call a taxi," she offered.

"No thanks, Mom. We have a ride already arranged." Mrs. Wyntrap looked concerned, but Tim smiled at her and the emotion vanished.

"Where will you be? At least let me know so I can write to you."

"We haven't received an exact address yet, but as soon as we get it, there will be a letter containg all pertinent information going out to all of the parents," Jamee chimed in. Mrs. Wyntrap nodded.

"I'll keep in touch," Dana promised.

"We'll take care of her," Tim assured her mother. "She's in good hands."

"Thank you."

Dana practically flew up the stairs, calling out, "I'm just going to get some stuff from my room. Then we gotta go."

"You're doing a great thing by letting her go," Jamee told Mrs. Wyntrap.

"Thank you, Jamee, but it's you who are going to do great things. I'm glad she's going to be a part of it." There was the thud of feet coming down the stairs, and Dana came into the kitchen carrying a small backpack.

"Ready," she announced.

"That was quick," he mother noticed.

"Almost everything is already provided," Dana told her.

"We really do have to get going," Xander said.

"Thank you for the wonderful hospitality," Tim added with another smile.

It appeared that Mrs. Wyntrap wanted to ask more, but with Tim smiling at her, she merely said, "Oh, I guess it's time to say goodbye." Wrapping her daughter in a fierce hug, she tearfully added, "Take care of yourself."

Choking back tears of her own, Dana responded, "I will, Mom. I love you."

"I love you too, honey." The four Signs walked to the door and stepped outside.

They walked down the path and Dana turned back to take one last look at her house.

"It's going to be weird not having flowers around," she said, and then they were off, with Xander leading them back towards the park. Dana was silent, hanging back behind the group, lost in thought. As they neared the park, though, she caught up with Tim.

"Listen, I'm sorry for yelling at you. That was incredible," she said. "I could feel you charming her, changing her mind. She definitely didn't want to let me go when I first started talking about the program, but I felt her thought pattern change when you jumped in. She barely even asked all the questions she normally does. She would have never let me go if it weren't for you. That's a great talent."

"I guess so," he admitted. "Each of us has a powerful talent, though. We just have to learn as much as we can about ourselves to use them correctly."

"Well, thanks for using yours. That was the most accepting my mom has ever been. If that's because of your talent, I'm all for learning more about our gifts."

"Glad to hear it," Xander commented. "It's time for you to experience another talent."

Dana looked from Xander to Jamee. "Whose?"

"Mine," he told her. "We have to travel to the location of the next Sign."

"What's it like? Do I have to prepare for it somehow?" she asked eagerly, hefting the backpack.

"It's indescribable," Jamee said.

"It's also dangerous. You have to stay in contact with one of us," Xander ordered. Dana opened her mouth, but he continued, anticipating her question. "I don't know what happens to someone who lets go and I don't want to find out. Always keep in contact."

"Okay, keep touching you guys. I got it."

"Good. Ready?" Xander held out his hands. Tim took one and Jamee took the other.

Dana asked nervously, "Right now?"

"Right now." Tim held out his other hand. Dana reached out and grasped it tightly.

"Ouch. Careful."

Her grip loosened a bit, but she had one more question. "Where are we going?"

"Curiosity killed the cat," Xander answered, and they were off.

Chapter 14

A tom cat stalked down an alley, his green eyes peering intently through the shadows. Nibbling absentmindedly on a stale piece of bread, a lone, unsuspecting mouse crouched at the end of the alley. Ever so slowly, the calico predator approached his prey, paws making no noise on the pavement. He had come just within striking distance when there was a sudden ripple through the air and four forms materialized almost on top of the mouse, who squeaked in terror and disappeared into a crack. These humans smelled strange, unlike most humans he had encountered. Unlike all humans, save one. Disgusted and irritated, the cat slunk off to the shadows to observe.

* * * * * * * * * * *

Dana looked around. "Weird."

"What is?" Jamee asked.

"Shouldn't there be a Sign here waiting for us? We have an appointment, don't we?" She threw a sidelong glance at Xander. "Weren't you supposed to take us to the Sign?"

Xander spoke. "There's a reason I didn't. It's up to you to find her."

"Me?"

"You or Jamee. Or both."

Jamee nodded. "It's up to the new recruits to find the next Sign," she told her. "I was supposed to help find you, but...I had trouble."

"What happened?" asked Dana.

"Just trust me when I say, don't do anything until it's explained."

Dana winced as she read the memory in Jamee's mind. "Got it." She turned to Xander. "How do I do it?" Xander started to explain, but she stopped him. "Don't tell me, just think about it. I can get a clearer picture of it that way."

"Sounds good to me," Xander agreed. While they communicated silently, Tim and Jamee observed their surroundings. They were at the end of an alley littered with trash cans and a large recycling receptacle. The street could have been any residential street in any city. In the midday light, the lack of noise was oppressive. He turned back to the alley to meet the gleam of two eyes watching from behind a trash can. Adrenaline rushed through his chest and he moved cautiously towards the shadows, gesturing surreptitiously to Jamee. Both of them had almost reached the cans when Dana said, "Okay, I think I got it." They whirled around. "What are you two doing?"

"We saw something," Jamee said. She searched behind the cans, but there was nothing there.

Dana was already glowing red. "Come on. Let's go find the next Sign." Golden flickers appeared among the red. "Over that way." She took off down the street. After a block, Dana gasped.

"She's in danger." She broke into a run.

"Danger?" Tim panted.

"Yes, but not far away." They dashed down three blocks, made a sharp right and stopped before a small house with a nice gated yard in front. Cats of all shapes and sizes swarmed the Signs as they opened the gate. The yowling rose to an ear-splitting cacophony. Dana sped by the feline population and through the open front door. Once inside, they heard a woman's voice upstairs and loud thumping noises. Dana took the stairs two at a time, the other three on her heels. Making a quick left at the top of the stairs, they burst into the master bedroom where pandemonium reigned.

Tim counted six astranihl in human form, draped in the familiar grey attire. Near the corner of the room, a small, blonde woman struggled with one of the grey-cloaked figures. Three more astranihl were spread throughout the room, involved in battles of their own with various cats, hissing and spitting. The final two figures were pinned against a wall by snarling jungle cats – a snow-white leopard and a midnight-black panther. Before they could witness the demise of the two cornered enemies, the four Signs sprang into action.

Xander and Tim grabbed matching candlesticks and bashed two of the figures over the head. Tim watched in satisfaction as his victim crumpled to the ground. Xander's fell just as quickly, a grunt escaping from her mouth. Jamee had latched onto an astranihl and quickly twisted his cloak into a noose that she pulled tight, effectively choking him to death. She continued to choke him with vicious glee until Xander hauled her off, leaving her to stand there, panting. A scream reminded them of the other dangers, and the three Signs turned to see Dana deck the blonde woman's attacker in the jaw, who went down without a sound. Dana shook off the pain and saw the others staring at her, open-mouthed.

"High school boyfriend," she explained simply. She faced the blonde woman. "Are you alright, Miss...?"

"Avella," the woman answered in a low, throaty voice. "Rhys Avella."

"Dana Wyntrap," Dana said, and went on to introduce the others. Rhys nodded at each of them. Now that they were just standing there, Tim noticed that she was even smaller than him. Suspicion and gratitude warred for dominance in her expression. Eventually, gratitude won out, but she did not move any closer to the Signs.

"Let's move to a different room and then maybe you can explain to me what you're doing here and who these people are. We'll get you some ice for that hand." She looked around the room at the dead and unconscious bodies.

"Good idea. But I don't think we should stay in the house," Jamee suggested. "Those two over there won't be getting back up." She gestured to the two figures the big cats ripped apart. Looking at the purple-faced figure at her feet. "Neither will he. But those three might recover at any time." Indeed, they were showing signs of animation.

"Smart thinking," Xander agreed. "Home?" The others nodded.

"Wait just a second," Rhys protested. "I don't know who you are or why you're here. I'm not going anywhere until I get some kind of explanation."

Dana sighed impatiently, but Tim agreed. "Fair enough."

Xander turned to the others. "I have to take advantage of the fact that we have the enemy in our possession. You guys answer any questions that she has. I'll be right back." With that, he grabbed a hold of one of the astranihl and vanished. Rhys blinked, then walked cautiously to the spot where he had been. She whirled around.

"Look, I deal with trauma on a daily basis, but I don't know what the hell is going on and someone better explain it now." As if to accentuate the point, the jungle cats growled menacingly.

Jamee took over. "What do you want to know? More importantly, what do you need to know so that you'll be comfortable coming with us? We don't have a lot of time."

Rhys looked as though she was curious about what she had just seen, but instead she asked, "First, where would we go?"

They exchanged glances. "It's complicated," Jamee explained.

"It's a place where you'll be safe," Dana added.

"A place that houses all kinds of people," Tim put in.

"People like us?" Rhys asked alertly. The others started. "Come on, I know I'm not ordinary and clearly, you aren't either."

Tim turned to the other two. "Does everyone know our secret?"

Rhys smiled. "I have informants."

"You have informants on us?" Jamee asked, surprised, but Dana had already figured out the answer.

"The cats! You can communicate with cats!"

It was Rhys's turn to look surprised. "How- how did you know that?"

"I have my own informants," Dana told her smugly.

"She's a telepath," Xander explained, re-appearing in the room with a hard look at Dana. They didn't want to alienate this woman. "She reads thoughts. Only surface thoughts, so when you talked about your informants, you were thinking about the cats and she picked that up."

"What about you?"

"We change things," Jamee said, flashing into James. Dana and Rhys stared.

"Well, that explains why your mind felt so weird," Dana muttered.

Rhys heard her. "The cats mentioned the double nature, but I didn't understand what they meant."

"Nice to meet you, ladies," James said, grinning. "I hope it wasn't too shocking."

"No more so than the rest of this," Rhys said. "What about you guys?"

"I charm people," Tim told her.

"And I travel," Xander finished. "Speaking of, we really have to get going before the rest of these guys wake up. Will you trust me when I say that we're friends? There's a lot more to tell you, but we can't hang around here."

"Hold on. If I go with you, I need the Brownings and Donne with me. Can you accommodate them?"

"Who are they?" Jamee asked.

Rhys pointed to the jungle cats who were in the corner cleaning the blood from their muzzles. "Meet the Brownings: Robert and Elizabeth Barrett. The leopard is Robert and the panther companion is Elizabeth. They're always together."

Dana started moving towards them. "Are they tame?"

Rhys laughed and the Brownings raised their heads. "Of course not!" Dana halted in mid-stride as Robert licked a drop of blood from a whisker. "They're friends of mine, though. We respect each other. Oh, and speaking of friends, meet my most trusted confidante." A silver, orange, and black calico tom cat stalked into the room with a mischievous air about him and his tail cocked to one side. She reached down and picked him up. He butted her chin with his head and stared at the Signs with bright green eyes. "Tim, Xander, Jamee, and Dana, meet Donne. He says you scared his prey away earlier."

"We'll make it up to him," Xander promised.

"He says saving me is thanks enough," Rhys said, hugging him tightly.

"Robert and Elizabeth Browning. Donne. As in John Donne?" Jamee mused. Dana and Rhys whirled at the sound of her voice.

"That's going to take some getting used to," said Dana.

"You're quick," Rhys said to Jamee. "Cats are fascinated by human poetry. They take names that reflect their favorites."

"They can read poetry?" Xander looked incredulous.

"Of course. How do you think they learned our language?"

"Makes sense. The musical *Cats* is based on T. S. Eliot poems," Tim pointed out.

"Yes, well, actually, they aren't overly fond of that musical." Rhys coughed delicately. "They say it doesn't portray them in their best light."

"We can discuss feline politics later. Can we get out of here now?" Dana was hopping from foot to foot in her impatience.

"Yes, of course. Donne says that you are to be trusted, and I always follow his advice." An insistent meow came from outside the door and another cat entered. "Hello, Sylvia." Sylvia went directly to Tim who stared at her in shock.

"Harmony!"

"You know Sylvia?" Rhys asked, surprised anew.

Tim swooped down on the feline and swept her into his arms, feeling her purr vibrate against his chest. "Well, I never called her that; I called her 'Harmony', but I couldn't talk to her to find out her real name."

"Her taken name is Sylvia, after Sylvia Plath, but she says that she prefers Harmony. That's a great honor to you, Tim. It's rare for a cat to permanently take the name a human has given them." Tim hugged the little ball to him.

"How in the world did you get here, Harm?" She meowed.

"She says she sensed danger coming when she saw the astranihl. Then I unconsciously sent out a call and she responded." Rhys stopped and looked at Harmony. "I did? I sent out a call?" The cat meowed again. "I didn't even realize I did that."

Tim protested, "But I needed help, Harmony. How come you didn't stick around to help me?"

More meowing. "She says I needed her more. Cats have their own way of foretelling the future and she says she knew that you would come here. The astranihl was an omen, so she took off. She says she's sorry she caused you grief."

Tim tried to be hurt, but he was so happy to see her again that he merely said, "Oh, it's fine, I guess. But no more running off after this, okay?" She meowed and he could swear that he understood that to be a promise. A groan from the floor startled them all and Jamee grabbed one of the discarded candlesticks, whacking the woman over the head and knocking her out again.

"Let's go," she said. "I don't want to have to keep doing that."

"I agree." Rhys started for the door.

"Not that way," Xander said. "As I said, my gift is travel." He looked at the big cats. "Will they be able to stay in contact with us? It's important."

"Naturally. They understand us, but only I can understand them."

"Cool!" Dana exclaimed. "You're a telepath like me, but with cats."

Rhys smiled. "True. I never thought of it that way." Donne meowed. "They're ready to leave." Robert and Elizabeth walked to stand by Dana and Jamee. "Please put a hand on each of their backs," she told them.

"They have to stay touching throughout the entire journey. Dana and Jamee might have to grab onto their fur," Xander warned.

"We'll try to be gentle," Dana promised. Jamee nodded.

"They understand," Rhys said. The two large cats made soft growling sounds and Rhys chuckled. "They will try to be gentle as well." Her meaning became clear as Robert gripped Dana's jeans in his teeth and Elizabeth did the same with Jamee. The girls put their hands on the Brownings' backs and Dana clasped Xander's hand with her free hand. Rhys moved in and took Dana's forearm in her hand while cradling Donne in the crook of her arm. Jamee mimicked Dana and Tim mirrored Rhys.

"Brace yourselves and don't let go," was all the warning the newcomers received.

Traveling was, in itself, an amazing experience. Traveling with non-human souls was another experience altogether. Tim held tight to Harmony and she dug her claws into him as the house dissolved. When the merging happened, the pain of her claws disappeared, but a new sensation took over. Tim felt predatory and powerful with an incredible sense of self-assuredness and importance. It was such a unique feeling that Tim forgot to search for the other Signs. The merge ended and the pain of her claws returned. They were back in the hallway outside of their rooms in the astrology wing. Tim and Rhys put the cats down and they immediately began exploring. The big cats released their holds on the girls and sat up, watching Rhys intently.

"This is where we live. We call it The Gathering," Xander said. "Or home. You'll come to call it home as well, I'm sure."

"You all live here?" Rhys's head was swiveling to take everything in.

"Well, Xander's lived here his whole life..." Dana started.

"His parents are members of The Gathering," Jamee interrupted.

"...and Dana, Jamee, and I just recently became members," finished Tim.

Rhys looked at the three of them, amused. "Do you do that a lot? Construct sentences together, I mean."

They burst out laughing. "Not usually," Xander answered over their laughter. "Look, there's a lot to explain, but you should probably get a chance to settle in. We can show you to your room." Donne began rubbing his leg. "I'm sure Donne would like to explore his new home. Afterwards, we can answer any questions you have."

Rhys hesitated, then nodded. "Okay, that seems like the best course of action. Which room is mine?"

Xander led her to the room diagonally across from Tim's. Opening the door, he said, "We'll meet in my room in an hour. Make yourselves comfortable."

"Thank you." She and the cats entered the room and closed the door.

"How did you know which one was hers?" Jamee asked. "We never found out which Sign she was."

Xander smiled. "Only one Sign would have command of the feline world. Leo, the Lion."

"Oh."

"Can I see my room?" Dana asked.

Tim jumped in. "Me too."

Dana turned, a little confused. "You haven't seen your room yet?"

"It's a long story. The short version is that we've already had a brush with the enemy and I didn't come out of it looking too good. I've only seen the inside of the hospital wing so far."

"Your rooms are at opposite ends on opposite sides of the hall," Xander told them. "Remember, my room in an hour."

"Deal," Jamee said. The other two nodded.

* * * * * * * * * * *

The room was spacious and aesthetically decorated with cool colors. The queen size bed was covered with a large comforter displaying the Libra glyph, and numerous pillows at the head of it. In the corner was a beautiful desk made of rowan wood. On top of the desk, as promised, sat a flat-screen computer begging to be used. He decided to check his email later though. A matching rowan wood bookshelf and dresser stood off to the side, the former filled with books, the latter already filled with clothing. There was a huge walk in closet, also filled with clothing, some of it his, some of it new. The wall sported a flat screen TV and DVD/VCR player. A sofa stood along one wall with a coffee table in front of it. Two big easy chairs framed the sofa. The bathroom was large, with a Jacuzzi tub and shower. All of his hair and skin products sat on a shelf next to a mirror. Slipping out of his clothing, he eagerly started the Jacuzzi. Suddenly remembering the last bath he had, he cautiously dipped a finger in the warm water. Reassuring himself that this was a completely different situation, he slowly allowed himself to relax.

Recent events swept through his consciousness and he gave them free reign. Dana was impulsive, but intelligent. Rhys seemed less impulsive, but just as passionate. The thought reminded him that Fire Signs are supposed to be passionate. He had met almost half of the Signs and different members of The Gathering. The thought that there were still seven Signs to find was dizzying, but exciting in the prospect. He already missed Nell and his parents, but the presence of Harmony went a long way to comfort him. As if she had read his mind, he heard Harmony pawing at the door. Glancing at the clock on the wall, he saw that he had a little time to spend with her.

Walking back into the main bedroom, he reveled in the feeling of the plush area rug on his bare feet. Harmony jumped onto the bed, meowing with pleasure. Tim threw on clothing and laid down next to her, smiling as she nuzzled his chest. If he closed his eyes, he could imagine that they were back in his apartment. After a few minutes, however, he reluctantly heaved himself off of the bed and went to find Xander's room.

* * * * * * * * * * *

"So what do you think?" Dana asked. She and Jamee occupied the couch, while the boys held the bed.

"Of her?" Tim shrugged. "She seems nice. Older than us though."

"She's the oldest of the Signs, but then again, she's only twenty-nine – not that much older than you or I," Xander said. "Anyone want a snack?" Reaching into a drawer, he pulled out candy. He tossed two bags to the girls, keeping the others on the bed.

"That's really weird," Dana said, tearing into a chocolate wrapper. "I mean, by the calendar, shouldn't I be the oldest? I mean, I am the first sign of the zodiac."

"True," Xander agreed. "Still, there are those who say that Aries is also the youngest of the zodiac. I don't know why we're in the order we are, but maybe certain Signs needed more time to develop their talents."

"Rhys definitely has an interesting talent," Jamee noted, shoving a handful of candy into her mouth.

"It comes in handy," Rhys confessed, entering the room and taking a seat in a big chair, Donne strutting along behind her. He meowed once at them. Harmony meowed back from her position at Tim's side on the bed. He hopped up onto the couch next to Jamee and fell asleep with her scratching his back.

"Hello, Rhys. Candy?" Xander offered.

"Yes, please. Chocolate." Xander arced a bag in her direction. Deftly snatching the bag out of the air, she ripped it open and devoured one.

"Is your room okay, Rhys?" Xander asked.

"More than okay, Xander, thank you. I was surprised to find extra rooms for the cats, and I never expected those rooms to contain outside environments. The Brownings were thrilled to find their natural habitats and immediately went gallivanting about, but Donne said he'd stay with me and explore later." She looked fondly at the sleeping cat. "He's so loyal. What I don't understand, though," she continued, "is how you knew to provide the rooms for the cats. After all, you had no idea of my talent before you met me, had you?"

"No," Xander admitted. "Not until Dana read your mind and we wouldn't have had a clue if she hadn't told us." Dana beamed. "The rooms are equipped to fulfill the occupant's needs. If you need a bathroom, the bathroom will be there. It will always be there when you need it. When you don't need it, it'll disappear. The room sensed your need for an outside environment, so it provided one. There will be a litter box for Donne as well when he needs. Harmony, too."

Tim swallowed a mouthful of licorice. "How does it do that?"

"It's a form of telepathy," Xander answered, and Dana perked up. "The rooms were enchanted when The Gathering was constructed. All of the rooms here do it."

"Cool!" Dana exclaimed.

"So the room knew of my talent even when you didn't?" Rhys queried.

"In a fashion, yes. We had no way of knowing previously," Xander told her.

"In fact, we didn't even know which one you were until your talent was revealed. Xander figured it out," Tim said.

Rhys was bewildered. "Which one I am?"

"Leo," Jamee said.

"You were born on August 11th, 1970, right?" Tim asked.

Her confusion grew to frustration. "What do you do here? Research people's lives? I mean, yes, I'm a Leo, but that doesn't mean..."

"Not *a* Leo," Dana interrupted. "The Leo. Leo personified."

"What?!"

As Xander launched into the familiar story, Tim tuned out. *I'm already tired of hearing this.* Carefully guarding his thoughts from being broadcasted to Dana, he reflected further on meeting Rhys. She seemed like a confident person, but he could tell that she was shaken by this experience. Harmony nuzzled his hand, seeking attention. Tim obliged, wondering just how much the cats understood what was going on. That thought made him wonder just how much *he* understood what was going on. Glancing at Rhys's expression, he knew he understood a great deal more than he had a few days before. *What's it going to be like when we're all Twelve here together?* he asked himself. Dana glanced in his direction and raised an eyebrow. Hastily, he cleared his mind and smiled at her. She half-smiled back.

"This sounds impossible!" Rhys burst out.

"We know it does," Tim reassured her.

"It's jarring, but it's the truth," James added, sympathy in his eyes.

Donne raised his head and focused on Rhys, meowing insistently. Rhys glanced at him sharply. He made a low growl in his throat and she nodded, resigned.

"Yes, of course, you're right," she said softly. She faced Xander. "Donne has informed me that he and the Brownings will do anything they can to support your cause and he says I should do the same." Harmony meowed. "Oh, and Harmony. Sorry, Harmony. Cats have a strong sense of responsibility and loyalty but most of all, they have an incredible survival instinct. The feline world is fully aware that the Star Child is on her way and with her comes a strong potential for destruction." She laughed suddenly. "Donne says that he isn't surprised to find that I am to be a protector of this great power. Thanks, Donne. Your confidence in me is overwhelming."

"Are you okay with all of this?" Xander asked her.

"Yes," she said firmly. "I'm fully on board. Where the cats go, I go." Chewing thoughtfully, she added, "It's time I did something exciting with my life."

"Yeah, fighting a bunch of astranihl wasn't exciting enough," Tim chimed in wryly.

"Oh, yes, who were those people?"

"They are astranihl, messengers of Merel. Merel's goal is to keep the twelve Signs from coming together," Dana told her.

"That's the short-term goal," Xander corrected. "The ultimate goal is to gain control of the Star Child and use her to destroy the universe as we know it."

"Why would anyone want to do something like that? Wouldn't that destroy them as well?" Bags flew through the air as the Signs exchanged candy.

"Eventually. The Star Child's responsibility will be to keep the universe in balance. Merel wants that power and that upsets the balance to a dangerous amount. With nothing to counter it, the universe will collapse into a large black hole, taking Merel with it. There has to be a balance of both sides for the universe to remain stable. "

Rhys laughed. "I'm sorry," she apologized quickly. "It's not funny. I just never dreamed that there would be real 'good and evil' situations."

"It's not really as much of a 'good and evil' thing as it is an 'us and them' situation," James observed. "It depends on how you define 'good' and 'evil'. Our side wants to preserve life the way it is; their side wants to destroy it."

Bags switched hands again. "That's a good way of looking at it," Rhys agreed.

"So, in the traditional sense, 'good' and 'evil'," Dana said.

James laughed. "Yeah, I guess so. Glad to have you aboard, Rhys."

"Yeah, welcome to the club," Tim added.

Xander yawned. "If you need anything, just ask."

"Thank you all," Rhys said gratefully. "It appears as though you four could use some sleep."

"Oh, we weren't up too early," Xander demurred, grinning at Tim.

"You're the one who just yawned," Tim retorted.

"Either way," Jamee said, heading off the potential argument, "I'm sure we have time to grab a short nap before dinner."

"I think I'll need the nap after today's adventure," Rhys admitted.

"We'll all sleep well tonight," Dana promised, handing Xander the bags of candy from the couch. Tim knelt and began cleaning up the wrappers.

Xander stashed the bags back into their drawer. He paused. "You said before that you're used to dealing with trauma."

"I'm a nurse," Rhys told them. "I've had some interesting experiences."

"Just wait, Rhys. Initiating a Sign is an experience you won't forget," Jamee said. "Trust me."

"Don't make us sound like some kind of fraternity," Xander admonished.

"Well, aren't we?" Dana countered.

"I guess, but it sounds so mundane," Xander complained. The others laughed.

"How do you know which one is next?" Rhys inquired.

"We know that we need the Fire and Air Signs before the other six. We don't know why exactly. We have all three Fire Signs now. Dana, you and me. After tonight, we'll have all three Air Signs and we can concentrate on finding the Water and Earth Signs."

Rhys was paying close attention. "How much time do we have?"

Xander grimaced. "Not much. We know that the birth of the Star Child is at the turn of the millennium. That's why we have to gather the rest of the Signs together by the end of the year. Once the year turns, we have to be on the lookout for the Star Child."

This was news for the other Signs as well. "Doesn't The Gathering know where she's going to be born?" Dana asked.

Xander shook his head. "The prophecy only says that it'll be at the turn of the year, but it doesn't say where."

"How are we going to find out?" Tim asked.

"Dad said The Gathering is working on the problem, but so far, they haven't made any headway." The door banged open, making them all jump. Lisa stood in the doorway, anger clearly written across her face.

"Sagittarius," she said in a deceptively quiet voice. "What exactly did you think you were doing?"

"Lisa, come on. We have Signs to recruit." Xander tried to keep a cool composure to belie his guilt.

"I see. Do you think it might have been a good idea to tell The Gathering that you were leaving, let *alone* inform the hospital wing that you were taking one of our patients?" The other Signs suddenly found focal points elsewhere in the room.

"I was going to. It was a last minute decision. I didn't want to wake anyone." *Except me*, Tim thought. "I thought you'd be happy that I went to get them so quickly. And it was a good thing I did, Lisa, or else you'd have had another patient. Rhys here was under attack from astranihl. There were a whole bunch of them in the room and if we hadn't shown up when we did, we might have brought her back injured, or worse, not brought her back at all. What would you have done then?" he challenged.

Lisa sighed. "Sagittarius, to go off without checking in was incredibly irresponsible and caused no end of panic around here. You weren't just risking Libra. We could have lost all of you."

Tim opened his mouth to tell her that he felt fine, but she whirled and cut him off with an imperious glare. "You. Back to the medical wing. Now."

"I want to stay in my own room," he argued. "I feel fine."

Rhys stood, assuming a regal manner. "We appreciate your concern for our safety, but as Tim clearly stated, he has recovered. He was well enough to fight off my attackers and has shown no sign of relapse since our return."

Lisa's expression clearly displayed that she wasn't convinced, but she forced a smile and held a hand out. "I'm Lisa Weisman."

Rhys smiled pleasantly, but kept her regal mien. "Rhys Avella. I'm happy to make your acquaintance, Dr. Weisman."

"Not doctor," she corrected. "I'm a healer. And please, call me Lisa."

"Lisa," she repeated. "I am Leo."

"And I'm Dana Wyntrap," Dana interjected. "Aries, at your service."

The healer shook her hand as well, then turned to Tim. "I'll discharge you, but I will be keeping tabs on you. You may stay in your own room from now on. Would you like me to show you where it is?"

"No need," Tim declined. "It's just two doors down." Harmony, sensing that they were about to leave, stretched and jumped to the floor. He laughed. "Well, I guess someone's ready to go."

"I think we're all heading out," Jamee said. "I'm gonna go see if Mr. Pears is free."

"I'll be glad to show you some of The Gathering," Lisa offered to the new Signs.

"Cool," Dana accepted.

"I would like to see the medical center," Rhys agreed.

"I'll see you guys later," said Tim.

He returned to his room and crawled under the covers, not bothering to undress first. Harmony leapt up onto the bed and, after her usual circling routine, finally settled into a niche made by the curve of his body. As if Harmony were a feline dream-catcher, Tim's sleep was dreamless.

Chapter 15

Tim itched to leave The Gathering. The protective walls had become a prison and he longed for the outside, but Lisa forbade it. Unfortunately, she had swayed the other members of The Gathering to her side and even Professor Galten agreed that he should be confined to the building. Additionally, for safety reasons, they required all of the Signs to be together, which threw both Xander and Dana into a snit. The Signs argued until they were blue in the face, but The Gathering stood firm. Although they could not physically prevent Xander from using his power, his loyalty kept him from leaving. That was only part of it. Though it galled him to admit it, he confessed to Tim that he agreed with the decision on some level. As much as he wanted to go get Aquarius as soon as possible, he recognized the wisdom of having as many Signs together in order to face possible danger. However, he was not above making a little mischief of his own.

Tim sat at his desk, checking emails. He sent off messages to Nell and his parents, reassuring them that all was okay. Harmony was snoozing on the bed, but she raised her head sharply as a pounding echoed through his room.

"Hey Tim!" Xander called through the door. Tim finished the last sentence of his email to Latwanda, hit SEND, and moved to answer the door. When he opened it, Xander grinned at him with a sparkle in his eyes. "Up for some fun?" he asked.

Curious, but wary, Tim thought before asking a question of his own. "What kind of fun?"

"You'll see." He grabbed Tim by the hand and dragged him down the hall to the stairs. Tim tried to pay attention, but after traversing a maze of hallways and doors, he was thoroughly lost. Eventually, they stopped before an ancient door with a large lock.

"Where are we?" Tim wondered.

"Professor Galten's office. I want to show you some of the potions she makes."

Tim nervously peered up and down the hallway, expecting the professor's form to appear at any moment. "What if she's in there?"

Xander leaned against a wall. "She's not. I just saw her leave with my parents and Sereny. They won't be back for awhile. It's the perfect chance."

"I didn't know you were into potions."

"I've lived here my entire life. You think I haven't explored?" Xander's grin was infectious. "Besides, I told you that I had places to show you." He took Tim's hand. "Let's go." There was a brief shimmer of color and then they stood within the office. Xander flicked on the light. Shelves upon shelves of multicolored bottles lined the walls. Each was carefully labeled, and Tim began to move among them, fascinated. Meanwhile, Xander moved towards a shelf opposite Tim and snatched down a long-necked, golden bottle, holding it up to the light. Prismatic light spread across the floor. Tim watched as Xander hunted among the shelves, finally locating a squat, blue-green bottle. He placed both upon the desk.

Tim stepped up to the desk and looked more closely at the bottles. There appeared to be nothing magickal about them. "What are you doing?" he asked.

"I had an idea," Xander bragged. "Most of us get to experience our own talents, but you don't know what it's like to be charmed. So I thought maybe you'd want to feel what it's like from the other end." He looked hopeful and excited as he held up the golden bottle. "This is a mirror potion. It makes the drinker experience everything another person experiences. You can drink it and charm me and you can feel what it's like." He appeared proud of this idea.

"If I drink that and I feel what you feel, what happens when we want to stop?" Tim asked, worried about the long-term effects.

"It'll wear off eventually. And if we want to stop it earlier, we have this," Xander answered, holding up the blue bottle. "It's a dampening draught. It'll stop the emotions from getting through until the mirror potion wears off."

Despite his nerves, Tim was excited. "Cool. It might even help me understand how to charm better." He stretched out his hand and took the golden bottle. Fighting briefly with the stopper, he finally opened it and golden vapors hissed through the air, filling his nose with an overripe smell. "Wait," he said, "what happens when the professor finds out that it's gone?"

"Already covered." He pointed to the shelf, where another golden bottle had appeared. "The professor keeps a stockpile of them and they're automatically replaced."

Tim was impressed. He raised the bottle to his lips. "Bottoms up," he said and tilted the bottle. The spicy liquid filled his mouth, rushing past his tongue and down his throat, burning as it went. His nostrils flared as the vapors assailed them.

He tried to cough, but the liquid had coated his throat and he could feel it working its way through his body. He opened his eyes. The world had a slightly golden tint to it. Xander's eyes had changed from blue to green with the mix of gold.

"Wow, Tim. Your eyes are yellow," Xander said. Tim could feel Xander's surprise filling his chest and working its way out to his limbs. Unprepared for a direct assault, he fought to keep a hold on his individuality. Xander was watching him, concerned, and Tim felt that concern like a battering ram against his mind. He tried to shut it out and sent a thought deep down inside of himself, searching for that part of him that was authentic Tim. His awareness snagged on a chunk of personality that grounded him firmly in himself and the pressure eased slightly.

Tim slowly let a crack open in the shell he had made for himself. *This is like searching for another soul,* he thought and suddenly, the exercise was much easier. He exerted the same control that he had when searching for Dana and felt Xander's heart beating within his chest. He could still feel his own heart and the double beat left him breathless at first, but he clamped an iron control down on his lungs, forcing them to work at normal speed. He reminded himself that there wasn't any more blood being pumped through his body; it just felt that way.

"You okay?" Xander asked, and Tim nodded. "Okay, start charming."

"Right," Tim muttered. He focused on Xander, but nothing came to his mind. "I don't know what to say," he complained.

"Doesn't matter," Xander told him. "Just try telling me something I don't want to believe. You'll feel it."

Tim took a breath and smiled charmingly at the Sagittarius, picking the first thing that came to mind. "Xander, listen to me. The Star Child is not important. That was a ploy by The Gathering to distract you from their true mission." He had to pause as Xander instinctively fought him and the other boy's shock and outrage washed over him. After all, he had not only challenged Xander's dedication to the Star Child, but he was slandering the very organization that Xander had trusted his entire life. He stiffened his resolve and kept his smile beaming. A shudder went through Xander as his belief was shaken. The shock vanished as quickly as it had come, but the anger refused to depart as easily. The golden light was developing lavender edges.

Tim decided to try a different tack. "With your help, we can figure out The Gathering's true mission and stop it. Xander, I can't do this without you. Please, Xander." His smile changed from reassuring to pleading and another shudder went through Xander as sympathy hit Tim in waves and he could feel the layers of resistance peeling away. He went in for the kill. Wielding his smile like a weapon, he said firmly, "I can show you the proof. You have to trust me." All resistance suddenly vanished. A bolt of emotion shot through the both of them and tears welled up in Tim's eyes. Despair was radiating from Xander and Tim felt his own heart scream. Sadness hit him again and again. Tim's smile disappeared and he crumpled to the floor, hugging himself and crying uncontrollably. Xander stood straight and tall, but tears were streaming down his face. Sobbing, Tim crawled to the desk and yanked the blue bottle's cork out, drinking deeply.

As the ice-cold liquid trickled down his throat, the despondency was gone and he was able to stop crying. He placed the bottle back on the desk and wiped the tears from his face, using a chair to help him rise. Xander was rigid, staring straight ahead with unseeing eyes, tears still streaking his face, his hands balled into fists that shook slightly. Tim stood cautiously and slowly approached him. Xander made no move as he drew closer. Tim's hand made its way to Xander's upper arm. At the touch, Tim could again feel the despair, but it was muted. "Xander?" he whispered. No response. He shook him, gently. "Xander. Talk to me. I don't understand."

"No, you don't." Xander's voice was barely audible. Tim stepped back, breaking the physical contact. The sadness disappeared, but it hovered at the edge of his consciousness. Painstakingly slow, Xander opened his hands and moved to sit at the desk. Tim stood nearby, hardly daring to breathe, lest he scare Xander off. The boys stayed that way, neither moving, neither speaking, for a while. The air was thick with unspent emotion. Then, Xander turned a watery eye on Tim. "I'm sorry," he said. "It's not your fault. You couldn't know."

"Xander, what is going on?"

Xander took a ragged breath. "I told you," he began slowly, "that my parents made sure I had a normal education." Tim didn't respond. "They bought a piece of property in Oklahoma City and enrolled me in the school system there when I was old enough to travel. We never lived in that house, always coming back here to The Gathering. The house was proof of residence for the authorities. I don't even know what the inside of it looks like. I went to public school from the time I was eight until I was seventeen.

"I began my senior year of high school. High school wasn't anything special for me. I wasn't popular, but I wasn't unpopular. I was your average student - did pretty well in school; played baseball and lacrosse. People knew who I was, but I kinda kept to myself. Every so often, I'd go out with a few acquaintances or some girl to make my life look normal, even though I knew it wasn't and it never would be." He turned away from Tim, staring across the room, lost in memories. "Until I met Danny." Tim felt an iron fist squeeze his heart.

"Danny transferred during the summer between my sophomore and junior years, but I didn't meet him until second semester junior year. He was in my English class. He sat down next to me the first day. In the middle of class, he passed me a note saying something about how dull the class was and I passed one back. Every English class became about passing notes back and forth." He gave a small, bitter laugh. "We almost got caught a few times, too. We started to hang out outside of class. Danny became my best friend. My only real friend, actually. I started making excuses for missing occult lessons at night to hang out with him. We'd go to the movies or play video games in his parents' basement. I felt like a normal kid. It was great.

"The middle of the next summer, we were playing video games again in his basement and he was losing. He started to tickle me in the middle of the game so I would lose. I dropped the controller and tackled him. I remember rolling around, wrestling with him and I pinned him – like I did with you – and he kissed me." The fist tightened. "I had never kissed a boy. I was scared. All of my training in the occult and some of the most frightening phenomena known to man and what scared me more than anything else was that kiss. I had to get out of there, so I left Danny sitting on the floor and went outside. I traveled to the first city that came to mind. I didn't care where I was going; I just wanted to be alone. I stayed there for hours, just walking around. Wandering around the city, I replayed what had just happened over and over in my head, and the more I thought about it, the less afraid I became, and the more excited I was by the idea that Danny was interested. I hadn't ever thought of him that way, but now I entertained the idea and found that I liked it. A lot. I traveled back and knocked on his door. When he opened the door, his eyes were red from crying. I didn't let him say anything, I just pulled him close and kissed him." His tone was wistful.

"We began to date. As senior year started, we were both very careful not to let anyone in school know what had happened over the summer. There were small changes. Both of us stopped going on dates with anyone else. We were together almost everyday after school. I told my parents about Danny. They were mad." He laughed. "But they were mad because I had been blowing off lessons to be with him. They didn't care whether I was gay or straight. My mom said, 'Honey, the important thing is not who you love, but that you love.' I've never forgotten that.

"It was far from perfect. I couldn't bring Danny home. Telling Danny who I really was would change everything and I didn't want it to change. He met my parents over dinner at a restaurant. I had been careful to tell him little lies that never revealed where I lived or anything too personal about me, but the longer we were together, the more persistent he became. He wanted to know everything about me. He complained that I held parts of myself back. 'Without trust,' he told me, 'this relationship will fail. I love you, but it's not enough. You have to trust me.'" Tim gasped as he realized that he'd echoed Danny's words. "And I trusted him. Told him everything. He wouldn't believe me until I took him to The Gathering. Mom and Dad were furious. Most of The Gathering was, but I didn't care. Danny finally knew me. All of me. He was shocked, but he gradually came to accept who I really was and stayed with me. I was so happy."

"What happened?" Tim whispered. Xander turned to him.

"Danny was going to take me out for my eighteenth birthday. He had these big surprise plans that I wasn't allowed to know about. All I knew was to meet him at his place at 6:30. When I got there, there was a limo parked outside with a note taped to his front door that said, 'Your ride awaits'. I couldn't believe that he'd hired a limo. I went to the car and opened the door. It took a minute for my eyes to adjust to the low lighting." His voice became hollow. "Danny was there, not moving. His throat...his throat had been slit. There was a red rose still in his hand," he whispered brokenly. "I don't remember much after that. I remember the limo starting but then there was shouting and Professor Galten was screaming in my ear to get back to The Gathering." Xander's eyes were bright. "I killed him. I trusted him and he died. That's why we can't tell anyone the truth about us. Because they die." Tim stretched his hand to place it over Xander's. "I vowed never to trust anyone like that again. I never have. Until now."

At the touch, Xander's emotions came flooding into Tim. The sadness was still there, but it had taken a backseat to more powerful feelings. Affection, interest, mingled with guilt. Tim didn't know what to do with all of them. His heart, already full with his own feelings for Xander, swelled with the onslaught of the other boy's emotion. Xander pulled back, realizing the transfer that had taken place. He blushed scarlet and before Tim could say anything, stood and dashed out the door. Tim stared after him.

"He's kept that buried for a long time." Tim yelped and whirled around. Professor Galten stood there, her eyes focused on Xander's exit.

"You scared the shit out of me!"

The professor gazed at him. "It's my office," was all she said.

Tim fought to get his pounding heart under control. "What happened to him?"

The professor sat down. "I met Daniel. He was a nice boy. Bright. He knew the dangers even if Alexander did not. Merel was simply waiting for the right moment. Fortunately, John had a last minute vision and immediately, a team went out. We arrived just as Alexander entered the limo. There was a scream and the limo began to pull away. A telekinetic held the limo in place, but astranihl were converging upon us. I ignored them and headed straight for the limo. There was a strong, sulfuric smell that pervaded the interior. Paralyzing vapors. Alexander was frozen, staring at Daniel." Tim pictured it. The image was terrifying.

"I dragged Alexander from the limo and away from the vapors, forcing an antidote down his throat. Then I ordered him back to The Gathering. It took awhile, but eventually, he disappeared, and I went back for Daniel, but there were too many astranihl. A few members of The Gathering had already been lost. There was nothing more we could do, so we returned to The Gathering. Alexander was already being checked over by healers."

"What are paralyzing vapors?" Tim asked.

"There is a potion for everything, Timothy. This potion exudes vapors that render the individual helpless, unable to move or speak, while leaving all feeling intact. The person becomes imprisoned in his own body." Tim shuddered at the thought.

"Why did Merel need the potion?" Tim wondered.

"Merel was not there. This was a job left to the astranihl." There was a pause.

"Alexander did not speak for a year after the incident. It was only through constant sessions with psychics who helped him to deal with the incident that he was able to regain some of his old self, but he was a much more somber person after that year. He couldn't go back to school and never graduated, although his education continued here. None of us realized just how deeply he had repressed the murder."

Her violet-brown eyes probed his. "In stripping away his resistance, you broke down the walls he had put up around that incident. I can only imagine what it must have been like for him to have that wound brought to the surface again." She took his hand in her gnarled claw. "He cares about you and he needs you. Be careful with him. He'll need time to recover from this. He's been dealing with it on a subconscious level all of these years. Now you've come along and not only have you forced Daniel to resurface, but you are occupying a similar role in Alexander's mind and heart." Tim began to protest, but she held a finger to his lips. "Don't deny it. You have no more control over his feelings towards you than you have over your feelings towards him. You are something good for him, Timothy. You just have to give him time." She rose, bones creaking. "Let's go to dinner." As she reached the door, she paused.

"There are far worse potions to encounter than the mirror or paralyzing potion. You'll find that out firsthand if I find you in here again."

Chapter 16

That night brought the usual whispering along the dining hall as Professor Galten ambled up with Tim. Xander was sitting between his mother and Jamee and did not look at him when he sat down, but he was composed again, all traces of sadness buried.

"Professor, will you be joining us for dinner?" Mrs. Conlyn invited.

"That was the idea, Rachel," came the grumbled reply. The woman lowered herself ungraciously into a chair. "So the Fire Signs are complete," the professor said to Sereny, ignoring the others.

"Yes, Blanche, they are," Sereny said with a smile for the two new Signs. "Dana has requested help in learning how to send thoughts. I've done what I can to help her and she has made significant progress so far."

"Only with pictures," Dana murmured. "No sound yet."

"That's still progress," Jamee told her.

"Excellent." The professor focused her eyes upon the group before her. "Tonight, you seek out the Aquarius." It was not a question. She looked over Sereny's shoulder. "I see the instructor for Aries has arrived."

"Yes, we had to call him back early from his trip since our son saw fit to bring Dana and Rhys here as early as possible," Mrs. Conlyn said, looking at Xander. There was mild rebuke in her tone. Xander managed to look slightly guilty.

"Sereny isn't my instructor?" Dana asked.

"Of course not, dear," Mrs. Conlyn told her. "She was just filling in until your instructor arrived. I'm sure he will make you feel right at home. He's at the table over there." She pointed to a midpoint between them and the door. They all followed her finger to see a group of mid-twenty-somethings hunched over their food, chatting in low voices. One young man with his back to them suddenly straightened and looked back at them. A sharp intake of breath came from Dana.

"Chris?" Incredulity was clear in her voice. "Is that Chris?" The young man left his table and strode over to her, a broad grin on his face.

"Hey cutie. Sorry I'm late."

"What are you doing here?"

He shoved his hands deep into his pockets. "I'm a part of The Gathering. Always have been. *You're* the newcomer." She stared at him, speechless. "I couldn't tell you. It's one of the reasons we, um, well, anyway, it's good to see you."

She blushed. "Same. Um, these are Xander, Tim, Jamee and Rhys."

"I know Sagittarius. It's nice to meet the rest of you." The Signs nodded at him. He turned back to Dana, smiling expansively. "I gotta get back to the table, but we can start working tomorrow. I'll see you then." She nodded dumbly, and he returned to his table.

Before anyone could ask, Dana spoke up. "We used to date. It was getting kind of serious, but I felt like he was hiding something from me. Which he was. This." She looked around. Xander avoided her eyes. "I guess I understand now."

"He's your instructor?" Jamee asked, amazed.

"He's been trained in the workings of the psychic mind, specializing in telepaths," Mr. Conlyn explained. "Dana is a telepath in a class by herself. The most powerful telepath this world has ever seen. She has asked for help with her gift and with his help, she will be able to do things with her mind that many people can't even dream of." He beamed at Dana.

"Dear, don't exaggerate," Mrs. Conlyn chided him with a fond smile playing about her lips. "The mind is extremely delicate and complicated. With training, she will have great skill and power, but she won't be omnipotent."

"Please stop talking about me as if I'm not here," Dana begged. "Seeing Chris...well, that just wasn't something I was ready for." Tim tried to catch Xander's eye, but Xander seemed to sense it and deliberately kept his focus on Dana.

"There are going to be many things that you need to be ready for, surprising or not. From here on out," Mr. Conlyn warned, "things will become more difficult. The astranihl that you brought in," and there was an emphasis on this statement to let them know that they had not yet been forgiven for leaving without notification, "was interrogated."

"Interrogated how?" Dana's interest was suddenly very aroused.

"We have methods...," Mr. Conlyn began.

"...but that's not something you need to know," Mrs. Conlyn finished with a severe look at her husband.

"Oh, fine." Dana settled back with a pout. Mrs. Conlyn, satisfied that her message had gotten through, continued the conversation. However, Tim watched Dana's expression change into one of surprise and then to smug confidence. Glancing around the room, he saw Chris surreptitiously steal a glance at Dana, then return to his meal, smiling obscurely. Wondering what had been said between the two telepaths, he tried to refocus on the conversation at hand.

"Merel must be aware of the fact that we have one of the astranihl," Sereny was saying. "They are going to redouble their efforts to eliminate the rest of the Signs. It's a race. Luckily, they don't have the advantages of travel that we do." She winked at Xander, who gave her a weak smile. Tim got the feeling that the adults knew what had transpired and were doing their best to keep away from the topic.

"They have their own methods of travel," Professor Galten countered.

"You're just full of good thoughts," Mr. Conlyn commented sarcastically.

"Having all three Fire Signs puts me in a good mood," the professor responded, not seeing his irony. "Soon we will have all three Air Signs."

"Hopefully, soon we'll have all twelve Signs here safe inside The Gathering," Mrs. Conlyn said.

"That was delicious." Rhys placed her utensils upon her empty plate. "What's to keep them from attacking The Gathering? If they know we're here, wouldn't it be a better plan to wait until all of the Signs are in one place and attack there?" It was a frightening suggestion.

"The Gathering is not so easily attacked," Mr. Conlyn argued. "The building does not actually exist in the material world. From what Jamee has told us of Merel, they are set up in an actual building that is obscured from view and protected by some kind of energy field that prevents easy access. The Gathering is not like that. This building has no fixed location." Dana was beginning to nod, but the other three looked blank.

"It's like a ship," Dana explained. "It shifts constantly, floating past locations in the real world, but there's something about it that protects it from view, just like Merel."

"That is a powerful talent," Mrs. Conlyn murmured.

"They're all powerful talents," Professor Galten said. "It'll be a lot of power here once we have all Twelve."

"And speaking of, we have another Sign to bring in," Xander said.

"Then let's get to it," Jamee said, wiping her eyes.

"Yes!" Dana pounded the table, upsetting plates and glasses. Then, "Sorry."

"When do we leave?" Rhys asked.

"You leave now," Professor Galten informed them bluntly. As they stood, Rhys suddenly cried out.

"Donne! I need Donne!" The professor turned a discerning eye on her. "He is permitted to go, isn't he?" Professor Galten said nothing, but Donne came padding into the dining hall, Harmony trotting along behind him. Rhys and Tim scooped the felines into their arms. "I'm ready now," Rhys announced.

Barely anyone looked up as they joined hands and disappeared from the dining hall.

Chapter 17

The air was hot and muggy as they emerged onto the dusk-lit street. They blinked rapidly, getting their bearings. Xander turned to Rhys.

"It's up to you to find the Aquarius."

"Me?" She recovered quickly. "You all had to do it too, didn't you?" They nodded. "Very well. Donne!" she called.

"Not that way," Jamee stopped her.

"He can find people without being noticed," Rhys said.

"Yes, but we have ways of finding each other on our own." The instructions began. Rhys closed her eyes. Tim watched as a golden glow came into play around her, then turned to examine his surroundings. The area was quiet, clean, and suburban. Beautifully mowed front lawns, trash cans neatly placed in rows at the end of smoothly-paved driveways, nice stone work on the houses – it was a pretty neighborhood. Not a person in sight. *They're all probably inside, enjoying dinner on an evening like this*, Tim thought enviously, picturing families sitting around the table, safely unaware of the impending danger. There was an abrupt crash and Tim beheld Donne lying in a heap of trash playing with a small piece of cloth. The door to the house opened and a woman came storming out, glaring at the cat.

"Get out of here, you rotten animal! Get out! Shoo!" Donne ignored her. Tim glanced around for Harmony, but she was nowhere to be seen.

Still glowing, Rhys opened her eyes. "Excuse us, madam. The cat is mine and he's usually much better-behaved." She haughtily snatched the cat from the ground, wrinkling her nose at the smell.

Tim was sick of feeling helpless. He stepped towards the woman, smiling winningly. "Yes, please forgive us. We're new in this lovely town of yours and we would never do anything to mess up one of the prettiest and obviously well-kept houses on the block." Dana and Xander bent quickly, uprighting the can and stuffing the trash back inside of it.

The woman's harsh expression softened a little. "I'm sorry. I didn't realize that he was your cat. However, we have certain standards to live up to in this community."

"We completely understand," Tim placated her. Rhys gasped. The others shot looks at her as she held up the cloth that Donne had been playing with. *Astranihl,* she mouthed.

The woman misunderstood the nature of her concern and stepped in to reassure her. "Oh, don't worry, hon. He didn't have it in his mouth too long and he wouldn't have touched it if it were dangerous. As I was saying, our neighborhood..." Tim felt something brush against his leg. Harmony looked up at him and meowed urgently. Donne meowed back from Rhys's arms.

"Yes, thank you so very much, but we really have to go," Xander interrupted her, with a worried look at the others.

"Yes, we must go," Tim agreed, still smiling, "but you've been very kind and helpful. Thank you so much." He wondered if he was pouring it on a little thick, but the woman smiled back.

"You're quite welcome. Please stop by when you get a chance." Harmony gave one last meow and left.

"We'll certainly try," he promised as a struggling Donne broke free of Rhys's grasp and took off down the street after Harmony.

"Donne!" she called after him, breaking into a run of her own. The others quickly followed, leaving the woman staring after them, bewildered.

Donne tore around a corner and out of sight. Rhys stopped at the corner, leaning against a wall, gulping in air. Xander tried to follow Donne, but the other three stopped to help Rhys. After a moment, Xander came back.

"I lost him. Damn, that little bastard is fast!"

Rhys took a ragged breath. "It's okay. We're always in contact. He and Harmony smelled two astranihl. They're going after the Aquarius. We have to get there first!"

"Anybody have any ideas?" Jamee asked.

"Maybe I can charm them into thinking I'm a comrade of theirs," Tim mused. "Xander, do you think you could get the cloak from the guy we brought in this morning?"

"Sure thing." Xander vanished.

"Dana, you think you could read their minds?"

Dana shrugged. "Shouldn't be a problem, s'long as they're surface thoughts."

"What if something happens?" Rhys worried. "What do we do?"

James grinned. "If it comes to that, I'll be ready." He slapped a bat against his hand.

"Where did you get that?" Dana asked.

"Made it. It used to be trash."

Xander reappeared, holding a cloak. "Here," he said, handing it to Tim without really making eye contact. If any of the others noticed, they didn't say anything. "Great. How do we catch up with the cats?"

"Your talent," Tim answered.

"I need to know where I'm going," Xander pointed out.

"I know," Tim said. "Rhys, where is Donne right now?"

"Donne is just behind the astranihl. He and Harmony are tailing them," she answered.

Tim became business-like. "Send them on ahead of the astranihl." She nodded. "Can you get a picture of where they are in your head?" She nodded again. "Dana, can you get that picture from Rhys's mind and send it to Xander?" Dana was surprised, but she nodded. "Good. Do it!" He wrapped himself up in the cloak. "Xander, take us to where the cats are!"

* * * * * * * * * * *

Two grey-hooded figures strode down the sidewalk. Doing their best to appear nonchalant, they made their way through the perfect-seeming neighborhood, single-mindedly focused on a particular address. One of them jumped as, out of nowhere, two cats streaked past, yowling. A deep, guttural laugh erupted from the other.

"Scared?" he mocked. "They're just cats."

"I dislike going about in broad daylight," she snapped back. "We could be discovered."

"Who would dare disturb us? We can protect ourselves," he reminded her.

She growled, "If we were allowed to use our abilities in the first place, this would be much easier."

"We can't use them until we reach the water-freak's house. You want to bring The Gathering down on our heads?!"

"Of course not." They continued along for a block before she spoke again. "I wonder what will be done with him."

"We know all of the plan that we need to know," the man rebuked her. "It is an honor to be chosen for the duty."

"Yes," she agreed, chastened.

"A greeting, my brother and sister," said a new voice. The two were suddenly confronted with another astranihl. The newcomer stood hooded and unmoving.

"Why have you come?" the male astranihl demanded. "This is our assignment. There was no mention of a third member."

"And are you privy to all plans?" sneered the newcomer.

"We were chosen and sent with no information other than our instructions," the woman admitted. She was immediately hushed by the man.

"Then perhaps you won't challenge another member of your group so lightly."

The man quickly attacked back. "We will have no challenge so long as you can tell us the codeword given to us specifically for this mission. If you are a true member of the faith, you should have no problem." There ensued a moment of silence. Tim's hands began to sweat inside the stolen cloak and his breathing quickened. The two astranihl leaned in maliciously. Suddenly, Dana's voice exploded in his mind.

Feigning a calm he certainly did not feel, Tim replied, "Not at all. Retrograde."

They seemed almost disappointed at the word. "You are indeed a true brother," the man grated.

Tim had to exert a steel will to keep his legs from turning to jelly. "You are on your way to Aquarius now?" he inquired.

"We are."

"Excellent. How do you plan to kill him?"

"To kill him? We are under no orders to kill him." The woman eyed him suspiciously. "Someone sent directly would know this."

"I was making sure you knew the mission. I had to make sure that you were true members of the faith," Tim said somewhat desperately.

"We know our mission," asserted the man. "If there had been a change from the mission, we'd have been informed."

"That's why I'm here," Tim told him. "The mission has changed."

"Has it?" The man smirked. "What is our new mission, brother?" There was an emphasis on this last word that told Tim that he was in trouble. He thought quickly.

"Aquarius has already been captured," he lied. "The new target is..." He racked his brain, but he could not think of a Sign that was not already a member of The Gathering.

Virgo! Dana scream-thought.

"Virgo," Tim finished, relieved.

The woman laughed harshly. "Virgo was brought in ages ago and has since been put under constant surveillance."

Tim's mouth was dry. "I...just returned from a special mission. I wasn't informed of the Virgo's capture."

"Yet you were informed of the Aquarius capture?" Her tone was filled with scorn. "I doubt that." Alarms were going off inside of Tim's head. "If you truly knew–" She was cut off by the thud of her companion hitting the pavement. Her eyes went wide with shock even as James's bat connected with her head. She crumpled to the ground beside her partner. James brushed his hands off and began transforming the bat back into trash.

Tim pushed back the hood of his cloak and stared down at the two bodies. "Well, that was fun," he muttered sarcastically. "Good aim," he said to James. James just smiled.

Rhys stepped in. "Tim, take off that ridiculous cloak and give it to Xander. Xander, get the bodies and the cloak out of here. Be quick. We don't have a lot of time." She didn't say what everyone else was thinking: Virgo had already been captured. Xander took the cloak from Tim, placed a hand on each of the bodies and disappeared.

The cats had returned and were sniffing the spot where the bodies had been. Tim bent down to scratch Donne and Harmony on their heads. "Thanks, guys. Way to send an image back for us. Rhys without your talent, we could never have gotten ahead of the astranihl. Thank you." Donne and Harmony nodded. Rhys smiled.

"And me?" Dana pouted. "Didn't I do something?"

"You were key," Tim assured her.

"There's plenty of credit to go around," James said, tossing the trash into a nearby can.

Xander flashed back into existence. "Hey."

"Everything taken care of?" Rhys asked him.

"Yeah. They'll be joining their friend. Did you find Aquarius?"

Rhys closed her eyes and the golden aura flared with bright blue shining sporadically. "Just up another block. We cut it really close with those astranihl. Follow me." Then she laughed. "Rather, follow the cats." She pointed to the felines striding up the block, tails and heads held high. The others chuckled and obeyed.

They came to a house very similar to the rest of the neighborhood. The only difference with this house was that the front lawn was decorated with a large fountain and numerous statues of figures holding urns filled with water. From inside the house loud music blasted with a heavy beat that caused ripples across the water. As they walked up to the front door, their bodies began pulsing with the beat of the music. Dana knocked on the door, but there was no response. She pounded on the door while Rhys rang the doorbell. Almost immediately, the music ceased and they heard a man shout, "Just a minute!" There was the sound of running about the house and then the door opened to reveal a large African-American man wearing red sweatpants and a puzzled expression. Sweat poured from his forehead into his dark, almost black eyes. He wiped a hand across his brow. "I'm sorry, I was just exercising. Uh, can I help you folks?"

James cleared his throat. "Um, yes. My name is James Holm. These are Alexander Conlyn, Timothy Dalis, Dana Wyntrap, and Rhys Avella. Oh, and Donne and

Harmony," he added, indicating the cats who were inspecting the man's feet. "We would like to talk to you about...well, something very important and it involves you."

"Involves me? Have I done something wrong?"

"No, not at all," James said quickly. "It's just that...um, can we come in?"

"I'm sorry. I'm not in the habit of inviting strangers into my house." The man stood firmly in the doorway, blocking any view they might have had of the inside.

"We completely understand, Mr.?" Rhys prompted.

"Price. Cole Price. Please call me Cole, Miss Avella."

"Rhys."

"Rhys. As I was saying, you all seem like very nice people, but I just don't see what you're talking about and I'm afraid I'm not of a mind to invite you in without an idea of what you want from me. Unless you can explain it to me here, I'm afraid I can't help you."

"It's a little far-fetched and it's more than a little complicated." Rhys took a deep breath.

"We're all Signs," James added, trying to be helpful.

"Signs of what?" Cole looked even more confused. Tim groaned inwardly.

Rhys tried again. "We're all specially talented members of a group. As are you."

"I'm what?" *This was not going well,* Tim decided.

"Geez, I wish this was easier," Dana muttered.

"I apologize. I know this seems difficult to understand," Rhys said loudly with a hard look at Dana, "but what we're saying is true." Cole's expression, if anything, became even more skeptical and wary.

His recent experience reminded him that trust was important, so Tim tried to find common ground. "Excuse me. What do all of these statues represent?"

Cole relaxed marginally. "I'm a history professor with a penchant for mythology. These are all water deities. It's part of my job to research gods, but I have a special fascination for the gods of water."

"Really? I had no idea that there were so many." Tim wasn't faking his interest.

"Most polytheistic religions have a god or a goddess of water. Water is a powerful Element in religions throughout the world. The tears of a deity, the parting of the seas, the healing powers of water, the Fountain of Youth, etc. The list goes on."

"The figure of the Waterbearer has its place in astrology as well," Xander pointed out, hoping to steer the conversation back.

"Yes, Aquarius. I've a statue of him over there." He pointed to the corner of the yard. He chuckled. "My friends joke that he kind of looks like me."

"There might be a reason for that," Dana muttered before being silenced by another glare from Rhys.

"Cole, please understand," Rhys pleaded. "You're part of our group."

"What group?" Cole asked, the enthusiasm sparked by the water discussion diminishing.

"Guardians of power," Xander explained simply.

"What kind of power?"

"Power to stop the end of the world." Cole's expression became outright disbelief and he began to close the door.

Dana obstinately stopped him by jamming a foot in the way. "We have powers too."

Cole raised an eyebrow. "Power to stop the end of the world," he repeated, unconvinced.

"Yes, special gifts," Jamee said. Cole jumped at the sound of her voice.

"You – are the boy," he said hesitantly. Jamee nodded. "This is an elaborate illusion."

"No illusion," said Rhys gently.

Cole still looked skeptical. "It is some kind of trick..."

"We aren't lying!" Dana exclaimed heatedly. Rhys placed a hand on her shoulder, warningly.

Cole saw that and spoke directly to Rhys. "You are certain that what you tell me is pure truth?"

"Absolutely."

He saw the resolution in her expression and nodded. Taking her by the hand, he led them into the foyer of the house and pointed to a statue of a young boy with a large urn in his hands. "There is an ancient belief in four demi-gods of the Elements. These deities were said to be able to bestow gifts upon those who would follow them. The texts on them are scarce and often indecipherable, but from what I've gathered, the demi-god of water was the Mer-Child, Niole. He was the youngest of the Four." Looking again, Tim saw that the boy had a tail. "I don't know all of the gifts they gave, but I know one of their abilities was discerning the truth through their Elements. The water in the urn Niole carries is one of the few samples said to be taken from His original lake. It is water in its purest form. If you are telling me the truth about all of this, please dip your hand in the urn and make your statement. As long as you are telling the truth, you will not be harmed."

"What would happen if someone lied?" Dana asked.

Cole shrugged. "Niole punishes as He will. If you have doubts, you don't have to go through the test."

"Hah! I'm not scared of a little water." She started for the urn, but Rhys pulled her back. Dana saw the expression on Rhys's face and did not protest. Rhys stepped forward to the urn. Slowly, carefully, she lowered her hand into the water.

"Cole Price, you are a member of this group. As I am Leo, you are Aquarius." She withdrew her hand. "There you are. I spoke truly."

There was a strange ripple across the water, but Cole remained calm and controlled. "You did indeed. Please," he welcomed them, "let's sit down and you can tell me more." Rhys smiled and followed him into a large room where couches of blue and green surrounded a small fountain. Donne and Harmony remained by the door, preferring to stay as far away from the water as possible. Cole excused himself and came back wearing a white polo shirt and jeans. When he had found a spot on the couch next to Rhys, Xander began the familiar story.

"I've always had a connection with water," Cole said when Xander had finished. "It would respond to my emotions when I was very young, but I've discovered that I can work with it in other ways." Tim understood the ripple across Niole's urn; Cole's surprise had caused it. "I never dreamed that there was anyone else with such gifts."

"Join the club," Dana muttered.

"Aren't you an Air Sign, though?" Tim asked. "I mean, I know we were supposed to get all of the Fire and Air Signs first, and you have a talent for water."

"Aquarius is the Sign of the Waterbearer, just as Libra is the Scales or Aries the Ram. I suppose it only makes sense that I have the gift of water magic," Cole answered him.

"What kinds of things can you do with water?" James asked.

"Oh, goody, a demonstration," Dana chimed in.

Cole smiled at her, but spoke to the Gemini. "Put your hand into the fountain, James," he instructed. James looked apprehensive. "Don't worry, there's no danger of punishment."

The Gemini stretched out his arm towards the water. "Hey! I'm not getting wet!" They could see the water bending around his arm and then continuing on its natural course. He removed his arm, feeling it. Dana leaned over to feel as well.

"That's so cool!" Suddenly, she was doused with a spray of water from the fountain. "Hey! Cole!" she complained. Cole laughed.

"Don't worry," he said again. "It's easily fixed." The dampness vanished and Dana patted herself in surprise.

"Cool!" she repeated. "What else can you do?"

"I can tell if a person is telling the truth or not. Although Niole is a real mythological figure, the water in that urn is no different from the other water found on this property."

"You might find where we're going interesting, then, Cole," Tim said with a smile. "There is plenty of information on the Mer-Child and his associates."

"You know of Niole?" Cole asked, surprised. "Aside from those of us in the field, I've never come across anyone who knows anything of the four demi-gods. Even my colleagues and I don't know what religion they belong to."

"They don't actually belong to a religion," Xander informed him. "And they aren't usually referred to as 'demi-gods'. We call them Patrons. Patrons of The Gathering."

"Yes, you mentioned that place in your story. Where is it?" The others looked at each other. "That shouldn't be a difficult question, should it?"

"Unfortunately, it is," Rhys said. She explained to Cole about The Gathering's unique situation. Cole seemed enchanted by the idea.

"A powerful method against attack," he mused. "You said there are more of us. Are they there?"

Rhys shook her head. "You're the last one of the masculine Signs. Half of the Signs have come together; the three Fire Signs and the three Air Signs. We need to find the others and bring them together as well." Her demeanor grew solemn. "We just learned that Virgo has been captured."

"We have to go after him or her!" Dana commanded.

"No, Dana," Rhys disagreed. "We have to secure the other five before they are captured as well."

"What if they kill Virgo?" Dana argued.

"They won't. They said the plan was not to kill the Signs."

"Oh yeah." Dana considered. "Then why? Ransom? Torture?" Tim, Xander and James all shuddered with the collective memory of their time under astranihl lock and key. Dana caught the thoughts. "Sorry."

The room went silent except for the sound of the fountain.

"If I'm to understand it correctly," Cole began slowly, "it sounds as though they're playing a double-or-nothing game. Were they to kill the Signs, they would take control of this Star Child. If they're attempting to capture the Signs, it must mean that they have some way of harnessing our power as well. I don't know what they would attempt to do with that power, but they want it, and it seems that they can't get it from a dead Sign. Virgo will be safe for now, although he or she will not be comfortable. It is imperative that we seek out the other Signs and see them safely back to The Gathering before the astranihl find them." Rhys looked at him appraisingly. Even Dana couldn't argue with that.

"Yeah, you've got a point," she conceded.

Xander jumped in. "Meanwhile, we have to get back to The Gathering ourselves. Cole would probably like to learn more about The Gathering and we have some research to do."

"And Cole hasn't seen our talents in action," James added.

"Oh, I don't need a demonstration," Cole demurred.

Dana smirked. "But you want one. In fact, you're wondering what my talent is right now." Then she giggled. "No, it has nothing to do with sheep!"

Cole turned to the others with a wry smile. "Mind-reader?"

"I prefer the term 'telepath'," Dana replied loftily.

"Okay, Dana, that's enough," Rhys admonished mildly. Dana pouted dramatically.

"We're able to change things," James told the new Sign. He picked up a small statue from a side table, a woman with a jar carried upon her head. He concentrated intensely and the figure morphed into a delicately fluted champagne glass which James then held out to the fountain, catching some of the water in it. "Drinkable?" he asked their host, handing him the glass. Cole nodded and took a sip. He passed the glass to Rhys, who also took a sip and passed it around.

"That's quite a talent," Cole admitted. "But please change it back before you go. I had to bargain quite skillfully in order obtain that statue of Pere."

"Another water goddess?" Tim asked.

"Polynesian, yes. What do you do, Tim?"

"I have the talent of charming, but I'm still learning how to use it." He resisted the urge to look at Xander. "I won't perform a demonstration here."

"But it's pretty powerful," Dana butted in. "He made my mom trust him."

Cole smiled. "I'm sure it's something to see," he said politely. He turned to the woman next to him.

"I can communicate with the feline world." She pointed to the cats by the door. "Donne and Harmony accompanied us here and helped to find you."

"Harmony originally was my cat," Tim told him. "I mean, we lived together." It was hard to think of ownership when he and the cat could communicate through Rhys. Harmony didn't really belong to him anymore; she was more like a friend.

"Do you command them?" Cole asked. The cats hissed. Cole jumped, then laughed. "I guess that was my answer."

"I don't command them," Rhys confirmed. "But we're friends and I could ask them to do things just as they can ask things of me."

"Even something they wouldn't normally do?"

Rhys was confused. "Like what?"

"Well, I noticed that they're staying far away from the water. Could you ask them to jump into the fountain?"

Donne growled. Rhys sighed. "Donne says that if you really need a demonstration, he will do as you wish, but only this once." With that, the tom cat ran towards the fountain and leapt into the water.

"Damn!" Cole swore. "I didn't expect him to do that." Suddenly, the cat was standing on the dry stone base of the fountain, with the water diverted around him. There wasn't a drop on him. He stepped out, meowed at Cole and returned to his spot by the door.

"He says, 'thank you'," Rhys translated.

"Thank you as well," Cole said directly to the cat, who unmistakably bobbed his head once.

"My talent is traveling," Xander said. "You'll get a demonstration of that in just a few minutes when we go home to The Gathering. We really should check in with them."

"I see. We have the power, but they control us."

Xander snapped. "Look, I've lived there my whole life and no one has *ever* controlled me. These are the people who support us."

"Hey, hey. I didn't mean anything by it." Cole held up his hands in a surrender gesture.

"We know," Rhys jumped in. "It's a strange situation for all of us."

"I apologize, Xander."

"No apology necessary," Xander said hurriedly. "I'm just a little sensitive. It's been a recent issue."

"I understand. I only meant that if we don't have to return tonight, perhaps we should go after another Sign before our enemy becomes more active than they already are."

"Yay! Good plan," Dana cheered his suggestion.

"A noble idea, for sure, but we need to know more before we go after the other half. Besides, I want to know more about the Star Child and where she's going to be born. We still don't know that," Rhys pointed out.

"Cole should see The Gathering and get settled in," Tim agreed.

"Oh, screw that," Dana said. "I want to go after another Sign."

"Dana, as much as I want to go find another of our group, it's probably best that we get back," James said. "Maybe the astranihl that we met earlier today have more information than they let on, and I also want to know more about the Star Child. I want to find that book that locates the libraries of Anderson Baker. Perhaps one of them has a clue about where the birth is gonna be."

"Yeah, if we could find them," Dana muttered.

"Libraries?" Cole was very interested.

"Libraries that have been lost to civilization," Rhys explained. "There is a book that reveals their locations but the title is in a language that no one can understand and disguises itself with a nondescript title so no one will recognize it. It's complicated."

"I'd like very much to see that."

"You're about to get the opportunity," Xander told him. "It's time to go. Dana, don't look so glum; we'll go after the next Sign soon."

"Fine," she conceded in a sullen tone. Xander gave the usual warning to Cole about keeping contact. They joined hands and were swept up in a swirl of blue and green hues. Tim always felt strange while traveling. He didn't know if it was that he just wasn't used to it yet, or because there was a new awareness along each time. The usual merging felt familiar, yet foreign because of the additional person.

This is quite a talent, his mind thought. It took him a moment to realize that the thought hadn't been his own, but Cole's.

We can communicate? he thought, surprised.

So it would seem, Rhys thought. *It appears that in our merged state, we can share Dana's talent and send and receive thoughts if we wish to.*

Humans, a wry thought interrupted. *Just discovering the advantages of a group mind.*

Donne? Dana asked, incredulity radiating in waves from her mind.

Who else? You all have your odd mode of communication. Cats are much more practical and versatile. Sometimes there are things that must be communicated that can't be put into words.

Naturally, purred a female voice. *I spent a few nights trying to communicate through dreams.*

You were trying to tell me something! Tim exclaimed.

Ouch! Tim, don't shout. That was James.

This group mentality is very useful, Xander remarked, but Tim could sense that he was guarding himself.

A guy could get used to this method of travel, Cole commented. *I usually travel by water when I can.*

Boats? Dana asked.

Sometimes. Mostly, I just lie on the water and let it take me where I want to go.

Cool.

There was a painful separation and a somewhat violent push into reality. It was a more pronounced separation than they had ever experienced. The loss of the comforting presence of each others' minds was unsettling. They found themselves in the dark hall outside the library. There were a few members around, but no one paid them any mind. "This is the library," Xander said to Cole.

"Is it open now?" Dana asked.

"It's open all the time. There are three librarians and they take shifts. Miss Balcombe is usually working this time of night."

"You know, I don't think I'm really in research mode right now," Tim said. "Today was a long day and I'm kind of wiped out."

Dana was curious. "Why? What did you do today?"

Tim immediately began doing complex mathematical calculations in his head, avoiding Xander's eyes but knowing that he was doing something similar to block Dana. "Just exploring and learning new things about this place," he answered evasively. Dana must have sensed the mental walls because she didn't press the issue, for which Tim was thankful. "Let me know if you discover something interesting. Goodnight."

Rhys and Cole were deep in conversation and barely heard him, but Dana smiled and James said, "'Night." Xander gave no sign that he had heard him, but he felt Xander's eyes on him as he started up the stairs towards the astrology wing. He felt an irrational flicker of jealousy as he saw Harmony follow the group into the library, but he brushed it aside. When he reached his room, he locked the door and headed into the bathroom to brush his teeth. He stripped down and climbed into bed, grabbing a pillow and hugging it to his chest. Only once he was safely under the covers did he let the tears come. The magnitude of what he had done to Xander hit him full impact and he squeezed the pillow tightly against his body as tears flowed sideways across his face to dampen the pillow underneath his head. Slowly, exhaustion overtook his guilt and he fell asleep.

He stood on a beach. Harmony was playing in the sand and staying far away from the waves that lapped the beach. He watched her bat a piece of seaweed back and forth, then shake her paw, annoyed, when it stuck to her. He laughed at her and waded out into the water. An eerie calm settled upon the ocean. There was no wind, no waves. The water was clear and he could see right to the bottom, but there was only sand. No shells, no life, no seaweed, nothing. He saw his reflection on the surface writhe and shift independent of the water's slight movement to form the image of the dream-boy. The boy seemed desperate to communicate something to him. Tim was startled to hear the image speak. "Book. Cat," he said. A shaft of sunlight reflected off the water, making Tim squint and when he looked again, his own reflection was back. The boy was gone. He moved quickly out of the water and headed for Harmony. He picked her up, brushing the sand from her fur. "Who is he, Harmony?" he asked her. She purred and rubbed her face against his repeatedly. His mind climbed back towards consciousness as he felt a hand imitating the dream cat's movement, brushing the hair from his forehead. A familiar smell filled his nostrils.

He rolled onto his back without opening his eyes. Another hand traveled down the length of his left arm, lightly skimming over the muscles until it reached his hand. Fingers interlocked. He felt the touch trace his jaw line from ear to chin, finally coming to rest on his lips. He leaned into the hand during its journey, rolling more onto his left side. He could feel a fingertip running over the outline of his mouth, and then the finger disappeared, quickly replaced with the heat of two lips, hesitant, careful, barely touching his own. Tim inhaled the other boy's sweet scent and, letting go of the hand, he reached up, placed his hand behind the boy's head and pulled the lips closer to his own. He felt a hand rubbing his lower back through the covers. Lips parted, tongues exploring and caressing each other. Suddenly, the other boy pulled away and sat up. Tim opened his eyes.

"Alex?" he whispered.

"I'm sorry," Xander said, not facing him. "I thought...I don't know what I thought."

Tim sat up and placed a hand on Xander's back. "It's okay."

"No, it's not. I'm sorry." Xander stood. "I'm just not ready. I thought I was, but I'm not. It's still too fresh. I just...need some time."

Tim's heart strained against his chest, but all he said was, "I understand."

Xander faced him, his eyes bright with unshed tears, but a smile on his face. "Alex," he repeated softly. "You called me 'Alex'."

"I didn't realize. I don't even know why."

"No one's ever called me that before. I like it."

Tim smiled briefly and took a breath. "About today. I didn't mean to–"

"I know." He bent down and lightly kissed Tim. "Give me time."

He vanished. Tim shivered and laid down again, pulling the covers more tightly around him. He didn't fall asleep again for awhile.

Chapter 18

When he awoke the next morning, he found he was not alone in bed. Shifting his weight carefully so as not to disturb the cat, he made it out of bed and went to the bathroom. He started the shower with both a pang in his heart and a smile on his face. He didn't know what would happen, but he knew he would give Xander all the time he needed. Harmony peered at him as he emerged from the bathroom drying his hair with a towel. He took his time getting dressed, all the while conscious of Harmony watching him. He wondered if she knew what had happened the previous evening.

"It would be nice to have Rhys's gift," he mused aloud. Harmony meowed and left the room through a cat-door that Tim was sure hadn't been there a second before. In fact, as it swung shut, he saw the wall become solid once more. Marveling at the versatility of the room, he opened the door to see James standing there with his hand raised.

"Sorry!" James gasped as Tim stepped back hastily. "I was just knocking to let you know that we were going down for breakfast, if you wanted some."

"Sure. Thanks." They started down the hall, Tim lost in thought.

James broke his reverie. "Miss Balcombe has been showing me books on chemistry and stuff so Jamee and I can sort of understand what happens when we change one thing into another. It's strange to change things now. I'm starting to become aware of the atomic makeup of different objects and it's helping me develop control. Jamee says she feels it too. I want to get to the point where we could even be able to change something halfway or even change two things at once by using both of our brains. It won't matter who has control of the body! Miss Balcombe also introduced us to Sharon Cledume, who's been studying transformations." He was really excited. Tim laughed and grinned with him, sharing in the ebullience. Dana met them at the end of the hall, rubbing sleep from her eyes. Tim quickly began doing math again in his head, blocking her telepathy. He wanted to keep what had happened private. Dana glanced at him with curious, if bleary eyes, and gave both boys a hug.

"Where are the others?" she asked.

James answered her. "They're already downstairs. You guys are the sleepyheads. Did you stay up late last night or something?"

The square root of 169 is 13, Tim thought strongly. "I went to bed early, remember?" he reminded them. "Guess I slept too much."

"I just couldn't sleep. I was too excited," Dana said.

"I know what you mean," James agreed. "Miss Balcombe showed me..." They descended the stairs, James talking enthusiastically.

"Tim," Dana whispered under her breath, "I know you're trying to hide something. You did the same thing last night. I don't know what it is, but don't you think keeping secrets is kind of dangerous?" There was a twinge of hurt to the tone and not just a little bit of anger.

Tim almost stopped on the stairs, but caught himself and did his best to appear as though nothing was happening. He kept all thoughts of Xander deeply buried. "I'm not trying to keep secrets from you, Dana, but I'm still working some things out in my head. I just don't want to discuss it yet."

"How do I know that you aren't plotting against us?" she demanded. "You could be a spy pretending to be a Sign."

He sighed, quickly covering it with a nod at James, who glanced back in excitement. James continued his story and Tim muttered, "You felt my talent, remember? When I charmed your mother."

Dana responded, "Oh, yeah, I forgot. But you are keeping secrets, Tim, and that's not fair."

"Look, Dana, I'll let you know when I feel comfortable. I promise. In the meantime, stop prying."

"Fine," she grumbled.

"...and then I told Sharon about changing your sheets into ice cubes, Tim, and she said it was such a radical change and we shouldn't be able to do that yet. She brought out a bunch of sheets and made me do it again, but slowly this time so that I could feel the fabric change into water molecules. It was an incredible feeling. It's weird though. I could do the change from fabric to ice cubes, but Jamee can't. Sharon says it's because of our different energies. It's like my trouble with the soul connection. Jamee gets that with no problems at all. Maybe because she was actually born in the body. I don't have as much trouble with our talent though. I mean, transforming the sheets was easy for me. I could actually sense the fabric molecules shifting, changing one by one into water molecules that then froze together. I mean, I don't know enough about chemistry to really understand it yet, so I'm going to the library after breakfast to see if Mr. Pears can recommend more books."

"Sounds like a good plan," Tim said as they entered the dining hall and made their way to the usual table. The other Signs were sitting with Xander's parents, already eating.

"Nice of you to join us," Mrs. Conlyn greeted them, smiling warmly.

As they sat, her husband picked up the conversation. "So my vision was correct? It was a feminine Sign that was threatened."

"And taken," Rhys confirmed. "Virgo is a prisoner of Merel."

"You must go out at once to rescue him or her!" Mr. Conlyn declared.

"That's probably not a good idea," Sereny said from behind the new arrivals. She took a seat next to Tim. "We still don't know where Merel is and Xander can hardly travel there if an energy field surrounds the building. It would be next to impossible to attempt a rescue mission with no idea of where to go or what we're up against."

"Sereny has a point, John," Mrs. Conlyn said. "What's the next Sign to be obtained?" she asked Sereny.

"At the moment, none of them."

Eight pairs of eyes stared at her. "I have cast the dice, read the cards, everything I could think of, but nothing related to the Signs came up. It's possible that we're supposed to concentrate on something more important at this point."

"What could be more important than getting all of the Signs together?" Dana asked. No one had an answer to that.

Finally, Mrs. Conlyn said, "I suppose the best thing for all of us to do is to continue trying to learn all that we can. I will see if the astrology wing has come up with anything new." They all agreed to that plan. More food arrived for those who'd just joined the table.

"So, Cole, what do you think of our facilities so far?" Mr. Conlyn asked, pride evident in his voice.

"I confess I'm quite impressed," the Aquarius answered. "I had not known such a place existed. If I had, I assure you that I would have been here in a heartbeat, asking for information on the numerous water deities, especially the Mer-Child, Niole. I explored the library briefly last evening and I see there is an entire section devoted to the study of deities, ancient and modern."

"As well as an extensive selection on the Elements themselves," Xander's father agreed. "We obtained most of our newest books regarding the deities from Anderson Baker. He was a great believer in the Patrons and most of the books concerning them lie within his libraries. There are even some rumors that he was able to contact the Patrons before he died."

The Aquarius nodded. "Yes, Miss Balcombe mentioned Mr. Baker. I had heard of him in passing from one of my colleagues. She had come across a text that was translated from one of his books regarding the Mer-Child. I researched what I could about him, but found very little. It was rumored that his libraries were destroyed when he died. Miss Balcombe assures me, however, that this is a fabrication of the masses."

"Mr. Pears told us the same thing," Xander said.

Sereny chimed in, "The libraries were not destroyed at all. They were preserved, sealed until the time came when they were needed again. A spell was woven about them that encouraged man to overlook them when he came across them. Over time, the libraries, and, unfortunately, Anderson Baker were forgotten. We do not know much about him beyond his love of books and his libraries, and even that is not a great deal of information. He was reputed to be kind, but increasingly reclusive as his years wore on."

"Is there any way to break the spell? The information contained in those books could give us the advantage that we desire," Cole suggested.

"The key lies in finding the libraries," Sereny informed him.

"Speaking of libraries," James interrupted, "I've wanted to get in some research before I go talk to Professor Galten. She said she might have a potion that would help me. Excuse me." Sereny nodded again. He rose with barely controlled eagerness and quickly left the hall.

The mention of potions reminded Tim of his last lesson and he blanched, glancing at Xander, but Xander was talking quietly with his mother. However, Dana caught the look and raised an eyebrow. Tim slammed mental shields into place and saw frustration flare in her eyes, but she said nothing.

He cleared his throat. "You know, I think I'll take a walk." Dana's expression soured further, but no one protested as he stood.

Sereny also rose. "I think I'll join you," she said.

"Oh, I don't need a guide. I know my way around The Gathering," Tim said quickly.

"I'm sure you do," she agreed smoothly. "I haven't really had a chance to talk to you since you arrived, and I thought this might be a good opportunity."

Tim hesitated a moment. Then, "Okay. Sure."

They exited the dining hall together and headed towards the stairs. A few people looked up as they passed, but most ignored them, continuing about their own business. They started climbing and Sereny said, "You don't have to hide this from her, you know."

Tim flushed. "I'll talk to Dana when I'm ready to talk."

"What's going on between you and Xander is your business." He turned, surprised and annoyed. "It doesn't take psychic abilities to see what's going on. Besides,

Professor Galten told me. It's good that it happened. He's been repressing Danny for a long time."

"What's that got to do with Dana?" He knew he was acting like a brat, but he couldn't help it.

"Dana can sense that you're holding out on her. The Signs have to trust each other and right now, she thinks that you don't trust her."

"But I do!" he protested vehemently. "It has nothing to do with trusting her or not! I just–" He stopped, unsure of whether he wanted to reveal anything. Sereny walked on without saying anything. He sighed. "It's just that since I met you, everything has been about the Signs and the Star Child and what's the next thing to be done and planning and research and everything. What's going on between me and Alex–" He halted, and Sereny smiled at the name. "I mean, Xander, has nothing to do with the Signs or The Gathering or any kind of mission. I just wanted to have something to myself for a little while. Besides, nothing's definite. It's not like we're getting married or something."

Sereny exclaimed, "Trines and quincunxes! Nothing 'definite', you say. Why, it couldn't be more definite if it were written in the stars. Tim, after Danny's death, Xander was a shadow of his former self. He barely spoke, rarely smiled, and never laughed. He's gotten better over the years, but the past few days have seen a radical change in him. Ever since he met you, he's almost been the same Xander he was before the murder. There's no doubt in anyone's mind why he's regaining his old personality."

"Everyone knows? But, I never meant to...I mean...and his parents must think..." Tim floundered helplessly.

"His parents have noticed the change, but they wouldn't dare say anything for fear of upsetting either of you. Of course, they're thrilled to see him come back into himself. It almost destroyed them to see him after the murder. Tim, you are bringing their son back to them. They wouldn't jeopardize that for all the world. Besides, they're fond of you. They've mentioned how highly they think of you."

"Great, so everyone's talking about me," he murmured, taking note of where they were. They stood in an enormous hallway filled with mirrors of all shapes and sizes.

"Don't be an ass," Sereny reprimanded him. "There are far more important matters for The Gathering to discuss. The reason I'm bringing this up to you is to point out that your desire to have something private is hurting Dana. I understand you wanting something to yourself, but allowing Dana to know about it doesn't make it any less yours. You might as well get used to people knowing about your private affairs. There isn't much that happens in The Gathering that isn't known by at least ten people within minutes of the occurrence. No one would dream of interfering though. Your business is still your business, Tim."

"Yeah, thanks."

Sereny stared him in the eyes. "Tim, you aren't doing yourself or anyone else a favor by keeping this to yourself. Xander understands the importance of having no secrets between the Signs."

"You've talked to him?"

"His parents have. Promise me that you'll at least think about what we've talked about."

Tim sighed. "I promise. I don't like it, but I promise."

"Good."

"Where are we?" Tim asked.

"The Hall of Mirrors," Sereny told him. "I sometimes come here to think and most people avoid it because of the noise."

Tim listened, but no sound reached his ears. "I don't hear anything."

"That's because you are listening with your ears," Sereny told him. "Listen with your mind."

He closed his eyes again and tried to clear his thoughts. As he concentrated, he began to get the hint of a whisper. And then another voice broke through.

Tim! The shout came loud and clear.

Dana?

Come to the library!

Why? What's going on?! But she was gone. Tim turned. "Sereny–"

"I heard. Let's move!" Suiting action to word, Sereny dashed back down the hallway. Tim was swift to follow. As they hurried through the maze of hallways, Tim's mind buzzed with curiosity. What was happening? Perhaps it was a way to rescue the Virgo. Taking the last three steps in one bound, Tim suddenly found himself in a sea of people, chatting animatedly. He pushed his way through the crowd, ignoring their attempts to engage him in conversation. Finally, he reached the library door and almost ran headfirst into Xander's father.

"Oomph! Sorry, Mr. Conlyn!"

"Tim, get inside. The others are there."

"What's going on?" Ignoring him, Mr. Conlyn turned to the crowd.

"Ladies and gentlemen!" Slowly, the crowd began to quiet down. When the room was almost silent, he began again. "Ladies and gentlemen, as many of you already know, an incredible discovery has been made. We've found the key to the Baker libraries." There were many exclamations of surprise. Tim didn't bother to hear the rest of the speech. He spun around and raced through the stacks, calling to Dana with his thoughts. He came upon her and most of the Signs in Middle Eastern Literature crouched around a fairly ordinary-looking book lying on the ground. Donne was pawing at it. Another group, including Mr. Pears, Mrs. Conlyn, Professor Galten, and Chris, was standing just beyond the group on the floor, speaking in low tones. Sereny joined them as Tim knelt next to Dana.

"Hi," she said curtly.

"What the hell is going on?"

"Donne found Anderson Baker's book," Rhys told him.

"Donne?!"

"Well, technically, James found it," Cole pointed out.

James looked slightly embarrassed at the attention. "I didn't mean to. I came into the library to see what I could find on chemistry and molecular structures, remember?" Tim nodded. "Donne followed me, but I didn't know that. We were in the science section and I was looking up stuff, taking different books out and skimming through them to see if they had the kind of information I wanted. Well, one of the books had a section on ancient Egypt and the study of chemistry from back then. I thought it would be a good idea if I started with where chemistry began; that way, I could understand some of the more basic concepts before working up to the harder stuff. I asked Mr. Pears what section to go to and he said to come here." The other group had ceased their conversation and were listening to James. Mr. Pears nodded. "So I'm hunting through the shelves, seeing if I can find anything that has to do with chem., when Donne here starts meowing and pawing at this book on the bottom shelf. I was trying to shut him up when Rhys came running in, with Mr. Pears chasing her."

"Well, it is hardly proper for the young lady to be dashing about through the stacks," the librarian muttered somewhat defensively.

"She ran in, grabbed the book and laid it on the floor, telling me not to touch it until everyone else got here," James continued.

"I didn't want him to do anything in case there was a counterspell or something," Rhys explained. "So I yelled for Dana–"

"You yelled for Dana?" Tim asked, confused.

"Mentally," Rhys explained.

Dana jumped in, excited. "Scared me outta my mind!" She paused. "No pun! I was halfway down the stairs before she finished explaining what was going on. That's when I screamed for the rest of you." She paused and flushed with pleasure. "First time I've ever sent sound."

"I arrived just a few minutes after Dana," Cole said, "and I still don't understand what's going on."

"Neither do I!" Tim agreed fervently. "I mean, I heard the first part of Mr. Conlyn's announcement about the discovery..."

"...and now we're going to find out exactly what that discovery is," Mr. Conlyn finished from behind Tim. Tim turned sharply to see Xander and his father standing there. Xander smiled shyly and sat down next to him.

A fuzzy body leapt over Xander, landing in Tim's lap. Tim laughed and hugged Harmony against him. Glancing back, he saw that the Brownings were keeping watch at each end of the aisle. No one would interrupt this meeting.

"The entire Gathering is aware of the situation, of course," Mr. Conlyn said with a smile. "However, I've managed to persuade them to give the Signs some privacy for this important moment. There will be a full report of what is learned here to those parties that need informing. Beyond that, the information found here is to stay confidential." He looked at each of them. "Yes?" They all nodded, including the cats. "Now," he said, rubbing his hands together with barely suppressed eagerness, "what exactly is it that we have discovered?"

"The book is written in Feline," Rhys told them. An astonished silence greeted her announcement.

"It appears to be written in English, Rhys," Jamee said, finally, pointing to the book's title: *Cat Gods and Goddesses of Ancient Egypt.*

Rhys smiled. "Well, Mr. Baker has quite a sense of humor," she noted wryly. "The book is actually written in ancient hieroglyphics." She opened the book to reveal unfathomable symbols covering the pages.

"But hieroglyphics have been interpreted," Chris protested.

"Yes, but in this case, they have not been interpreted correctly," Rhys told him. "In olden times, the Egyptians worshipped the cat. They created a language of pictures based upon communication with the feline world. Modern man came to understand the pictures within the contexts of their own languages and as such, the hieroglyphic took on an omnilingual quality. However, the feline world knew better. They can recognize these symbols for their true meanings." She glanced fondly at Donne. "As soon as Donne saw the writing, he called out to the others and to me. He was sure that this was what we had been searching for."

"Wait, I don't get it," interrupted Xander. "This book is written in a language that humans don't understand, but we can read it anyway?"

"The book is written in a language that people misinterpret," Rhys explained.

Mr. Conlyn was jubilant. "Now we can disenchant the book so that anyone can read it!"

His wife took his arm gently, but firmly. "Dear, we don't have to disenchant the book. We have an interpreter." She indicated Rhys, who blushed.

"Not really," she demurred. "Donne and the other cats are the true interpreters. I just happen to be the conduit, it seems."

"Think, John," the professor chimed in, "You were just saying how precious this information is and then swore us all to secrecy. I agree that there are some outside of this group that would need the knowledge contained in that book, but let's not rush off to tell them anything until we know what it is. With our own interpreters, we can preserve the information found here."

Mr. Conlyn looked abashed. "Of course, you're right. I just got a little excited."

"We know, dear." His wife moved her hand from his arm down to entwine his fingers with her own. Tim watched the intimate gesture with a twinge of jealousy. *Not now,* he told himself. Out loud he said, "So, what are we waiting for?"

"Yeah, let's find out what Mr. Baker has to say," Dana said.

"How did you want to do this?" Cole asked.

Chris spoke up. "I have a suggestion, if no one minds." All turned to him. He cleared his throat. "Well, Dana and I have been working on simultaneous reception and projection of thoughts. I feel that this might be a good exercise in that. Between the two of us, we should be able to cover everyone in this room." Dana looked surprised and opened her mouth. "No arguments, Dana. Your training was cut short today because of this."

"So I get extra lesson time?" she complained, but her heart wasn't in it, and Chris knew that.

"You'll do just fine."

"Excuse me," Rhys interrupted. "What do I have to do?"

"Just listen to Donne with your own mind. Dana and I will pick up the thoughts and transmit them to the others so that it will seem as though we are all hearing Donne. Dana will transmit for the Signs and I will take the rest of you."

"It's worth a try," Mr. Conlyn said.

Rhys stroked the cat in her lap. "Very well. Get comfortable, everyone. This should be an interesting experience. Donne, are you ready?"

The feline meowed once and long. *Naturally.* Tim heard the voice in his mind. It sounded somewhat altered from the Donne he had heard while they were traveling and he realized that the tone was being colored by Dana's mind. *Maybe that's something that's worked out with more practice,* he thought to himself.

Yes, it takes some time before one can transmit in an objective way, Chris answered him. Tim was embarrassed into mental silence. Meanwhile, Donne was speaking.

You humans do take forever to make a decision, don't you? Donne sounded both irritated and amused. *Ah, well. I suppose this is a cumbersome way to get something done, but so be it. Rhys, I must ask you to turn the pages.*

How will I know when we come to the end of the page? That was Rhys.

What about a musical chime as the signal for a page turn? James joked.

I'm not a musical instrument, Donne reprimanded him.

Sorry, Donne. Joke. When I was younger, there were these books on tape–

No one cares, his twin broke in, surprising them all. *I want to know about Anderson Baker.*

Yes, let's begin, Donne agreed. *When we reach the end of the page, I will simply say "page".*

Rhys opened the book, and Donne began to read. After a while, Tim no longer noticed Donne's cues for a page turn.

Chapter 19

I was fortunate to be born into a wealthy family. I was more fortunate that my parents never made it obvious that they were rich. They did their utmost to see that I was raised without special treatment. No butlers and nannies for me. I went to public school with all the other children and no mention of money was ever made in my presence. All in all, we lived a fairly normal life.

"Is all of this really necessary?" Xander asked. Several people hushed him.

It is, Sagittarius. Both the present and future are affected by the past. If you are to prepare for what is to come, you will need to know what has gone before.

"How did he do that?" James wondered aloud.

Visions.

"He had visions too?" Tim asked, confused.

No, Libra. The spell that surrounds the book is one of retroactive vision. I can see you all there even as I write this. Now, where was I? Oh, yes, fairly normal life.

I was a well-behaved and studious child. My parents took an active interest in my education and taught me to read at a very early age. I moved quickly through the usual baby books and by the time I was five, I was reading at a high school reading level. My parents encouraged my reading habits, but they worried that I was becoming too introverted. I didn't have many friends, and I filled that void with books. Books held worlds I could only dream of; worlds I longed to explore. At first, I was strictly a western kind of boy. The old time fighting, complete with its classic icons of ruggedness and dainty beauties fascinated me. Soon after, I began to dive into science fiction and fantasy. Pistols and spurs were replaced by planets and spells. As I grew older, I found my niche in mysteries.

I spent countless hours in the school library – so much that the librarians knew me by name. I used to add up the clues in my head in an attempt to solve the mystery before it was revealed. I became quite good at it, actually, and would often discuss the mysteries with my parents and, on occasion, with the librarian on duty. Once, one of the librarians made a passing comment about my ability to remember all of the clues, and it was around this time that I started to realize I was a mnemonic, although I didn't know the word for it. I, of course, had thought everyone could remember the clues the way I did. I soon noticed that my memory was much more advanced than most people's, not just with mystery books, but in everyday life. Around this time, I developed a pointed interest in the human mind and its workings and began to study books of a more psychological nature. My teachers saw this and encouraged me to major in psychology in college. Yes, I realize that I'm skipping over most of my school years fairly quickly, but if I were to explain my whole history in detail, we'd be here all night.

I took the advice of my teachers and enrolled in college as a psychology major. I was an unusual student, however. I wanted to study the effect of the environment and the Elements upon the human mind. I wondered whether my perfect memory was something that was ingrained inside of me, or whether it had been bestowed by some other power. I hesitate to use the idea of a Supreme Being, but I suppose I was delving into the nature of something like that. I began to study the earth and heavens, as well as more occultish studies, attempting to divine a reason for such a specific talent.

It was in my second year that I met Esme. I ran into her in the library – no surprise there. We were both in the New Age section; she was looking for a book on Wicca, while I was searching for a Neo-Pagan text. She had straight, straw-colored hair that fell to the small of her back, light brown eyes, an almost white complexion with pale pink lips. She wore a peasant-type shirt with shorts and a pair of shabby sneakers. Right from the start, I thought she looked beautiful and I told her so.

"Beautiful?" She smirked. "Do you always start conversations this way?"

"Well, no," I admitted. "I don't usually start conversations at all, but I wanted to start one with you, so I thought it was a good idea to begin by saying what was on my mind." As you can see, I wasn't socially graceful.

"Hmmm. I see," she replied, continuing to scour the shelf. This wasn't going well. I decided to start over.

"Hi," I said brightly, holding out my hand. "I'm Anderson."

She looked at me for an uncomfortably long moment. Then, sighing resignedly, she quickly shook my hand. "Esmerelda," she introduced herself, and returned to the shelf.

"What year are you?" I asked.

"Sophomore," came the perfunctory reply. "Women's Studies."

"I'm studying Psychology. How come I haven't seen you before?"

"I transferred this year." She snatched a book from the shelf and examined it, seeming satisfied with the choice.

"Oh." I paused to regroup. "Well, if you're doing Women's Studies, why are you in the New Age section?"

She faced me and said, "I'm currently doing a report on the position of women within various societies. Wiccan society is the next one."

"Funny, you don't look like a witch," I joked.

Her mouth tightened and something flashed in her eyes, but otherwise, her voice was quiet and steady. "I suppose not." She started off down the aisle, book in hand.

I hurried to catch up. "Hey, listen. Do you wanna get a cup of coffee or something sometime?"

She kept moving towards a table and picked up a large canvas bag stuffed to the hilt with books and papers and other assorted items. "No, I don't think so."

I grabbed her arm and she whirled around, quick as an adder. Immediately, I dropped my hold. "Look, I'm sorry if I said something to upset you, but I'm really not so bad, once you get to know me. Just one cup of coffee and then you can ignore me if you like."

"Why would I possibly want to go out with someone who starts a conversation by telling me I'm beautiful, which is even too crappy to be a line, and then compares me to a witch?"

I spoke without even thinking. "Because the conversation can only go up from here."

The corners of her lips twitched. "I'm not so sure of that."

"Well, if it does get worse, at least it won't be boring, I can tell you that," I promised.

She stared at me again and finally shook her head. "Okay. One cup of coffee, Andy."

"Um, it's Anderson."

"I like Andy." And that more or less ended that.

* * * * * * * * * * *

"So, Andy, what where you doing in the New Age section? Kind've an odd place for a Psychology major," Esmerelda noted through a mouthful of fries. She said that if we were going to go out, we might as well go whole-hog (her term, not mine) and get a meal instead of just coffee. So, here we were at the local diner.

"I was trying to find information on the Elements," I answered.

"The Elements? What do they have to do with the mind? Isn't psychology a study of the way that the mind works?"

"Yes, but since we don't completely understand how the mind works, I'm wondering if there are outside influences that affect the mind, causing certain reactions within that we could never get otherwise."

She looked curious. "What kind of influences?"

"Well, outside forces. The Elements, for one. Does our environment affect the way we think?" I took a sip of my soda.

"What about, like, beings? Like, deities and stuff?"

I hesitated. This was crossing into dangerous ground for me. "I haven't really explored the idea of God or gods, actually."

"So you don't believe in a higher power?"

I backpedaled. "I didn't say that. I'm just exploring my options and seeing what's out there. I believe that there's more to this world than what we see and it has an effect on our minds. After all, we only use like, what- ten percent of our brains?"

Esme snorted. "Probably less."

"The point is that we don't use our entire brain. Who's to say that we're experiencing all that this world has to offer? My supposition is that we aren't and that leads me to believe that there are forces out there that affect us without our being aware of it. Whether that's a deity or nature or something that we haven't even explored yet, I think there's more out there." I began to warm to my subject. "I'm starting with the Elements. I think the ancient ideas of Earth, Air, Fire and Water might have something to do with how we behave."

"And Ether."

"Huh?"

"Stars are made of Ether. There are actually five Elements, but the fifth usually goes unnamed," Esme pointed out. "Sometimes it's called Ether or Spirit or Void or any other number of titles, but there is a fifth Element. It's elusive, though and most of the time only the other four are used." She seemed put out by this last statement.

"How do you know about this?"

"I told you, I've been studying women throughout different cultures and some of my research has led me into the roles of women in different religions. Wicca explores this idea of the fifth Element." She shoved another handful of fries into her mouth.

I was excited. "I wonder if that fifth Element is a main instigator in the abilities of different people!"

"What kind of abilities?" Esme wanted to know.

"You know, special abilities," I replied evasively. Things were starting to go well and I didn't want her to know about my memory and start to treat me like a science

project as others had in the past. "Some people have psychic abilities and stuff like that."

She seemed almost disappointed. "Oh." Then she thought of something else. "So you believe in psychic abilities."

I thought about it for a moment. "Yes, I guess I do."

She pushed further. "And you're open to the possibility that there's more out there?"

I was taken aback by her insistence. "Well, yes. Aren't you?"

"Of course. You just didn't strike me as the type of person who would believe that though."

I paused in the act of eating a nugget. "What type of person am I?"

"Well, you're very blunt. And very practical. And, if you don't mind my saying so, you're not the most socially graceful of people." She eyed me speculatively. "But I guess there's more to you than I thought."

I smiled, albeit a little uncertainly. "And I'm not boring," I joked.

"No," she agreed. "You're not boring. I'd like to know more about you, Andy Baker. Why don't we go out again this Friday night?"

Of course, I said yes. After that, Esme and I began spending a lot of time together. I had never been on a date so I didn't know what was expected of me. I didn't really have any friends, so there wasn't anyone who could tell me how to behave on one. Esme was content to take the lead in most of what we did, and she didn't seem in a rush to define us, so I never knew if she considered us dating or not. We mostly just hung out a lot and talked. There was usually food involved and occasionally a movie or two. I knew Esme had a few other friends, but I never met them. It was always just us.

We had a lot of conversations about the nature of reality and the human mind. We also talked about the role of women and the differences between the genders. Sometimes, we would laugh about different theories one of us would come up with. Other times, we would get into heated fights and I wouldn't know why.

A year passed this way and I had never been happier. I still stuck to my books, but they weren't an escape anymore. They were pure enjoyment. My room filled quickly and my parents began buying me bookshelves on a regular basis. I made quite a few treks to my parents' house with books in tow in order to make space in my room for more.

I continued my studies of the Elements, coming across numerous theories for special abilities like mine. In early summer, I received a nondescript package with no return address. Suspicious, I opened it with careful rips. A book fell out upon the desk with a muted bang. It had no title; just a picture of the four Elements. Breathlessly excited, I flipped open the book and began reading. The book delved into the nature of the Patrons and their Elemental powers. I was still avidly reading *two hours later when Esme walked in. She took one look at me and gave me up as a lost cause. Instead, she moved to the desk and picked up the package wrapping. When she turned it over to examine it, a piece of paper fell out. I watched as she read the handwritten words, her eyes widening.*

"What is it?" I asked.

"It's a poem," she responded, handing it over to me.

I read the words that prophesized the Star Child's arrival. "What does that mean? Does that have something to do with this?" I held up the book, explaining about the Patrons.

"It looks like someone is trying to help you with your thesis," she said.

"More than that," I said. "I think someone wants me to get involved with this child."

"Be careful, Andy. You don't know where this is from."

"Hey, I've got you to protect me, right?"

Esme looked at me and said, "Andy, have you ever had a girlfriend?"

The question caught me off-guard. "No," I admitted.

She moved closer to me on the sofa. "Have you ever wanted one?"

"In a general sense, yes," I said.

And closer. "Never a specific person?"

I swallowed. "Well, I – it's never really been an option. Girls don't usually go for guys like me." I laughed self-consciously.

And closer. "But what do 'guys like you' go for?"

"I guess we go for what most guys go for." I was being evasive and I knew it.

She knew it too. "You said when we first met that you thought I was beautiful. Do you still think so?"

"Yes."

"I think you're beautiful too, Andy." And she kissed me. It was my first kiss and after that, I never wanted to kiss anyone else. I realized then that I had fallen in love with Esme. I felt stupid for not realizing it earlier, and from her actions, it appeared that she loved me back. There were a lot of firsts that night and I'm thankful for my perfect memory that I can recall that night so vividly.

Oh! said Jamee and Dana together. The rest of them smiled mentally.

It was not unnoticed on campus that Esme and I were an item. On rare occasions, we went out with a few friends of hers, who quickly accepted me into the group. I didn't say much and I laughed at the appropriate times, but I liked being alone with Esme more. Social occasions were still foreign ground. We ended up getting an apartment together in our senior year. I thought this would have been bliss, but I saw her even less than I had when we lived in separate places. She told me it was because of her thesis and she needed time to work on it. When she was home, she was often irritable and exhausted and her diet changed completely. She was constantly hungry and ate throughout the day. The only moments where it was like old times was when we were discussing my thesis.

In late February, I received another anonymous letter. With her eagerly looking over my shoulder, I ripped open the letter and stared.

"What is this written in?"

"They are ancient runes, often used in Norse mythology," she answered.

"What do they say?" I asked her.

She smiled. "I never said I could read them, only that I recognize what they are. Think one of your books might have information on this?"

I shrugged. "If not, I can always get another one."

"Just what you need, another book." She rolled her eyes, took my arm and steered me in the direction of the library. This was the old Esme and I was glad to have her back. I went directly to the familiar New Age section. "Look at all of these alphabets. Norse runes, Ogham, Arabic, Hebrew, Egyptian hieroglyphics – these could all be very useful to learn."

"Don't get distracted," she admonished me, grabbing the book on runes. She sat down in the middle of the aisle and opened the book on her lap. I sat next to her and looked at the paper. Painstakingly, we matched up the symbols. It read:

The memory of the mystery is the key to the mystery of the memory.

"What the–?" Esme was clearly confused. "What does that mean?"

I hesitated. I had just gotten Esme back and now I was going to lose her again. "I have a perfect memory. I can remember anything I want to. It's one of the reasons that I been studying the effects of the environment on the brain. I want to know where this talent comes from." I looked at her sadly.

"Oh. That's different." She looked thoughtful.

I wasn't prepared for this reaction. "'That's different'? That's all you have to say about it?"

"Well, it's not something I'm used to and I know a lot of different talents. After all, I'm a witch." She stood up and put the book back. As I sat there gaping at her, she added, "Well, you're the one who knows where we're going, Memory-Boy. Let's go." She started off down the aisle.

I recalled our first meeting. Funny, you don't look like a witch. Things suddenly fell into place. Her strange knowledge of various occultish things. Her odd opinions on the roles of women in society and their power, especially in religions. I suddenly understood. She was just like me, keeping her identity hidden lest people treat her differently. Protecting herself from a society that doesn't accept the unusual. I hurried after her. Catching up, I turned her face and kissed her deeply. When the kiss broke, I said, "We're heading back to school."

"We're in school, dummy," she said, putting her hand in mine. We walked out of the library into the bright sunshine. I had to squint to find my car.

"Not this school," I corrected her. *"My old school. My grade school. That was where I first learned I had a special memory. I remember I was in the library and I had just finished a mystery.* Mike Harber and the Case of the Missing Notebook. *The librarian came up to me and asked me what I thought of it. I told her that it was good, but I had the ending figured out by the middle. She laughed and asked me how. When I proceeded to list all of the clues and the pages they were on, she looked at me strangely. 'How do you remember all of that?', she asked me. 'Well, it's easy,' I told her. 'Don't you?' I can still remember that look. Half-awe and half-fear. It was then that I began to suspect that I was different."* I held the door open for Esme, then climbed into the driver's seat and started the car.

"I don't have a perfect memory, but I know that look," she said softly as we headed down the road.

"She brought over another woman. Her name was Joan Selding, and she asked me a bunch of questions about different books. Then she started asking questions about my memory in general. I felt like a science experiment. I never saw her again and the librarian avoided me whenever I was in the library."

For awhile, neither of us said anything, lost in our memories. The sky was a clear, crisp blue and the trees were just beginning to bud. Splashes of brown and green flew by as we headed for my hometown. I had been there many times, of course, but this time, there was a sense of excitement and apprehension that had never been there before. The old town was suddenly new and I didn't know what to expect. Esme was humming softly, but I couldn't make out the tune. I glanced over at my companion, thinking about her announcement earlier. I wondered what kind of things she could do. I had never considered the possibility that there were real witches in the world, but there was no reason why not. It did make a perverse kind of sense, after all. I couldn't be the only one in the world with special abilities. I wanted to ask her about it, but her expression didn't invite conversation. So I kept the silence.

As we passed the town borders, my heart jumped. Familiar sights from my childhood whizzed by. Post office. Playground. Shopping mall. I turned down an old road which led to a large, gray building. On a weekday afternoon, the school would be filled with screaming, laughing children running all over. On this Saturday, however, there were just the few deserted cars of teachers who had come in to do some work in preparation for the next school week. I pulled into an empty parking space and we got out of the car. The school was much smaller than I remembered it. We walked up the marble steps to the front door and peered in. No one was about. I opened the door and we headed into the main hall.

"The library is this way," I said, my voice echoing. I led the way down a small hallway to the back of the school and through two metal doors. The library had been painted since I had last been there, but everything was still in the same place. The memory of the mystery, *the note said.* I moved among the stacks, looking for anything unusual. "Do you know what we're looking for?" I whispered.

"No," she whispered back.

"Maybe it's time for something witchy," I suggested.

She stiffened, and I thought I had insulted her, but what she said was, "There's someone else here. I'm going to go check."

"I'll come with you," I said.

"No. Do you think I can't handle myself? You keep looking. I'll be right back." She gave me a brief kiss and disappeared. I stood for a moment, relishing the kiss, then continued along the stacks. *The memory of the mystery...* I suddenly had an idea. I headed for the mysteries section and a quick search revealed Mike Harber and the Case of the Missing Notebook. *I took the book off the shelf and opened it. There, written on the inside cover was a note that said, "Solve the mystery."* I automatically started to flip to the page where the big revelation took place, but before I got there, a startling voice made my heart start to pound.

"Anderson." At the end of the aisle was an older woman, slightly bent from age, but I still recognized her.

"Joan? Joan Selding?"

She moved a little closer to me so that I could see her face. "Yes, Anderson. I knew you would come. But we haven't much time. You are in danger. I came to warn you."

My fingers were still flipping through the book as I involuntarily took a step towards her. "Danger? What kind of danger?" Without warning, Esme came running around the corner behind me and screamed. There was a loud crack and the stacks toppled over, crushing the older woman beneath their weight. I moved forward quickly, the book still in my hand, but there was a sudden pop and the scene before me vanished. I found myself in a large hall with Esme's screams still ringing in my ears. I looked around me, terrified anew. It was a large hall made of stone, with various doors leading to places unknown. A man stepped forward from the shadows and I instinctively raised the book over my head like a weapon. "Who are you?" I growled.

He looked at me sympathetically and said, "Don't be afraid." All of the pressures of my recent adventures overpowered me and I began to laugh hysterically.

"I'm sorry," I choked out, "but in light of recent events, that is a very funny thing to say." He took a step forward and I held the book even higher. "Don't come near me!" I warned. Though the book was not a formidable weapon, he stopped immediately.

In a calm voice, he said, "Please let me introduce myself. I am the librarian, Mr. Pears."

Everyone turned to Mr. Pears, who coughed, embarrassed. "I was the most logical choice to meet him. He had an interest in books. It only seems fitting that the person he would trust most easily would be a librarian and a mnemonic, like himself."

Exactly, Pears. And trust was vital at this stage.

"Where am I?" I asked him.

"Home," he answered. By now, my friends, you have probably guessed that I was in the hall directly outside of the very library you are in right now.

It took awhile, but eventually, I relaxed enough to let him lead me through the building, explaining all the while. I kept an eye out for weapons just in case. Though I was beginning to like Pears, I did not trust him. On top of that, I was concerned for Esme's safety, but Pears reassured me that with me removed from the situation, anyone else would be safe. Since it didn't appear that I would be returning to Esme's side without the assistance of my new acquaintances, I decided to learn as much as possible.

The Gathering fascinated me. It was a lot of information for my brain to take in at that time, but Pears knew that I would recall it perfectly and be able to sift through it later. We ended the tour back at the doors outside of the library.

"Would you like to see it?" he asked me. I nodded. He opened the large doors and I walked into the largest library I had seen to date. Even my own collection was second to this. Pears stayed at the entrance, gesturing for me to explore. I moved among the stacks, marveling at the new titles, running my hands lovingly over old favorites. I asked permission to take out a few and, given the affirmative, selected books on the history of The Gathering, the four Patrons, and a number of books on special abilities. Pears then led me to a bedroom where I gratefully sank into a chair. Before I would rest, however, I needed questions answered.

"What happened to Joan?" I asked. "Did she always know about me? How did you find me? How did I get here?"

"Joan was a remarkable member of The Gathering," Pears said, sadly, and I knew from that moment that Joan was dead. I didn't know how I felt about that. "She was a returner, which is a branch of telekinetics. Returners can attach a certain point in space to an object or a person. They can then take the object anywhere with them. At any time, they can send that object and anything in contact with it back to the aforementioned point. It is a useful talent when one has important information that might need to be removed from a dangerous situation at a moment's notice. Just as she did with you."

"She said I was in danger and then Esme screamed, the stacks fell, and I was here. Is she the one who sent me the book?"

Pears' expression was grave. "Let me make it clear to you that you are, indeed, in danger. Joan knew this. She informed us that you would be coming to see her soon and that she would bring you here. We have known of your existence since you first told her about your special ability. Our special ability," he corrected himself. "Our astrologers have looked at your chart and it appears that you are vital to our cause. We cannot have you out there without information and take the chance that you might fall under certain influences."

"Influences?"

"You must be careful with your gift. Does anyone else know about it?"

I thought about Esme. I still didn't know what The Gathering's goals were and I wanted to protect her in case there was malicious intent. Therefore, I made a foolish choice for love. "No," I said. "No one knows."

Pears seemed relieved. "Good. It must stay that way. Joan sent you back here to protect you and we will not take that sacrifice lightly. I believe that is all the information that you need right now. Please do not wander about. If you need anything, there's a phone for your use." He indicated the phone on the bedside table. Shutting the door, he added, "Welcome to The Gathering, Anderson Baker."

I looked around my room. It seemed a fairly normal bedroom with the usual furniture: bed, table, lamp, rug, chair, etc. I decided to learn all that I could about the place and, taking up the first book, I settled in to read. I had been reading for a few hours when I picked up a handwritten journal and found a passage that disturbed me deeply:

> From almost the moment that this world came into existence, a great danger entered it. It has hidden among the dominant life on Earth, adapting its form as each race died out. Now, it has taken human form, but it is not human. Its power grows and will continue to do so until it has the ability to affect the entire universe. This absorption of power creates an imbalance; it will destroy the universe and everything in it. We have discovered a prophecy that, come the millennium, a child will be born with enough power to counter this being. We must begin preparations for her birth. That means preparations for the guardians as well.

This was the first I had heard of Merel or the prophecy and I was naturally curious. I read through a few other books, hoping to find more on this elusive subject, but my eyes began to tire and I reluctantly closed my book and went to bed.

* * * * * * * * * * * *

Over the next few days, I met different members of The Gathering and I learned a great deal about different abilities. I asked about the Star Child at every chance I got. It was fascinating and the members really seemed to care about me, but I knew Esme would be worried about me and I constantly asked to be allowed to go back to school, begging a need for normalcy and routine. Along with numerous reminders of the importance of secrecy, I was given a phone number to call if I should ever need help and a birch leaf. The next thing I knew, I had appeared by a birch tree just outside of the campus with the leaf in my hand and a backpack filled with books that Pears had loaned me. I popped my ears and headed back towards my apartment.

Esme had vanished from the campus. I hunted all over for her. I spoke to the few friends of hers that I knew. I talked to her professors. She hadn't told anyone that she was leaving. I thought about The Gathering and considered calling them, but at that point, I wasn't completely sure that they hadn't taken her. My days were consumed with my hunt for Esme and research on the Star Child. Even during the night, I dreamt of an infant crying out to me. Fortunately, spring break fast approached, offering a brief reprieve from my hectic life. I was getting ready to head home for the week when I heard the front door open.

Esme appeared in the doorway like Hamlet's ghost. My glad shout stuck in my throat when I saw her face. "What did you do to me?" she whispered.

"What do you mean?"

She moved into the room. "What did you do to me?" she repeated.

I didn't know what she was talking about. "I– where have you been?"

"That's a question I could ask you too," she retorted. "But I don't care about that right now. What did you do to me?"

"Esme..." It was then that I noticed she was wearing skin tight clothing, something she hadn't done since we had moved in together. I had a sudden sinking feeling. "Esme, what did you do?"

"I took care of your mistake," she told me. "You put that thing inside of me."

I was dumbfounded. "You're pregnant?"

"No," she told me roughly. "I was pregnant. I'm not anymore. It was a parasite, feeding off my energy, taking my life. I couldn't let that happen." This wasn't my Esme. This was a monster.

"You...killed...our baby?" Fury built inside of me. "You were pregnant and you didn't tell me and now our baby is dead?!" I launched across the room, my hands extended towards her throat, and saw stars as I smashed into an invisible wall.

"I'm a witch, you idiot. You won't touch me ever again." As I raged helplessly against the invisible wall, she moved about the room, placing items into a suitcase. "I could feel him sucking away at me. That was your plan all along, wasn't it? To take

*away my power? You wanted it all for you and your son. Well, you won't get it now."
She laughed. "I am in control."*

With a contemptuous sneer, she swept out of the apartment and out of my life.

*The following years were a blur of helpless despair for me. Esme's cruel double
betrayal left me empty and I clung even more tightly to my books, searching harder
for an explanation of my curious talent. Using resources from The Gathering, I was
able to complete a comprehensive thesis, which resulted in an invitation from the
university to join the teaching staff. I found solace in my work, helping to impart
wisdom throughout the day, but at night, a child haunted my dreams. I would wake
up, sweating and guilt-ridden. Rationally, I knew there was no reason for my guilt,
but I couldn't stop the dreams.*

*I began to notice a strange phenomenon. My dream child was aging. I realized
that this could not be the Star Child as I had originally thought. This was the child I
had lost. Yet, even when he reached the age where most normal children would be
speaking, he remained silent and distant. Twelve years were spent this way, teaching
by day and watching my son grow by night. Yet, on an oddly humid night in March,
I heard my son's voice for the first time. It floated in his upper register, but crackled
with the hints of manhood.*

"Hi, Dad," he said.

*A name floated into my mind. I had never considered it before, but I
automatically knew my son's name at this very moment. "Hi, Kelsey."*

*He ran to me and hugged me. I held him tight. We just stood there. When we
broke apart, I could see tears on his face that mirrored my own. "What happened to
you?"*

"I'm Pisces, Dad. The Dreamwalker."

"She..." I had to fight a lump in my throat to say it. "She killed you."

*He shook his head. "She didn't. She tried, but my powers took over and I came
here. The Dreamworld. From here, I can go into anyone's dreams. I know about The
Gathering and their dreams told me a lot. I stay away from her dreams." He
wouldn't say Esme's name. "She'd come after me if she knew I was alive."*

*I simply reached out and hugged him again. I couldn't believe that my son was
alive. My life regained a sense of meaning and I began to take pleasure in living
again. Every night, Kelsey came to visit me and we would talk. I became a real
father, even if it was in the Dreamworld. Our father-son relationship had only one
odd component: we spent a great amount of time talking about the Star Child.
Once again, books became important for research. I searched for any information
that would help my son with his mission. I bought books in enormous quantities,
easily filling my library room and starting to fill the empty room of my lost child
with the surplus. Over those years, I took the money that I earned and gifts from my
parents and built four libraries.*

Those four libraries have become the stuff of legend. I reconnected with The Gathering, explaining my situation and asking for help. They were happy to offer books, historical artifacts, and anything that might contain the key to Merel's downfall. On several trips to The Gathering, I clandestinely removed several of these items and placed them among my own collection, making sure to keep them in separate libraries. On my travels, I also collected any artifacts of occult origin, placing them in the libraries. The libraries are key. They hold secrets that will help you protect the Star Child.

Due to the warnings from my son, I have secured protection for the libraries to ensure that only those whose intent is to protect the Star Child would be able to enter and partake of the knowledge and power to be found there. As time has passed, I've learned of attacks on the libraries, supposedly by a powerful force that did not gain entry. I am pleased to hear that the spells have worked, but worried that I know who was behind the attacks. The psychics at The Gathering have been dreaming of Esme, or so Kelsey tells me. He says that they've had visions of her attempting to gain more power. The latest rumor is that she has tried to contact the Patrons themselves and has been denied. I assume this is what prompted the attacks on the libraries. Since then, she has been reserving power, building up for another attack.

I decided it was vital that you, the Signs, would know that one among you is of the Dreamworld. In addition, you had to know your enemy. So I began this writing. I have asked The Gathering to spell the novel so that as I speak the story, it is automatically translated into paper.

News has reached me recently. News of various Gathering members that have been horrifically murdered. Kelsey has informed me that people fear I will be next and I hasten to finish this before it comes to pass. Esme– There was mental silence.

"Why did you stop?" Dana asked. Donne meowed.

"That is all there is," Rhys translated. She looked sad.

"You mean, there's nothing left to the story?" Jamee demanded. "How are we supposed to find the libraries? We can't find the Star Child without them!"

"I think–" began Tim. Everyone looked at him. "I think we have to talk to Kelsey. I'm pretty sure he's been in my dreams. Has he been in anyone else's?" He looked around. Nods from all the Signs.

"I just didn't know who he was," said Cole. "I couldn't figure out why this strange boy kept showing up. He tried to talk to me."

"And me," added Xander. "But he was having trouble."

"Perhaps you have to want him to really be there in order to hear him," Mr. Conlyn suggested.

"Or he's being blocked somehow," Professor Galten countered darkly.

"Yeah, by Esmerelda," Dana declared.

Jamee looked confused. "Esmerelda? Merel! Esmerelda is Merel!"

Cole nodded. "We're up against someone who has no problem killing..."

"...or torturing..." added Jamee.

"...and already has one of us captured..." Xander reminded them.

"...and another one is in Dreamworld," finished Tim.

"It's time to get the other Signs," Rhys said.

The others agreed.

Chapter 20

"I'm telling you that eight is what came up," Sereny said.

"But Merel has one of the Signs!" Mr. Conlyn protested. It hadn't been more than ten minutes since the reading was completed and the old argument had begun anew.

Mrs. Conlyn intervened. "John, we did say that the Earth Signs would be the hardest to recruit and that the Water Signs would probably be next on the list. Besides, there's one less Sign to collect now. Kelsey Baker has tried to make contact with the Signs. We just have to find a way to communicate with him."

"I think I can do it," Dana offered. "I mean, if I have mental powers, I should be able to control my dreams."

"No," rasped Professor Galten. "Telepathy does not cover dreams."

"What about us?" James asked. "Maybe if one of us is asleep while the other one is awake...no, that won't work. We can't communicate if one of us is asleep."

"But you can if there's a telepath involved," Chris volunteered.

Dana looked at him. "I thought you said–"

"You can't connect to a dream figure if you're asleep, Dana. But you might be able to connect to someone who is asleep and speak to Kelsey that way."

"Do we try it now?" Xander asked eagerly.

"Is anyone actually tired?" Cole countered. They all smiled ruefully and nodded their heads. There was too much excitement in the air for any of them to sleep.

Sereny spoke up. "I suggest that you go after Scorpio and try contacting Pisces later tonight."

Mr. Conlyn opened his mouth, but Professor Galten cut him off. "That is a good idea. John, why don't you go outside and do crowd control while the Signs go on their mission?" Her tone brooked no argument and Mr. Conlyn shut his mouth with a small pop. Mrs. Conlyn smiled surreptitiously at the Signs.

"I think you should be on your way," she said.

The group hurriedly got to their feet. Mrs. Conlyn was already leading her husband towards the doors of the library and Chris moved quickly to follow as the Brownings rejoined the group. Mr. Pears and Professor Galten had moved to the side and were having a quiet conversation of their own. The Signs were left alone with Sereny.

"The Scorpio is next," she said. "Eight was first, then twelve, then four. No matter what anyone says," she warned, "the Water Signs are your priority. We can and will rescue the Virgo, but we have to make sure that no more Signs are taken! Go quickly!" She turned and joined the librarian and professor in conversation. The Signs looked at each other.

"There's something I don't quite understand," Dana ventured. "I don't want to say it, but how can we be sure that Virgo's not dead? After all, they're trying to keep all the Signs from coming together, right?"

"I've been thinking about that," said James. "There must be more to it than just keeping the Signs apart. That could easily be done. Merel is holding a Sign hostage. There's something she's going to want in exchange. Now that we know where the libraries are–"

"We don't know where the libraries are," Dana pointed out.

"Well, we know of a way to find them," James stated.

Dana groaned. "We don't even know that for sure. We're going on a possibility. We need to get in touch with Kelsey."

"No," Rhys contradicted her. "We need to get Scorpio and Cancer. Sereny said to."

"And you do everything Sereny says?" Dana accused.

Tim cut in. "She's been right about everything else. She even predicted the order that we all came here and we have to trust someone!"

"Oh, that's so easy coming from you!" she shot back.

"Guys!" That was Xander. "We can't start bickering. We need to get moving and find another Sign. Since none of us are tired, that rules out Pisces." Dana looked mutinous. "For now," he amended. "This leaves the other Water Signs and the Earth Signs, and one is captured. Does anyone have any ideas about how to rescue the Virgo?" Blank looks. "Fine, Virgo and Pisces are both out. I know where to find Scorpio–"

"How?" James asked.

"Yes, I've been curious as to how you know where each Sign is," Cole said.

Xander was taken aback. "I– just do. I hadn't really thought about it, but your locations come to me in a dream...a dream! Kelsey!"

"But how does he know who is next?" Tim wondered.

Dana smacked her forehead, her fight with Tim forgotten for the moment. "The visions! Sereny's visions. If he's the Dreamwalker, he can enter anyone's dreams, day or night. The visions must be just enough of a dream for him to get in! He's been helping us all along."

"Or at least trying to," Tim added ruefully. "I haven't been paying enough attention."

"So, he's saying to go after Scorpio too, because I don't have the location for anyone else in my head," Xander said.

"Then let's go after Scorpio!" Rhys declared.

"Yeah, I can't stand around here talking anymore. It's making me nuts," Dana muttered under her breath.

Xander reached for her hand. "Alright, then. You know the drill." They all linked and the library vanished.

* * * * * * * * * * *

The group materialized in a graveyard at dusk. The dusty, orange light slipped over and around the gravestones, casting hazy shadows across the grounds. Tim shivered, despite the warm weather. The rest of the group was glancing around and no one appeared particularly happy about their surroundings. The cats, big and small, immediately went exploring, sniffing the air.

Xander turned to Cole. "Your turn." He began to explain about each Sign's obligation to find the next one. Tim tuned him out and sought out Dana. He found her off to the side, leaning against a tall gravestone with an angel on top.

"Hi."

"Hi." They stood for a few minutes in silence, watching the others help Cole concentrate.

"Look," Tim ventured, "I'm sorry that I shut you out. It's not that I don't trust you, but I'm just dealing with a lot here."

"And I'm not?" she returned.

"No, we all are. But–"

"But what, Tim? I grew up with parents who didn't even want to understand me, let alone trust me. I don't need another family like that. So whatever it is you're dealing with, get over it. I don't like being shut out." She walked away to rejoin the group. Tim sighed and, after a moment, followed her. As he arrived, he saw a deep blue aura flow into existence around Cole. One by one, the others started to glow as well and their colors came to manifest in his aura. Cole looked around him with wonderment and each Sign nodded, acknowledging the bond. He faced a few different directions and suddenly, a deep crimson streaked his aura. Rhys called to the cats as he began to walk, the rest in tow. They picked their way among the graves towards the exit, reaching it just as the sun kissed the horizon. Cole paused for a moment and then crossed the street, heading for an area where a herd of mobile homes lazed about in the grass. There was a worn path through the area that wound its way among the trailers. Cole led the way, passing various states of degeneration. Occasionally, voices could be heard from inside, some pleasant, some not. Cole walked on, seemingly oblivious to everything but Scorpio's call.

"Hey, folks!" a voice called from in front of them. "Where d'ya think you're goin'?" The voice belonged to a middle aged man. His flannel shirt hung open, displaying a large gut, yet one could see that there was still some muscle to him. He eyed the Signs with curious dislike.

"We are here to visit a friend," Cole answered calmly.

The man laughed harshly. "Don't seem like you folks would be friends with anyone around here. Awful nicely dressed for this area, ain't ya?" Greed showed plainly on his face.

"I promise you, we will not harm you. We only came to see a friend." Cole moved to walk on, but the man blocked his way.

"You ain't got no friends here." He spat on the ground. "We've had your kind here. Makin' offers. Trying to get us to move off our own land. Well, we ain't movin'. We like our place here."

Other people were starting to come out of their homes. There was hostility brewing in the air and Tim moved up next to Cole. He smiled, pouring all of his talent into it. "Please, sir." The man's eyes came to rest on him. "We're just coming to see a friend and then we'll be on our way."

The man blinked, feeling the weight of the Libran power on him, but, recovering, he shoved his face into Tim's. Tim struggled to hold onto his charming smile. "You ain't goin' to see nobody. And stop smiling at me. I ain't no goddamned fairy!" This was emphasized by a swing at Tim, who was pushed out of the way by Cole, but before anyone else could make a move, there was a loud crack and the man squealed in pain. He crumpled to the ground, clutching at his arm, where already, a thin line of blood was welling up. Tim got up from the ground and saw a girl around his own age.

She had black, greasy hair and pale, ivory skin. Her gray eyes were heavily laden with dark makeup and her lips were touched with a deep violet color. Her face was long, with a strong jaw and high cheekbones. A torn tank top and pair of jeans hung on her razor thin frame and she stood over six feet tall in a pair of combat boots. She wore long, black gloves on both hands, the left lightly holding onto a long whip. It was clear that this was the cause of the man's wound. She stood, feet slightly apart, appearing at ease, but with an air of alertness. In the diminishing light, she almost looked ethereal.

"What do ya want?" Her voice came out like a low growl and though not unfriendly, was definitely a warning.

"Please, miss," said Cole. "We would like to speak with you."

Her expression did not change. "Yeah? About what?"

Cole coughed delicately. "Would like to speak to you in private."

"I ain't bringin' no one in my home 'til you gimme a good reason why."

Tim caught the faint sound of Dana's voice in his mind, like a memory, and he knew she was talking to Cole. *She's curious about us*, she sent. *She has no friends and she wants them, but she would never admit that.* Meanwhile, Cole was speaking.

"My name is Cole. My friends and I thought we might be able to help you."

"I can take care of myself."

"We can certainly see that, miss, but we were also hoping you might help us." The girl did not move, but her eyes narrowed slightly.

She thinks you're going to offer her a job, Dana thought. *She's been hired as muscle for various jobs. Protects some big name people.*

"We've got a situation that needs taking care of and we could really use your services," said Cole. "We promise large rewards if we achieve success."

"Large rewards, huh? You don't really look like the dangerous type."

"We are more formidable than we might appear. May we discuss this in private? As you said, you can take care of yourself."

"Is that a threat?"

"No, miss. We mean you no harm. Search us if you like, but you seem to be pretty apt at your weapon there and you are welcome to hang onto it while you discuss with us."

A hint of a smirk showed on her lips. "Like you could take it from me. Fine. Boys, search 'em and then let 'em come." She turned and walked back to the trailer at the end of the road, disappearing behind it. A few local men grabbed the Signs and efficiently, though not gently, searched them for weaponry. The cats snarled when Rhys underwent the treatment, but she assured them of her safety. The men disappeared as quickly as they had come and the Signs walked down the road to the trailer.

"If Earth Signs are tougher than her, we're in trouble," Jamee muttered.

"Scorpio is known to be intense," Xander agreed.

They circled the mobile home and found the girl standing facing them, ready as before. "What do you want from me?" she asked.

Cole stepped forward again. "You have a gift. A special talent."

A shadow passed over the girl's face, but she recovered quickly. "So what?" she sneered. "What's it to you, anyway? I ain't usin' it for this kind of thing."

"No, you misunderstand. We do not need you for your usual services."

Her eyes and mouth narrowed to slits and the hand holding the whip began to move back and forth, dragging the whip along the ground. Tim was hypnotized by the serpentine movement of the whip and he wrenched his gaze away. "Whatcha gonna use me for then?"

Xander jostled his way to the front of the group. "Let me show you something. Don't blink and don't be scared." A muscle twinged in her jaw, but otherwise, she kept silent. Xander shimmered and disappeared, reappearing behind her. "We have abilities too," he said. She gasped and whirled around, snapping the whip, but Xander was already disappearing again. He reappeared where he started. "Please don't attack. We don't want to hurt you," he repeated. She whirled again, and though she did not crack the whip, it was raised.

"What the hell!? Who are you?"

"We are friends and we're in need of your help," Cole said. "You have an ability. We know this. We have abilities as well."

"Yeah? How do you know what I can do? Why should I even listen to you?"

"Your name is Rory," said Dana, moving up so the girl could see her. "But no one here knows that."

Rory's hand froze and all of the anger seemed to drain from her. "How do you know that?"

Dana stepped forward, moving slowly towards the girl, who retreated. "You've been living here for eight years. You keep your distance from everyone else and though they all look to you for protection and guidance, you shy away from the public eye. You only come out for extreme situations and since you've honed your skills in combat, people pay you to protect them. When people ask for you, they ask for Styx. You keep to yourself to protect your secret and you just figured out that I'm a mind reader." She stopped in front of Rory who had grown even paler with each sentence.

"You–" She looked at the rest of them. "You all can do stuff like them?" She indicated Dana and Xander. The rest of the group nodded. Cole stepped forward again.

"Miss, each of us is gifted with certain abilities and we are on a mission–"

"To save the world?" she asked sarcastically. "You got any idea how crazy you folks sound?"

"We do," Cole answered sincerely. "Nevertheless, you are a part of our little group. We haven't a lot of time. We need you to trust us."

"Why should I even begin to trust you?"

"Because," said Tim, stepping up, "with our talents, we could have easily attacked you and brought you in by force." Rory began to glare. "We didn't. We are asking you, respectfully, to join us. In return, we are offering protection and we are a group of friends who you don't have to hide from." He did not smile, but he couldn't help pouring his talent into his words.

Rory considered a moment. "What do I have to do? Tell me exactly and don't leave anythin' out." Cole stepped in and explained to the newcomer about the Signs and the Star Child. By the end of it, she was thoughtful. "Well, either you folks really are crazy, or you're really good storytellers, or you're serious and I'm in deeper trouble than I thought when I first saw ya. But I don't run from a fight, so if you can take me to this Gathering place, then I'm in."

"That won't be a problem," Xander assured her. "You ready to go now?"

"Let me just set some stuff in motion. I'll be right back." She headed around the trailer.

"Should we be keeping an eye on her?" Jamee asked.

"Don't worry," Dana said. "I'm tracking her mentally."

"Besides, we have a way of finding her again," Cole added. The Signs waited nervously for Rory to return. When she came around the trailer again and saw their faces, she laughed.

"Man, you all thought I'd run out on ya, huh? You must really want me to be a part of this."

"Where did you go?" Jamee asked.

"Had to make sure this group was taken care of," she answered. "Talked to Matt – that's the dumb ox that welcomed ya when ya came in – made sure he would look after the place. Before we go, though, ya mind showin' me the rest of your stuff? I mean, I saw him disappear and she can read minds, and I think you used something when you were talkin' to me," she said to Tim. Tim agreed and explained about the charm. "What can the rest of ya do?"

I have an idea, thought Dana, quickly explaining to the Signs.

Rhys asked the cats to go into the trailer and bring out seven articles of clothing. They did. Then Jamee became James and he changed the clothes into mugs and handed one to each. Cole called forth a spring of water from the ground, causing it to fountain up.

"Would you like to taste it? It's pure," he assured Rory. She held out her mug and filled it, then drank deeply.

"It's sweet!"

"The purest," he agreed. "Perhaps you wouldn't mind filling for the rest of us?" He held out his mug.

Rory's face clouded over. "I don't think that's a good idea," she said in a low voice.

"Why? What's wrong?" James asked.

Rory was silent. Finally, Dana spoke. "Her gift is Poison," she said. Cole hastily withdrew his mug. "Her body is constantly producing poison, deadly to anyone if it gets inside their body. Skin to skin contact is just as deadly, but takes longer."

"It didn't start 'til I was eight. I was makin' cookies with my ma for the first time. I was so proud of 'em and I said everyone had to try one. Ma said to wait until after dinner, but I couldn't wait. I took one to each person in the house. My folks were all dead within minutes." Her voice had a hollow quality to it.

Xander nodded sadly. "The Scorpion's sting," he said.

"I ran. I didn't know what to do, so I ran. I was on the streets for awhile. Found a group of kids on the street and we would steal whatever we wanted. Was out there six years. Tried to stay under radar, but I got older and men began to notice me. Had to run away a few times. This one guy came after me, grabbed me and held me down in an alley. Started to kiss me. He was dead a minute later." There was no expression on her face.

"I started to figure out what was goin' on. I knew it was comin' from me and I knew it could happen again, so I stole extra money and went to find a fightin' class. From some friends, I learned about this weapons master guy. Could fight really well, but didn't teach or nothin'. Was the only news I had to go on, so I showed up at the guy's place and told him I wanted to learn to fight. He laughed in my face. I camped outside his door for a week, waitin' 'til he would see me again. Finally, he came out, grabbed me by my shirt and shoved me inside. I told him I would do whatever he wanted if he would just teach me how to fight. He didn't say nothin', but handed me a quarterstaff, grabbed one himself, and started slappin' at me with it. I wasn't even fightin' him. I was just tryin' not to get hit. He kept at me for about fifteen minutes and then put his staff down.

"'Alright,' he said. 'You train with me during the night and you work as a maid for my wife during the day. I won't accept any lip and I won't let you slack off. You do what you're told and if anyone asks you, you're eighteen.' Well, I was all set to leave when he said, 'You agree and I'll make you the finest fighter you can be.' That stopped me right there 'cause I really wanted to learn to fight."

"Why, though?" James asked. "You have a natural weapon. And what about a gun?"

"I have a deadly weapon. That's true. But guns are for killin' and I'd had enough of killin'. I may take jobs to protect somebody or fight somebody, but I don't take no jobs where I gotta kill. I only wanted to know how to protect myself. What my teacher didn't know was that I was protectin' anybody who'd mess with me from gettin' too close." James nodded.

"So I studied with him. There was one point where he wanted to send me back to school, but I wasn't goin' to no school. I didn't remember what it was like and I told him I wasn't goin'. He put up a fight, but once I set my mind to somethin', that's that. His was a nice place to be. I liked learnin' to fight. I mastered the quarterstaff and a few other weapons, but I got my favorite right here." She held up the whip. "We been together for five years now. If I take the gloves off, I can send the poison down to the end so she kills instantly. But I can keep it back so she just hurts, like I did with Matt."

"But you're wearing gloves now. Won't that keep the poison from getting on the mugs?" Xander asked.

She shook her head. "I won't serve food or drink to no one again. I won't take that chance."

"How did you end up here?" Rhys asked sympathetically.

"Came home one night last year and found Teach and his wife dead on the ground. Guy'd been hit with a mace and the wife had been stabbed with a sword. I had my whip out, ready to go and when the attack came, I was ready. Thing is, it wasn't a person. Not at first. Seemed like some kind of thing with a long coat comin' off of it. I snapped my whip with the poison and the thing dropped like a stone. When I went over to look at it, though, it was a person. Some guy I'd never seen."

"Astranihl," said Rhys, and the rest nodded.

"What's an astranihl?"

"The enemy," Dana said. "We'll explain in a bit. How did you end up here?"

"I ran again. Took a few weapons, threw 'em into a bag and hit the road. Somehow, I found my way here and folks were kind enough to set me up with my own home. 'Specially since I protected 'em when the land officials came."

"Land officials?" Cole asked.

"Not really supposed to be camped here. Against the law somehow. I don't understand all that bullshit, but I know that the folks here are good people who are just tryin' to get by. So I stayed. Told 'em my name was Styx on account of a band I heard of once. Don't tell 'em much more than that. They don't need to know. 'Sides, none of 'em can get too close anyway." She indicated her gloves.

"We might be able to help you with that, but we really need your help," said James.

"Please," added Rhys.

"Yeah, well, not much else to do around here anyway. Guess I might as well go with you folks. How we gonna get there?"

Xander answered her. "That would be my department." He told her about the importance of contact.

"Who's gonna want to hold onto me?" she muttered, eyes downcast.

Cole took her gloved hand in his own. "Not a problem," he said. She looked up at him in surprise and though she did not smile, her face softened in gratitude. "Just make sure you hold on tight," he added. She nodded.

"Okay, everyone," Xander announced. "Let's go." They linked up and Xander whisked them into nothingness. The felines of their party took advantage of the group mind to say hello to Rory and the group could feel her delighted surprise. They landed together in the hallway outside of their rooms. Rory was given the room between Tim and Xander, across from Rhys.

"Meet at my room in about half an hour?" Rhys offered. The rest of them agreed and she turned to Rory. "If you need anything before that, just come across the hall," Rhys told her. The newest Sign thanked her and disappeared into her room. The rest of them split to go to their own rooms, but instead of doing the same, Tim followed Dana to hers.

"Dana, can we talk for a moment?"

She paused with her hand on the doorknob. Tim could feel her at the edges of his mind and he made no move to resist her. Finally, she opened the door and walked in. "Come in." He entered the room, found it much like his own, but surprisingly, with flowers all over. She noticed him looking. "I guess I miss them more than I expected to."

"I didn't realize. I'm sorry."

"I know," Dana said.

"Listen, Dana, the other day with Xander...I know we're all dealing with a lot, especially on short notice, and I already feel like you guys are my family. But Xander's different."

Dana sat down on the bed. "I know, Tim. I knew without even reading your mind. Anyone with half a brain can tell there's something between you two. I don't know all the details of what's going on and I don't really care. None of that is what upset me. I don't like being shut out. You deliberately kept something from me. If I didn't have my talent, I might not have felt it so keenly, but I did. We're going to have to trust each other. Maybe even with our lives. One of the Signs is already captured and though I don't even know Virgo, I care. I've seen what secrets can do to a group of people. I can't– I won't let it happen with us. You don't have to tell everyone everything, but if you don't tell someone something, we can't do anything to help you. Whatever you're going through, don't you think someone to talk to might help?"

Tim stood there, feeling frustrated and guilty. She was right. Sereny was right. His resistance broke and he told her what had happened. She made sympathetic noises every so often, but otherwise said nothing. By the end of it, he was sitting next to her. "So I don't really know where to go from here," he concluded.

"Sounds like he has some stuff to work out before he can truly figure out how you two are gonna work," she said. He nodded, disconsolate. "Don't worry. He'll come around. Otherwise, you're both nuts. Trust me, I know about head cases." She grinned and he had to laugh. The tension of the original discussion gone, she hugged him and went to the door. "Come on," she said. "We have a meeting. I promise to stay out of your head unless you ask for my help." She paused. "Well, I promise to try."

"I guess that's all I can ask," he conceded. "Thanks."

"No sweat." She flung the door open and they headed towards Rhys's room. Cole was just coming out of his room. Dana walked up to him. "So, what do you think of the new Sign? Kind of depressed, isn't she?"

"She has good reason to be," Cole answered quietly.

"Yeah, she's had a hard life," Tim said. They knocked on Rhys's door. "I wouldn't be the happiest person if I had grown up like that. I wish we could help."

"You folks carin' is more than enough," Rory said from across the hall. "I was startin' to get kinda lonely." Now that she had showered and changed into clean clothing, Tim couldn't help but notice that she was a beautiful girl. *A femme fatale*, he thought to himself, noting the whip at her side.

Rhys opened the door and welcomed them in. Her room was nothing like the others Tim had seen. There was a majestic, king-sized bed, populated by pillows of crimson and gold. A glittering Leo symbol surrounded by a plethora of cat images bedecked the ceiling. Behind the bed, there was a running stream and beyond that, there was a lush jungle where, if one looked closely, the Brownings could be seen amidst the greenery. All around the room were places to sit, each one plush and vibrantly colored. The purple carpeting was at least two inches thick and covered the entire floor. A roaring fire kept the chill of the stone walls away.

"Whoa. Nice room," Dana exclaimed.

Rhys moved to join Donne on the bed. Stretching out, she said, "I've always wanted luxury. I just couldn't afford it. A girl could get used to a place like this. Please, have a seat." She gestured to the furniture as a queen would address her court. Dana and Rory took a divan. Tim stretched out on a chaise lounge with Harmony while Cole lowered himself into a large, throne-like chair. The Signs waited for the remaining two, chatting about different experiences and answering Rory's questions. After a short time, Xander entered, talking animatedly with James. They sat together on a divan and turned to the rest.

"James and I were talking about your talent, Rory, and he has a pretty good idea of how to help you so that you don't have to wear gloves all the time." Rory looked at them, face expressionless, but hope shining in her eyes.

"Jamee can probably explain it better," James said, and then she was there.

"Now that's a neat trick," Rory said.

"It helped us escape from Merel," Jamee told her. "We were originally trapped, like the Virgo, until Xander and Tim showed up."

"We didn't really do much to help you," Tim demurred. "If anything, you helped us."

"Well, who helped who isn't the point here. Do you remember the bracelets that they made us wear?" Tim nodded. "Rory, they have bracelets that negate our abilities. I was thinking that we could make a pair of those bracelets, but we alter them so that they have a switch to turn on and off." She considered a moment.

"Well, I probably couldn't, but James could. Then you'd be able to turn your talent on when you needed it and you'd be okay the rest of the time."

"Those bracelets were dangerous," Tim argued. "You don't know what you're doing."

"What if we had a pair of the bracelets to study and work from?" Rhys asked.

Cole agreed. "We're going to have to rescue the Virgo. Do you think Merel would have used the bracelets?"

Xander nodded. "I'm almost sure of it. Merel isn't going to get involved unless she can have all the Signs and astranihl don't have enough imagination to change the process. The Virgo will almost definitely be in bracelets."

Rory was looking from one to another. "Control over my ability? Man, I never thought I could do that."

"This is all still hypothetical," Tim pointed out. "You might want to speak to Professor Galten about this. She has experience with potions and I'm sure that she has experience with poisons."

"I'm also going to talk to Sharon and see if she has any suggestions," Jamee told him.

"We still need the bracelets to work from and we're not going to get those until we can get Virgo," Rhys reminded them. She explained to Rory about the captured Sign. "Plus we still have to talk to Pisces if we can get in touch with him."

Rory's stomach growled and Dana laughed. "I think we might want to do that after dinner. Somebody's hungry."

"Actually, I'm kind of hungry too," Tim admitted.

"Let's head to the dining hall and welcome our new family member to her new home with a good meal," Rhys suggested. They all exited the room and traipsed downstairs, Xander leading the way and pointing out different parts of The Gathering to Rory and anyone else who was paying attention.

Dinner was a relatively quiet affair. The adults at the table greeted Rory as she sat down and asked a few preliminary questions about her. Jamee brought up the bracelet idea. Professor Galten said that there had been advances in the creation of objects with sympathetic properties, but there had been no significant progress to date. She offered to share her texts with Jamee and James and, with Sharon Cledume's help, study the principles behind it. Rory asked to join in the study session. As dinner ended, the conversation turned to what the next move should be. Sereny voted that they should conduct the dream experiment that evening to see if they could contact Kelsey. Mr. Conlyn was silent, but Mrs. Conlyn pointed out that they were probably too tired. Dana argued that that was the point.

"I mean that you're probably too tired as well, dear," Mrs. Conlyn said. "Remember, you're going to have to stay awake and we can't risk your health."

"I'm fine," Dana disagreed. "Besides, we have to go after Cancer as soon as possible and we can't find out where that's going to happen without Kelsey's help."

"She's right, Rachel," wheezed Professor Galten. "Sereny told us the order and Pisces is next. Then Cancer. We don't have much time left."

"I have an idea how to help," said Chris. "Come with me." The two telepaths stood. "We'll meet the rest of you in the meditation center at midnight." They left.

"I feel like I should eat more, but I'm too excited to see if this bracelet idea will work," Jamee admitted.

"I know what ya mean," Rory agreed.

"Well," said Professor Galten, "then let's go see if we can make this work." She rose with the two Signs, moved to another table, and spoke quietly to a woman who Tim assumed to be Sharon Cledume. The four left the dining hall.

"I would like to take a closer look at Anderson Baker's book. Maybe there are some clues that we missed," Cole said.

"I think that's a good idea," Sereny agreed in a soft voice. Tim glanced at her. There were circles under her eyes. She caught his eye, smiled reassuringly, and joined Cole as he rose.

Rhys pushed back her chair. "You're going to need my help." Donne meowed. "Our help," she corrected herself.

Soon, it was just Tim and the Conlyns sitting at the table. Mrs. Conlyn looked at the three men. "I have some work to do at the lab, so I'm afraid I'm going to leave as well. John, come keep me company."

Mr. Conlyn looked from his wife to his son and back. "Right. I need to see if I can find out any more information on the Virgo anyway." He pushed his plate away and followed his wife from the room. The two boys sat at the table for awhile, not speaking, not looking at each other. Finally, Tim broke the silence.

"Well, that was...contrived," he said. No response. "And this is awkward."

"Yeah. Sorry. It's just the first time that we've been alone together since..."

"Yeah." Tim looked around. "Well, it's not like we're really alone together. There are lots of people still eating around us," he joked.

Xander didn't smile. "I've wanted and dreaded being alone with you again."

"I know." Tim thought a minute. "It shouldn't have to be so hard."

"But it is," Xander groaned and put his head on the table.

Tim stood up. "No, it's not." He looked at his watch. "We have time before the dream session. Want to go watch a movie? I have a TV and DVD player in my room." Xander lifted his head. "Come on. It's just a movie."

Xander thought for a moment. "Okay. But I get to choose the movie."

"As long as it has nothing to do with planets, stars, or space," Tim amended.

"Deal."

Chapter 21

The meditation center was laid out like an enormous garden. There were stones and bonsai in various patterns, designed to please the eye. Soft music played to soothe the ear. Mats and mattresses dotted the room. There were also secluded areas if one desired privacy during meditation. According to the sign posted by the door, guided group meditations were available and if one wanted a personal guided meditation, appointments could be made. The room was dimly lit and a selection of candles stood by the entrance for the taking.

A number of mats had been grouped together in a corner. Chris and Dana each sat on one. Dana looked at Tim as he and Xander entered together. She smiled faintly, but Tim could see she was nervous. One by one, each of the other Signs entered and took a mat. They made small talk and Jamee told them the exciting news that the bracelet idea just might work. "If we can get a hold of one, of course," she added. Then, from one of the private rooms, an enormous bear of a man entered. He wore a robe of beige and his long, dark hair was tied back.

"A greeting," he rumbled. "I am Unega Wahuhi. I have been working with the Aries on her meditation exercises. It is my hope that she will be able to enter a trance state with the rest of you, keeping you all mentally linked. Because of the situation, I will be leading you in a guided meditation where you will attempt to meet your friend on the astral plane. Aries will be your leader. It is vital that you develop a group mind. There will be times where you will need to think as one. You must enter into this group mind with trust and understanding. If there are any grievances that you hold onto, speak them now for release." Tim looked at Dana, suddenly very glad that he had spoken to her earlier. No one spoke. "Very well. Please lie back and close your eyes." There was a nervous energy among them, but they did as requested. Harmony curled up beside Tim. Chris reached out and took Dana's hand.

"Please take a few deep, centering breaths. Breathe in through your nose and out through your mouth. You find yourself growing relaxed." The deep voice was drowsily soothing. "Please take a moment and check your body for any unwanted tension that you may be holding. Breathe in deeply and release that tension on the exhale." Tim heard exhalations all around him and he did the same, releasing his lower back. He felt pleasantly relaxed. "Take the aware, conscious part of you and move it to the center of your body. Feel yourself settle comfortably just behind your navel. Let yourself float there for a few minutes. Your body is your home and you are secure inside your favorite room in the home. Look around the room. You see familiar furniture, pictures of loved ones, favorite toys from your youth. There is a door in this room. It's an ordinary looking door and you walk over to it. Open the door."

"As you open the door, you see a beautiful garden with a path that leads downhill. You step onto the path and feel the sun shining down on you. It warms your body as you start down the path." Tim could feel the sunlight. The voice sounded farther away.

"You see beautiful flowers and trees around you and there are birds singing. The path leads to a sparkling fountain with padded benches around it. As you come upon the fountain, you meet your companions. Everyone is happy to see each other. You all sit and watch the fountain, feeling the spray of the water on your skin." The voice was fading.

"Then, as one, you move past the fountain and follow the path further down. The leaves are tickling your ankles as you walk. You feel the warm breeze on your face..." The voice disappeared. Tim could only hear the birds in the garden around him. He followed his companions through the garden, Dana in the lead. They came to a grove of willow trees. Dana chose the largest of them and moved into its shade. The rest of them followed. They sat in a small semi-circle around the trunk and waited.

"Dana, do you know what you're doing?" Jamee finally broke the silence. Tim felt her voice more than he heard it.

"Jamee, leave her alone. She's concentrating." That sounded like James. Surprised, Tim looked over and saw that both of the twins were present.

It was Xander who asked what was on all of their minds. "How?"

The answer came from above them. "Because this is a dream. They have separate minds and both minds are dreaming. So they both appear here." The Signs looked up. Kelsey Baker was sitting in the branches.

"Hello, Kelsey," said Tim.

The dream boy began to descend. "I should be welcoming you," he said. "This is my domain: the Twelfth House."

"The what?" Rory asked.

"This is the Twelfth House. There are twelve slices of reality. Each Sign has a House that is their home. The Twelfth House is the Dreamworld and everyone visits here on a nightly basis. You've all been here and I've known all of you for longer than you've known me."

"Good point," James muttered.

"Yes, you have. Why haven't you spoken to us?" Rhys asked him.

Kelsey joined them on the ground. "I couldn't. For me to actually speak and be heard, there has to be strong emotion from the dreamer. The stronger the emotion, the more influence I have. That's how most dreams work. For those who have no interest in me, I'm rarely noticed. Most members of The Gathering have a strong investment in the Signs and since I'm part of that, I can influence them in their dreams. The more aware you became of the Signs and our task, the more noticeable I became in your dreams." They all nodded. "The cats and I have been in constant communication, though." He smiled fondly at the felines of the group.

"You can talk to the cats?" Rhys asked, put out.

"Only in dreams," he reminded her. "In dreams, we all speak the same language. I don't think I would be able to, were I to manifest in the real world."

"Has it been lonely?" Rory asked. She was gazing sympathetically at Kelsey. He came over and took her hand.

"No more than it has been for you, my fellow Water Sign. Now that we have found each other, we won't be lonely again." He gestured to take in the entire group. Dana made a small noise of frustration and with a sharp glance, Kelsey noted her struggle. "We do not have a lot of time. She is using all of her concentration to make sure the group stays together. Circumstances have changed. The libraries–"

"You know where they are?" James asked.

"Yes, but they are not as they were," was the cryptic answer. "I will show you dreams of them, and the locations that you see are the same as their locations in the real world." He looked at Xander. "You should be able to travel there with these images. I will take you to the first one now." The air around them became formless. Unlike traveling with Xander, this was a somewhat frightening sensation. There was no comforting presence of other people, no colors, no lights. Just void. It reformed into a large building which was on fire. The Signs stared at the inferno, fascinated and horrified at the same time.

"Is this one of the libraries?" Rhys asked.

Kelsey nodded. "This is the first."

"But it's on fire!" Xander said.

"It is and is not. If you look again, you'll see that it's not burning down. Nothing is being destroyed." They peered through the flames and saw that he was right.

"This is Andoleen's work. He is protecting this library." Many of them looked blank, but Tim spoke up.

"Braith's Vision!" he exclaimed. Kelsey looked at him. "Professor Galten was telling me about Braith's Vision and how each of the Patrons was associated with an Element. Andoleen was the Fire-Spirit who created the telekinetics. Each of the Patrons helped to create a different branch of the psychic world."

"Who created my talent then?" asked Rory, almost accusatorily.

"No one," Tim answered. "She said that we are products of the zodiac, not the Patrons. How are the Patrons involved in this?"

"Let me show you." The flaming building vanished and was replaced by a giant pile of branches and vines.

"Where's the library?" James asked.

"This is the library," Kelsey answered.

"It's like Sleeping Beauty," Jamee observed.

"There is no princess inside," Kelsey said. "Still, it is under the protection of the Dryad, Rythsinda."

"Patron of the healers," Tim added for the others. "Are all of the libraries protected this way?" As if it were an answer, the scene changed and they now stood before a seemingly ordinary library. When they stepped forward, however, a howling gale came out of nowhere and nearly blew them all over. "This must be under Manaran's protection."

"Air's library," Kelsey agreed. "The Seed-Keeper is just as effective as the others."

"Who is She the Patron of?" asked Rory.

"Telepaths," Dana wheezed. They all looked at her. She was pale and sweating.

"We need to get her out of here," Cole said, supporting Dana's weight with his body. "She can't hold up much longer."

"I need to see the last library," Xander insisted.

"We don't have time, Xander! She needs to get out of here now!"

"Go. See one more," Dana croaked out. Without waiting for another argument, Kelsey replaced the scene before them with an ocean coast. He pointed into the water.

"Just beneath the surface of the water is the last library. It was submerged by Niole, the Mer-Child, Patron of the precogs. When I approached it, Niole told me that only when three Signs of the Element approach will they, and they alone, be given access." He turned to the rest of them. "So you see why it is so important that we find and retrieve all of the Signs. Without Cancer, Rory and I cannot get to this library. The Earth library is currently lost. Right now, we're only able to gain access to Fire and Air and that's not enough."

"What happens if they kill Virgo?" James asked.

"They won't. I have been visiting him. He's okay. For now. They're keeping him as bait. We'll need everyone if we're going to get him back." Dana began to shake violently and Kelsey changed the scene back to the garden. The sun was low in the sky, creating an orange glow on their faces. Kelsey took Dana from Cole "Quickly, go back to your houses and return to consciousness. I will take Dana." He began to lead her away. "Go!"

Tim saw the others running for various paths and he dashed for his own. He sped up the path, reaching the door within minutes and opening it quickly, but gently. Slipping into the familiar room, he dropped into a comfortable chair. He could hear his heart beating as a gentle pulse throughout the room and slowly, over that sound, a series of words reached him.

"...settling back into your center. Let yourself expand to inhabit your body again. Feel your awareness in each part of your body and gently move your fingers and your toes. Let yourself feel the mat underneath you. Let yourself sense the people around you and when you feel comfortable, open your eyes."

Tim let his awareness explore his body, flexing and contracting muscles here and there, gently shaking his fingers and finally, opening his eyes. He saw the huge, domed ceiling, beige and covered in intricately intertwined shapes. His eyes drifted along the patterns, following until it came back to where it began. He was pleasantly drifting when he heard a gasp next to him and he sat up quickly. Jamee was staring across the circle at Dana, who was a greenish-gray color, her hair damp and sticking to her face. She clung to Chris, who looked up at their guide. Unega watched Dana for a long, tense moment. Then, with a sympathetic click of his tongue, he motioned for Chris to lift her. He turned to the Signs. "She is exhausted. With rest, she will heal." He left. Chris took Dana tenderly in his arms and followed Unega out of the room. The rest of them glanced around at each other.

"What do we do now?" Jamee whispered.

"We can't do that every time we want to talk to Kelsey," Tim agreed.

"We must find another way to contact him then," suggested Cole.

"We can't worry about that now. We have to get the other Signs," said Rhys.

"And quick," Rory added.

"Well, we can't do it without Dana," Xander pointed out. "Kelsey was nice enough to leave me a clear picture to locate Cancer, but finding a new Sign is something we should do as a group. I'm going to have a talk with Sereny. Maybe she has more information we could use."

"I'm going with you," said Tim quickly.

"And me," Jamee said.

"I would like to speak to Sereny as well," Rhys said.

"Well, I don't know if I understand what's goin' on, yet, but I do know that girl is hurtin'," said Rory. "I'm gonna go make sure she's all right."

"I will go with you," said Cole.

"Wait," said Jamee. "I want to know that Dana's okay, but James really wants to know what Sereny has to say."

"How about we meet you in Dana's room after we talk to Sereny?" Tim suggested to Cole and Rory. They nodded and Jamee looked relieved. They all left the meditation center together, but at the end of the hall, Cole and Rory headed left and the rest of the group headed right. Not knowing Sereny's location, they had to ask a few people and they finally found her in the Hall of Mirrors.

"I don't remember seeing this on the tour," Rhys said.

"Neither do I," Jamee confessed.

Sereny turned towards them. For the first time since he had known her, Tim could see her age in her face and manner. "It's not a common place to convene. Mirrors are very special, very temperamental objects. They are used for many different practices, but most of all, by the seers. Some mirrors have been dipped in specific potions to give them their powers. Others were found in powerful places on the earth or along ley lines."

"Ley lines?" Jamee asked.

"Lines of flowing power. These mirrors are the strongest. Other mirrors have been trained to answer simple questions. There is a mirror here for almost anything you wish...and some things that you don't wish," she added in a soft voice. "Most do not come here because of the noise." Tim was already concentrating, but he was having trouble hearing anything out of the ordinary.

"Uh, Sereny–" Rhys started.

"I know you don't hear it right now because you are listening with your ears. Listen with your talents." Tim closed his eyes and tried again to listen without his ears. The others followed suit. He could feel himself slipping into the mental state where his talent came easily and suddenly, it came easily. It was faint, just a whispering at the edge of the mind. So faint that he wasn't completely sure that he heard it at all. But then it grew louder. Metallic voices, sharp voices, smooth voices, hard voices, sifting through his brain, speaking, whining, screaming. He strained to listen with his ears again and the roar diminished considerably, but did not depart.

Sereny looked at them. "They are the mirrors, speaking to us. Because of the power that they are infused with, they have developed sentience. Personality. Just as there are those that believe that machines of today have their own intelligence, these mirrors truly have evolved into beings of their own." She stretched out a hand and stroked the gilded edge of a large mirror. "They are powerful and impartial. You may ask them questions and though they will always give you a true answer, it may not be the answer you seek. I come here when I wish to think or when I need hard truth."

"Sereny, are you okay?" Jamee asked.

"My mother has passed," Sereny said sadly. The Signs all made sympathetic noises. "It was time and she was ready, but it is not easy. I would not say this to Rory, but I suppose it is fitting that her addition to the family is heralded by a death. Scorpio is, after all, the sign of death and rebirth."

"Do you want me to take you home?" Xander offered.

"That is very kind of you, but there is nothing there for me now," Sereny said. "I am needed here. She has been laid beside my father and she would want me to continue with my work." She looked around her. "It is time that I left this hall. The mirrors have shown me echoes of my life and I am tired." Tim offered his arm and she took it gratefully. They moved back through the hall towards the psychic wing and it was awhile before Sereny spoke. When she did, it was in a near whisper. "Before I forget, I have new information for you." The Signs became instantly alert. "You will find Virgo last, of course. After Cancer, you must find Capricorn and then Taurus. With all complete, you will be able to enter the libraries and claim nascregala." They had reached her room.

"What's nascregala?" Jamee asked.

"I don't know. The word comes from the last vision I had before my mother passed. I only know that the libraries hold the answers that you are looking for and that to enter them, you must all be together." She opened the door, slipped inside, and gently closed it.

"Well, that doesn't really give us any more information," said Xander as the Signs left to find the astrology wing. "We already know that we need to get into the libraries."

"But we didn't know that there's something specifically for us in there," Jamee pointed out.

"Didn't we?" Xander argued. "The libraries are protected and it'll take three of each Element to get in. Makes sense that there's something just for us."

"At least we know the order of the last three Signs," added Rhys. "This is an improvement."

"As much as can be expected, I suppose," responded Xander. He seemed disgruntled, but he shook it off as they reached their hallway. He paused with a hand on the doorknob. "Should we just go in? What if she's sleeping?"

"Come on in!" they heard Dana call out. Xander looked at the rest of them and, grinning ruefully, opened the door. Cole and Rory sat on chairs, munching on snacks and Chris stood by the bed. Dana herself was laying back against the pillows. She still looked exhausted, but she was awake and smiling as they entered.

"You mind-read me," Xander accused her. "Guess you're feeling better."

"Much," she agreed. "Professor Galten gave me a potion. It tasted gross, but it opened my chakras or something like that so when they had a healer stop by, she was much faster healing me than it would be normally."

"Professor Galten's great," Tim declared. "Don't tell her I said so, though."

"My lips are sealed," Dana assured him.

"What did Sereny say?" Cole asked.

"She said that we have to find Cancer, then Capricorn, Taurus, and Virgo is last," Rhys told him.

"And that there's something called nascregala!" Jamee exclaimed.

Confusion flooded Rory's face. "What?"

Tim sighed. "Sereny told us that we'll need all of the Signs to get into the libraries–"

"Which we already knew," Xander interjected.

"–and we would be able to claim nascregala," Tim finished.

"She didn't explain what that means, did she?" Cole asked. They shook their heads.

"We gotta get into the libraries then," stated Rory.

"Maybe Kelsey knows something about them," Jamee suggested.

All eyes went to Dana. She bit her lip. "I'm not ready yet."

Chris came to her rescue. "That's okay," he said, giving the rest a look that dared them to defy his words. "It's late anyway. You need to rest. You all need to rest," he amended. "When you're feeling better, you can go after Cancer." Tim saw Xander's frustration and reached out, taking his hand.

"I could use some sleep," Tim admitted and watched relief creep into Chris's eyes. Xander's hand tightened, but he did not speak. "Let's go after Cancer in the morning." Reluctantly, Xander nodded and Tim motioned to the others. As Tim reached the door, he looked back and saw Chris mouth, "Thank you." He shut the door gently behind him.

* * * * * * * * * * *

Tim's dream started the moment his head hit the pillow. The garden was exactly as he remembered it. Lush plant life everywhere, birds chirping, beautiful sunlight. He walked along the path, taking in the beautiful scenery and feeling his body happily relax. The pressures of the world seemed far away and there was almost a bounce in his step. Bounding from branch to branch above him was Harmony, taking deep pleasure in the freedoms of the outside world. He saw figures through the leaves walking along, but he could not make them out and he did not strain to do so. He came upon the fountain and sat down on one of the benches. Harmony gleefully leapt into his lap. *How am I back here?* he thought.

A shadow fell across him. "You are dreaming," Kelsey told him. Tim squinted up to see the tall boy eclipsing the sunlight. "I thought it was a good idea for us to get together since we were interrupted last time." Tim looked around to see the other Signs coming down different paths and he became alarmed.

"Dana–"

"I'm okay," she said, sitting down next to him. The rest of the Signs had arrived and a few were looking at Dana with concern. "Really, I'm fine," she restated.

"You're not hurtin'?" Rory asked her.

Dana shook her head as Kelsey answered for her. "She is in an actual dreaming state now. The last time that you came here, it was a conscious effort on everyone's part to join the Dreaming, but especially for Dana to keep you all together. Now, when you dream, I will be able to easily find you and bring you here together. We've established a strong connection." As he spoke, an aqua aura came into play around him and each of them could see swathes of their own colors mixed in. "We haven't a lot of time. You need restful, dreamless sleep for you to fully recover and be ready to find the next Sign."

"I already have the general location but it's a little hazy," Xander informed him.

Kesley nodded, but his look was grave. "The Cancer, Emily, is in trouble."

"She's been captured!" Jamee gasped.

"No, that's not the problem," Kelsey told her. "I can't completely get a read on where she is and I think it has to do with her talent. She can shut me out to a degree and her dreams are strange, but I was able to garner a close enough picture of where you need to go." The environment around them shimmered to reflect a peaceful meadow with a building on the hill.

The image brought a chill and Tim immediately thought of Merel. "That looks like where we were kept," Tim said hesitantly. He looked at Jamee.

"We never saw the outside," she said. "We were unconscious when we were brought in. Maybe if we saw the inside, we would know."

Kelsey shook his head and explained, "I can't get any closer than this or it becomes hazy." To demonstrate, he motioned them closer and suddenly, the grass beneath their feet became blurred and it felt as though they were stepping into mud. They retreated quickly.

"Maybe I'll be able to reach her mind," Dana suggested.

"Be very careful if you do," Kelsey warned her. "Her dreams are not pleasant ones. She suffers almost constantly." He shuddered. "It's horrible to see."

"Well, we're going to get her out of there," Rhys declared. The cats yowled in response.

Kelsey nodded again. "You have to and quickly. Then the Waters will be complete."

"Do you know where Capricorn is?" Cole asked Kelsey. "That's the next Sign after Cancer." In response, the area around them vanished and was replaced with a cliff overlooking a terrifying drop. One could see clouds drifting lazily below them. The air was thin and cold and many of them were left breathless at first.

"He's kind of a loner," said Kelsey.

"Capricorn seems to prefer his Element," Dana remarked.

"He and Taurus both do," Kelsey told her. "You'll see that when you find her."

"Kelsey, do you know anything about something called nascregala?" Jamee asked hopefully.

He looked at her. "Nascregala?" He searched his mind. "Roughly, that translates into 'gift of birth' or 'birthright.'"

"A birthright?" Now Jamee was excited. "What kind of birthright?"

"Where did you hear about it?"

"We were talking to Sereny and she said something about finding nascregala in the libraries," Rhys explained

They all waited tensely while Kelsey considered. Finally he admitted, "I haven't heard anything about a birthright and no one has been dreaming of it. If Sereny said something about it, though, it must be from a vision of hers. There are some visions that I can't get into. I guess it's information I'm not supposed to have right now." He looked frustrated.

Jamee was disappointed, but she said, "It's okay. I'm sure we're gonna find out as soon as we get into those libraries!"

"Signs first, nascregala after," Rhys declared. "We won't find anything if we don't get–"

"–all of the Signs together," Dana interrupted. "Yeah, we know. I'm kinda sick of hearing it. If we're gonna do it, let's do it."

"You need to recover," Tim told her.

"Then you have to have dreamless sleep," Kelsey said. "Dana, you need it the most. I'll make sure that happens."

"Wait!" Tim cried. "What if we need you?"

"Then dream," Kelsey said, and the scene faded from view.

Chapter 22

Tim awoke feeling rested and remembering everything from the previous night's dream. Yawning, Harmony stretched and hopped off the bed. Tim followed quickly, getting ready for the day. They were coming down to the end. He could feel it and it made nervous energy run rampant through his body. As soon as he stepped into the hall, he was hit with waves of the same anxiety coming from the other Signs. With the exception of Rory, they had all gone out to find other Signs before, but never knowingly walked into danger. Tim wondered whether there would be astranihl. *What if Merel shows up?* he thought to himself. He was careful to keep these thoughts below the surface. From the look on Dana's face, she was still not fully recovered and he didn't want to aggravate her or any of the other Signs with his apprehensive wonderings. The Signs chatted about the dream of the night before and though they all went down to breakfast, very few of them ate. When each plate had been pushed to the center of the table, they convened in the hall.

"Ready?" asked Xander. They all nodded and held hands. The hall dissolved with a familiar swirl of colors. Tim felt the collective worries of the group envelop him and he did his best to stave them off. For the first time, he was glad to feel the separation as they materialized in the meadow. Xander turned to Rory and explained about the new Sign's responsibility to find the Cancer.

"But we already know where she is, don't we?" Rory protested, pointing to the building on the hill.

"We know the general location," Rhys agreed, "but we need to find her and quickly and as Signs we have the best compass ingrained in us for finding other Signs." Tim watched as Rory began to emanate with crimson light. Slowly, flickers of other Signs came into play, but then Rory screamed and fell to the ground, clutching her chest.

Everyone immediately converged on her, but Jamee was closest. As Tim neared, he could hear her saying, "Focus, Rory. Concentrate only on me. Find my soul." It was an echo of the words Xander had used when she herself had experimented too soon. Rory's scream cut off and she began shaking violently. Jamee looked up at them. "It isn't working!" she cried, panic showing in her eyes.

Cole knelt down to lift her. "Careful," Dana warned. "No skin to skin contact. You don't want to get poisoned." Cole glanced at her sharply and backed off.

"How are we going to move her?" he asked the group.

"Maybe we don't have to," Tim suggested. "Someone has to stay here and watch her while the rest go after Cancer."

"I could take her back to The Gathering," Xander offered. "They might be able to help."

Jamee shook her head. "She's moving too much. The healers won't get close enough to Rory without endangering themselves and besides, I doubt this is something that they'll have seen before. This connects to Cancer. We have to get to her. She might know how to fix this."

Rory began to laugh hysterically, throwing her head from side to side.

"Who stays with Rory then?" Rhys asked.

"I'll do it," Cole volunteered. "I don't think my talents will be of much use up there." He indicated the building.

The two large cats growled. "The cats have offered to stay with you," Rhys told him as they padded over to sit nearby. Harmony and Donne sat up alertly and Cole smiled gratefully at them. "Don't worry," Rhys assured him, "we'll figure this out. Let's go." She started across the meadow towards the hill. The rest of them followed. As they drew close to the top, they heard voices and halted, listening.

"...started screaming again," said a light female voice.

"Emily Halsbern? I thought she was on the recovery list," responded a fluty alto voice.

"She was, but they've seen relapses with her before, so they were giving her time to see if the new drugs helped." There was a sigh. "Those drugs were really working. But just a little while ago, she started screaming again and grabbing her chest."

"You saw her?"

"Well, I didn't see it happen, but I heard from Margie who was on the shift. Said a shudder went through her and she almost glowed or something. Then she started screaming again."

"She glowed?" asked the alto voice skeptically.

"Well, Margie likes to embellish, but she said Emily just lifted her head and there was this glow and then she started hollering. They're gonna have to sedate her if she keeps this up." The voices were moving away. "Shame though. She's such a pretty little thing..."

The Signs looked at each other. "It's an insane asylum," Dana whispered in horror.

"We have to get her out of there," Rhys whispered back.

"At least now we know what happened to Rory," Tim added. "She tried to connect and whatever she did negated the drugs that Emily's taking. I wish I knew what was wrong with her."

"Maybe I can find out," Dana said tentatively.

"No," Rhys told her. "We can't risk losing you too. I think we have to go in there if we're going to get her out."

"How are we gonna do that?" Xander asked.

"I think we'll need a little charm." Rhys looked over at Tim. "You up for it?" Tim swallowed and nodded.

They moved across the grounds towards the white marbled building. Silently, they marched up the stone steps to the front doors and Rhys opened them. The lobby was large and cold. Bronze tile reflected the garish fluorescent lighting. There were a few patients in wheelchairs being attended by nurses in white. Long hallways led away from the lobby in opposite directions. Screams echoed throughout the building.

"I guess that's our girl," Jamee muttered.

They walked up to the front desk. The receptionist was a tired older man with very little hair on his head, but a full grey beard. He looked up from his book as they approached and smiled an oily smile. "How can I be of service?"

Tim moved to the front. "Excuse me, sir. We're here to see a friend of ours. Emily Halsbern."

"No visits unless you're family." He returned to his book.

"We're family," Dana told him.

The man snorted. "I highly doubt that." He returned to his book.

Tim tried again. "Excuse me, sir," he repeated, smiling and tapping into his talent. A lavender light illuminated the man and he raised his head, blinking. His expression softened. "We really need to see Emily. Do you know where she is?" A particularly painful scream sounded through the halls and the receptionist grimaced.

"Oh, she's making her presence known. What do you need her for?"

"Another friend of ours has been showing the same symptoms as Emily," Tim improvised.

"Which friend?" the receptionist asked, eyeing each of them critically.

Tim continued to smile. "She's outside. We didn't want to bring her in without confirming it. We need to see Emily and check her charts." The man was beginning to melt. "Her parents sent us," he added on a whim. That did it. The man really didn't want a confrontation and was willing to bend the rules if it would make his job easier.

"You can't stay long, but she's down the hall to the left." He consulted his notebook. "Room 4C."

"Thank you very much, sir," said Tim, but the man was already engrossed in his book. Tim led the way down the hall, all of them trying to look as though they were supposed to be there. When they drew near to 4C, they encountered a nurse coming out of the room.

"Oh! Hello."

"Hi," said Tim. He went into the charming routine again and by the time he was finished, the woman was smiling broadly.

"How nice for you to visit Emily! She never gets visitors. I'm afraid she's terribly lonely." She held up her hands, preventing them from moving towards the door. "I'm sorry, but you can't go in. You can talk to her through the window there." She pointed to a rather large window that gave them full view of the room. "Don't worry. There are three sheets of Plexiglas there. There's no way to get through it." Xander started to smile, but stifled it. Tim maintained his smile as they all moved towards the window.

Emily was a voluptuous, dark-skinned woman with large olive eyes and a head of curly hair. She was dressed in a hospital gown and though a bed had been provided for her, she laid upon the floor. She stared at them through the glass and her mouth opened in an incoherent howl. Clawing at the floor and contorting her body painfully, she pierced the air with her screams. Her body froze in a catatonic state, but a moment later, she was pounding on the glass, enraged. The Signs recoiled with each hit. A minute later, she was rocking on the floor, humming contentedly.

"I thought the drugs were helping," Tim said to the nurse with a sympathetic smile.

"They were," she replied. "But it's a new experimental drug and it's difficult to know the full effects. She relapsed only this afternoon. We don't know why." The Signs managed slightly guilty expressions, but Tim kept smiling throughout. "The doctors said that this might happen though and to up her medication. Would you mind keeping an eye on her while I go and get a stronger dose?" She smiled sweetly at Tim and he mirrored her.

"Of course."

She practically pranced down the hall and Jamee turned to watch her go. "That was weird," she noted. "Since when does a nurse leave a patient in the care of people she's never seen?"

"Since there's charm involved," Xander answered, vanishing and reappearing on the other side of the glass. Emily tore at her hair, weeping.

"Xander!" Rhys exclaimed. "They probably have cameras everywhere!"

"You got a better idea?" he asked, picking up the struggling Sign and blinking back into the hallway. "Now, grab onto me and let's get out of here before they sound alarms or something." A siren began to wail throughout the building, drowning out the Cancer's cries. They hurriedly held onto each other and Xander whisked them back out to the meadow where Cole and Rory were waiting.

He faced Xander. "I can hear sirens. Did you–? Is that–?"

"Yes, we did and yes, it is," Xander yelled over Rory and Emily's cacophonous howls. "Now, grab a hand!" Cole took Rhys's hand as the felines moved to various humans and Cole grabbed quickly onto Rory's boot. The siren sound vanished, but a new turmoil began. Tim felt as though emotions were passing through him at a rapid rate. He could not fully experience one before another took over. The feeling was overwhelming and it was with relief that he felt himself return to material form. However, the experience had shaken a memory loose and as soon as they became corporeal again, he yelled at Dana to call Professor Galten.

"Tell her to bring the dampening draught!"

She looked startled, but closed her eyes, concentrating. People were coming into the hall from all areas, drawn by the screaming. After a tense wait, Professor Galten herself came stamping up through the crowd. She handed a bottle to Tim and turned towards the Cancer. Tim moved to Rory. He hesitated, not wanting to touch the writhing girl, then poured some of the liquid directly onto her shrieking face. She gasped and spluttered, but ended up swallowing some of it and her body relaxed just enough for her to focus. She stared at him, whimpering.

"Here," he said, holding out the bottle. "Drink more of this. It will help." She reached out with a shaking hand and took it from him, tipping it into her mouth. Immediately, the shaking stopped and though horror was clearly written across her wet face, she was silent. The whole hall had become quiet except for the murmuring of the crowd. Tim straightened up to see that Emily had stopped screaming as well and was now sitting up, gulping in large breaths of air.

"How did you know to do that?" James asked Tim.

Tim continued to watch Emily and Rory closely. "I learned a lesson."

"Good thinking, boy," the professor praised him. "Alexander, you should take these ladies out of the public areas. We will discuss at dinner." She handed him a vial of the icy liquid, adding, "You might want to hang onto this. She's a sensitive." With that, she stomped towards the crowd, motioning them away with her hands. "Move out! Give them room." The crowd reluctantly began to withdraw.

Xander carefully pocketed the vial and told the rest of the Signs, "Meet in our hallway." He carefully made contact with each of the girls and vanished.

Tim picked up the other vial from where Rory left it. "What does that mean?" he asked. "A sensitive?"

"Only one way to find out," James said, and started up the stairs.

* * * * * * * * * * *

The Signs were bombarded with questions as they made their way towards the astrology wing, but they fended them off with minimal issue. Tim explained to the rest of the group about the dampening draught, but did not reveal Xander's past. They passed a few theories back and forth as to what a sensitive might be. Jamee thought that it meant Emily's skin was so sensitive that everything hurt. Cole suggested that she was in touch with the Earth and anything being done to the Earth affected her. Rhys thought that maybe she understood crazy people. Tim was silent, remembering the feeling of emotional overload he had felt while they were traveling. When they reached the Sign hallway, Xander was waiting for them.

"Hey, guys. Let's meet in Rory's room. She says she's feeling up to company." They went and knocked on the door.

"Come on in," Rory called. The Signs filed in and took various seats around the room. Rory was sitting up on her bed. She looked better, but there was still a skittish air around her. This experience had shaken her confidence.

"How are you feeling?" Cole asked her.

"I feel better," she told them. "But I'm thinkin' I don't wanna go through that again." She shuddered.

"You won't have to," Rhys reassured her. "It's up to her to find the next Sign. If she's well enough to do it."

"Yeah, what's wrong with her anyway?" James asked.

"Professor Galten said she's a sensitive," Tim put in.

Xander answered. "She is. That's what The Gathering sometimes calls empaths. It means that she can feel what other people are feeling. Apparently, she can't control it and emotions just run through her, unchecked." He looked worried. "They must have had her on some pretty powerful drugs to have kept her talent from operating."

"But it was operating today," Dana protested. "We all saw her."

"I felt it when I was connectin' with her," Rory said. "There was this poppin' sound and then everythin' just went crazy."

"You must have reawakened her talent when you found her," Cole said.

"Well, I'm sorry I did. I don't like having no control of what I'm feelin'," Rory declared.

"So, she's got emotional Tourette's?" Dana joked, but no one laughed.

"Two questions," James said. They looked at him. "First, how is that talent of any use to us if she can't control it?" There was silence in the room. "Okay, then, question two: do you think the dampening draught is gonna keep her talent subdued?"

"The dampening draught should work, at least for a while," Tim ventured. "But I don't know how much use that's going to be in the long run. She has to learn to control it."

"Nascregala!" Jamee said through James' mouth. "We're going to need Emily to get into the Water Library. Maybe her nascregala will help her control her talent!"

"I guess she'll have to stay dampened for now," Xander suggested.

"I guess I will." They all whirled around to see Emily leaning tiredly against the doorframe. "Whatever that means." She examined each of their faces. "I didn't realize that I was going to be the topic of so much discussion," she said.

"Emily," said Rhys. "We didn't know you were up."

"For the first time in a long time," Emily replied. "Sorry if I don't come hug you all, but I've spent most of my life in an institution and now I'm somewhere with people I don't know. Not that I'm not grateful for the rescue or whatever, but I haven't been able to talk to anyone for most of my life without constant interruptions. Something weird is going on here. Want to clue me in?"

Rhys answered her. Others jumped in to add information, but Tim quietly watched Emily as the familiar story unfolded. Her guarded demeanor melted as she realized that they weren't out to hurt her and she seemed delighted by the demonstration of talents, but grew cautious again when the dampening draught was mentioned.

"So you drugged me," Emily accused.

"It's not a drug," Tim responded. "It's a potion. It'll keep other people's emotions out of your body."

"Which is exactly what the drugs did," Emily shot back. "They kept me numb. Mindless."

"Emily, with all due respect," Cole said, "you are neither numb nor mindless in this present moment. Nor besieged by others' emotions."

She blinked. "You're right," she admitted. "Sorry. It's been a long time since I've felt feelings of my own; it's hard to keep control of them. How does this potion work?"

"You'd have to ask Professor Galten," Tim told her. "She makes the potion. We're hoping that what we find in the libraries will help you get control of your talent."

"Yeah, you mentioned those. Can we go to them now?" Her voice caught in her throat and Tim ached for her. Even Rory's deadly talent seemed like a blessing compared to Emily's. "The idea that I could maybe control this on my own is something I've only dreamt about."

Xander shook his head. "We need to get everyone together before we can do that. Capricorn is next. When you and Rory feel better–"

"I'm ready," Rory declared. "I may not look it, but I'm ready for another Sign."

"I...don't know," said Emily. She seemed a little shy now that she understood the situation.

"We won't force you, of course," Xander assured her.

James grinned. "It's actually kind of fun. Well, not in your case," he admitted, "but other times have been fun."

"It's much easier from this side," Dana agreed.

"Can we eat first, though?" Rory asked. "I'm starvin'." Others murmured the same.

"We have a little time before the next meal. We'll grab some snacks from my room and then what about a tour, Emily? Everyone can kind of relax for the afternoon and I'll show you around. I promise you, it's a lot bigger than your old room with better furniture." Xander grinned at her. "We can discuss how you're feeling about the next Sign over dinner."

Post snack, Tim spent the afternoon curled up with Harmony and his books from The Book Nook. He learned all he could about each of the Signs. He tried to think about them in the context of the people he had met. He wondered just how much of their lives were shaped by the stars and how much was a result of their experiences. *No matter what*, he thought, *we have a destiny. And that's definitely influenced by the stars.*

Chapter 23

Dinner was an event that now required a long table, instead of the usual circular one. Emily seemed much more at ease, joking and laughing with the rest of the group. She talked to Professor Galten about the dampening draught and asked about various other kinds of potions that could be made. The adults seemed very happy to know that all of the Water Signs were accounted for. Only Sereny appeared out of sorts; her usual cheery expression missing. Tim wanted to talk to her, but she was sandwiched between Rhys and James and he couldn't say anything without alerting the entire table. He got the impression that she preferred it that way, so he contented himself with a sympathetic smile in her direction. She ended up excusing herself halfway through the meal. When dinner drew to a close, Xander turned towards Emily and raised a questioning eyebrow. She hesitated, then nodded.

"Anyone who wants to change clothing might want to do it now," Xander warned the Signs. "We're going into high altitudes. Meet in the hallway in ten minutes." A few of the Signs got up and headed for their rooms.

"Capricorn next, huh?" Mr. Conlyn asked his son.

"Yeah, and Taurus after that. Depending on how it goes tonight, we might just continue and pick her up as well."

"Don't overdo it," his mother warned him.

"We won't," he promised.

A few minutes later, they were in the hall and ready to go. Emily still looked a little nervous, but she held onto James' hand and they were off.

* * * * * * * * * * *

The cliff hadn't changed since they saw it in the Dreamworld. Thinner air immediately forced Tim to gasp. He took a few minutes to get his breathing under control. He wished he had gone upstairs with some of the others to grab warmer clothing. This was a different part of the world and the sun hung low in the western sky. Tim risked a glance over the cliff's edge. He couldn't see the bottom through the layer of cloud cover and he shuddered to think how far he would fall if there was a misstep. Pines stood in clusters, speaking softly to each other with deep throated creaks. The cry of a hawk pierced the quiet, making Tim jump. When he refocused on the group, he found Emily shaking her head.

"I know it's the responsibility of the new Sign, but I don't think I'm up for it."

"We have other ways to find the Capricorn," Dana reminded them.

"We also have someone here who hasn't done it yet," Xander noted, looking at James.

"What? Oh, right. I guess I didn't, huh?" he admitted sheepishly. "I still don't think I'm gonna be much help here. I'll put Jamee on."

There was the usual blur and the female Gemini stood before them. "Okay, I'm ready to give it another try, but just be ready to grab me if my mind snaps."

"Gotcha covered," Dana said, grinning.

Jamee stuck her tongue out, winked, and then closed her eyes. Tim watched a coppery orange slip in amongst Jamee's yellow. "He's strong," she said, and began to walk. The group followed her into the wooded area. Tim reexamined his surroundings. There were squirrels and birds flitting from tree to tree above them. Rustlings in the foliage around them suggested other animals inhabited the area and were cautiously observing. Tim traipsed along with the group for a good while before they came out into a clearing. A group of boulders stood sentry over a beautiful, sparkling lake.

"He's around here," Jamee whispered. They spread out slightly and began searching the area. Suddenly, Tim heard a gasp behind him and he spun around only to find he couldn't move or speak. He saw various others of his group frozen in different positions and locations. *I guess we know what his talent is*, Tim thought. There was movement from amongst the trees and he saw a stocky man with dark eyes approach. His long brown hair was tied back in a ponytail and Tim could see the coppery orange glow around him. This was their Capricorn. A whimper sounded to his left and Tim strained his eyes to the side but he couldn't see who had made the noise.

The man spoke. "What do you want?" His voice was low and quiet, but it had hidden strength.

"We need your help," was the timid response. Tim groaned inwardly. The voice belonged to Emily, the only one of them whose talent was inactive.

"My help?" The man laughed scornfully. "This is just more trickery. I am sick of your games!"

"Please," Emily begged. "I don't know what you're talking about."

He stopped for a moment and eyed her appraisingly. "You're good. You're much better than the others."

"Others?" Emily asked, bewildered. "Please, I don't know what you mean and I don't know a lot about what's going on, but these people helped me when no one else would. They're...friends. I don't know how to explain it, but–"

"Stop," he commanded her. "You and your *friends* are not welcome here." He turned to go.

"You may not be able to help us, but at least you can let them go!" Emily cried at his back. She took a few steps forward, bringing her into Tim's line of vision. "They haven't done anything to you!"

He stopped and turned to face her again, his face a mask of ire. "They have been attacking me! You and your friends with the grey cloaks!" *Astranihl!* Tim thought, alarmed.

"That's not us!" Emily practically screamed.

The man searched her face. "If you really aren't part of that group, then prove it." He sat down on a boulder and waited patiently, but alertly.

Emily cast about for some way to show him she was telling the truth. "Listen, you're our Capricorn! My name is Emily and I'm the Cancer and that's Xander and he's the Sagittarius..." Increasingly hysterical, she went through each member of the group, but when she got to Jamee, the man stopped her.

"Why does she glow?" he asked her. "You've never glowed before."

Emily seized the advantage. "She's a Sign! You're a Sign! We're all Signs!"

"Then why aren't you glowing?" he asked shrewdly. "If what you say is true, then you and the rest of your companions should be glowing as well."

Emily looked stricken. "I wasn't ready. I'm not ready." The man shrugged smugly and started to get up. "Okay, wait!" Emily took a deep breath and closed her eyes. Tim watched carefully, willing her to succeed. There was a flicker of light playing about her. Slowly, but surely, she began to glow with silvery light. Her face was pinched tight, as if she expected the worst, but when it didn't come, she cautiously opened her eyes. Relieved, she smiled, but her smile faded when she looked around and saw her companions were still frozen. "Why haven't you let them go?" she demanded angrily.

"So you glow," the man responded. "I still don't see how this connects to me."

"You want to see what this has to do with you?" Emily threatened. "Fine!" She stared at him and with an almost audible pop, the orange copper color of his aura shone through her silver and he gasped. "Do you feel that?" she asked him. "That's *your* glow. That's what this has to do with you."

The man immediately got up and moved towards the lake. His reflection confirmed Emily's claims and without a word, he turned around. Tim and the rest of the Signs suddenly fell to the ground, groaning and massaging limbs. One by one, auras flared into existence until there was a veritable rainbow in the clearing. "You really are Signs," he said in wonder.

"As are you," said Emily. "You are our Capricorn."

"That's quite a powerful talent you have," Rhys added, cracking her knuckles. The felines growled. "The talent of freezing people."

"Well, time, actually," the man corrected. Now that he wasn't holding them hostage, there was a warmer quality to his voice. "I can manipulate time."

"A gift from your ruling planet, I'd bet," Xander offered. "Saturn is Father Time in Greco-Roman mythology."

"Well, you know all of our names, but we have yet to learn yours, sir," Cole said.

"I'm sorry. My name is Stephen Wyonne. I apologize for freezing you. For the past few days, I've been attacked at my home by these creatures..."

"Astranihl," Tim interjected. The others nodded, but Stephen looked blank. "Frightening and flying with grey cloaks?" Now Stephen nodded. "Astranihl," Tim repeated.

"I didn't know what they were or what they wanted, but I didn't want to find out, so I froze them in time. More came to attack and yesterday, I abandoned the house. I came out here and camped out. Next thing I know, you guys show up."

"But why didn't you freeze all of us?" Emily inquired. "Why did you leave me?"

"I wanted to see if it was a trick. They've attacked every day, but they always looked the same. I didn't know if they could assume human form."

"They can," said Jamee.

"I wasn't sure, but I figured I could always freeze you if I had to," Stephen said. "I took a chance."

"You took a big chance," Rory told him. She cracked her whip nervously and looked around as if expecting an attack.

"We need to get out of here," Dana said, picking up on Rory's energy.

"Anyone up for a double header?" Xander asked them.

"Right now?" Rhys asked. "Is that wise?"

"They've already been after Capricorn and they've got Virgo. We can't take the chance that they'll get Taurus as well."

"He's right," Tim said. "Let's go." The group came together around Xander.

All except for Stephen, who was trying to follow the conversation and failing. "I don't understand what you people are talking about. You still haven't explained to me what you're doing here, who those creatures were, and what I have to do with any of this!"

With a look that clearly said, *We don't have time for this*, Dana stepped in and took the lead. "I know this seems strange to you. Hell, it's been strange for all of us, but we're running out of time and I can explain it to you on the way."

You can do that? Tim sent her.

Worth a try, she sent back with a mental shrug.

"I'm not going anywhere with you until I have some sort of explanation," Stephen stated adamantly.

"Okay, here's the short version," Jamee said. "We're all Signs; we all have powers. We have to save a child that's going to be born soon. To do that, we need to get everyone together and we need to go now. The rest can be explained on the way." She turned to the others. "Did I leave anything out?" she asked them.

"Yes," said Xander. He reached out and grabbed Stephen. "Hang on."

* * * * * * * * * * * *

As it turned out, Dana was able to transfer information to Stephen mentally, so that by the time they landed, Stephen was fully aware of the situation. He stepped away from the group as soon as he could and stared at them, breathing hard.

"Nicely done," Tim complimented Dana.

"Thanks."

"Mind if I take a small turn?"

"Go right ahead."

Tim moved towards the suspicious Capricorn. He smiled gently at Stephen. "We know that probably wasn't the best way to gain your cooperation, but we're a little pressed for time. I'm sorry that you have to have things thrown at you, but we do need your help." He was careful not to overdo it. He wanted Stephen's trust; not his blind compliance. "The most important thing right now is to find the next Sign. She's the last one we have to locate before we rescue the Virgo."

Stephen held up a hand. "Look, I can feel your talent working and you don't have to do that. Don't use your talents on me and I won't use mine on you. Agreed?" Tim nodded. "I just need to sort things through in my mind. Either way, I'm along for the ride now, aren't I? It's not like you're going to send me back home any time soon."

"Back to the astranihl who're waitin' for ya?" Rory pointed out. "Nah, we won't do that. Not unless you want us to."

Stephen sighed. "I guess I don't really have a choice." He faced Emily. "If I hadn't felt your soul, I wouldn't be here at all."

"Guess you can blame me if things get really bad then," she joked.

He had to smile. "Very well. What do I do now?"

"Now, you get to find the next Sign," Emily told him. They walked him through the familiar routine and almost before the orange glow appeared, there was a green streak in it.

"That was fast," Jamee remarked.

He opened his eyes. "I'm a quick study. She's over there." They began to walk towards a public garden. There were colorful flowers everywhere and statues dotting the lawns.

"Reminds me of my house," Cole said.

"Mine too," said Dana.

"Reminds *me* of Kelsey's dream," said Tim.

Stephen strode along the paths, ignoring the passersby. He crossed a bridge and strolled underneath an arch formed by two maples. Bushes surrounded a statue of a woman holding an apple. A group of women perched, gossiping, on a park bench. Two young lovers held a picnic nearby. A family of five played happily together in the greenery. Stephen stopped.

"She's around here. I can feel her."

"Why aren't any of them glowing?" James wondered, scrutinizing all of the people around them.

"Kelsey said it was a girl," Rhys noted.

"We don't know how old she is," Dana said. "She could be an older woman."

"That doesn't make sense," said Cole. "We're all around the same age."

"And Sereny said that the planetary alignments happened once a year for twelve years. Which means that she fits one of the missing years." Tim pulled out the paper that Sereny had given him. "The first one was on August 4, 1970."

Rhys started. "That's me."

"Right," Dana said. "I remember Xander saying you were the oldest. Who's next?" she asked Tim.

"February 14, 1971," he read.

"Me," Cole responded.

"January 15, 1972," read Tim.

"That's me," Stephen responded.

"March 16, 1973." There was no answer. "What Sign is in March?"

"Oh, that's Pisces," Xander said. "Kelsey." There was a small hiatus while they explained to Stephen who Kelsey was. During this time, the ladies left the area and a few people came by, but none of the women glowed.

Tim returned to the list. "December 3, 1974."

"Present." Xander held up his hand, grinning.

"And I'm October 11th of '75," Tim acknowledged. "So who's November 7th of '76?"

"That one's me," Rory claimed.

"May 16th of '77." Silence. "Taurus or Virgo?"

"Taurus," Xander answered.

"She's twenty-two," Cole said, peering around.

"What about the Virgo?" Dana asked.

Tim, who was looking around as well, glanced back down at the paper. "June 6, 1978?"

"That's us," said Jamee.

"July 1, 1979?"

"No, that's me," Emily said.

"April 5th, '80?"

"Me," said Dana.

"So, I guess Virgo is September 10, 1981. The youngest of all of us."

"Great. Leave it to the baby to get into trouble," Dana joked.

"Meanwhile, where's Taurus?" Cole wondered aloud. There were very few people around them now.

"I sure don't see anyone who looks twenty-two," Rory said, mystified. Her hand hovered near the whip.

James turned to the others, nervous. "You don't think…"

"No, she's here," Stephen reassured them. "I just can't figure it out. Maybe it's cuz I'm new at this."

"Hey, guys. Come here." Emily was standing a small distance from them. They moved as a group to stand by her and she pointed to the statue. What had been hidden by the greenery before was now vivid against a backdrop of blue sky: a green aura surrounding the figure. "I think she's been here the whole time."

"The statue?" Rhys asked incredulously.

Dana walked up and knocked on the statue's shoulder. "Dana!" Tim admonished.

"What?" she said. "It doesn't look like she can feel it."

"Just great," James said. "Someone turned our Taurus to stone."

"I don't think so," Xander contradicted him. He moved around the statue, observing her from different angles. "Taurus is known for its stubborn nature. Wanting a Taurus to do something and getting them to do something are two completely different things. If they want to, they can become completely unmovable on a topic." He laughed. "A statue. That's a pretty clear demonstration of immobility."

"Then we have a bit of a problem," said James. "If she doesn't want to join us, we're between a rock and a hard place. Speaking of rocks, how do we get her to stop being one?"

"You ask nicely, of course," was the statue's reply. The granite color faded into a flesh tone and white dress. She moved gracefully, but purposefully towards a bench. The Signs quickly looked around, but the Taurus had picked the right moment; there was no one around them to witness the strange occurrence. She seated herself and took a bite of her apple. "Now," she said through a mouthful, "why don't you start at the beginning?"

* * * * * * * * * * *

Since there seemed to be no immediate threat, the story was told yet again. Tim reveled in the fact that, except for the Virgo, this would be the last time he would have to listen to it. Stephen also paid close attention. The two Earth Signs were silent as they took in the information that was being handed to them. Finally, with a small demonstration of talents, the Signs were able to get their new member to open up.

Elizabeth Medina, or Izzy, had the power to become stone, unmovable and impervious. She had used it at different points in her life when she felt threatened. This explained her state of being when they found her. "I was sitting in the park when I felt something strange lock onto me. I didn't know it was you," she apologized to Stephen. "So I found a good spot and went stone. I could feel you guys getting closer and closer. I was just gonna wait for you to go away, but then I heard you talking. You mentioned something about a Taurus and I knew this was something different. Then Emily discovered my secret." Emily blushed.

"So you're on board?" Xander asked her.

"I'm on board," Izzy answered.

"And we thought the Earth Signs would be difficult to get," Jamee remarked.

"Stephen wasn't exactly easy," Emily pointed out.

"And Virgo's another challenge," Rhys added. "A rescue mission."

"Yes, how do you plan on rescuing him?" Stephen asked. The group looked uncomfortable.

Cole spoke. "We don't exactly have a plan yet. We've been told to focus our efforts on you."

"We need to get back to The Gathering," Xander said. "Maybe they have a plan ready for us."

"I think we gotta talk to Kelsey too," Rory suggested. "He might have some idea of what we're headin' into."

"But I still have a life here," Izzy protested.

"Trust me, Izzy," said James. "Merel's already got one Sign and she's looking to collect. If she gets you, it's not much of a life."

Frustrated, Izzy saw both sympathy and resolve in their faces. It was Stephen who finally helped her decision. "I'm not too comfortable with this either, but you don't want to see what the other side has to offer."

Suddenly, Dana and Emily screamed and fell to the ground. Tim was about to ask when he felt it: the Virgo. They were slowly draining him of his energy and talent. All of the Signs were reeling, but Dana and Emily were especially affected.

Tim snatched at the bottle of dampening draught and poured it into their mouths. The screaming subsided, but now people were beginning to converge on the group.

"We need to get out of here," Rhys said.

"Now," Xander agreed, holding out his hands. Terrified, the Signs, including Izzy, grabbed a hold and vanished from the spot.

Where are we going? Tim asked.

A brief stop at home for supplies and then we're going to get our last family member, Xander replied.

They landed in the main hall. Dana sent out a mental shout and a group of people came running. At the front of the pack were the Conlyns, Sereny, and Chris, with Professor Galten bringing up the rear. Xander asked Rhys to explain the situation while he went for weaponry. His father forestalled him. "We're ready for this, son."

"What?"

"Your father had a vision," Mrs. Conlyn explained.

"Damn good thing, too, by the looks of it," the professor added. "Everyone ready?"

"Yes, and we have our own transportation, so don't worry about us," Mr. Conlyn said. He pointed to the conjurers standing by.

"But you don't even know where they are," Xander protested. Tim watched the conversation with disbelief. Were they really going to head into an full scale battle?

"We've been busy since you left. Once I got my vision, I was able to determine a few things about the terrain and the surrounding area to realize that I knew the place. Surprised you didn't, actually. They've been right by that house we bought when you were young."

"In Oklahoma?"

"Outside of the city," Mr. Conlyn agreed. "An old, abandoned mansion."

"I know that mansion! Dad, we have to go now!" Tim looked around to see people already beginning to vanish from the hall as the conjurers got to work.

His father nodded. "Just go in and get the Virgo. Fight only if you have to! We can't lose any of you." The hall was only half full now as more and more people vanished. "And don't worry about us! We'll see you on the other side. Now go!"

The Signs all moved into their usual traveling formation. Tim could feel Dana's hand, tight and tense in his own, and he squeezed reassuringly. Professor Galten was already gone. Mrs. Conlyn blew them a kiss. Mr. Conlyn waved. The world changed.

Chapter 24

They found themselves in the midst of chaos. All around them, people were fighting, yelling, bleeding. The air was thick with astranihl. Tim saw a member of The Gathering carried into the air and dropped from a great height. He landed nearby in a heap and did not move. Rory had already removed the glove from her whip-hand and held her weapon ready. Tim saw Rhys grab a rock from the ground and take aim at the airborne enemy. He gripped her wrist, stalling her throw. She faced him in angry surprise and the cats hissed warningly.

"Don't fight unless we have to, remember?" Her face did not lose its fury, but the rock dropped from her hand. Tim turned towards Xander to see Jamee already pointing out a route. Xander gestured to the rest of them and they ran through the battle, dodging people and astranihl alike. Tim had no way of knowing who of the humans was a friend and who was an enemy, so avoided them all. He could see that they were headed for the side of the building. As he ran, he thought he detected a faint iridescent glow surrounding the mansion. *The energy field,* he thought and he was very glad that he was not wearing the deadly silver bracelets. It was a maze to get through all of the fighting. Most were involved in their own battles, but the large group running together drew attention. The big cats did their best to fight off these attacks, but before they knew it, an astranihl snatched Jamee and, with a cry of triumph, began to rise. Screaming, she struggled against her attacker. Cole leapt for her, but missed. Rory was faster. With a crack of her whip, a thin line of red appeared on the astranihl and it faltered.

"First blood," Rory mused aloud. Jamee's captor recovered quickly and resumed its deadly climb. Other astranihl were converging on the spot as Jamee's screams were growing fainter. Rory's whip blurred as she lashed each attacker that came within range. The Brownings were leaping and pouncing on others. Izzy had turned to stone and Stephen was freezing as many as he could.

"So much for not fighting," Tim muttered.

"What are we gonna do?" Emily cried.

Rory continued to strike out, keeping the astranihl at bay. "Just wait," she said.

"We're just supposed to wait?!" Dana screamed hysterically. "Wait for what?" She was breathing heavily and glaring at Rory.

With a swift stroke, Rory sliced her whip across an astranihl's neck, causing it to fall to the ground, and turned to Dana. "Smaller dose of poison," she responded and pointed to the sky. Those who were not fighting tilted their heads upwards to see two figures plummeting towards the ground. Rory, meanwhile, had returned to the fray.

"Stephen!" Rhys bellowed. Stephen turned and saw the problem. He moved quickly, peering up at the sky. Jamee's screaming was audible again and becoming more so with each passing moment.

"Gonna have to time this right," Stephen muttered. They waited, hardly daring to breathe, as the battle raged around them. Jamee was falling face down, spread eagle, fingers splayed as if she thought it would hurt less if she were spread out more. Stephen took a deep breath and focused his talent. The astranihl hit the ground with a sickening crunch. Jamee froze a foot from the ground, her eyes wide open and her body tense. Xander moved towards her and picked her up in his arms.

"Geez, she's heavier than I thought."

"Most statues are," said Izzy, returning to flesh. "Even the living ones."

A thought occurred to Tim. "Uh, Stephen? She's not gonna keep falling when you unfreeze her, is she?"

"Actually, no. Stopping time seems to stop physics." Stephen looked thoughtful. "Kind of a strange phenomenon. I've been meaning to research that."

"Yeah, fascinating," Dana said. "Unfreeze her so we can get inside!" Startled, Stephen obeyed and the small girl was suddenly screaming in Xander's arms. Xander quickly clamped a hand over her mouth.

"You're safe," he said. Mute, eyes wide, she nodded and he removed his hand and set her on the ground. Her legs wobbled and she shifted into James.

"She needs some time to recover," he said. "That was *not* fun!" He looked around at the astranihl that littered the ground around them. He turned to Rory and the Brownings. "Nice job," James complimented them.

"Thank goodness there weren't more. That was about all I could handle," Rory admitted.

"Well, that's helpful to know," said a familiar voice. Tim whirled around to see Lena standing before them with a group of human-form astranihl behind her. Rory stepped forward, reaching for her whip. "I wouldn't if I were you," Lena warned.

From within the group, a pair was brought forward, bound and gagged. They were not familiar to most of the Signs, but one Sign knew them all too well.

"Nell! Gary!"

Nell's head snapped up and she stared pleadingly at Tim. Gary thrashed about, but his captors held him firmly. Lena smiled a cold, cruel smile. "Why, they just happened to come into the diner and Nell mentioned how much she missed you. Of course I had to arrange a reunion, didn't I?"

"Let them go," Tim growled at her.

"What's the matter, Tim? Aren't you happy to see Nell again?"

The other Signs kept silent, recognizing the personal interest and allowing him to handle it. None of them knew Nell or Gary, but they knew this would affect Tim. It seemed Merel was happy to incapacitate a Sign however she could.

Tim tried to summon his talent, but there was a white hot knot of anger in his chest and his attempt at a smile was more of a grimace. "They have nothing to do with this, Lena."

"Oh, but they do, Tim. They do. You see, I'm happy to make a trade. The Virgo for these two."

"You don't want those two," Tim said.

Lena grabbed Nell's chin and turned her so she could examine Nell's face. "No," she said. "I don't." She let go and Nell's head dropped. "But *you* do. I bet you don't want to see your dear friend cooped up with me this whole time. So, I'm offering you a choice. You can either take someone you've never met or you can save your childhood friend." Tim's mind went blank. "Of course," Lena continued, "this is a limited time offer. I wouldn't want to see harm come to any of them, but if you don't choose soon, I can guarantee that it will." A few members of her band raised weapons. Tim thought he recognized the doctor who had used the *psyphagyte* on him. He couldn't think. He willed his brain to function, but it was resistant. He couldn't meet Nell's eyes, but he saw a tear slip down her cheek and his heart squeezed. He knew what he had to do and he stepped forward.

Stall, Dana's voice sounded in his head. He tried not to show his surprise.

"Well?" Lena asked.

"I'm thinking! This isn't easy, Lena. You can't expect me to make up my mind on something like this in just a few minutes. Nell's my best friend, but it's not just her life at stake. It's the whole world. The whole universe, in fact."

"Then choose to take the Virgo and we'll be done," Lena told him, but Tim could see she was nervous.

"It's not that simple. I can't just hand Nell over to you knowing what you'll do to her and Gary. I need more time. At least let me see the Virgo."

"Oh, that's not possible." Lena spread her hands. "You see, he's keeping an appointment with a technological friend of yours." The doctor grinned at Tim from the midst of the crowd. "The longer you wait, the worse it gets for him."

"You're gonna kill him." It was not a question.

"Eventually. We have lots of experiments to do first. Most will take a while. All of them are painful." She was obviously enjoying this.

They're torturing him, Tim thought to Dana. *We have to get him out of there.*

Almost ready, she promised.

"How do I know that's really Nell and Gary?" Tim asked, his mind racing. "They could be someone else magicked to look like them or something."

"Perhaps I can help persuade you." Lena pulled out a wicked, three-pronged blade and held it against Nell's side. Tim knew that blade's touch all too well. Nell struggled to get away from the cold steel pricking her flesh, but Lena held her with an iron grip. "Do you really want to take the chance that it's not Nell?" she inquired. Tears were streaming down Nell's face and a muffled screaming could be heard through the gag. Lena walked Nell forward a few steps so that Tim could see the tiny drops of blood that had started to appear on Nell's side.

Tim was sweating and his heart was hammering against his ribs. It was anguish for him to see Nell in this predicament, especially knowing that he was the cause, and it was taking all of his willpower to remain outwardly calm. He waited for a word from Dana, but nothing came. He tried to think of something, anything that would stall what seemed to be the inevitable, but his mind seemed to be numb. The silence took on an almost physical tension between them. Lena pressed harder and Nell's screaming grew louder.

"Choose or there won't be anyone left to choose from," she warned. All around them, the battle raged, but Tim could only look at Lena, locked in a deadly stalemate until he came to a decision. Dana's voice exploded in his mind.

Get Nell!

Without thinking, Tim lunged forward, grabbing Nell. Lena, unprepared for such a sudden move, moved a hair too late. There was a wind across the back of Tim's neck as he bore Nell to the ground. He looked up to see a large handle protruding from Lena's neck. She coughed, blood spurting from her mouth and fell to the ground. Tim's gaze turned towards Jamee, who stood there with a matching blade in her hand.

The Gemini's eyes glowed with righteous hatred. "Bitch."

The astranihl leapt into action. Tim pulled Nell to her feet and ran towards Gary. His two captors stood stock still and offered no resistance as he pulled Gary free from their hold. Tim looked back to see Stephen wink as he froze yet another astranihl. Izzy had returned to statue form and astranihl struck her repeatedly with no result. Others fell to Rory's whip. Jamee was fighting viciously with her knife.

Xander came running over and Tim shoved Nell and Gary towards him, yelling at him to get them to safety. Xander nodded and the trio vanished. Tim turned back towards the fight and, concentrating, tried to charm an astranihl, but he had never charmed the deadly enemy before and fearful anger blocked his talent. He rushed over to where the Brownings were protecting Dana and Rhys as Xander returned. He shouted over to Tim, "Safe at home!" Tim's body sagged in relief, but the relief didn't last long.

Cole ran over as the last of Lena's group fell. "We have to go!"

They wasted no time in dashing towards the mansion, dodging bodies as they ran. Tim was terrified and furious. His mind kept replaying Nell's terrified face, fueling his rage, spurring him on towards the mansion. He could see the vague iridescent haze that was the energy field. There was no one around. All of the astranihl were involved in the battle, leaving the energy field unguarded. Pushing himself to move even faster, he leapt towards it and fell to the ground, winded, as the energy field proved to be solid. It took a few moments for him to get his breath back. Confused and dizzy, he looked to the left and right of him and saw the rest of the Signs painfully picking themselves up off the ground.

Rhys walked up to the energy field and put a hand on it. "This is a wall," she said.

"We're so stupid!" Dana exclaimed. "Xander..."

She turned towards Xander, who was already tense with concentration. "I can't get through it!" Xander cried.

Jamee joined him at the field. "It wasn't like this before. They must have changed it."

"Well, how are we going to get through?" Emily asked. Tim felt the first pangs of panic.

"I can try to freeze it," Stephen said. "It looks like it's made up of energy particles constantly moving around which is what creates that light coming from it. If I can freeze the particles, it might create a hole for us to go through." Yet, he looked doubtful.

"We don't have any other options," Dana said. "Do it!"

Stephen concentrated. There was a shimmer in the energy field. They all held their breath as he moved to touch it. His hand came up to the field and met resistance. He shook his head. "I was wrong. This light isn't created by moving particles. It's actual light. Somehow, Merel has a way to make light solid."

"We gotta get through solid light?" Rory asked, skeptical. "That's impossible."

Cole stepped forward. "There might be a way." The ground began to rumble beneath them and a few Signs cried out in alarm, but instead of the danger they were all expecting, a geiser of water burst from the ground. It quickly eroded the land around it and before they knew it, the energy field was bisecting a fairly large lake. Cole immediately dove into the lake, submerging himself in the clear water.

They watched his shadow travel underneath the iridescent barrier and emerge on the other side. "Water refracts light," he called to them. "Even a solid wall of light can't continue straight down. The water deflects it. Swim under."

They did as they were told and Cole used his talent to dry them off. As the last Sign emerged from the lake, Emily screamed. An astranihl was zooming towards them, but came up short against the barrier. Cole waited patiently until it plunged into the water. The lake disappeared as quickly as it had come, leaving the astranihl in an earthly tomb. Emily shivered.

"Nicely done, Cole," Rhys complimented him.

"And a little scary," Tim added. The idea of being buried alive had always terrified him.

Jamee was already moving amongst the mansion's columns, searching for a door. When she found it, she beckoned to the rest of them. "This will lead into the hallway on the ground floor," she whispered. Izzy took the lead, glowing softly.

As the Signs filed through the open doorway, Tim turned to Dana. "What happened back there? And why didn't you tell me what was going on?"

"You were trying to figure out what to do. I didn't want to give you too much information or it would have shown on your face." She shivered as they moved from the daylight into the dark, torch-lit hallway. "Besides, I had my mind full explaining to Izzy how to get the Virgo while keeping everyone updated on Jamee's situation."

Tim was completely thrown. "Jamee's situation? What was wrong with her?"

"Nothing," Jamee answered him, quietly closing the door behind her. "I needed time to make those weapons. Those knives didn't come from thin air. I had to make them out of grass and that took time."

"Sorry I didn't tell you," Dana said.

"Blades of grass into blades of steel," Tim said, grudgingly admiring the humor. "Well done."

Jamee shrugged. "She had it coming." They turned in time to see Izzy's green aura take on a white streak. "She's got him. Let's go."

Chapter 25

Tim's stomach twisted as the stale air flooding his nostrils brought back hideous memories. He felt Jamee stiffen beside him and he knew she was reliving her torturous stay. As they moved further and further into the bowels of the beast, Tim developed an almost heightened awareness of his surroundings. Every shadow seemed to hide an enemy waiting to strike and it was with great apprehension that he found himself standing before a large, locked, wooden door.

"He's in there," Izzy whispered.

"How do we get in?" Rhys asked.

"Why ain't it guarded?" Rory wanted to know.

"I can't get us in, but I can get us out," Xander said.

"I can get us in," Izzy said, "but it's gonna be noisy." There was a scream from behind the door.

"Sounds like it's already noisy," Dana said. "Get us in there."

"Okay. Stand back." Tim's anxiety increased exponentially as he watched Izzy run and leap at the door, changing to stone in midair. The impact caused the door to explode into splinters. Astranihl came pouring out of the room like bats scared from their cave. Fighting on the battleground was fairly difficult. Fighting in an enclosed hallway was near impossible. There were enemies coming from all angles and more than once, he found himself face to face with another Sign before realizing who he was fighting. He could hear grunts and yells from all around him and every scream, be it friend or foe, sent a chill through his bowels. There was blood splattering everywhere and he was constantly tripping over bodies.

Tim's heart pounded in his throat as he faced enemy after enemy. He wanted to use his talent, but he could barely concentrate. There was a scream to his left and out of the corner of his eye, he saw Dana fall. He moved to help her, but was sent reeling by a blow to the head. Dizzy, he stumbled towards a wall and that's when he saw the Virgo. Strapped to a table with a psyphagyte sitting on top of him, he struggled wildly against his bonds as the malevolent machine penetrated his chest. He felt someone grab him and he whirled, prepared to fight, but it was Stephen.

"I can freeze it, but you gotta get it off of him!" he yelled over the din. Tim nodded and ran towards the table.

From his right, he saw an astranihl approaching him, but there was a loud crack and Rory screamed, "Keep goin'!" He focused on the scene in front of him. Both the boy and the machine were still, frozen. He grabbed the machine, wincing as he pulled it from the boy's prone flesh and hurled it to the ground, hard. Satisfied, he turned to free the boy, but he heard Izzy's voice.

"Tim! Look out!" He whipped around to see the machine in one piece skittering quickly towards him. On instinct, he kicked out, catching the machine unaware and sending it across the room where it landed in front of Izzy. Horrified, he watched the machine climb her body and the needles emerged. They jammed into her...and broke off. Izzy had turned to stone. The machine jabbed at her again and again until she suddenly brought her arms in and hugged herself, smashing the psyphagyte against her stone chest. Breathing heavily, she rushed to the table and began untying the Virgo. "Help me!" she pleaded.

Tim automatically obeyed. Together, they released the young Sign as more of the Signs came pouring into the room, some still fighting. James appeared at Tim's side and, concentrating hard, was able to transform the Virgo's silver bracelets into harmless hunks of metal.

Dispatching another astranihl, Xander called out to the Signs and like one entity, they moved, grabbing hold of each other along the way. Cole was carrying the limp form of Dana in his arms, blood leaking through the hand he had pressed to her chest. Rory was last to reach them. She sliced an astranihl across the chest and placed her gloved hand around Stephen's arm. The mad scene in front of them dissolved into a different kind of chaos.

Where are we going? What do we do now? What happened to Dana? Did we get the Virgo? Is he okay?

The questions flew from mind to mind, creating a building tension throughout the group. With a jolt, they landed in the great hall of The Gathering and Xander immediately called for the healers. There was no response. Now that they were safely back in the castle, the battle trauma overcame Tim. A wave of nausea washed over him and he vomited. Izzy laid the Virgo on the floor with his arms out and was anxiously checking him over. His wrists were decorated with red burn marks; a parting gift from the bracelets. Cole clutched Dana close to him, trying to stanch the bleeding. Rhys moved between them, examining each of the unresponsive Signs as tension built in the hall.

"What happened to Dana?" Emily cried.

"Astranihl's knife," Cole said bluntly.

"We need the healers!" Rhys yelled into the room. It echoed hollowly.

"Someone has to be here," Xander stated firmly, but Tim could see he was shaken. "There has to be someone to protect The Gathering."

Stephen shook his head. "Doesn't look like it."

"But the healers–"

"–left to take care of those that were hurt," Sereny whispered from a corner. They all jumped. She emerged from the shadows with slow, measured steps as if she did not trust herself to walk. Her face was a haggard mask of pain and misery.

"We thought there was no one here," Jamee said, relieved.

Sereny laughed a bitter little laugh. "No one here. Only me. I'm all alone."

Tim moved cautiously towards the psychic. "Sereny," he said gently, "we need the healers. Dana is hurt."

Her eyes seemed to look through him. "They all left. Not coming back," she said sadly.

"Sereny!" He grabbed her by the arms and shook her. "We need help now! How do we get the healers?"

"Can't," she whispered. He let her go and she sank down to the floor, staring straight ahead. "Can't see."

"She's gonna die if we don't find someone," Cole said.

"I can..." said a faint voice. It was the Virgo.

"You can't do anything," Izzy told him compassionately. "You're too weak."

"Can heal," he insisted softly. "Need to touch her." The fingers of his outstretched hand twitched. Cole looked to the others, then carried Dana over and laid her down next to their newest member. They could see her heart through a gaping chest wound, weeping blood. A few shut their eyes for a moment, but none of them could turn away. The boy turned his head gently to the side and saw the unconscious girl before him. He stretched his fingers towards Dana.

As his fingertips brushed her skin, a violent shudder wracked her body. Cole moved towards her, but Rhys placed a hand on his chest and he halted, a cry of protest dying on his lips. Her upper body rippled. They watched in fascination as her chest muscles stretched towards each other over her heart, obscuring it from view. Izzy watched anxiously as the boy gritted his teeth, sweat breaking out on his forehead. Dana's skin formed, closing the wound, and the boy broke the contact, exhausted. Izzy and Cole immediately examined their respective charges, checking for further injury.

Cole looked up. "There's no scar, no mark. Nothing," he said in wonder.

"Can heal," the boy repeated and fell unconscious.

* * * * * * * * * * *

"So what are we going to do?" Emily asked, biting her lip. The Signs had gathered in the hospital wing near the prone newcomer and were conversing in hushed tones. Sereny hovered at the edge of the group, rarely contributing, except to repeat her declaration of solitude. There had been what little ministrations they could do with the absence of the healers, who were now attending those on the battlefield. The castle felt drafty without the constant noise of its members and more than a few Signs were on edge.

"We only have one choice," Jamee stated. "We have to go to the libraries and get our birthrights."

"We don't know if they can help," Stephen protested.

"Yeah, but without them, we don't have a clue what to do," Dana countered.

"He's not ready," Izzy said, indicating their new member.

"We don't have a lot of time," Rhys added. The cats growled in agreement.

"Well, the only one who can heal is the one who's injured. Perfect," Tim muttered sarcastically.

"You're not helping," Cole told him. "We simply have to find a way to heal him. There must be something that we're missing."

"We've already searched the room," Dana complained.

"And there's nothing here that any of us understands," Rory added.

"Not any of us," Xander agreed, "but maybe someone else." He faced the psychic. "Sereny, do you know of anything here that could help us revive the Virgo?" She stared at him, silent. He grabbed her by the arms and shook her. "Sereny! We need help now!"

"Transference," Dana said. The others looked at her. "She thought about transference. What does that mean?" she asked the woman.

"Transference." Sereny tasted it on her lips. "Release. Transference." She laughed aloud; a wild cackle that erupted from the depths of her throat. "Yes, freedom." She continued to laugh. "I can do transference."

"What is she talkin' about?" Rory asked aloud.

"The healers do a kind of energy transference..." Xander began, but Dana cut him off.

"No. She's talking about a total transference. Her energy goes completely into his. There's nothing left."

"That's what she means by freedom," Emily said, horrified. "She's going to kill herself."

"She can't do that!" Tim exclaimed.

"She can and will," Sereny argued in a quiet voice. Her eyes were filled with sorrow, but the cloudiness was gone. In her hand, she held a vial filled with brightly colored, viscous liquid. "My mother was the last of the great seers. She said something before she died that I never understood until now. 'You will heal the healer.' I'm going to do this."

"No!" Tim grabbed for her, but she dodged and moved to stand beside the unconscious Virgo.

"It's time," she said simply and uncorked the vial. She examined each of their faces, noting the fear and sadness. "I will miss you. Don't be afraid to create a better future for all of us." She lifted the vial as though in a toast, then tipped it down her throat. Her features began to blur, transforming the woman into an amorphous blob. From where her mouth had been, a sigh escaped and they could see it form in the air before them. The sigh seemed to pull her body along and for a brief moment, there was a struggle between the visible breath and the fading body. The breath won and what used to be Sereny was completely encompassed by that swirling gust of air. It flowed around each of the Signs and finally came to hover over the Virgo. Tim felt a thought tickle at the edge of his mind.

Goodbye.

Chapter 26

"Welcome back," Izzy said warmly. Tim was jealous of her ability to smile in light of such a loss, but he reminded himself that she hadn't really known Sereny. He brushed tears aside as they gathered around the boy, who was now opening his eyes.

She wanted this, Dana told him. *The loss of her mother affected her more than we thought. For all of her dedication to The Gathering, she didn't want to be here anymore. That's why she spent so much time in the Hall of Mirrors. She was happier in her memories.*

How do you know all of this? Tim asked.

I've been picking it up for awhile now, but Sereny asked me not to say anything. Let her go. She's happy now.

Sereny would want them to move on to the next step. So he focused his attention on the newest Sign.

"Thanks," the boy whispered.

"How do you feel?" Emily asked him.

"Tired. Wired. Both," he responded. "Never felt this way after a healing. Did something go wrong? Is she okay?"

The Signs looked confused, but Dana picked up his thoughts. "He means from healing me," she told them. "I'm fine," she reassured the boy. "Thanks." She seemed embarrassed by her recent recovery.

"I'm glad you're okay, Dana," the boy said, sitting up. The sores on his wrists were fading quickly.

She seemed startled. "How did you–?

He appeared a little surprised as well. "I – I don't know. I just knew your name. And I know who we are. I didn't know about any of this before. Trines and quincunxes, what's going on?" His eyes were wide.

Tim recognized the odd phrase. "Sereny," he breathed. "She gave you her life, so you must have access to her memories or something!"

"Do you have visions too?" Jamee asked eagerly.

The boy was silent, internally searching. He raised his eyes to them. "Doesn't look like it. I don't have all of her memories either. Whoever this Sereny person was, she only left me memories that have to do with us."

Cole was awed. "How did she manage to do that?"

Tim smiled. "Thanks, Sereny," he said softly.

"Well, since you know all of us, how about an introduction?" Rory asked him.

"Oh, it's Michael. Michael Conway."

"Nice to meet you," Stephen said politely.

"Same here." Michael cocked his head. "There's something about nascregala that's floating at the front of the memories. I don't know what it means."

"Told you," said Jamee. "We have to get to Kelsey; he might have found out more about the birthrights."

"Who's Kelsey?" Michael asked.

Xander spoke up. "I already have the library locations in my mind. We don't have time to check in with Kelsey. Michael, do you think you can travel?" Michael looked as though he would have liked to ask more, but instead, he nodded. "Good. Everybody link up."

* * * * * * * * * * *

The group stood at the Library of Fire. It was just as they had been shown by Kelsey. Little glimpses of a building peeked through the great inferno. From the center, an explosion of flames leaped towards them, making them back up and rub their stinging eyes. When they could see again, there was an elderly man standing before them. He wore a robe of iridescent orange that flickered as he moved, mimicking the fire behind him. Smiling beneficently upon the Signs, he held out a hand in a gesture of welcome.

"Aries, Leo, and Sagittarius, step forward," he said. His voice crackled. Rhys and Dana stepped forward immediately, Xander close behind them. Andoleen nodded approvingly. When he spoke again, it was in low tones that only the three of them could hear. The cats growled and returned to the group. Without Rhys, Tim had no idea what Harmony was trying to tell him. The three Fire Signs turned towards the building and walked forward into the inferno. Tim's heart squeezed as he watched Xander disappear, but his mind trusted the Fire Patron. Andoleen watched them go with a proud bearing, then turned back to the group. "You have your own challenges to face." And so saying, he smiled at them and the scene before them burned up, replacing it with the Library of Earth.

The vines were still there, and there was a stirring among them. From within the vines, a beautiful woman with skin the color of deep rosewood and an oaky fragrance emerged. She carried three flowers in her hands. "Taurus, Virgo, and Capricorn, I have something for you." She spoke in smooth, dulcet tones. Izzy, Michael, and Stephen moved towards her and she handed them each a flower. Once again, there was a hushed conversation between the Earth Signs and the Dryad, then they moved towards the building. The vines parted for them, revealing a doorway, and closed immediately behind them. Rythsinda looked at the cats and nodded. "I will care for the animals until this is over." They ran to the Dryad and rubbed against her happily. She took the cats back amongst the vines, blending in and soon lost to view. The earth began to shake and a crack appeared before them. The crack quickly filled with water, spreading and transforming the scene before them into the ocean and leaving them standing on the shore. The six remaining Signs looked at each other.

"Guess it's your turn," Jamee said to the three Water Signs. Tim looked again. *Three?* It was true; Kelsey was present, though somewhat hazy and, upon closer inspection, disheveled. Kelsey caught him looking.

"There have been attacks on the Dreamworld," he said. "I've been using all my power to keep it intact, but she's getting stronger." They had no need to ask who *she* was.

The head of a young boy broke the surface of the water. "Hi!" he said brightly. "Um, can I talk to Cancer, Scorpio, and Pisces?"

The three Water Signs moved forward towards the cherubic creature. He spoke once again in a low voice, smiling impishly all the while. He gestured behind him and Emily, Rory, and Kelsey vanished beneath the water with barely a ripple. The boy slipped underneath after them and the Air Signs were left by themselves.

"What now?" Jamee asked.

All of a sudden, there was a splash and the boy reemerged. "Sorry!" he called out. "I forgot." With a flick of his fin, a tidal wave rose and sped at frightening rate towards the shorebound Signs. Tim involuntarily cried out.

"It won't hurt us," Cole promised his companions. Niole disappeared as the tidal wave crashed over them. Just as Cole had assured them, there was no feeling as the wave touched them, but as the water swept through them and they were left on the other side, they found themselves at the Library of Air.

The marble building looked no more unusual than any other. Without warning, the wind began to blow around them, lifting their clothing and hair, but not uncomfortably so. It whipped into a frenzy, becoming a howling gale that shook their surroundings with its force. Suddenly, they found themselves in the eye of the storm accompanied by a middle aged woman whose body appeared to be constructed of petals. She spoke:

"Gemini, Aquarius, and Libra, welcome to the Library of Air. I am Manaran, Seed-Keeper." Tim felt he was in the presence of something wondrous and he bowed, folding awkwardly from the waist. Cole performed a more fluid bow and Jamee, unsure of what do, ended up half-bowing and half-curtsying. Manaran smiled at them. "The curiosity of the Air Element is legendary and I know of thine eagerness to begin, but be forewarned. Each must earn thy nascregala through a test of talent and character. Demonstrate prowess and the nascregala is won. Fail, and all is lost."

"What does the nascregala do?" Jamee asked.

"Thou shalt discover the purpose of the nascregala when it is within thy possession," the Patron informed her. "None may help on this perilous journey. Pay heed to thine instinct and have caution. Yet, ye shalt not go without gifts. Here." She reached in among the petals and held out her hand. In her palm were three seeds. "Take one each. These are seeds of thought. Use them if there is need."

"How?" Cole wanted to know.

"Swallow the seed and it will take root," Manaran told him. "Now, go." She gestured towards a large cloud. "Through there lie the answers ye seek." The three Signs looked nervously at each other and together, they stepped towards the occluded entrance.

Tim thought of something. "How will we find the others?" he asked, turning around, but there were only a few petals on the wind to hint that Manaran had ever been there. The Signs shared another anxious glance, slowly vanishing in the layers of mist.

Chapter 27

He stood in a cavernous marble hall with enormous windows that stretched from ceiling to floor. The library appeared to be on the peak of a mountain and clouds were the only things in view. Inside, there were beautiful statues of birds, faeries, sylphs, and other creatures associated with the air, including an enormous Pegasus in the middle of the hall. Paintings and drawings bedecked the walls and the constant tinkle of hidden wind chimes sounded in his ear. A gentle breeze lazily danced through the area. Swatches of cloth caught the breeze and partnered it in a colorful pas du deux. Tim looked around him, fascinated by all of the beauty. As he moved about the room, however, he noticed something peculiar. Every window showed exactly the same cloud pattern regardless of where he was in the hall. It gave him an eerie feeling to know that these were not true windows to the outside world.

A feeling that intensified when he realized that he was alone.

"Jamee?" he called out. "Cole?" The chimes tinkled merrily in response. Tim crossed the entire room, still calling for his friends. He halted suddenly before the Pegasus statue. The mane was moving. It was ever so slight, but the mane rippled as though it were blowing in the wind. He moved to the hindquarters. The tail was moving as well. Returning to the front, he reached out hesitantly to touch a leg. Stone cold. He focused upon the mane again and the statue winked. Tim gasped, quickly backing away. He hurried over to a statue of a faery and examined it closely. No movement. Cautiously, he crept back towards the Pegasus. The statue unmistakably winked again. Cautiously circling the statue, Tim saw that there was writing on the stone block beneath the winged creature. He read:

"Horse of poet, horse of Muse,
Ridden by the dawn.

Ride! For I am yours to use,
If you can stay on.
Charm me into waking light;
Fly upon the hour.
For nascregala, you must fight.
Trust in your own power."

Tim ran his fingers over the words etched into the stone. His gaze returned to the powerful lithic creature before him. "I have to ride Pegasus to earn my birthright?" The idea seemed absolutely ludicrous. "Jamee? Cole?" he called hopefully. He really wanted someone to help him. Manaran's words came floating back to him: *none may help on this perilous journey.* He exhaled explosively, venting his frustrations, and eyed the statue before him with anxiety. He had never ridden a horse, let alone a flying one. How was he to stay on? *Trust in your own power,* the poem said. A decision was made within him. With a swift movement, he climbed up onto the stone beast's back and settled himself between the wings. Tentatively, he took a hold of the creature's mane and with a deep breath, he tapped into his talent. "Wake up," he said. He felt warmth spread through the stone and with a whicker of joy and a terrifying beat of the wings, the animal leapt into the air. Tim emitted a half-scream and flattened himself to the creature's back.

Okay, he thought wildly, *I'm riding Pegasus. Now what?*

You must get to your nascregala, Pegasus answered him. Tim was so startled, he almost fell off the creature's back. Only by quick reflexes and an adjustment from the winged horse was he able to right himself.

"You can talk?"

In a manner of speaking, the horse said. *You have charmed me into life and for that, I will suffer you to ride me.*

"Great. Thanks. So, that's all I have to do and I get my birthright?"

No. You must get permission to enter the sacred hall, was the answer.

"How do I get that?"

They descended and Tim's breathing became easier. *Only one of the other statues can grant you access to the sacred hall. You must charm them into life as you did with me.*

"Which one?" Tim asked, frustrated.

I do not know.

His frustration growing, Tim directed Pegasus nearer to the ground, choosing a petite, sweet-looking faery. Smiling, he said, "Wake up." The faery opened her eyes, blinked once, and with a buzz of her wings was zooming around the room. Tim tried to follow her, but she was too quick. A buzzing began to fill his ears, however; suddenly, the air was filled with flying creatures zipping about the hall. "What happened?"

Waking one of them wakes them all.

"Why didn't you tell me that before?!"

You didn't ask.

Tim closed his eyes and swore, partaking of Nell's healthy breadth of curses. When he opened his eyes, he found himself face to face with a giant that stood almost to the ceiling of the hall. The giant's skin appeared to be moving and upon closer inspection, Tim saw that the giant was comprised of all of the tiny flying creatures that had been woken when he charmed the faery. In the giant's hand was a sword, scintillating with the glint from thousands of beaks and miniature swords. Tim had no doubt that those could do a great deal of damage to him if he got too close.

"I charmed the faery, so they should all be charmed, right?"

They are not beholden to the laws that govern me. I am required to serve the Master who can free me from my stone prison. The other statues are sworn to protect the sacred hall. They will do everything they can to prevent you gaining access to the hall.

"I was afraid you'd say that," Tim muttered. "Well, Pegasus, looks like it's time to trust my power. Let's go!" Pegasus flew up around the giant's head. Up close, Tim could see the tiny figures brandishing weapons at him and a score of arrows arced towards the pair. Pegasus dodged and Tim suddenly found himself sliding off the side of the horse. Scrambling for position, he felt himself slipping further until Pegasus maneuvered to resettle Tim solidly on his back.

I will not let you fall.

Only halfway reassured, Tim focused on the giant arm that was in front of him and, forcing a smile, he reached into his soul. To his amazement, he saw a pale lavender wave of light emanate from him and smash into the giant's arm. Where the wave had struck, creatures fell to the ground, dazed. Tim geared up for another attack. Another volley of arrows came towards them and many of them struck Pegasus on the flank, who squealed in anger and pain. A few struck Tim in his arm and he gritted his teeth. He sent out another wave, taking out a large chunk of the giant forearm. More arrows and tiny spears came flying towards him, but as they drew close, they were blocked by a number of flying creatures who suddenly appeared in front of Tim.

Charmed we are, they chittered, *and protect we will.*

Dizzy with success and support, Tim fired again, removing the creature's entire arm. Waves of lavender light swept through the air, washing over his airborne protectors without effect, but visibly smashing into his opponent, who diminished with each hit. Soon, Tim was surrounded by a cloud of flying fighters and the giant was missing both arms, half a head, and a huge slice of the left side. Pegasus darted in and out, allowing Tim to strike at several places with rapid waves and the giant faltered and stumbled. On very few occasions, an arrow or spear would get through and Pegasus would have to dodge, leaving Tim to cling tightly to mane and sides. Before long, the majority of the creatures were fighting with Tim and shortly after that, Tim faced the one faery who he had first awakened. She brandished her tiny sword at him and he sent a wave at her. She flew out of the wave's path and down the length of the hall, Tim and Pegasus in hot pursuit. She zoomed through an open doorway and Pegasus halted, almost throwing Tim over his head.

The sacred hall, he said. *I cannot go with you.*

"That's the sacred hall?"

Yes. You must go alone.

Tim dismounted. "Thank you, Pegasus. Thank you all," he added to the throng. Pegasus dipped his head and the creatures chittered. He walked into the sacred hall and the opening became a solid wall behind him. Frightened, but determined, he advanced and saw five figures before him. The faery was the middle figure.

"Where is my birthright?" he asked her.

"It is here in the hall. The nascregala is in the possession of one of the figures you see before you. Choose wisely and you obtain your nascregala." She went silent and Tim saw that she had become a statue once again, but of prismatic crystal that cast rainbows throughout the chamber.

"What happens if I choose wrong?" Tim asked. The faery did not respond. Tim wandered about the hall, examining the figures. He stopped before the left-most statue and sucked in a sharp breath. Nell, in crystalline form, gazed down at him. "What is this?" he asked, confused and frustrated. His frustration growing at the lack of response, he moved to the next statue. It was an infant and he recognized it as a copy of the stone infant that stood at the Sign's entrance to the astrolab. Clearly, this was the Star Child. The middle was the faery herself, with no indication that she had ever been animate. He nearly jumped out of his skin when he saw a crystalline Lena glaring at him from the next pedestal. Heart hammering wildly against his ribcage, he moved hurriedly to the last and viewed the crystalline Xander. He had no idea what any of these figures meant. "How am I supposed to choose one of you if I don't even know what I'm choosing between?" he cried. The statues stared at him. He banged a fist against the stone wall. Taking a deep breath, he considered the figures before him.

"Who would give me the birthright?" he asked out loud. There was no way that he was going to accept anything from Lena. She had betrayed him and tried to kill Nell. Nell was possible, but she didn't know a thing about the birthright, so he didn't see why she would be a logical choice. The infant would be make a lot of sense since she was the ultimate goal of this, but then, Xander had been helping and guiding him throughout the journey. Plus, there was the emotional connection. The faery seemed to be thrown in to make it more confusing. He shook his head, attempting to clear his thoughts and make an official decision.

He quickly ruled Lena out as a choice. In any multiple choice question, there was always a choice that didn't make sense. In this case, Lena was it. So he knew she didn't hold his birthright. There was also always a choice that was too obvious. That was the Star Child. She was too closely tied into the birthright for her to be the key. That left Nell, Xander, and the faery.

The faery seemed a likely choice. She was deeply connected to the Library of Air and Manaran. He had come in here to obtain his birthright and she was a natural creature of the edifice. She was also the one who had led him into the sacred hall. A guide would most likely have the key to his power. The word stuck in his mind: power. Suddenly, he knew why she was there. She was a representation of his power. As soon as he knew that, he knew she didn't have his birthright. Power alone wasn't going to do it.

Nell and Xander. He loved both of them, but in very different ways. Nell had been his friend for nearly his entire life, having been there through many questions and trials. Xander had only become his friend recently, but the emotions ran deeper than mere friendship. He had a new life and a new identity. Xander was a part of that. And he loved Tim. It was a complicated, confusing love as romantic love can sometimes be. Xander belonged to all of it: the duty, the power, the love. Tim's choice was easy.

He closed his eyes and reached down into his soul, down to where his talent waited to be awakened. He tapped into it and released it with a smile of confidence. A hand slipped into his own and squeezed. He squeezed back. "Hi, Nell."

"How did you know?" she asked.

He opened his eyes. Nell stood before him, flesh and blood, with no hint that she had ever been otherwise. "You have nothing to do with this," he said. "You have no emotional ties to it. You have no stake in it. At first, I couldn't even figure out why you were here, but when I saw you and Xander on opposite ends, I knew. Xander is everything that has to do with this life. You're everything that's not. You're just a person. An ordinary person and I love you for that. You're everyday humanity. You're what's at stake. If we don't find the Child, you're lost. That's the most logical person to give me the key to saving our world: just an everyday person."

Nell grinned at him. "All right, all right, don't give me a big head about it." Tim had to laugh. "Turn around."

He faced away from her and she lifted his shirt, placing a hand on his lower back. There was a stinging sensation and he jumped away from her. "What the hell did you just do to me?"

"Gave you your nascregala, silly." She produced a mirror and he twisted so he could see his back. There, stretched across the spine, was the glyph for Libra.

"A tattoo? My birthright is a tattoo?" He was disappointed.

"The tattoo is just a symbol, Timmy," she told him. "The birthright is inside you. That way, you won't lose it. Knowing you, that's a good thing."

"Shut up, Nell."

"Hey, you be nice to me. Remember, Libra rules the lower back, kidneys, and the butt. I could've put that tattoo somewhere else." She grinned mischievously.

"No thanks." Tim shuddered dramatically, then hugged his friend. It was nice to be joking with Nell again even though it was an unfamiliar situation. He released her and stepped back. "So, what does it do?"

"Part of earning it is learning how to use it," she answered smugly.

"You're enjoying this a little too much, Nell."

"Perks of the job," she said.

"Come on, Nell. Give me a hint," he begged.

She shrugged. "It's not anything you don't already know. The nascregala will make your talent stronger. You'll need that kind of power for the upcoming battle." Her expression became grave. "Figure out how to use it as soon as you can, Tim. A trip to visit the Patrons takes more time than you think. They don't obey the same rules that we do."

Tim groaned. "When Sereny talked in riddles, it was annoying. When you do it, it's creepy. How do you—"

"I'm sorry, but that's all the time we have, folks!" Nell announced cheerfully. Her features became distorted, blurry. The whole scene was bleeding into a swirl of color. Tim's stomach rolled and he closed his eyes. The last thing he heard was Nell's voice calling, "Break a leg!" and he smiled inwardly.

Chapter 28

"Did you get yours?"

"What did you have to do?"

"Do we know what they do yet?"

Tim opened his eyes. He was lying on his bed in The Gathering. Harmony kept watch from a nearby chair. Voices penetrated the closed door. Rising and heading over to a full-length mirror, he lifted his shirt and torqued his body so he could see his back. The symbol was still there, its dark ink like a slice of midnight against his skin. He thought about testing it out and looked around the room for a subject. Harmony's tawny figure caught his eye, but he couldn't bring himself to make her his guinea pig. He hardly even thought of her as a pet since she had spoken to him. She was a friend and part of the team. Almost as if she knew what he had considered, she jumped down from the chair and rubbed against his legs. He picked her up and held her tightly against his chest, feeling the vibration of her purring. Still carrying the cat, he opened the door to the hallway.

"Tim!"

"You're back!"

"Did you get your birthright?"

The greetings flew at him and he looked around at the faces, some proud, some curious, all of them happy to see him. Counting quickly, he counted only nine of the Signs, including himself. Stephen, Emily, and, as Tim anxiously noted, Xander were missing. He put Harmony down and Jamee came running up to give him a hug. "Did you get it?" she asked excitedly. He nodded and, releasing him, she jumped up and down. "That makes nine!" she crowed.

"Everyone got them?" Tim asked.

"Everyone so far," Kelsey answered. "Yup, I'm here in the flesh. Courtesy of my own nascregala," he explained before Tim could ask.

"Isn't that kind of dangerous?" Tim asked. "I mean, if the Dreamworld is being attacked..."

"*She* was looking for me to get access to the Libraries. Now that I'm here, I'm in no more danger than the rest of you."

Tim grimaced. "That's supposed to make me feel better?"

"We're all in danger and have been since the beginning," Rhys reminded them.

"Wasn't it weird when we disappeared?" Jamee asked him. "Where did you go? Do you think we were still in the same building?" Her curiosity was overwhelming.

Tim held up his hands. "Whoa. It was very weird. In fact, the whole process was weird, but I did get this nifty party favor." He turned around and showed them his back.

"So did I!" Jamee shouted. She turned to the side to show the Gemini glyph on her left shoulder.

"We all have them," said Cole. He rolled up a pant leg and the Aquarius symbol decorated his ankle. They all followed the pattern. Rhys's was on her upper back. Izzy's on the side of her throat. Dana's was patterned into her hair. Rory refused to show hers.

"We ain't close enough yet," she said simply.

"It's okay. We know where it is," James said, grinning. The glyph for Gemini was on his right shoulder.

"Has anyone from The Gathering come back yet?" Tim asked.

A door opened and Emily entered the hallway, seeming dazed. "Hi," she said.

"Are you okay?" Dana asked her.

"Yeah. Just feel different. Don't worry, I'm fine." She leaned against the wall. "Honestly, I'm okay. There's so much nervous energy in this hallway, I feel like I'm buzzed." The Signs all exchanged a look. "Here. Let me help." She gestured, palms out, and silvery beams flowed over the Signs. Tim was alarmed at first, but as he was enveloped by the light, he suddenly felt calm and content. He was confident in his own talents and in the abilities of his companions. The beams disappeared, but the feeling remained. "Ah, much better," she said, straightening.

"How did you do that?" Michael asked her.

"Empathic birthright. I can control it now." She smiled.

"That's amazing," said Izzy.

"Yeah. Oh, by the way, you can have this back." She took the vial of dampening draught out of her pocket and tossed it to Tim. "I don't need it anymore." Tim pocketed the vial just as Xander emerged from his room. Tim's nerves erupted in a remembrance of his former anxiety and were immediately washed away by a flood of relief. Xander walked over to Tim with a determined look in his eye and kissed him.

"Wow. What was your test?" Tim wanted to know.

Xander smiled at him. "You won't ever know. But this was a nice reward." Tim smiled back. Harmony meowed and the two boys became acutely aware that they were not alone. Feeling a flush rise up the back of his neck, Tim saw a myriad of expressions on the faces of the other Signs.

"Uh...," he said awkwardly.

"About time," said Dana. That seemed to sum it up.

Just then, Stephen opened his door. "Hey." No one said anything. "What? I'm the last one here and no one's glad to see me?"

"Oh, it's not you," said Jamee. "Xander and Tim just came out."

"Finally," added Dana.

"What?" Stephen looked utterly bewildered.

Tim burst out laughing. He couldn't help it. Xander's kiss had left him lightheaded. The confusion of the situation combined with the immensity of his recent trial and what was still before them manifested in an overabundance of emotion and he either had to laugh or cry. Xander glanced sharply at him, then he too started to laugh. It caught like wildfire and soon all of them were helpless with mirth. The sound of running feet and shouting sobered them and they instinctively drew closer together. The door flew open to reveal a very anxious Professor Galten. She did a rapid head count and relaxed marginally.

"Good. You're all here. It is time to go."

Tim took the lead. "Hello to you too, Professor," he said, mirth still bubbling in his chest. "How are you today?"

"No time, Timothy. You must leave and you must leave now."

"What's so urgent, Professor?" Xander asked her.

"The birth is what's so urgent, Alexander. The Child is to be born!" Her hand entangled itself in her beaded necklace.

"That's not supposed to happen until the year turns!" James exclaimed.

The professor frowned. "We are on the cusp of the millennium. It is December 31st." The Signs gasped collectively.

Rhys asked the question that was on all of their minds. "How is that possible?"

"That's what Nell meant!" exclaimed Tim. He repeated Nell's words to the others. He found that others had been similarly warned, but no one had understood until now.

"We've lost so much time!" Michael cried, dismayed.

Professor Galten repeated, "You must leave immediately if you are to find the Child."

"We don't even know where she's gonna be born!" Xander protested.

"We do. She will be born in England." She pulled a piece of paper from her pocket and handed it to him. It was a photograph of a tiny cottage, surrounded by verdant hills. "This is the location. Go and find her." Professor Galten was insistent.

"Xander!" a voice called from the hallway.

"Mom?" he yelled, running forward, but the older woman blocked his way.

"Xander, you must leave!" the professor said, grabbing his wrist.

"Xander!" his mother called again.

"Let me go!" Xander struggled against her. "Mom!"

Mrs. Conlyn appeared in the doorway, her hair unkempt, her eyes rimmed with red. Her clothing was in disarray and she walked slowly towards her son. Xander broke free of the professor's grip and ran to his mother. She clutched him close to her, tears spilling onto her cheeks.

"Merel has your father."

* * * * * * * * * * * *

Tim's heart ached for Xander. The group had moved into his room and he sat on the bed in his mother's arms, looking for all the world like a lost child. She was openly weeping, but Xander stared blankly ahead. The rest of the Signs stood or sat awkwardly around the room while Professor Galten paced angrily.

"You shouldn't have told him, Rachel. He needs to be focused. We don't have time for trivialities. The Star Child is going to be born and what then? Without all twelve Signs together, they will surely fail. And then where will we be? In a black hole, that's where! I told you that he shouldn't know until after the mission ended. Well, now you've told him and look where we are! Nowhere! They have to get going!"

"Shut up!" Xander yelled. He stood and faced her. "My father's been captured! Don't you understand that? He's my dad!" With a sob, he threw himself back onto the bed. His mother stroked his hair.

"You are being selfish and childish," the professor said contemptuously. "Do you think I feel nothing for John? Why, I would give almost anything to save him. But," and she took his chin in her hand and jerked his head up so he was looking into her eyes, "I will not sacrifice the world. Not even for your father, Alexander. I will not!"

"Leave him alone, Blanche," Mrs. Conlyn pleaded.

"No! We have a responsibility. So do they." She gestured to indicate the Signs. "Alexander has always taken his responsibility seriously. He believes in this cause and he knew the dangers of casualties. We have already lost many and we will lose everything if this persists. Time is running out. They must go. Now!"

"Xander, she's right," Cole said, and a few Signs nodded.

"Besides, it could be a trap," Izzy added.

"Yeah, how do you know Merel didn't capture your dad just so that you would be distracted and go chasing after him instead of the Star Child?" Dana put in.

Xander looked blearily at Tim.

Tim's heart squeezed. "They're right," he said.

Xander flinched as though he had been hit. "It's my dad," he whispered.

Tim thought of his recent encounter with Nell. "But there's more than that at stake. The whole universe depends on us. If we save your dad and we lose the Star Child, we've lost everyone, including your dad."

"Merel is doing the same thing," Professor Galten said firmly. "She may gain immortality, but she loses the entire universe in the process. She's too shortsighted to see this."

"Your father would want you to go after the Star Child," Tim added gently.

This seemed to put steel back in Xander's spine. His eyes burned with anger and frustration, but the light of determination could be seen within them as well. "Fine," he said petulantly. "But as soon as we get the Child, I'm going after Dad."

"Will you be okay?" Izzy asked him.

"Tim has the dampening draught," Jamee suggested. "It can help to dull the pain."

Professor Galten shook her head. "The sadness is his own. The draught will only work on outside emotion."

"I can do it," Emily offered. "I can take away the sadness."

Xander shook his head. "I need the pain to help me get through this."

"So...we're going to England?" Rhys asked hesitantly.

"Rightio!" Michael shouted. The rest of them looked at him and he blushed. "Never been there," he murmured.

Xander pulled the folded picture out and studied it. No one spoke as he quickly refolded it and returned it to his pocket. He hugged his mother and nodded to Professor Galten while the group grabbed coats from a newly materialized closet. They began to gather in their usual traveling formation, but Xander held up a hand, a grim smile on his face. "No need anymore. Nascregala privileges." Without explaining further, they all vanished.

Chapter 29

The smoke rose high into the crisp winter night before merging with the cloudy sky. The hills were covered with a light layer of frost that crunched underfoot. A warm, golden glow spilled from the windows onto the ground, creating sharp shadows. White candles lit the upstairs windows, giving those outside a flickering glimpse into the rooms beyond. A tree grew in the fenced-in front yard, bare branches beckoning to the visitors. All in all, it was an idyllic country scene.

Except for the screaming.

A single keening wail rose from the tiny cottage and tore through the night to torture the ears of the Signs. They stood upon the hill, huddled together for warmth. Emily winced as the woman's distress struck her but she quickly regained control. Stephen had his eye on his watch and was counting silently. Harmony and Donne took refuge in the branches of a nearby tree, while the Brownings stayed close to Rhys. Izzy stood by Michael, concern in her eyes at how the cold weather might affect him. Dana, Jamee, Rory, and Cole conversed in whispers, while Kelsey was somewhat separated from the group, a thoughtful expression on his face. Tim watched the cottage with Xander's hand in his own. He felt Xander squeeze his hand when the cry came, though whether from excitement or fear, he wasn't sure.

"Labor pains," said Emily quietly.

"Almost time," confirmed Stephen.

"How much?" Jamee asked.

"About an hour," was the reply.

"We should get in there," Izzy said. There were a few nods of agreement.

"Dana, how many are inside the house?" Xander asked.

She concentrated. "I can make out three minds, but there's a weird buzzing in my head."

Rhys stepped in. "Izzy's right. Let's get down there."

"Okay," Xander said, leading them forward, "but be careful. Merel could appear..."

There was a horrendous screeching and the air filled with astranihl. They arrived in droves, like locusts descending on the cottage until it was shrouded in a cloud of the flying terrors. Many lit upon the ground, taking their human forms while most preferred the air. The twelve Signs found themselves exponentially outnumbered by an army of enemies shouting, hissing, and screaming at them. The cats hissed and growled back. Near the cottage door stood a woman in a dark cloak.

"...at any time," Xander finished.

The woman at the door raised her hands. "I guess that means go," Tim muttered as astranihl came towards them. His heart was pounding against his ribs like a caged animal. He tried to smile, but his lips felt dry and limp and wouldn't obey him. His mind was racing so quickly that every second seemed to last a lifetime. His body automatically tensed for action and he saw the others prepare similarly. Reaching down into himself, Tim searched for his talent, but all he found was a cold pit of fear slowly spreading through his body, numbing his limbs and mind into inaction. He was paralyzed with terror, watching his death approaching. He opened his mouth to scream and a splash of silver haze washed over him. His body and mind calmed and he was able to move again. Glancing over at Emily, he saw her wink at him and turn quickly to face her foes. Grateful, he focused his energy inwards and tried to charm the first astranihl that came towards him.

Nothing happened.

Losing a bit of the calm Emily had given him, he tried again with no result. The astranihl came on faster with a wicked leer. Tim desperately tried to force a smile on his face, but his resolve faltered and panic overtook him as he came face to face with the deadly creature.

Caught unprepared, he felt searing pain as a knife sliced through his bicep and he lashed out wildly, his mind blank, his defense a mere reflex. The tattoo on his back burned with cold fire as a flash of lavender light smashed into the enemy and surrounding area in a wide arc. Those affected stood still with stupid, dazed looks on their faces, then turned and began to fight their brethren. The advancing astranihl were confused and hesitant as their former companions became enemies. Recognizing the new threat, they began cutting down the other astranihl with vengeful glee. Tim's tattoo was still burning and he tentatively searched for his talent. It was there, strong and ready, within him. He turned to face the astranihl who were cutting a wide swath through their former allies to get to him.

Tim heard screams from above him and he looked up quickly. Astranihl were descending from the sky. He prepared for another attack, but before he could release his talent, one of the astranihl was knocked from the sky. He blinked.

Another one fell.

The cats scampered from the tree as it lifted a branch and smacked a third astranihl from the sky. Tim watched in amazement as two more astranihl were taken from the air. Soon all of the branches were waving through the air, smashing through the enemy ranks and sending them crashing to the ground as broken figures. They did not get up.

I can charm trees? he thought.

His mind burned with the possibilities even as he emitted another wave of lavender light. It spread through the enemy ranks, also encompassing nearby trees and rocks, all of which turned to fight the seemingly endless supply of foes. He charmed another pile of rocks, which moved to form a low wall in front of the Signs, some of whom looked surprised, but happy to have it. Michael came running up to him.

"Here, let me get that for you," he said, gesturing to Tim's bleeding arm. In his excitement, Tim had forgotten, but with attention drawn to it, the wound sent a fresh flow of pain through him. Michael looked at it and the wound closed quickly and vanished, taking the pain with it.

"Thanks!" said Tim, but Michael was already running back down the wall. Tim saw each Sign involved in their own battle as astranihl swarmed over the grass towards the stone wall. He sent out another wave of charm, forcing enemies to become friends and tried to determine who might need his help. Xander was vanishing enemies as quickly as they arrived, sending them wherever he decided. At the edge of his mind, Tim heard the faint echoees of a mental scream. The astranihl who attacked Dana were grabbing their heads and falling to the ground, blood leaking from their ears. Dana smiled grimly as she concentrated, cheerfully overloading the brains of her enemies with mental sound. Tim shuddered.

A large section of the wall had gruesome statues decorating it. Tim was startled to see one of the statues moving. That was Izzy in her stone form, transforming her attackers into hideous sculptures. Any astranihl that made it through to the Taurus found itself crushed to death by the stone figure's arms. Izzy suddenly turned her attention to the skies and astranihl began to drop onto their companions, crushing them beneath their stone weight.

Disturbed, Tim noticed that other statues bedecked the wall, but these were of flesh and blood; that was Stephen's doing, taking them out of time. When he saw Izzy's strategy, he too focused on the flying enemies and soon it was raining astranihl of both flesh and stone.

A body slammed into the ground next to Tim and he jumped back as a second astranihl came screaming out of the air towards him. Quickly, he emitted another wave, this time spreading it upwards to the flying creatures. Many of them descended on their own kind, giving the Signs a brief reprieve.

A chain link fence sprang up behind him and curved over his head, allowing for a small gap in the front between the fence and the rock wall. It spread down the entire length of the wall and Tim saw Jamee finishing it with another astranihl body with one hand while the other hand transformed the enemy into more rocks, thickening the wall. She caught him looking. "I'm doing the fence while James works on the wall!" she explained. "We can change the animate!"

"I can charm the inanimate!" he yelled back and thought he saw her wink before she turned back to the battle. A loud roar sounded over the battle noise and his mouth dropped open to see thousands of animals attacking the astranihl. Squirrels, foxes, bears, birds of all kinds pecking and clawing and biting. The roar sounded again and he beheld an enormous lioness leaping from enemy to enemy, tearing throat after throat. He heard her call out in a loud voice he recognized as Rhys's, "Fight! Fight for your lives, your homes, your world!" She had become Queen of the jungle, with a firm command of the entire animal world. Tim worried for her safety, but then he saw Michael keeping close watch on all of them. When a stripe of red blood appeared on Rhys's flank, Michael healed her from a distance. It made Tim feel better to see Michael's talent at work.

Kelsey stood towards the middle of the wall, sparks of aqua leaping from his fingertips. Those whom the sparks touched suddenly opened their eyes wide and pointed at nothing, gibbering in terror. Nothing would move them and eventually, the other astranihl were forced to kill them as they became a second wall of defense. "Waking nightmares," he shouted by way of explanation.

The number of astranihl was dwindling, but so was time. Tim sent a wave towards more trees and they took up the attack. He quickly sent out a second wave as astranihl broke through the line of horror-stricken dreamers, forcing them to turn and fight. He saw a whirlwind of activity near the other end of the wall. Rory was a blur of motion striking again and again, but though he saw no whip in her hand, the astranihl around her fell, poisoned. She stung the closing ranks and was soon obscured by a pile of dead astranihl.

A cloud of dust took to the wind close to her and Tim saw Cole's mouth moving though he could not make out the words. He watched as an astranihl approached, faltered, and crumbled to dust in front of Cole. He shivered involuntarily as he realized Cole was leeching all of the water out of their bodies.

There was plenty of water elsewhere. Tim watched in amazement as a line of enemies suddenly halted and fell to their knees, sobbing and begging for death.

Emily stood before them, emanating silver light. The Cancer was forcing such strong feelings of depression forth that the astranihl had become suicidal.

All in all, each Sign had a formidable weapon bolstered by his or her nascregala. Looking out at the rapidly dying swarm of astranihl, he was very thankful for the gifts that had been bestowed upon the Signs and he marveled at the versatile fighting force they represented. He sent out another wave, noticing that odd objects had begun to appear on the battlefield. That was the work of the Gemini, changing astranihl into harmless objects.

Soon, the hillside was littered with the bodies of the dead and the incapacitated. Fortunately, the twelve Signs were mostly unharmed and what harm was done was quickly taken care of by Michael. Sweaty and exhausted, yet exhilarant with victory, the Signs met together mid-wall. They had proven themselves as a team and there was pride shining on every face.

The cry from the cottage brought them back to their senses.

The Signs sped down the hill, leaping over bodies and jumping the fence. Crossing the threshold, they dashed up the stairs and burst into the bedroom where a woman, pale and sweating, grunted and whined in the throes of childbirth. A midwife bustled about the room, muttering to herself. She didn't even look towards the door as the Signs entered. "Almost," she said soothingly to the soon-to-be mother. "Almost there." The woman only screamed through gritted teeth.

Tim did a swift survey of the room. Nothing out of the ordinary that he could see. Not a thing to show that this was a special birth. There was no sign of Merel. Something was wrong. He wasn't the only one who could feel it.

"This isn't happening," said Stephen.

"What do you mean?" Dana asked sharply.

He moved around the room, concentrating. "This isn't in real time. It happened already. Look." He walked over to the midwife and reached out for her midsection. His hand went right through her. Tim's eyes widened and there was a stifled gasp from someone behind him.

"Merel!" Xander exclaimed.

"Can you fix it?" Emily asked Stephen.

"Give me a minute." He closed his eyes. The scene before them shifted and shimmered. There was a hazy outline of another scene, a scene that contained a tall woman in a dark cloak. The two scenes fought for dominance as Stephen's talent tackled Merel's illusion. Stephen gritted his teeth in a similar fashion to the woman in the bed and suddenly the second scene came sharply into focus. He collapsed to the floor and Emily ran to him. "I'm fine, just exhausted."

"He's drained!" Dana said in horror. "It sapped his talent!"

"He'll recover," said a new voice. "Eventually."

Merel stood to face them as they appeared, her hood pushed back, and the first thing that Tim could think was, *She's beautiful.* The candlelight cast shadows over her pale, ivory skin. Straw colored hair spilled into the limp hood. Her hands, with long and delicate fingers, were outstretched as if in welcoming, a gesture echoed in the faint smile playing about her almost colorless lips. Only her eyes betrayed her anger. Her intense ire had warmed the brown irises to a dark yellow, gleaming in the firelight. Behind her, the bedridden woman was muffled, though she tried to cry out through it. The midwife lay beside the bed, her throat slit.

Merel watched, amused, as Michael rushed to the midwife. He looked up sadly.

"She's dead. I can't heal the dead."

Xander stepped forward, murder in his eyes, but Merel moved faster. She stretched out a hand and grabbed a familiar figure, bringing him into the light. "I wouldn't do anything if I were you," she warned. She tilted the man's head so that Xander could see him. Mr. Conlyn stared desperately at his son and strained against invisible bonds. His mouth opened, but no sound came out.

"What did you do to him?" Xander snarled.

"He's enchanted to kill any and all who do me harm," Merel answered smugly. "So don't do anything rash or we all die. Then where would the Star Child be? Untrained." Her tone turned light and sweet. "It's a nice little reunion, isn't it? And speaking of family reunions...hello, Kelsey."

Kelsey stood straight and tall. "Hello, Esme."

Her face darkened. "That's an idiot name your father chose to call me. I am Merel."

"You will not kill Mr. Conlyn the way that you killed Dad, Esme," Kelsey declared, placing a strong emphasis on the last word.

She smiled cruelly. "Oh, I wouldn't do that. I have different plans for him. There will probably be killing involved, but I assure you, it won't be the same way I killed your father."

What do we do now? Dana asked mentally.

Change her mind! Jamee thought back.

I can't! said Dana.

"You might as well talk out loud," said Merel. "I can hear you just fine either way. Did you think I would take no precautions against your so-called 'talents'? My mind is my very being. 'Change my mind?' Ha! That would be just as harmful as if you killed me outright! This human body, this shell, is just a costume. I am my thoughts and desires. I desire the Child for my own!" She pointed to the woman on the bed who was sweating with the effort of labor. "You cannot change that! I have existed for millennia and once the Child is mine, I will be here forever!"

"Not forever, Merel!" Rhys protested. "Don't you realize that what you plan to do will destroy the entire universe?"

"Destroy it? Of course not!" Merel scoffed. "Why, once I have the power, the universe will bend to my will! I will see that it does not end, but endures forever in service to me!" Her eyes were wild.

"Ain't gonna happen!" Rory growled.

"There's nothing you can do," said Merel. "You cannot harm me and without that, you have nothing. I will see you all dead!"

"You know something, Merel?" asked Dana. "I can hear your thoughts too." She faced the Sagittarius. "Xander, your dad is enchanted, but only with a spell binding him to Merel. She's right though. No one can harm anyone in this room; it's protected for the birth of the Child." She turned back to Merel. "Otherwise, you could have attacked us by now, huh?"

"I laid that spell on this room!" declared Merel in a loud voice.

"Then why don't you attack us?" Dana asked. Merel did not answer. "Because you can't," Dana said for her. "Just like us, you have to obey the rules of the room."

"I bow to no one's will!"

Out came the psychology major. "You are nothing, Merel," said Dana. "You're just a scared little girl who couldn't handle life so you're trying to run from it."

"I am a Star!" Merel bellowed in a crazed voice. "My light stretched to the corners of the universe and it will again! I will rule supreme! There will be no one who does not fear my name and all of the universe will bend to my will!" She continued to rant, moving about the room, gesticulating wildly, proclaiming her future reign.

Okay, while she's distracted, Dana mentally whispered, *anyone got any ideas?*

The word struck a memory in Tim. He felt in his pocket and found the seed Manaran had given him. He shoved it in his mouth, hoping the Patron's gift would bring the answer.

Well, we can't hurt her, said Izzy.

Man, I want to, though, put in Rory.

We need to incapacitate her without harming her, Cole said.

How do we do that? asked Emily.

A wild thought sprang into Tim's mind. *I have an idea,* he ventured. *It's going to be weird, but it could work.* He briefly explained the situation. There was an incredulous silence. Then they all spoke at once.

I can handle the mental state, said Dana.

I got the emotion, Emily said.

We can take care of the body, Jamee/James said.

I can help with fluids, Cole added.

Wait, said Xander. *I'm not even sure that I can do this.*

You have to, said Kelsey.

You will, added Tim.

It's time, Stephen told them.

There was a gasp from the woman on the bed and she squeezed her eyes tightly in pain. Merel halted, mid-rant, and moved quickly to the bed. "It's time!" she breathed.

"Yes, it's time," said Xander. Merel turned to him angrily, but her eyes widened in shock and she pressed a long fingered-hand to her stomach, which was expanding. She fell to the floor writhing with pain. "What did you do? You cannot harm me!"

"We aren't hurting you," Tim explained. "You're in labor. We transferred the Star Child to your own body, altering your mental, emotional, and physical states to accommodate her. We're doing exactly what you wanted. You said you wanted the Star Child to be yours. Well, she will be, at least for the next minute or so." Merel screamed in rage and pain. Her fingernails scraped against the floor as she struggled helplessly to escape the trap. Xander rushed forward to take his father by the arm.

"You–" she gasped. "You dare–"

"Yes, we dare," said Tim, standing over her. "You told Anderson Baker that pregnancy robs you of your powers, so there's nothing you can do. We have given you the honor of bringing the Star Child into this world. Then we will take the Child and we will educate her in The Gathering. Congratulations, Merel. You now hold the key to your own destruction."

Merel's face was contorted with effort. Rhys pushed Tim aside and knelt at Merel's feet. The Signs all gathered together, whispering quietly as Rhys took the midwife's tools and applied them in ways that Tim couldn't even begin to imagine and didn't want to. Michael, however, proved very curious and moved in. Rhys made to shoo him away, but then realized he had the potential to help and waved him in. Together, they delivered the Star Child and when Tim heard her first cry, he knew the world would never be the same. It was as if color had suddenly been introduced to a black and white world. Rhys handed the Child to Michael, who checked her over, but there was no requirement for his talent. Merel shoved Rhys away and reached towards Michael, murder in her eyes, but fell back in her weakened state. Michael quickly moved away, holding the Child tenderly in his arms.

"Emily!" Stephen cried out.

Emily had started forwards to the woman in the bed. Furious, Merel turned to the bed with a gesture.

The woman screamed and Emily was thrown back by some invisible force.

"She's recovering her powers," Dana warned. "We have to go."

"But–" Emily protested.

"She can't hurt her," Dana reminded her. "Time to go."

"Sorry we can't stay...," Jamee said.

"...and kill you," Rory finished.

"You will pay for this!" Merel snarled.

"I think we've got the ultimate insurance," said Michael, cradling the Child.

"I always wanted a sister," said Kelsey.

"Oh, and Merel," added Tim, "Happy New Year."

The Signs vanished into the night.

Epilogue

The first week of the millennium was a busy one at The Gathering. When the Signs first arrived, pandemonium ensued throughout the building. Everyone wanted to see and hold the Star Child, the bringer of hope. Michael was especially protective of the infant and was often found in the Star Child's room, talking to her, reading her stories, or playing with her. Tired of referring to her as "Star Child," he nicknamed her "Dawn." "She's the dawn of a new age," he explained, and the name stuck.

A banquet was held in Dawn's honor. It was the most lavish birthday party anyone had ever seen and Dana was overheard commenting, "It's not like she's gonna remember it or anything." However, Dawn loved the attention, giggling and burbling throughout the celebration.

Many wanted to know what had happened, so Tim and the other Signs found themselves repeating their story numerous times over. Mr. Pears was especially interested and he commandeered Jamee for long talks in the library. "I swear, I feel like one of his books!" she remarked once. The Signs were also beseeched for news of the famous Libraries, but when Xander traveled to them, they had vanished. Kelsey reported their disappearance in the Dreamworld as well. It was speculated that the Patrons had hidden them until they were needed again.

There was one detraction from the celebration: Merel's enchantment on Mr. Conlyn had baffled the healers. He remained in the medical wing, comatose. They had done everything they could think of to bring him back, but he seemed to be an empty shell. Michael was constantly trying to use his talent in order to revive Mr. Conlyn and as Dawn was roomed near the medical center in case of emergency, Michael eventually asked for a room in the same wing so as to be close to both of his charges. Some said that Mr. Conlyn's soul had been captured by Merel. Others said that she sapped his energy, leaving him too weak to be able to operate on a conscious level. The healer, Lisa, had a different theory:

"Being bound to such a dark power leaves an imprint on the mind and body. He was linked to Merel in ways we can't imagine and it's going to take time for him to destroy that link. Distance and proper attention should help him to heal, but it's ultimately up to him to break that connection and come back to us."

Mrs. Conlyn was devastated and retreated from the rest of The Gathering, speaking only to her son. Xander became impassioned and worked tirelessly with the healers and Michael to find a cure. Nothing seemed to work and Mr. Conlyn lay as though sleeping, pale as death. Only his chest rising and falling gave them any indication that he still lived.

Desperate to escape the confusing feelings of victory and helplessness, Tim and the other Signs took time to go and see their family and friends courtesy of The Gathering's conjurers and Xander's assistance. The Dalis family had a joyous reunion, although it was somewhat subdued by the fact that Tim wasn't able to really explain where he had been. He used a little bit of charm in the exchange to make things easier for them. It snowed during this time, enabling Tim and his parents to complete their Christmas ritual, albeit a little late. Tim no longer took coincidences so lightly and chose to believe that the universe was making up for his absence during the holidays.

He also made a special trip to go and see Nell. It was very strange to walk the familiar streets of his neighborhood knowing all that had transpired. He walked past the theatre, wondering what had become of the show and yes, even Cassandra's fate. A shiver ran down his spine as he passed Ilene's, memories of the elaborate deception that had occurred there. The Book Nook was open and he almost went in, but the sight of Mark and the thought of forced explanations forestalled that idea. Finding himself in front of Nell's door, he hesitated a moment, then rang the bell. He could see her through the tiny window, jumping down the stairs. She flung open the door and stared.

"You're not pizza," she said at last.

"Oh, is that what you're waiting for?" Tim asked rhetorically. "I'll leave then." He made as if to go, but Nell wrapped him in a fierce hug.

"Don't even think about it, you bastard," she said quietly.

He hugged her back, hard. "Missed ya, Nell."

"Is that the pizza?" a voice called from upstairs.

"Still with Gary, huh?" Tim accused her, breaking contact.

"We've been through a lot together, you know," she said.

"Yeah," Tim agreed. "I know." They spent the rest of the day together, laughing and crying about everything that had happened. Gary joined them for a small part of it, but in a remarkable show of sensitivity, he recognized their need to be alone together and left, claiming errands that required his immediate attention. Tim was happy knowing he could talk to Nell about things because she already knew parts of the adventure. They shared stories of Lena's respective betrayals and spoke of Nell's near-death experience.

"You never thanked me for saving you, by the way," said Tim.

"Yeah, well, you still haven't thanked me for that tattoo on your back!" she retorted.

Tim was dumbfounded. "That really was you? How did you get that kind of power?!"

"I thought I dreamed the whole thing," she admitted. "I knew I was there and I could sense everything, but it felt hazy. As if someone else were in control of my mind and body. Not in a bad way, though. Not like possession or anything. Just nudging me here and there to say certain things and move certain ways." She was thoughtful. "And then, when I gave you that birthright thing, whoa. There was this crazy power going through me and it was like pleasure and pain all rolled into one and I didn't know what was going on, but I kind of liked it and then it was over and you had that tattoo." She said this last bit in a rush.

Tim laughed. "I hope you had a cigarette afterwards." She punched him in the arm.

"Ow! You haven't changed, Nell."

"Would you want me to?" she asked sweetly.

"No," he said without hesitation. "Not at all."

It felt good to be back with his friend, joking as if nothing had happened. However, he had new responsibilities and the time came to leave far sooner than he wanted it to.

"Come visit soon, okay?" Nell invited.

"You got it."

"And bring your new daughter with you," she said. "I want to see Tim, the dad, in action."

"Shut up. She's not my daughter. I guess I'm more like an uncle. She is awfully cute, though."

"Well, goodbye, Uncle Tim." She held her arms out for a hug. He obliged, kissing her on the forehead.

"See ya soon, Nell." With a wistful pang in his heart for the ordinary life he used to have, he returned to The Gathering to find great excitement. He was led directly to the healing center where a handful of people encircled Mr. Conlyn's bed. Xander spotted him and ran over, a huge smile on his face.

"He's waking up! Tim, he's gonna be okay!" He laughed with delight. They ran to the bedside where Tim could see Mr. Conlyn's eyes fluttering. Tim squeezed

Xander's hand. Mrs. Conlyn was openly weeping and caressing her husband's hand. Lisa stood nearby, expressions of pleasure and disapproval at war.

"He shouldn't be crowded with so many people," she said. "He needs to recover before he can handle this much excitement." Surprisingly, the professor supported this.

"She's right. He needs quiet and we can't give him that right now. Get out." She glared at each of them. "Except for his wife and son, get out."

"And Tim," Xander corrected her. The professor threw him a sharp glance, but nodded. Tim smiled gratefully at Xander. The rest of the group muttered to themselves, but obeyed the professor's command. With a brief look to Mrs. Conlyn, Professor Galten stomped off after them, leaving Tim with the three Conlyns. Lisa stood watch nearby as Mr. Conlyn tried to push himself into a sitting position, but Mrs. Conlyn gently prevented that.

"You need to rest," she told him.

Her husband turned to his son. He seemed agitated and pulled Xander close, whispering in his ear. Xander paled and began to tremble as his father fell back, unconscious once more.

Mrs. Conlyn cried out, "John!"

Lisa immediately moved in, concern and frustration written clearly on her face. The room was silent as she performed her inspection. After a torturous wait, she looked up. "He's suffered a relapse, but he'll recover now that he's broken the link. Right now, he needs rest and that means no excitement." She emphasized these last words with a pointed look at the boys. Xander didn't move until Tim gently took his hand and led him from the room.

"Xander, he's going to be fine. Lisa said so. As soon as we can, we'll get Michael to take a look at him and make sure." He rubbed Xander's shoulder reassuringly.

As they moved down the hallway, Xander suddenly drew Tim into Dawn's room where the tiny infant lay, sleeping. He stared down at her for an uncomfortably long moment. Then Xander shivered and turned to Tim with a scared look in his eyes. "Twins."

"Jamee and James?" Tim asked, confused.

Xander shook his head. "Two Star Children. Dad said there are two Star Children."

Tim sucked in a sharp breath. "That's not possible."

Terror and understanding mixed in Xander's eyes. 'And yet be forced to share her,'" he quoted. "We thought that meant that everyone would share the benefits of the Star Child's birth. We were wrong. Tim, I only moved one child into Merel. There's another Star Child. A boy. And now Merel's got him."

As the boys stared at each other in horror, the infant slept on, blissfully unaware that a new player had entered the game.

Tim voiced what both of them were thinking. "What do we do now?"

JARED R. LOPATIN

Originally from Philadelphia, Pennsylvania, Jared developed an interest in astrology at age twelve when he picked up The Only Astrology Book You'll Ever Need by Joanna Martine Woolfolk. This book became the gateway through which he entered the world of the occult, touching on Tarot, numerology, metaphysics, and of course, further astrological exploration.

Around the same time, he embarked on a fifteen year journey through the theatrical world. This adventure took him to many places, one of which was Nappanee, Indiana. It was here in 2004 that Jared wrote the first few words that would become Rising Sign. The idea came to him in a dream that just wouldn't leave him alone and one day, backstage during a production of South Pacific (of all things), he began writing the story in a notebook. Thus, Rising Sign was born.

Five years later, Rising Sign is complete and enjoying a growing popularity among readers. Jared currently lives in New York City, and is attending school to get his Masters in Special Education, while continuing to write the Star Child Trilogy.

Made in the USA
Lexington, KY
22 June 2011